FULL
FATHOM
FIVE

■ ■ ■

FULL FATHOM FIVE

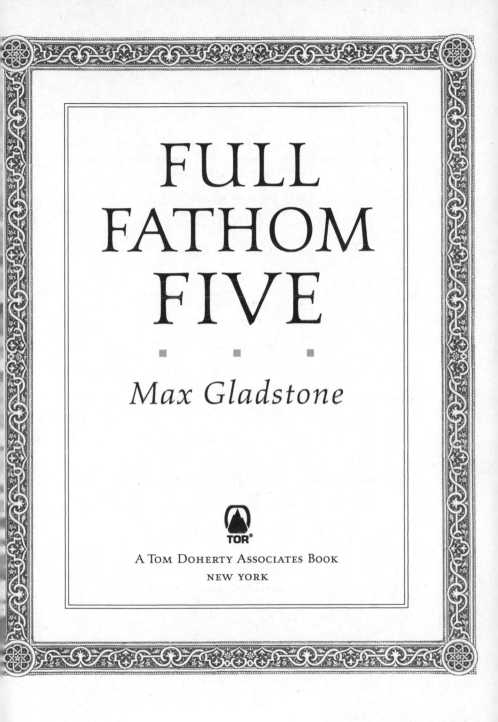

Max Gladstone

TOR®

A TOM DOHERTY ASSOCIATES BOOK
NEW YORK

FULL FATHOM FIVE

Copyright © 2014 by Max Gladstone

A Tor Book
Published by Tom Doherty Associates, LLC
175 Fifth Avenue
New York, NY 10010

www.tor-forge.com

Tor® is a registered trademark of Tom Doherty Associates, LLC.

The Library of Congress Cataloging-in-Publication Data
is available upon request.

ISBN 978-0-7653-3574-6 (hardcover)
ISBN 978-1-4668-2615-1 (e-book)

Tor books may be purchased for educational, business, or promotional use. For information on bulk purchases, please contact Macmillan Corporate and Premium Sales Department at 1-800-221-7945, extension 5442, or write specialmarkets@macmillan.com.

First Edition: July 2014

Printed in the United States of America

0   9   8   7   6   5   4   3   2   1

FULL
FATHOM
FIVE

■   ■   ■

1

The idol would drown that night.

"Death projected for half past one A.M.," ran the memo Kai read at lunchtime on the volcano's break room bulletin board. "Direct all inquiries to Mara Ceyla." Another business update among many, pinned between a recruitment ad for the office ullamal league and a pink poster for a lunch-and-learn on soul trading in the Southern Gleb. Few noticed the memo, and fewer read it. Kai did both, and took the news back to her office with her sandwich. Ham and cheese and lettuce on white bread digested easy. The news didn't.

Kai ruminated through the afternoon, and dinner, and the night. By 1:00 A.M. her work was done: three chickens sacrificed, one each on altars of silver, iron, and stone; a stack of profit and loss statements dispatched by nightmare telegraph; a prayer litany chanted balancing on one foot; a proposal drafted, suggesting an Iskari family shift their faith from the high-risk personal resurrection market to dependable grain-focused fertility. She scrubbed down the altars, washed her hands, brushed her hair, tied it back in a ponytail, and glanced again at the clock. One twenty.

Her office windows faced into the caldera. Two human figures waited on the shore of the dark pool far below, in the pit's center. Kai recognized their outlines, though rendered doll-sized by distance. Gavin, tall, round, peered into the deep. Mara beside him was a straight line with a slight bend at the shoulders; she paced in tight circles, nervous, desperate, already mourning.

Kai had long passed quitting time. The Order owed her a carriage ride home. In thirty minutes she could be brushing her teeth, and in five more abed and asleep, safe from everything but dreams.

Mara turned. Stopped. Twisted the toe of her shoe into broken lava. Stuffed her hands in her pockets, pulled them out again, crossed her arms, uncrossed them. She walked to the edge of the pool, glanced in, shuddered, retreated.

"Not my problem," Kai said, and realized she'd spoken out loud to her empty office—empty, at least, of people. The altars and prayer wheels and rosaries and fetishes and sacrificial knives kept their own counsel, as always. "Damn."

She walked the long lonely hallway to the break room and descended a winding stair to the caldera floor, to join the death watch. She paused at the foot of the stairs. She could still go. They hadn't seen her yet.

Leaving from her office would have been understandable. Leaving now was cowardice.

And anyway, Mara needed a friend.

Kai stepped out into the night, into view.

Cliffs above circumscribed a sky swirled with alien stars. Kai approached over lava five hundred years cool.

Mara's feet ground gravel as she turned. "You came." Her voice was at once relieved and bitter. "I didn't expect you."

"How are you holding up?" Kai asked.

"I'm fine." Mara sipped coffee from a white mug marked with the Order's black mountain sigil. Her free hand trembled. She turned the hand palm in, then out, spread her fingers, and watched them shake. She laughed a laugh of dry leaves. "I wish it would be over soon. Sooner."

Kai wanted to touch the other woman's shoulder, but hooked her thumbs through her belt loops instead.

Wind whistled over the crater's jagged lip. Gavin seemed not to have noticed Kai's arrival or overheard their conversation. Bent by the pool's edge, he watched the idol dying within.

"Waiting is the worst part," Mara said. "Knowing I'm helpless."

"There has to be something you can do."

Her laugh was short. "I wish."

"Your idol just needs a loan. A few hundred souls on credit, to keep her alive until the market recovers."

"No one knows when the market will recover, or if. Makes it hard to price a loan."

"Sacrifice to her, then. We can afford the soulstuff to get her through the next few days."

"Shame I'm all out of virgins and aurochs. What the hell's the plural of 'aurochs' anyway?"

"Use the Order's funds. You're a priest. You're allowed."

"Jace says no."

"Did he say why?"

"Does it matter?" She paced again, in circles. "He said no."

"Blaming yourself won't help."

"Who do you think my clients will blame when their idol dies: The market? Or their hired priestess?" She jabbed her thumb against her sternum. "The guilt's mine sooner or later. I might as well accept that."

"Your clients signed off on the trade. They knew the risks."

"I wonder what it feels like," Mara said after a long silence. "Losing half of your soul at once."

"Idols don't feel like we do." Kai knew as she spoke that it was the wrong thing to say.

Stars glinted in black sky and black pool—different stars above and below, not reflections. The shattered ground was a thin shell separating darkness from darkness.

Gavin turned from the pool and shuffled toward them over lava pebbles. "Won't be long now."

Kai replaced him on the shore, leaned over the not-water's edge, and watched the idol drown.

She was a wire-frame sculpture of light, flailing in the depths like a fish caught on a line: female in figure, almost human. Wings flared. Goat legs bent against themselves. The suggestion of a mouth gaped in a not-quite-face. Her heart had faded, and the fade was spreading.

Other idols swam and shifted around her in the pool. Bright outlines of men, women, animals, and angels danced through invisible currents, tied each to each by silver threads. No threads bound the dying idol. Mara had severed her ties to the rest already, to keep her from dragging them down when she died.

"It's beautiful," Gavin said. He shifted from side to side, and his shadow swayed, long and broad, broken by the ground. "And sad. It looks beautiful and sad."

The idol stared up into Kai and through her, desperate, drowning, and scared.

Idols don't feel like we do.

Kai turned from the pool.

Human silhouettes watched from office windows above. Curious enough to observe, callous enough to keep their distance. Kai was being unfair. No. She was tired. The situation, that was unfair. The idol was about to die, and take Mara's career with it.

"What's her name?" Kai asked.

"The file code's forty digits long. I've called her Seven Alpha." Mara sat on a rock and stared down into her coffee. "Jace's secretary already sent me the paperwork. Paperwork, can you believe it? I should have expected, but still. They die, and we fill out forms."

Kai shouldn't have come. Should have left early, or lingered over her altars and prayers until the worst was over. One more silhouette watching Mara pace, using distance to shield herself from pain.

Mara's despair hurt, as did the fear in the idol's eyes. In Seven Alpha's eyes. Kai ought to be home, swaddled in sheets. She felt swaddled, here. Arms bound to her sides. Helpless. Her own words mocked her: *there has to be something you can do.*

There was.

"You think they'll fire me tomorrow," Mara said, "or let me stay long enough to pack my things?"

Kai stepped out of her shoes. Sharp stone scraped her soles. She unbuttoned her blouse. Gavin and Mara would stop her if they saw. Especially Gavin.

But Gavin wasn't looking. Maybe the silhouettes were, above. Maybe someone was running down the winding stair even now to catch her. She unbuttoned faster. "You'll be fine," Gavin said, behind, to Mara. "This could have happened to anyone. Shining

Empire debt always goes up in price. Everyone knows that. Knew that."

"You're not helping, Gavin."

"One of Magnus's idols failed six months ago, and he was promoted. It's good experience. That's what Jace said. A leader has to know how it feels to lose."

Kai heard a rustle of stiff cotton as Gavin reached for Mara's shoulder, and an answering whisper as Mara brushed his hand away. Last button free. The hook on her skirt followed, and the zipper.

The idol in the water screamed.

All at once, Kai thought. Do not wait, or question. If they see, they'll try to stop you.

Do it, or don't.

She shucked shirt and skirt, stepped out of the fabric's warding circle, swept her hands above her head, ran three steps to the world's edge, and dove.

Mara must have noticed in the last second, too late to do anything but shout: "Kai, what the hells are you—"

Black water opened before her, and closed behind her.

There are many worlds, and one. A shadow cast is real, and so's the caster, though each is of a different order. Cast a shadow complex enough, and one day it will look up. One day it will tear free from the wall to seek the one who gave it form.

What might such a freed shadow feel, tumbling through spaces of greater dimension than its own?

Kai fell through the realm of gods and idols, on which rock and light and living flesh float like a raft on a cave lake. Diving, she kicked. Bubbles of reality jellyfished up to the distant surface. She swam deeper.

Idols drifted immense around her, sphinxes and chimeras, animals and men and women in lightning outline, planet-sized though they'd seemed small from shore. Every one was beautiful, and each terrifying. In their center, Seven Alpha flailed limbs of silver and samite. Sharp teeth glimmered in her open mouth.

Down Kai swam, down, the drowning idol nearer now, body

large as a mainlander cathedral. One sweep of a hand nearly sliced Kai in half; Seven Alpha was desperate and almost dead, scared as a lamb on the butchering floor, but still, here , strong as a god.

The next time the idol clawed in her direction, Kai caught one of the lightning-wires that formed her wrist.

Her shoulders jerked in their sockets as the idol's arm dragged her along. She rushed through empty space, and its hidden edges tore her flesh and mind. Around her in the black, paper-thin mouths peeled back lips to bare white fangs. Hungry ghosts, ready to descend. The idol's death called scavengers to whom a soul wrapped in flesh was a chocolate wrapped in foil.

Kai could not get Seven Alpha's attention this way. She was a gnat, a flitting nuisance. She needed perspective.

She held a piece of the idol's wrist, but that piece moved with the rest of the wrist, and so by holding it she held the wrist itself, and if she held the wrist her hand had to be large enough to hold it, and if her hand was large, then, since the rest of her felt proportional to her hand, the rest of her was also large. Mountainous in fact, and strong, but still struggling against the whirlwind of Seven Alpha's death.

Never, ever (Kai's mother'd told her when she was four and emerged dripping from the water with a half-drowned boy in tow) grab a drowning man. Death's approach lends strength even to the weak. A drowner, crazed, will pull you with him. Hold back, find a rope or plank or life preserver, and let the poor bastard save himself. Herself. Itself.

Seven Alpha kicked Kai in the side and she felt her rib break. The idol cut her, and burned her, as she pulled her into an embrace. Up so close, the idol's face was all geometry, perfect planes and curves. She spasmed in Kai's grip, transformed to fire, to thorn, to stinging jellyfish, to billion-armed insect, and back to woman, final form no less painful than the rest. Goat legs sliced Kai's calves and thighs to the bone. Blood seeped into the water.

The idol buried her teeth in Kai's left shoulder. A scream bubbled from Kai's mouth and bloomed, rising. The god-realm's darkness rushed into her lungs. She gagged and felt her body start to die.

The idol withdrew her teeth and pressed Kai in flaying embrace as they fell. Worlds' weight crushed them together.

No time to waste. Kai kissed Seven Alpha on the mouth.

Cold tangled her tongue. Hunger caught her. Desperation pulled at her soul. She let it. She gave, and gave, and sank. Her soul surged into the idol's mouth, torn from her by need, an insignificant scrap against Seven Alpha's vast hunger.

The idol took Kai's soul, and pulled for more, but there was no more to give. They fell, dying, bound by flesh and spirit. The idol sagged. Anger gave way to loss.

Perfect.

Kai crafted a contract in her mind, and offered it to the idol. A simple trade: a seven million thaum line of credit, enough to save them both for a while, provided Seven Alpha return as collateral her only asset, Kai's stolen soul. Jace may have forbidden Mara from using the Order's funds to save this idol, but he'd said no such thing to Kai.

Seven Alpha was about to die. She had no choice but to accept, and save them both. Simple self-preservation.

Any minute now.

Thought came slow to Kai at such depth, weighed down by dream and deep time. They'd fallen so far even acceptance might not save them. Too late, too deep. Stupid. Her spinning mind shuddered, slowed, and soon would stop.

Her spinning mind shuddered, slowed, and soon

Her spinning mind shuddered,

Her spinning mind

Her

Yes.

A key turned in the lock of the world.

Kai's eyes snapped open. Power flooded from her, and her soul flowed back along the contract that now bound her to the idol. Light broke through her skin. Seven Alpha spread her wings, pulled from their kiss, smiled a spring morning. The idol's tarnished heart began to heal, to shine.

Kai shook with joy.

Then everything went wrong.

Arms seized Kai from behind: human arms, fleshy, strong. They pried her from the idol, pulled her back and up. Seven Alpha tried to follow, but slow, too weak to resist the not-water's weight. Kai fought, but the arms did not give. She knew her betrayers by their grip. Mara, slender and corded with muscle, fingernails biting Kai's wrists. Gavin, an immense weight of skin and meat. Jace, too, their master. He was the one who held her neck.

"Get off!" She yanked at their fingers. "Let me go!" They did not.

Seven Alpha fell as Kai rose. The contract that bound them stretched, frayed. Star eyes beneath curling horns stared up at Kai in dumb hope. The idol did not begin to scream until the cord snapped, and water closed in to crush her.

Fighting and clawing and biting and bleeding, Kai heard sense inside that shriek. There were words amid the fury and the fear, senseless and mad, impossible words, but words nonetheless.

Howl, bound world, Kai heard as the idol fell, as she died.

Kai cried out in answer, in frustration, in rage. Still they pulled her up, as Seven Alpha dwindled to a distant ship on fire, a cinder, a spark, a star, then gone.

Kai's friends dragged her to shore. She screamed them back and lay curled on sharp stone, bleeding, coughing, vomiting dreams. Warmth returned, the shadow bound once again to its wall. Traitor hands wrapped her in a sheet and lifted. Jace held her. His chest pressed through the sheet against the wound the idol's teeth left in her shoulder. Bloody fabric rasped over her wrecked skin.

She tried to tear free, but lacked the strength. They carried her from the pool: glass-flat, undisturbed by the idol's death.

"It's okay." Jace's voice, strong, level, sad, so unlike her father's. "It's okay. You're safe."

"No," was all she said.

2

Izza went to the Godsdistrikt to buy incense for the funeral. She found the shopkeep snoring.

The old man slept with bare warty feet propped up on the glass counter of his coffin-sized store. His head lolled back against his chair. One long wiry arm swung loose from his shoulder, and at the bottom of each swing the tip of his middle finger grazed the ground.

He wasn't losing customers. The distrikt dreamed through the day around him. Foreign sailors and dockworkers stayed away 'til sunset, and no Kavekana native would risk trafficking with gods in broad daylight. Still not prudent, though, to nap.

Izza slipped through the shop's front door without ringing the bell. The man's mouth slacked open as the door shut. His snort covered the hinge's creak. Izza waited, awash in smoke and scent. Her fingers itched. She could steal half his stock and leave before he noticed. Could swipe the dreams right out of his head.

She could. She didn't.

That was the point.

She walked to the counter and rang the bell. The old man snarled awake and staggered to his feet, machete suddenly in one hand. Izza strangled her urge to flee. Her reflection stared back from the machete blade, and from the glass incense cases. Ripped and dirty clothes, lean and hungry face.

Neither of them spoke. The old man's chest heaved. Heavy gray brows cast shadows across his bloodshot eyes. Incense smoke weighed on the sweltering air of a Kavekana afternoon.

"I'm here to buy," she said.

"Get out, kid. Your kind don't buy."

She wondered whether he meant street kids, or Gleblanders, or refugees, or poor people in general. All of the above, most likely.

She reached for her pocket.

"I'll cut your hand off and call the watch." The machete trembled. "You want to test me?"

"I'm here to buy incense." She pronounced the words with care, suppressing her accent as much as she could. "I want to show you my coin."

He neither moved nor spoke.

She took from her pocket a thin beaten disk of silver, with an Iskari squid god stamped on one face and a two-spired tower on the other. She sank a piece of her soul into the coin, twenty thaums and some change, and tried to stop herself from swaying as the shop grayed out. Running low. Running dangerous.

The old man's eyes glittered. He set the machete down. "What do you want?"

"Something nice," she said. Forming words took effort. She didn't like spending soul, not straight like this. She didn't have much to go around.

"Twenty thaums gets you nice." His head bobbed. His neck was freakishly long, and spotted like a giraffe's. "What kind of nice? We have Dhisthran sandalwood here all the way from the other side of the Tablelands, send men into rutting elephants' heat." Her face must have twisted, because he laughed, creaking like a rusty dock chain. "Smells for all occasions. Murder, sacrifice, passion, betrayal."

"I need incense," she said, "to mourn a god."

He lowered his chin and watched her through the bushes of his eyebrows. This was why Izza'd come herself, rather than sending one of the other kids: enough refugees had flowed through from the Gleb at one point or another that the request might not seem strange.

"Old festival coming up?" he asked. "Some god dead in your wars?"

"Give me the stuff." She didn't want her voice to shake. It shook all the same.

"Which one are you mourning? Or would I know its name?"

"A god that doesn't talk much."

He shrugged, and stepped into the back room, taking the machete with him. Thin trails of smoke rose from smoldering joss sticks, twisting in and out of light. Izza's head hurt from the soul loss. She hoped that was the reason. Maybe the old man had drugged her with smoke. He might be out the back door now, running to call for the watch, for the Penitents. She had done nothing wrong, but that didn't matter much.

She stayed. She needed this.

The man returned, machete in one hand and a slender black wood box in the other. He set the box on the counter and slid it across to her.

She reached for the box, but he placed the machete edge against the lid. His eyes were a lighter brown than Izza's own.

She laid her coin on the glass beside. He snatched the coin, walked it down spidery fingers, up again, kissed the milled edge, then dropped it into one of his four shirt pockets.

She grabbed the box, but he pressed down with the machete and the blade bit into the wooden lid.

"How old are you?" he said.

"Fifteen."

"Old for a street kid."

"Old enough to take what I pay for."

"You should be careful," he said. "The Penitents start grabbing kids about your age."

"I know." If she could have burned him with her gaze, he would have been dust already.

He lifted the machete. She tucked the box into her belt, and ran into the street, trailing doorbell's jingle and wafting incense and the old man's laughter.

Soul-loss visions haunted her down the block. Recessed windows stared from plaster walls, the eye sockets of sun-blanched skulls. Bright sun glinted off broken glass in gutters. The alley stank of rotting mangoes, stale water, and sour wine. Her headache wouldn't leave. She'd almost died of thirst once, in the desert, after her home burned, before she jumped ship for the Archipelago. Soul loss felt the same, only you couldn't cure it by drinking.

She was so far gone that her shaking hands woke the man whose purse she slit minutes later, an Alt Coulumbite sailor drowsing on a couch outside a Godsdistrikt gambling den, long pipe propped on his stomach. He caught for her wrist, but she ducked, faster strung out than most sober, grabbed a handful of coins, and ran down the alley. Stumbling to his feet he called for the watch, for the Penitents, for his god's curse upon her. Fortunately, neither watch nor Penitents were near, and foreign gods weren't allowed on Kavekana Island.

She ran until she collapsed, beside a fountain in a palm-shaded courtyard, and drank the dregs of soul from the sailor's coins. White returned to the walls of surrounding buildings, red to their tile roofs, joy to the fountain's babble, heat to the air, and life to her body.

A single dull gray pearl hung from a worn leather string around her neck. She clutched it tight and waited for the pain to pass.

She wasn't whole. She did not remember what whole felt like anymore. But she felt better, at least.

Izza met Nick at the corner of Epiphyte and Southern an hour and a half before sunset. He crouched by a lamppost, thin, bent, eyes downcast, scribbling in dust. He looked up when he heard her coming, and did not wave, or smile, or even speak. She often forgot he was younger than her. Keeping quiet made him seem smart.

Together they turned north, and walked up Southern toward the mountain.

They soon climbed out of the city. The bay emerged behind them, peeking over red roofs, and before long they could see the two Claws, East and West, curved peninsulas stretching south to shelter the harbor. They walked fast in the shade of overhanging palms, past large green lawns and sprawling houses. The mountain slopes weren't priests' sole property anymore, but real estate was expensive here, and the watch quick to sweep up loiterers.

When houses gave way to jungle, Izza and Nick left the road. Izza stepped lightly through the undergrowth, and only where she could see soil. Trapvines and poison ferns, ghosts and death's head centipedes lived in these woods. Nick moved slowly through the foliage, and made more sound than Izza liked. Any sound was more sound than Izza liked. She walked softly until the trees gave way to solid rock, and the mountain's roots rose from the earth.

She scampered up the stone, and held out a hand to help Nick after.

"I wish," he said, breathing hard, as they climbed, "we could do this back at the docks."

"The mountain's holy," she said. "There were gods here once, even if the priests build idols now. Where else should we hold the Lady's funeral?"

He didn't answer. He didn't know what they were doing. Neither did she. No one had ever taught them how to pray: they made most of it up as they went along.

They cleared the trees and spidered up the scree, exposed to sky and sun. Izza fought her urge to hide. The mountain, Kavekana'ai, was a holy place, but it wasn't hers. For all she knew the Order's priests could feel them crawling flealike on the cliff face. Or a Penitent might see them exposed against the stone: their jeweled eyes were sharp as eagles', and hungrier.

They climbed. Izza helped Nick, and he helped her. A dragonfly watched them both from its stone perch, then buzzed off, wings scattering light to rainbows.

By the time they reached the funeral ledge, the sun had just kissed the western horizon, and the mountain's shadow lay long upon the ocean to the east. The other kids were here already, ten of them, representatives of the rest. They'd built the pyre, and crouched back against the rock. Izza felt their eyes, eyes of every hue in faces of every color, all hungry, all watching her. She'd heard them whispering before she reached the ledge. They fell silent now.

A row of ash smears lined the cliff, one for each funeral past, and in their center stood the pyre, a small pile of twigs and palm thatch. On the pyre lay a jade-breasted bird with folded blue wings.

Ivy had found the bird outside a hotel, neck broken. At least, she claimed she found it dead. The girl had a crooked sense of humor, and an even stranger sense of worship. She hugged herself and smiled grimly at Izza. Breath whistled through the gap between her front teeth.

Izza crouched beside the dead bird. Nick took his place with the others, and waited with them.

Izza felt her age. At fifteen, she was the oldest, had been since Sophie was taken for a Penitent after the Green Man died. So the story was hers to tell.

The others waited. Little Ellen curled her legs up under her chin. Jet ground his teeth, and picked at the side of his sandal where a strip of rubber had come loose.

Izza licked her lips. She'd seen Sophie do this before, for other gods. Her turn, now. That was all.

"The Blue Lady," she said, "is gone."

The others nodded. "Yes," a few whispered. There was no ritual beyond what felt right, and nothing did.

She told the story as she'd thought it through. "She died helping us. The way she lived. Tired of waiting for his dead boys to do his work for him, Smiling Jack himself came down the mountain to hunt her children through the streets. When he caught them, he threw them into his sack, and shut the sack, and when it opened again there was nothing inside." This had never happened. She'd made the story up days before, a patchwork of invention and theft and half-remembered dreams. None of these kids had been caught, and none had seen Smiling Jack. Still, they listened. "He caught me in a dead end, with stolen gold in my pocket. I offered him the gold, and he said he didn't want gold. I offered him my next night's take, and he said he didn't want that, either. I asked him to spare me, and he refused. He came at me, with the sack open—it looks like burlap outside but inside is all needles." Heads bobbed. They knew, though they'd never seen. The sack, the needles, both felt true. "The Lady fell on him from above, tearing and pecking at his eyes. I ran, but as I ran I felt her die."

More nods, emphatic. They'd all felt the death, and heard her scream.

"She saved me. I didn't deserve that. I didn't deserve her."

The backs of Izza's eyes burned. She tried to breathe, and realized she was gulping air. She looked down at the bird, and saw everything it wasn't, everything it should have been. This small feathery stand-in never sheltered her in sickness, never whispered promises to her at sunset, never caught her when she fell. Her heart beat double-time in her ears, loud and distant at once. The whistle of breath through Ivy's teeth sounded like a scream.

"We didn't." Nick, again. She hated the confidence in his voice. As if he believed this made-up ceremony would help. "None of us." Izza's heart kept up its strange double-beat—physical, an echo as if she stood too close to a loud drum. A familiar feeling. Her blood chilled. "When I first met the Blue Lady, I—"

Izza lunged for Nick. He hit the cliff face hard, and swore, but she clapped a hand over his mouth, and raised one finger to hers. He understood then, and froze.

The others did, too. Jet stopped picking at his sandal.

Izza's heart beat in her chest, but the echo she felt was not a heartbeat. And that high keening was not the whistle of breath through Ivy's teeth.

She released Nick, and uncurled herself on the ledge. Spread flat, she edged out her head so she could see.

A hundred meters to their left, a Penitent climbed the slope.

The Penitent was built on the model of men, but larger: a statue three meters tall and almost as broad, features carved of planes and angles, two massive three-fingered hands, two feet like slabs of rock. It did not climb like Izza and Nick had climbed, feeling for handholds, testing and trusting. It marched up the mountain as if stairs had been carved into the eighty-degree slope. Joints ground rock against rock. Dust drifted down behind it. Jewel eyes in its stern stone face scanned the mountainside.

With every step, the Penitent screamed.

Izza wondered who was trapped inside. Some dockside tough too smart or drunk or angry for his own good. Dope peddler, or murderer, or a kid old enough to be tried like an adult. Maybe that was Sophie. You couldn't tell from looking which Penitents held men and which women. You could only guess from the sound of their cries.

Penitents made you better. That was the line. You went in broken, and came out whole.

They just had to break you more first.

Izza did not shake. She'd given up shaking when her mother died, when her village burned. She did not make a sign to ward off bad luck or evil spirits. She'd tried all those signs, one after another, and none had worked for her before. Staying still, though, had.

So she stayed still, and watched the Penitent climb.

It drew level with their ledge.

She stopped breathing. Its steps slowed—or else her terror slowed time.

The Penitent climbed on.

Ivy shifted, dislodging gravel. A whisper of a sound, but Izza glared at her nonetheless, and the girl's pale skin paled more.

Footsteps receded. Faded. Vanished up the mountain.

Wind blew soft and cool over shaded slopes. The sun set, and the first stars pierced the sky.

The dead bird lay on the pyre. The kids watched her. Scared, and waiting for direction. For their leader to tell them what happened next.

"I can't do this anymore," she said.

No one spoke.

"Let's go," she said. "We don't need gods who die and leave us afraid. We don't have to be the ones who survive."

Their eyes glistened in the light of new-risen stars.

"Okay," she said. "Fine. But this is the last. Care for the gods yourselves from now on. I'm done."

She fished a coin from her pocket and handed it around. Each of them sank a piece of their soul into the metal, and by the time Nick passed it back to Izza, the coin pulsed with heat and life.

She took all their soul scraps, and held them, and touched them to the thatch. The dry grass caught at once, and burned, and the bird burned, too. A thread of sickly smoke rose to the sky. Izza removed two incense sticks from the black box, and lit them in the pyre. They smelled of the desert after rain, of blood shed on cold stone, of empty temples pierced by shafts of light through ruined roofs. Beneath all that, she smelled burning feathers.

Nice, the old man had said. She wasn't sure.

One by one the others left. Ivy stayed longer than the rest, curled into a ball against the ledge, chin propped on her knees as reflected fire and burning bird made a hell in her pinprick pupils. At last even she climbed down, and only Nick remained.

Izza could barely breathe. She told herself it was the smoke.

They climbed down together, and through the woods, and strolled along Southern past rich folk's houses until plaster walls closed in again and streetlamps put the stars to flight and they could walk easy, camouflaged by drunks and madding crowds.

"What did you mean," he said, "that you can't do this anymore?"

"What I said. I won't wait around to be locked in one of those things, just for one of you to take up as storyteller after me and get locked up in turn. I won't be Sophie for you. For them. I have to go."

"You can't."

"Watch me."

"They need this. They need you."

"They shouldn't," she said, and walked away down Southern toward the beach. He didn't follow. She told herself she didn't care.

3

Kai met the Craftswoman a week later in a nightmare of glass. She sat in a glass chair in front of a glass table and her fingers trailed over the slick armrests without leaving a trace of oil or sweat. In one corner a glass fern stood in a glass pot, glass roots winding through glass soil. Other identical rooms stretched above, below, and to all sides, beyond transparent walls, ceiling, and floor, and in those rooms sat identical Kais and Craftswomen. As Kai crossed her legs beneath the table her infinite other selves crossed their legs, too, a susurrus of stockings breaking the silence of the dream.

In the distant waking world, she lay bandaged on a bed. Here, no injuries bound her except the ones she earned herself.

She'd set her hand on the table's edge as she sliced her palm to the pink, a long deep wound that healed at once. The blood on the table stayed, though. Millions of red streaks surrounded her on millions of tables, catching the nightmare's sourceless light.

"Before we discuss the idol's death," said Ms. Kevarian, "please explain the services your firm provides."

"Our Order, you mean."

"Yes."

Myriad reflections offered Kai a choice of perspectives on her interviewer: a severe Craftswoman in a gray pinstriped suit, with black eyes, short white hair, and a thin wide mouth. Ms. Kevarian sat statue still. Her eyes held neither pity nor humor, only a curiosity like Kai had seen in birds' eyes, alien, evaluative, and predatory.

Behind Ms. Kevarian sat her client, a shadow in a white suit, a smudge of gray with a broad and gleaming grin. Fingers like wisps of smoke never seemed to rest. They laced together and unlaced, and trailed down his lapels and along the chair's arm without seeming to care whether the glass edge cut. He hadn't spoken since they shook hands; nor had the Craftsman Jace sent into the dream to protect and advise Kai, a round-chested skeleton who bore down so heavily on his note-taking pad that Kai wondered if he might be writing with rips instead of ink.

"I thought your clients would have told you," Kai said, and the Craftsman shot her a sharp look. *Don't get cute*, Jace had cautioned her. So much for that.

Kai wished she looked nearly so cool or collected as Ms. Kevarian. She had a choice of perspectives on herself, too, and didn't like what she saw: tan suit rumpled, a few strands loose from her tied-back hair, her round face strained. Gray circles lingered under her eyes, and a haunted look within them. Her mouth was dry. A glass of water stood on the table before her, but she feared its sharp edges and didn't drink.

"I am asking you," Ms. Kevarian said. "For the record."

She felt small in front of this woman, and hated the feeling. When she remade her body she should have made herself taller. "I've never worked with your clients directly."

"In general terms, then. What do priests do here on Kave-kana Island?"

"We build and sustain idols—constructs of faith—for worshippers."

"Would you say that you build gods?"

"No," she said. "Gods are complex. Conscious. Sentient. The best idols look like gods, but they're simpler. Like comparing a person to a statue: the resemblance is there, but the function's different."

"And what, precisely, is the . . . function of your idols?"

"Depends on the idol and the client. Some people want to worship fire, or fertility, or the ocean, or the moon. Changes from client to client."

"What benefits would a worshipper derive from such a thing?"

Even such a simple question might be a trap. "The same as from a god. A fire idol might confer passion. Strength. Return on investment in various heat-related portfolios."

"Why would someone work with one of your idols, and pay your commission, rather than deal with gods directly?"

"Each pilgrim has her own reason. Why don't you ask your clients theirs?"

"I am asking you."

"The mainland's a dangerous place," she said. "If you live and work in the Old World, gods demand sacrifices to support themselves. If you're in the New World, the Deathless Kings and their councils charge heavy fees to fund police forces, utilities, public works. If you travel from place to place, a horde of gods and goddesses and Craftsmen chase after pieces of your soul. You can give them what they want—or you can build an idol with us, on Kavekana, and keep your soulstuff safe here. The idol remains, administered by our priests, and you receive the benefits of its grace wherever you go, no more subject to gods or Deathless Kings than any other worshipper of a foreign deity."

"So, you believe your idols' main function is sacrifice avoidance."

The water glass tempted, despite its sharp edges. "I didn't say that. We offer our pilgrims freedom to work and worship as they choose."

"And part of that freedom is the assurance you will care for the idols you create. That you will protect the souls with which your clients trust you."

"Yes."

"Is that why you jumped into the pool?"

"I thought I could save your clients' idol," Kai said. "She was drowning."

"By 'she' you mean the construct designated Seven Alpha."

"Yes."

"Were you familiar with Seven Alpha's case history?"

"I was not."

"Would you say your High Priest Mister Jason Kol is a competent judge of an idol's health?"

"Jace? Yes. He trained me."

"And Mara Ceyla?"

"Of course." She'd said that too fast, she knew, when Ms.

Kevarian made a note of it. Or else she hadn't, and Ms. Kevarian was making notes at random to confuse her. "Our Applied Theologians are the best anywhere."

"What made you second-guess your coworkers?"

"I didn't." She bristled at the implicit scorn. Jace had cautioned her, and their Craftsman, too: *keep your answers short, within the limits of the question.* As if she were a child to be led. She swallowed her anger, and it cut her stomach. "I thought I could do more."

The Craftswoman's client produced a full moon from his sleeve, walked it along his fingers, and vanished it again. His fingers left black trails in the air. Ms. Kevarian nodded. "What could you do that they could not?"

"First, I was willing to run a big risk to save Seven Alpha—I needed to let her take my soul so she would have collateral for the contract. That's more than Jace could expect or ask of Mara. Second, I believed I could survive in the pool long enough to save the idol. There wasn't time to contact your clients, but if I approached Seven Alpha just before she died, she might have accepted the deal out of sheer animal self-preservation." She stopped talking. *Wait for the questions,* they'd said, *even if you chafe at silence.*

"Why could you survive longer than the others?"

"Because I'm better in the pool than most of them."

"Better than your teacher?"

That cool doubt was bait, but bait Kai happily swallowed. "I remade my body there, completely—Jace didn't. Not many people do, these days. As a result, I'm more comfortable in the pool than most. It's in my marrow." The Craftsman beside her tensed. Let him. "I thought I could last long enough to save her."

"By 'her,' you are again referring to the construct. The idol."

"Yes."

"You imply that it has gender and personhood."

"Language is weird like that," Kai said. One corner of Ms. Kevarian's mouth tweaked up, acknowledging, rather than agreeing. "Archipelagese has a fine set of gender-neutral pronouns, but mainlanders don't like them for some reason."

"What about personhood? Are the idols conscious, or self-aware?"

"No. Complex behavior doesn't emerge from a simple system, any more than lumps of iron can speak. The idols we build have a few believers at most; however much soulstuff they store, their behavior only gets so complex. About the level of a dumb rat."

And yet, and yet. What about that scream, and the words within it, the memory denied: *howl*, Seven Alpha said there at the end, howl, bound world. Words hidden within the death cry, steganography of fear between two beings that recently shared a soul. No, keep to the question. Don't hesitate. Don't hint. Ms. Kevarian did not ask about the words, because Kai had not written them into her report, and no one else had heard them. This was not the time, not the place, to raise the subject.

Anyway, Ms. Kevarian had already proceeded to her next question. "But you have affection for these constructs."

Kai let the words go. Breathed them out, with her memories of the dark. "We build them by hand. We're paid to worship them, to love them. We tell their stories. It's easy to get attached."

Another note, another nod. "You said you were stronger in the pool because you'd remade yourself completely. What did you mean?"

The Order's Craftsman cleared his throat, a sound like gravel being stirred. "That's a personal question," he said. "I don't see how it's relevant."

"I want to understand Ms. Pohala's decision-making process." Ms. Kevarian's smile lacked the warmth Kai typically associated with that expression.

Kai met those black, unblinking eyes. "Back before the God Wars," she said, "priests entered the pool during initiation—they met gods there, learned secrets, changed. Inside, spirit and matter flow more easily from shape to shape. Now the gods are gone, but we still go down. The first time priests dive, we change—we fix the broken bodies we inhabit. These days most changes are small: one priest I know corrected her eyesight; another cleaned up a port wine stain on her cheek. In the past more priests went further, like I did. That's where the tradition came from, after all. These days full initiates aren't as common, but there are a few of us."

"How did you remake yourself?"

"I was born in a body that didn't fit."

"Didn't fit in what way?"

"It was a man's," she said. Defiant, she watched Ms. Kevarian's face for a reaction: a raised eyebrow, a subdermal twitch, a turned-up lip. The Craftswoman seemed impassive as calm ocean—and Kai knew how much, and how little, one could tell from an ocean's surface.

"Ms. Kevarian," she said, "I tried to save your client's idol. I failed. Why are we here? Why not let this go?"

"You are bound to answer my questions," Ms. Kevarian said. "I am not bound to answer yours. But I will, out of good faith. My clients, the Grimwald family"—a forked tongue twitched out from between the gray man's jagged teeth—"suffered operational inconvenience due to their idol's death. We're investigating whether this inconvenience was avoidable. Your actions intrigue us. You believed the idol could be saved. Mister Kol did not. Do you think your judgment was wrong, or his?"

Kai stood so fast the chair toppled behind her; its edge sliced the back of her legs and blood seeped into her stockings. She didn't need to be a Craftswoman to see the threat in that question: if Kai was right, then Jace was wrong, and the Order liable for Seven Alpha's death. And if Kai was wrong, why did the Order employ priests so incompetent as to risk their lives on a lost cause? "I tried to help your people. So did Mara. And you want to use that against us."

"Kai," the Craftsman beside her said. "Sit down."

Kai did not. Nor did Ms. Kevarian seem at all perturbed. "Many have sat, or stood, across this table, and claimed they only wanted to help. They rarely specify whether they wanted to help my clients, or themselves."

"If you want to accuse me of something, say it."

"I am not accusing you or anyone." The Craftswoman ran her pen down the margin of her notes, nodding slightly at each point. "I am simply asking questions."

Kai reached for the water glass. Its edges pressed against her palm, the blade of its lip against hers; she drank the pain, and when she set the glass down only a drop of blood remained at the corner of her mouth. She licked it, and tasted salt and metal.

"There's no question here," she said. "Jace and Mara were right. I was wrong. I made a mistake, and put myself in danger." Strange that she could keep her voice level as she said the words. Humiliation was like ripping off a bandage: easier to endure if you took it all at once.

"And yet you have not suffered a formal reprimand. You still hold your position in Kavekana's priesthood."

"That's not a question."

"Based on your actions, do you think you deserve disciplinary action?"

"I'm still in the hospital," she said. "It's early. Do you have any more questions?"

"There are always more questions, Ms. Pohala."

"Get on with it, then."

Ms. Kevarian lowered her pen.

Time broke after that, and she tumbled from moment to moment through the dream. Questions flowed on, in that same round-voweled alto voice. Light pierced her from all sides at once. She drank, and was not sated; turned from Ms. Kevarian but found herself staring into another Ms. Kevarian's eyes. She sat not in one room reflected to infinity, but in infinite rooms, asked in each a different question, her answers blending to a howl.

She woke in her sickbed in Kavekana'ai, panting, tangled in sheets. Ghostlights glimmered from panels and instruments on the walls. A metronome ticked the beats of her heart. The ticks slowed as she breathed. In the polished ceiling she saw her own reflection, a sepia blur swathed in hospital linen.

Paper rustled. She was not alone.

Jace sat in a chromed chair by the wall. He folded his issue of the *Journal* so Kai couldn't see the date. He looked worse than she remembered, thin and sunken, clad all in black. He set the paper down, poured her a glass of water, and lifted it to her lips. She tried to take the cup from him, but bandages wrapped her hands. She drank, though the taste of glass shivered her.

"How'd I do?" she said when he pulled the water away. Her voice sounded flat and dull, an instrument left too-long idle.

"You were great," he said. "Rest, now. If you can."

She lay back, and knew no more.

4

Izza dangled her legs over the edge of an East Claw warehouse rooftop, and drank her stolen beer. Kavekana's city lights reflected in the black bay below, long false trails to freedom. A few years and forever ago, the two illuminated peninsulas cradling the harbor had welcomed her like her lost mother's embrace. They'd turned, since, to teeth, and the black water to the fanged mouth's inside. Clocks chimed two in the morning; Izza had spent the last hour deciding how to leave.

She was no stranger to moving on. Life was movement. She'd lied to herself thinking otherwise. The kids would miss her, fine, but the kids could find their own way, like she had. They didn't need her.

So she sat, and thought, and hated herself, and drank. She didn't drink as a rule, but there was a time for breaking every rule. She'd stolen this beer from a fat woman who ran a stall five blocks inland in the Godsdistrikt, selling cigarettes and cheap booze. The woman, caught up in a red-faced hands-flailing argument with a Kosite over the price of cigarettes, hadn't noticed the bottle's disappearance. She did notice Izza's sudden retreat from the stand, and shouted, "Thief!" after her, but Godsdistrikt crowds ran mudslide thick and fast. Izza vanished down a side alley before anyone could hear the woman's cry, not that anyone would have helped.

The beer needed a bottle opener. Fortunately the slums around the Godsdistrikt were well supplied with drunks. Izza stole a church key from the belt of a broad-backed sailor girl distracted by a clapboard prophet preaching doomsday, and found a rooftop where she could drink in peace.

She ran a finger along the frayed leather of her necklace, and wondered how to leave.

In the last four years she'd grown too big to sneak shipboard. As for work, well, sailors sang old pre-Wars songs about signing on with whalers and the like, but after singing they complained how the bad old days were gone. Shipmasters wanted papers, résumés, union cards. Stealing enough to buy herself a berth—that might work, but so much theft would attract attention. She could talk the kids into helping her, but she didn't want to, not for this. Pawning everything she owned wouldn't make up a ticket price. She didn't own much.

So she paced the passages of her mind, in the small hours of the morning, until she heard the fight.

Fights were common in East Claw. Sailors brawled, and local toughs, and sometimes if the scuffles spread to riot the Watch came, with Penitents to reinforce them. But solitude and alcohol had gone to her head, and this fight was loud and near. Stone footsteps thundered down dockside streets, multiplied by echoes: Penitents, running. Two, maybe more. The Penitents terrified, but they put on a good show.

So she rambled along the roof and, after checking her balance and relative level of intoxication, sprinted and sprang across the narrow alley between this warehouse and the next. She ran to the building's edge, and lay flat with her head jutting over the drop.

At first she did not understand the scene below.

The Penitents were familiar at least: two immense stone figures, broad and thick as battlements, blunt features formed from planes of rock. The Penitent on Kavekana'ai had marched up the slope with grim determination, but these moved so fast the word "movement" didn't seem enough. The prisoners within cried and cursed from the inhuman speeds their statue shells forced on them: one man, and, Izza judged from the voice, one woman. Their howls scraped the back of her skull, tightened her limbs, and locked her joints.

This much she'd seen before. But the thing—the woman—the Penitents fought was new.

She was quicksilver and smoke and swift water. Green eyes burned in the mask of her face, and great razor-pinioned wings flared from her back. She flowed as she thought: a Penitent swung at her with a granite blur of arm, and she ducked beneath the blow and rose off the ground with a knee-kick that struck the Penitent's bare rock torso and sent it staggering, chest spider-webbed by cracks. The woman turned to run, but the second Penitent blocked her way. She tried to dodge around, a mistake: the Penitents were faster than they looked, their arms broad. A stone hand swept out, and she jumped back. Wings flared to catch her in the air and send her spinning down again to earth.

Izza had fought before, wild, bloody backstreet brawls, gouging eyes, biting wrists, bashing stones into skulls and vice versa, combatants a haze of limbs and fear. The winged woman fought different, fast and fierce but tight, too, as if every movement served a higher purpose.

And still she was losing. As she fell, the first Penitent's stone fist pistoned out and caught her by the arm. With her free hand the woman grabbed the Penitent's elbow. Wings flared and beat and at the same time she pulled sideways. Stone broke, the joint bent backward, and the Penitent's scream—the man's—shivered the night. It released her, and falling she kicked viciously at its knee. The Penitent stumbled, and collapsed. The woman landed, but one arm hung limp from her shoulder. The second Penitent struck; she dodged, too slow, and the fist clipped her side. Izza heard a crunch of breaking bone.

The woman struggled to rise. With eyes of green fire she glared into and through the Penitent above her. A granite arm rose, and fell; the woman caught the Penitent's wrist. Stone ground and creaked. Inside the Penitent someone sobbed.

Izza'd never seen anyone last this long against one Penitent, let alone two: she had thought the stone watchmen invulnerable to everything but Craft. This winged figure was no Craftswoman, though. She did not drink the light around her, or wrong the ground on which she stood, or crackle with eldritch sorcery. She was brilliant, and she was doomed. The Penitent bore down, and she bent under its sheer strength.

Izza should have run. In a few days she'd be gone from Kavekana anyway. But when she stood, instead of slipping away across the rooftops, she slid onto a fire escape, and clanged down five stories to drop from ladder to cobblestone street, shouting the whole way, "Stop! Thief!" She ran across the street behind the fight, still shouting, to the shelter of the alley opposite and inland. If she had to run, she might be able to lose the Penitents in the warrens. Might. "Stop!"

The Penitent's head swiveled round to Izza. Gem eyes gleamed, and Izza felt herself seen: five six and skinny and scared, standing in the open on flat ground before monsters. She stopped breathing.

A silver streak struck the Penitent in the side of the head, and again. One jewel eye went dark. Stone crunched. The statue swayed, stumbled, and fell. It lay twitching across from its brother with the broken leg.

The silver woman stood over them both, cradling her useless arm. One wing hung from her shoulder at a bad angle. She limped around the fallen Penitents and away, up Izza's alley.

As the woman left the street, her silver tarnished and broke. Black cotton shirt and denim pants showed through widening gaps in her mirrored carapace, and pale skin too, bruised and dirt smeared. One human eye, also green, paired with the eye of emerald fire. Blond hair, cut short. Muscle and sharp lines. The wings melted last, and the silver woman was silver no more. She lurched down the alley, clutching her injured arm, favoring the side where the Penitent hit her. She swore to herself, words too low for Izza to catch. Their eyes met as the woman passed, black into green and back again.

That should have been the end of it. The woman limped half the alley's length, gait weaving and uneven, then stopped, slumped against a red brick wall, and bent her head to breathe.

This was not Izza's problem. She'd helped enough already. Time to run.

The Penitents' cries rose to an impassive sky. More would come soon to aid their comrades.

Izza knelt before the woman. Green eyes stared through strings of golden hair, not at Izza but around her, refusing to focus. Sweat slicked the woman's face, and she breathed so heavily Izza thought she might throw up. Izza snapped her fingers twice in front of those green eyes. "Hey," she said. "Hey. We need to get you out of here."

"Who?" The voice was cloudy and unfocused as her gaze. Izza'd heard that vagueness before, from sailors rising out of opium dreams or divine rapture. Great. Whatever this woman was, she was in withdrawal. The Penitents must have smelled the god on her, and come hunting. No foreign gods allowed on Kavekana.

"The Penitents won't stay down long." Izza risked a glance back: the stone around the fallen statues paled and lost color as they drained its essence into themselves. Healing, fast. A few minutes before they recovered, no more. "Do you have a place to hide?"

She shook her head. "Not yet."

"Shit." Leave her. Or dump her in the Godsdistrikt with the other grace addicts. Hard-luck cases aplenty on this island. But none of them could fight off a Penitent, let alone two. "Follow me."

Izza offered her hand, but the woman slapped it away. She closed her eyes, and drew a shuddering breath. When she opened them again, she took a step, and this time did not fall. "Okay," she said. "Let's go."

Izza led her through twisting Godsdistrikt alleys, to mask their trail with the stench of trash and foreign joss. The woman followed, around Dumpsters, over unconscious sailors, beneath the red lights of hothouse windows, and through puddles of foul water. At last, trail good and lost, Izza turned them back west toward the bay.

"I don't know your name," the woman said.

"Izza."

"Cat," she replied in answer to Izza's unasked question.

Cat passed out across the street from the collapsed warehouse. Izza heard her slam into a trash can, and caught her before she fell farther. The woman weighed more than she looked, as if her skeleton were not made of bone. Izza crouched beside her in the stink of garbage and stale water, and waited for the road to clear.

When Dockside Boulevard was empty of Penitents and freight traffic all the way south into East Claw, and north until it joined the Palm, she draped Cat's arms over her shoulders, hoisted her up, and stumbled across the road. She ducked through a hole in the wall next to the warehouse's padlocked gate, and in.

Rats and beetles scrabbled away over the slab floor. Rotten crates and dust, muck and fallen beams and tangles of rusty wire crowded them round. Decay and wisps of incense hung on the heavy air, and stars shone through gaps in the half-fallen ceiling. This warehouse had stood abandoned as long as Izza'd known or anyone else could remember. Its roof fell in one hurricane season, wrecking whatever cargo it contained and ruining the owners; nobody had fixed up the place in the years since. Piled debris cut the warehouse in half, and as far as most knew, the shoreside half was the only one open enough for folk to walk or sit.

She laid Cat in a patch of moonlight, left her there, and went to clear a space for her to sleep near the debris wall.

When Izza turned back, she saw a thin figure standing over Cat's body. She forced herself to relax. "Nick. Hi." She recognized him by the way he held his shoulders: hunched forward, as if pushing against an unseen wind.

"Who's this?"

"I found her," she said. "She's hurt. Give me a hand."

She walked back to the moonlight and lifted Cat by her armpits. Nick did not move to help.

"Fine." She dragged the woman across the floor, into the space she'd cleared. Her heels left trails in the dust. Cat groaned, and Izza shifted her grip to put less pressure on the injured shoulder.

"I thought you were going."

"I am," she said. "But she needed help. What do you want from me?"

"Stay," he said.

So simple.

"I can't." She looked down at Cat. "I'll take care of her, for a while. I'll stay that long."

"You can't have it both ways. You can't say you're breaking up the gang, and then bring someone here to put us all in danger."

"We were never a gang, and I *am* leaving. Just. She knocked out two Penitents. She deserves our help. My help." Izza searched the warehouse, but they were alone. "And what's this 'all,' anyway? I don't see anyone here."

"Me."

"Except for you."

"The kids are hiding," he said.

"We're kids."

"No. We're not."

"I need to leave, Nick," she said. "Nothing's safe here. Not gods. Not us."

"Change your mind."

"No."

Cat groaned, and Izza returned to her side. The woman's eyes rolled behind closed lids, and her lips twitched. If they formed words, Izza couldn't read them.

When she looked up, the warehouse was empty.

She waited for Nick to speak again, from hiding. But he was gone, like her family, like her gods.

Izza left Cat unconscious on the warehouse floor, and went to look for water.

5

Kai didn't hear from Mara for two weeks. When the other woman finally made it up the steep cliff steps to the balcony where Kai lay convalescing, she waited out of sight by the stairs, presumably working up the will to speak.

At first Kai—pillow propped in bed, white sheets pooled around her waist, wearing a hospital gown and reading the *Journal*—ignored her. Mara didn't like pain, physical or emotional, always last to shed her blood on an altar stone. Kai'd mocked her reluctance, but fourteen days into recovery, she was coming to understand the woman's caution.

So she read the business section, waited, and pretended not to notice Mara. She ran out of patience halfway through the stock columns. "You should short Shining Empire bonds," she said then, loud so her voice carried. "Hard and fast. Today. Exchanges don't close in Alt Coulumb until eight. Plenty of time to arrange the trade."

"You knew I was here."

"Saw you climbing the stairs."

"Glad you're in good spirits." Kai didn't need to look to know the shape of Mara's smile: slantwise and sarcastic.

"The nurses won't let me anywhere near spirits." Kai turned the page, and scanned an editorial by some bleeding heart in Iskar, suggesting that all the other bleeding hearts in Iskar join a crusade to stop the civil war in the Northern Gleb. No plan, just hand wringing and noble rhetoric. Fortunately: Iskar didn't have a good history with crusades. "Alt Coulumb's index funds are up, and the Shining Empire debt market's rebounded. Turns out the rumors of open trade on their soul exchange were wrong after all."

"Does that matter now?"

"False panics make for overcorrections. Shining Empire soul-bonds are trading twenty points higher than a month ago. The price will normalize in a week. Short-sell. Borrow against our AC index holdings to finance the trade. Act fast, and you'll make back everything the Grimwalds lost when Seven Alpha died. A peace offering. I'd do it myself, but nobody'll let me near the trading office. I had to take a nurse hostage to get them to give me a god-damn newspaper."

Mara strode past Kai to the balcony's edge. Slope wind whipped the hem of her dress like a luffing sail. "It's too late for peace offer-ings. They want a sacrifice."

"You mean the Grimwalds. And their Craftswoman."

"Yes."

"That's what it sounded like in my deposition, too," Kai said. "How'd yours go, by the way?"

Mara shuddered, and stared out over the rail, down the vol-cano.

Kai did not bother to look. She'd grown accustomed to the view. Kavekana, beautiful as always: stark black stone slopes, colonized even at this violent height by lichen, moss, and adventurous ferns. Farther down, grasses grew, and farther still palms, coconut, and imported date. Epiphytes flourished beneath the trees. Past those Mara would see signs of humankind, the fiercest invasive species, asserting presence with rooftop and stone arch, temple and bar and gold-ribbon road, traces thicker as the eye proceeded south until slope gave way to city and beach and the paired peninsulas of the Claws. In their grip the glittering harbor thronged with tall-mast clippers, schooners, the iron-hulled hulks of container ships an-chored near East Claw's point where the water was deep enough to serve them. Other islands swelled, purple ghosts, on the horizon. Craftsmen's spires hovered out there, too, crystal shards almost as tall as the volcano, flashing in the sun.

Kai had tired of it all in her first week of bed rest with noth-ing to do but watch the sea beat again and again on Kavekana's sand. Boring, and worse, a reminder of her own atrophy. No doubt the nurses thought the physical therapy they guided her through each day would help, but to Kai it felt like a joke. Raise this arm, lower it, raise it again. No weights, no failure sets, no rage, no fight, no victory. *If it hurts, tell me and we'll stop.* The first time she tried not to tell them, they threatened to give her even easier exercises unless she cooperated. Not that she could imagine easier exercises. Perhaps they would devise a system to help raise her arm, some elaborate contraption of counterweights and pulleys.

She set her newspaper aside and watched Mara's back. Her dress was the kind of blue desert folk said skies were: dry and pale and distant. A curve of calf peeked out beneath her skirt's drifting hem. Whatever bravery brought Mara here had given out, or else the scenery had crushed her into silence.

"If my mother saw you like this," Kai said, "she'd have you lacquered and mounted on a ship's prow."

"Do they do that? Living ships?"

"I think someone made real ones back in the God Wars, for the siege of Alt Selene. Forget whose side it was, or whether they kept the spirit's source body on ice for later. Probably not. It was a rough war. So I hear."

"I feel like that, sometimes. Don't you?"

"Mounted? Only on a good day."

She laughed, without sound. Kai could tell by her shoulders' shake. "No. Like those bowsprit figures, I mean." When Mara turned from the view, Kai saw she wore a blush of makeup. Interesting. She'd come armored. "Other people trim the sails and turn the wheel and the ships go where they want. The bowsprit woman's stuck. She's the ship's point. Whatever danger they meet, she meets it first. She can't even mutiny, or leave."

"Maybe she does," Kai said. "Maybe she bails, and takes the ship with her. Breaks it on rocks. Dashes it to pieces in a storm."

"Hell of a choice. Live imprisoned or kill everyone you know breaking free."

"Is it life if you're trapped inside it?"

"As long as you're breathing, that's life."

Kai touched her chest through the stiff scratchy gown. "I'm

breathing now. I don't know if I'm alive. Don't feel alive wearing this thing, anyway."

"It looks good on you."

"There hasn't been a person made that a hospital gown looks good on. They say I'll have my own clothes back next week, Seconday probably."

"That long?"

"Jace doesn't want me to leave before I'm healed, and he knows he won't be able to stop me once I can put on my own pants." Using her arms as a prop, she sat up, twisted sideways, and rested her feet on the stone floor. Mara stepped forward to help, but Kai waved her back, groped for, and found, her bamboo cane. She leaned into the cane, testing its strength and hers. Satisfied, she stood, though slower than she liked. "So, why did you come?"

"There has to be some secret motive?" Mara's face betrayed no pity, only the fear Kai had seen in her few visitors' eyes already, the fear of the healthy in the presence of the hurt. "I miss you. Gavin does, too, but he's afraid if he visited you'd get the wrong idea. You can't imagine the turnings in that boy's mind. He asked me how much I knew about your family, because he wants to come visit, but he wants to bring orchids because his mother always told him to bring orchids to convalescent women, but he wants to know if you were raised traditional enough to get the reference, because he doesn't want you to think that he's bringing you flowers because he likes you, not that he doesn't like you, but. You see. He thinks of conversations like a chess game, and I don't mean that in a good way."

Mara paced as she spoke, addressing cliff face and ocean and empty bed and her own hands, everything but Kai herself. "I'm glad you miss me," Kai said, "but that's not why you're here, especially not in that dress."

Mara stopped midstride. "I like this dress."

"So do I, but you dress fancy when you're scared. What of? Kevarian? The Grimwalds?"

"Of you, I guess. A bit."

"I got hurt. It happens sometimes."

"Hurt. People pull a muscle dancing, or break their arm rock climbing, or if they're having a bad year they tear a tendon. That's what hurt means. You, though. Do you even know what happened to you?"

"They read me the list. I recognized most of the words."

"You almost died."

"I almost a lot of things."

"I saw Jace's eyes when he looked into the pool as you were drowning. I didn't think he could feel fear. Or pain. You scared him down there. I've only seen him look that way in prayer: awed. By you, and what you'd done."

"Awe," she said, tasting the word. "Awful, maybe. I tried to help, and it didn't work. That's all this is. If I'm lucky Jace won't fire me."

"I wouldn't have done what you did."

"That's obvious." Kai saw Mara flinch, and regretted her choice of words.

"That idol was my charge, and I didn't try to save her. And don't say it's because I'm smarter than you." She held up a hand. "Don't say it. You talk tough, but you jumped into the water. I keep wondering why."

"The Craftswoman asked the same thing."

"She scares me."

"Me too."

"I read your deposition," Mara said.

"I didn't think they were showing those around."

"Do you really think you were wrong to jump in?"

"Does it matter?"

"Yes. Because if you lied, that's twice you've thrown yourself on a sword for my sake. By the pool, and in the deposition."

"Don't flatter yourself. We're all at risk here. Jace. Me. The priesthood. The island. It's easier if I was wrong."

"Why did you jump?"

I jumped because she screamed. Because her eyes were open. Because she was alone. Because you were frightened. Because no one else would. "You and Gavin were boring the twelve hells out of me."

Softness in Mara's eyes, and in the declination of her head. "Don't be cute. Please. I want to know."

Kai felt naked on that balcony save for bandages and scars, in front of Mara in her makeup and her dress. She ground the tip of her cane into the floor. Her left shoulder ached where Seven Alpha's teeth had torn her. "Haven't you ever felt sorry for a hooked fish on the line?"

Mara smiled slantwise once more, not sarcastic this time. Some weight kept her from smiling in full. She approached, heels on stone, and stood warm and near. Before Kai could pull away—cane, injury, two weeks' rest slowing her down—Mara grabbed her arms, then hugged her, pressing against Kai's bandages. Her touch was light, but Kai still bit down a gasp of pain. Mara withdrew. "I do now." Another step back, and a third. "I didn't come here to thank you. You took the worst moment of my professional life and added the guilt of almost killing a friend. And even if Jace fires you he never will look at me the way he looked at you drowning. I came here planning to cuss you out, but I don't have it in me. I'm glad you're alive, is all."

"Thanks," Kai said. And, because there was no other way to ask it: "Mara. Did your idol . . . did you ever hear anything in the pool? A voice? Words?"

"No," she said. "Nothing like that."

Howl, bound world, Kai heard again, on the mountain wind.

"Did you?" Mara asked.

Kai did not meet her gaze. "Will you make the trade?"

"Short the Shining Empire bonds, you mean."

"Yes."

"No."

"You should."

"You're no good at letting things go."

"So folks have said."

Mara stood still as a shoreside Penitent or a bowsprit maid. Then she shook her head, smile softer now and wistful sad, and walked away.

Kai sagged into her cane, but tensed again when Mara spoke behind her. "Get better. And be careful."

"I'll try." She listened to the wind and to Mara's receding footsteps. When only wind remained, she walked three-legged to the balcony's edge. The cable car descended the slopes below. Through its window she saw a flash of blue dress.

6

Izza tended Cat for three weeks. The woman slept for the first night and day, shaking and sweating in her nightmares. When she woke, she propped herself against a broken crate and drank water by the gallon. The only food she could bear was the blandest gruel, which was fine because that was all Izza could afford to bring her.

The next day Cat opened her eyes, and this time they focused, dancing around the room to settle on Izza. "I know you. Thank you for helping me." Her voice had rough edges and a New World Kathic accent, all rhotic *r*'s and dropped *g*'s.

"Don't get used to it," Izza said.

"I'm not." She reached for her pocket, and found a coin there. Izza had searched her, but hadn't robbed her yet. Cat sank soul-stuff into the coin, and flicked the coin to Izza, who plucked it out of the air. The woman's soul burned going down. As it dissolved Izza felt Cat's suspicion, and her hunger.

Izza knew hunger. "For saving your life?"

"For food," Cat said. "Can I stay here awhile?"

"What's awhile?"

"A few weeks. Maybe a month, worse case two. I need a quiet place to lie low. Then I'll move on. It's okay if you say no."

"How do you know I won't kill you while you sleep?"

"Have you tried?"

Izza crouched out of Cat's reach, and watched her. Being watched bothered some people. Cat wasn't one of them.

"What do you want?" Cat asked. "I can't offer much. I don't have any more soulstuff than what you've seen, and I won't go into debt for you or anyone."

Every cradle story Izza knew cautioned against pressing the issue of payment: travelers could be gods in disguise, or demons, waiting to avenge a breach of hospitality. Izza didn't want much, but she didn't know what a woman who fought Penitents single-handed could offer. "I want off this island."

"What's keeping you here?"

"Only the ocean."

"I can take you with me," Cat said, but her voice failed and she had to breathe deep and gulp more water before she could continue. "I can take you with me when I go."

"Stay then," Izza said. "Until you're well."

The woman lowered her head and slept. As she slept, she began again to shake.

Izza knew the shakes, the patterns of withdrawal. She was ready with a stolen bucket and a mop on the third day, when it turned bad. Cat threw up into the bucket, twice, and gritted her teeth. She convulsed, swatted at hallucinations, and sometimes babbled in a language that sounded more like grinding rock than a human voice. But the next night she slept, if not easy, then easier.

Cat became part of Izza's routine. She used the woman's soul-stuff to buy them food, and stole to supplement. Begged in West Claw, a little, when the Lunar New Year came and tourists danced mad dances and soul flowed like water.

Izza only regretted her decision to care for Cat when the children came back. One evening she returned to the warehouse and found Ellen and Ivy and a boy she didn't recognize seated in a triangle around Cat, asking questions. The kids looked ragged, and Izza could smell the boy beneath and through the warehouse rot. "Did the Blue Lady send you?" Ivy asked, and Cat looked at her, blank eyed, confused.

"No," Izza said from behind them both. Ivy's head darted around, and she stared at Izza, expectant first, then sad when she didn't find what she sought. "What are you doing here? I told you the game was over. I told you to get gone."

"We want a story," Ellen said.

She sank to her knees, so their heads were level. "No more stories. Come on. You want to waste time with this stuff? You have a life to worry about." The boy didn't look her in the eye. She didn't wonder what had happened to him.

"Who's she?" Ellen pointed to Cat.

"She's sick."

"Is she going to help the Blue Lady?"

"No one can help the Blue Lady," Izza said. "Not now."

Ivy sat, and crossed her legs. Izza returned her stare.

"I'm not leaving," Ivy said, "without a story."

So she told them a story. Gods help her, she told them a story, an old one about the Blue Lady saving a girl caught by Smiling Jack's dead boys. They listened, the three kids, and Cat, too. Izza kept waiting for the woman to interrupt, but she said nothing until the story finished and the kids nodded and left, padding softly over the warehouse floor. "Don't let me catch you back here," Izza called after them, but they did not seem to hear.

Once the kids were gone, she offered Cat a meal of rice and mangoes and something pretending to be pork, which she'd bought off a food cart down by the docks where meals came cheap. Cat ate in silence. Some of her color had returned, and yesterday Izza'd caught her doing push-ups one-handed beside her bedroll.

"You tell good stories," Cat said when the food was done.

"Too good," she said.

"Who's the Blue Lady?"

Izza did not answer.

"Okay," Cat said. "Why did you chase them off?"

"They need me."

"People need each other sometimes. Nothing wrong with that."

"I won't be around forever."

Cat laughed, but the laugh stopped when Izza looked at her. Not that Izza'd put any special malice into her eyes. She just looked, like normal. "You're young to say things like that and mean them."

"I'm leaving, aren't I? Soon as you're well."

"Why?"

Izza stood and paced, waiting for Cat to change her question. She did not. At last Izza stopped, returned, and sat again. "They don't put kids in the Penitents, okay?"

"Okay." Cat set the bamboo box aside. "You're scared."

"We're not all made of silver. We can't all fight those things off."

"You have to run," she said, "and you don't want them to be lost without you."

"Yes."

"Sometimes people have to work together, though."

"That why you left your god?"

Cat said nothing.

"I see the withdrawal. And I saw you fight the Penitents. A god made you. And you left him."

"I wasn't made," she said at last. "Not any different from you at least."

"But you had a god."

"A goddess. Yes. I worked for one, back onshore. Guess you could say we're separated now." She smiled briefly, after that, a pained kind of smile.

"What happened?"

"You know how I said people have to work together?"

"Yeah?"

"Sometimes the best way to work together is to be apart for a while."

Izza didn't understand, but she knew better than to ask questions. If Cat wanted her to know what she meant, she would have spoken plainly.

One night, Izza came to the warehouse and found Cat gone, the wad of dirty linens where she'd slept folded into a neat square. Not even footprints remained. Izza set down the box of rice and fruit she'd brought and searched the warehouse, even the little chapel hidden behind the debris, searched the docks beneath and the road outside. Nothing. Cat had vanished, quick as she came, and left her here.

She sank down beside the boxed rice, crossed her legs and hugged her knees, and stared over the horizon of her arms. Steam twisted out from under the box lid, rose a few inches, faded into air.

Of course. Cat needed food, and rest, time to recover. She hadn't ever meant to bring Izza along. Who would? Made as much sense as Izza bringing Ivy or Ellen. Or Nick or Vel or Seth or Cassie or Jet. Or any of the others.

Sunset purpled the sky. A single star gleamed through a gap in the roof. She didn't know the star's name. Her mother would have. Her mother was gone.

She remembered a song, and wished she hadn't.

Her jaw clamped and her arms tensed and her nails bit into her wrists and forearms. She would have stood and kicked the box across the warehouse, but she didn't want to waste the rice.

She stared instead into the steam and imagined fingers around a throat, and didn't know whose throat or whose fingers. A Penitent patrol marched by outside in thunderous array. She did not flinch. They passed. Even their echoes failed.

"Hey," Cat said a few minutes later. "Sorry I'm late."

Izza twitched to her feet, whole body taut at once. Her eyes were used to the dark by now. The mainland woman stood by the hole in the warehouse wall. Must have crept in while Izza wasn't looking. Stupid. Distracted, feeling sorry for herself.

She tried to look calm, but still she took a step back as Cat neared. The woman's limp was better, not yet healed. She moved slowly over rubble, into and out of light.

"I thought you left," she said.

"I went for a walk, got lost in the warrens. Too many side streets. I need you to help me make a map."

"I thought," she repeated.

"I'm here now." Cat spoke slowly, hands out. "I just took a walk, that's all. Trust me. When it's time to leave, you'll know. You'll be ready. Okay?"

"I brought you rice."

"Thanks," Cat said, and sat, and ate.

The next day, Izza stole a purse and did not sell it: kept it, rather, on the altar in the hidden warehouse chapel, under the gaze of dead gods. The day after that, she stole two, and the next two more. Building a little storehouse for the kids, tribute to whatever new gods they might find after she was gone.

She'd leave them ready. But she'd leave all the same.

7

Kai woke to find a folded letter on her sickroom sheets, parchment marked in spindly writing that faded as she read: "My office, one hour. —J." Economical. She placed the paper, folded again, on her bedside table, stood with aid of cane, and staggered to the bathroom. Sleep gummed her mind and body. At least Jace didn't come to her by nightmare. Her dreams the last few weeks had been dark and drowning.

Mara and Gavin had enlivened the bathroom with a few touches from Kai's house, but purple duck-shaped soaps and green towels did not soften the sterile white and chrome. Her hospital gown husk lay discarded on gray tile. Too-bright ghostlights reflected off her skin and off the mirror to her eyes: a worn, ill-used body made of meat, webbed with old and new scars. The bite wound on her shoulder looked like the angry outline of a blinded eye. More scars on her back, from the idol, as if she'd once had wings and someone sawed them free. They'd cut her hair short to operate, the clipped black fuzz grown out since to something like a pageboy cut. Mapping her scars, she imagined her next trip to the beach, once she'd healed.

What happened to you? the boys and girls would say.

Myself, she thought, and showered, and gritted teeth rather than accept the pain.

When Kai reached Jace's office he was in a meeting. She waited in the leather-cushioned foyer, paging through a two-week-old copy of *The Thaumaturgist* (garish lede: The Helmsman's Mistake, with accompanying full-color cartoon of an embarrassed Shining Empire theocrat draped in the kind of quilted robes no Imperial official had worn for two hundred years). Someone had left the door ajar, and she paid more attention to the argument within than to her article.

"Other members of the island council appreciate the merits of our proposal." She recognized the Iskari accent, nasal on vowels and heavy on consonants.

"Other members of the council," and that was Jace, "are more concerned with real estate profits and construction contracts than with theological security. That's where I come in."

"No one's proposing missionaries. We want a cathedral for our own merchants and diplomats to worship. The Communion of Iskari Faith will pay for construction, and land."

"I'd be more interested in your proposal, Legate, if your gods didn't have a way of wriggling into people's heads."

"The Old Lords do not corrupt. They call, and those blessed to hear decide whether to answer. I expected more than slurs from you, High Priest."

Jace's secretary cleared her throat; Kai was no longer even pretending to read. She returned her attention to the magazine, and tried to look as if she weren't listening. "Kavekana is neutral," Jace said, leaning into that last word. "We don't allow Craft firms to own land here, either. Even shipping Concerns rent their piers."

"A formality. Craftsmen's crystal spires stand three miles outside the harbor's mouth."

"And the nearest Iskari military base is fifteen minutes away on dragonback."

"That's hardly the same thing."

"Rent an office in the Palm, like everyone else. Or buy a skyspire suite. My duty's to keep this island safe until our gods return, and to protect our idols in the meantime. I won't risk exposure to mainland proselytizing." Jace checked his volume; his next words were so quiet she barely heard them: "I'm sorry, but it is what it is."

Kai couldn't make out the cleric's answer, if one came. She browsed business news until the Iskari legate swept out of the office, his purple robe trailing over stone. Gems glinted from the eyes of the squid god stitched into the robe's back. An attaché jogged after him, suited, holding a briefcase. Kai felt a pang of sympathy, watching the attaché go. Hell of a job. Sometimes literally.

She leaned onto her cane, pressed herself up, straightened her jacket and shirtfront, and stepped into Jace's office, closing the door behind her.

The High Priest's chambers stared south from the volcano summit over a more elevated version of the view from Kai's balcony: the slopes of Kavekana'ai, the city, East and West Claw pinching the harbor between them. The window was not made from glass, but rock transmuted transparent.

The office was almost empty. Upon his accession to the post, Jace had spent a week moving out his predecessor's junk. High Priests clung to life a long time, and most accumulated office mess like moss. Much of the cleanup was standard shred-or-store, but Jace's predecessor left arcane knickknacks in drawers and cabinets and trophy cases. An onyx statue of a beetle, when touched, came to life and began carving the mountain's stone into new beetles, who copied themselves in turn. A stack of papers in one corner had proved impossibly dense: seven hirelings strained to lift a single sheet. The papers had to be burned in place, and the resulting stink—of burnt hair and melted flesh and not of paper at all—lingered in the volcano's executive levels for a week.

After all that trouble, Jace kept his chambers spare. No furniture save for the magisterium wood desk, the leather chair he rarely used, and a small glass table. Four statues flanked the room, old Kavekana make, gem eyed and flat featured. No books. No pictures. Nothing to shield him from the demands of the job. Nothing to shield the job from him.

The chair was empty, the desk polished. Jace himself paced behind both, swift-moving silhouette against and above the island. He kept trim despite his desk job. Age showed only as frost in his short hair. She let the door close behind her; a pressurized arm guided it to soft rest in the jamb.

"Tough talk," she said.

He pressed his fingers together in front of his chest as he turned. "Gods spare me from priests. The Iskari have lobbied two decades for their cathedral and every year they get closer, no matter how many times I tell the council their gods' presence would warp our idols beyond repair. And the Iskari aren't the worst, either. You should see my inbox. Alt Coulumb keeps petitioning us to return a bit of their goddess they say we have. Same claim as all the others: back in the God Wars someone stole from them and stored it here. Their gargoyles ship us these big slabs of granite carved with their demands. Return the shards of Seril. I wish someone'd tell them paper was cheaper." He laughed. "I'm sorry. I love my job. How are you?"

"Ready for work," she said.

"What work?"

So that was the game. Since he wasn't sitting behind his desk, Kai saw no reason to stand in front of it. She joined him by the window and watched him oscillate, toward her, then away. "Building idols. Structuring trades. Solving problems. Your doctors have kept me prone as a roasting turkey for a month, and if you had your way they'd probably truss me like one. I'm ready to do my job."

"This isn't a job. It's a calling." He reached the apex of his round, and stopped, half in shadow and half out. "You're feeling well?"

"I am."

"You can walk without the cane?"

She tapped the bamboo against the floor. "Not for long. Physical therapy is slow."

"You haven't cooperated, I hear."

"It's hard to take seriously."

"You could have died. You almost died on the operating table, and before."

"I almost saved her."

"Saving her wasn't your job."

"This isn't a job. It's a calling."

"You plan to snap back at me. In this conversation."

"If you had good news, you would have told me; if you wanted to commend me, you would have. You owe me straight talk, Jace. Don't walk me through it like I'm some slave you're trying to teach math."

"I don't think you're a slave." His voice softened, and he approached her. His fingers trailed over the varnished surface of his desk. Easy to forget that he was a father, a lover, a leader. Easy to forget he was anything but a master. "I think you're dangerous."

"This is about Kevarian. And the Grimwalds."

"Of course."

"They won't win. We acted in their best interests, all the way through—Shining Empire debt looked like a safe investment, especially with the People's Congress coming up. No one expected the Helmsman to try to open the soul exchange over his own cabinet's heads. And we—I—went above and beyond to save their idol. I almost did."

"You would have died."

"I felt her healing."

"Blood loss, deprivation of oxygen and reality."

"What more do you want from me? I said I was wrong, on the record no less."

"You said you were wrong. Do you believe you were?"

She suddenly found the window and its view more interesting than the blacks of Jace's eyes. Ships rocked under heavy winds in the harbor. He let the silence weigh on her—respectful, maybe, or petty depending on how you looked at it.

"I heard something," she said at last. "Before the idol died. In the pool."

"What?"

"A voice. It said, 'Howl, bound world'—or something like that." The last equivocation added due to the weight of his silence, of the still air in the emptied room. She did not doubt the words, only her rightness in repeating them. "Have you ever heard things in there? Underwater? Words, I mean. I never have, before. The idols don't speak."

"Of course not," he said. "Are you sure you didn't dream these words later, or imagine them at the time? You were far gone when we pulled you clear. And the healing process can cause hallucinations."

"I know my own ears."

"And I know mine enough to doubt their evidence. Never trust an eyewitness, Kai. Or an earwitness, I guess."

"You think I'm making this up."

"You didn't mention it in the deposition. Or in your report."

"Has everyone read a copy of my deposition? I really did think those were private."

He shrugged.

"I wasn't asked," she said. "And I wanted to talk to you before I wrote down anything someone else might discover. I thought you might care."

"It's an anomaly."

"Which means you aren't worried, because you don't think I'm telling the truth."

"Which means we both have more pressing concerns." Jace sat in his chair, and leaned back. Wheels rolled over stone, and leather creaked. "What do you know about the Grimwald family?"

"I don't study our pilgrims."

"I wish I had that luxury. I'd sleep better."

"I saw one of them at the deposition. A man in a white suit, all shadows and teeth. "

"The Grimwalds turn up everywhere, on boards, at parties, in high halls of the Iskari Demesne. Their fortune travels through so many idols no one knows where it comes from in the first place."

"Important pilgrims."

"Dangerous pilgrims. They eat people."

"You're speaking figuratively."

"I wish. And as far as they and their Craftswoman are concerned, it looks like we're either incompetent, or mad, or playing them. What would you do, if you were me? What would you tell them?"

"That one of my priests made a mistake." Out over the ocean an albatross—she thought it was an albatross—beat west to the distant continent. "I gave you the opening in my testimony. Dock my pay. Put me on leave. Mandatory training."

"You think that would convince them?"

"What do you think?"

"They expect me to fire you."

That turned her from the view, and from the albatross. Her tongue felt like a piece of dry meat. "Will you?"

He watched her over his steepled fingers. "What do you think?"

"I love my work. I love my island. But sometimes people need to make sacrifices." She held out her hands, wrists together, offering them to be bound. She tried to smile. Her hands only shook a little. "Go ahead. Throw me into the volcano."

He laughed, once. "That'd convince the mainlanders of something. Not, I think, that we're a reliable investment venue. You're a great priest, Kai. Maybe a half-dozen people in the Order could have done what you did and come out alive. I respect you, I like you, and I can't keep you." He unlaced his fingers, stood, spun the chair around, and gripped the back cushion hard enough to dimple the leather.

"Because of Kevarian."

"In part."

"What do you mean?"

"I mean that even without Seven Alpha we would have had this conversation sooner or later." Before, she hadn't realized how dim he kept his office in daytime: no ghostlights, only the sun filtering through the window. "This isn't the first time you've run big risks. During the Kos situation two years ago, you stayed in the pool until the whites of your eyes stained black."

"That was a crisis."

"This spring solstice you danced for three gods at once. Almost burned yourself to a cinder. On the cross-quarter you negotiated a loan with the Iskari pantheon, solo. The squid gods just about took over your mind."

"We lose every exchange we make with the Iskari because we're too hands-off. Everybody knows it. That costs us clients."

"You're the last down off the mountain every night. You should have been home hours before Seven Alpha died. Even Gavin worries about you, and I don't think he's seen sunlight since he took holy orders. Do you see a psychologist? Any kind of head-shrinker?"

"You know I don't."

"When was the last time you went out?"

"Out?"

"For fun. To a bar. A play. Surfing. Whatever."

"I go to the gym every day. Went, I guess, before . . ." She indicated her healing body with a dismissive wave.

"With people, I mean."

"There are people in the gym."

"Kai."

"It's been a while."

"I spoke to your mother, when you were injured. She hadn't seen or heard from you in months. The island isn't so big you can hide like that without meaning to."

"Say what you want to say."

"I think you've been on a hard road for a while, and it's grown worse since you and Claude broke up." He waited for an answer that didn't come, and watched her, and she hated his watching her, because she knew he could see things she did not want to show. "You've always been brave, but this is something else. You stare alone into the abyss."

"That's what you pay me for."

"You're the best. Nobody's arguing. But the pool isn't all that makes a priest."

"Then what does?"

"People. Human beings who trust us to solve their problems, protect them from gods and Deathless Kings."

As a child, she'd built card houses with her sister. After a few thousand microcosmic catastrophes they learned to recognize the tremor of impending collapse, not in the structure but in the builder: first in her fingers, then in the bones of her forearm, and at last in her chest. She felt the same change now. She tried to ignore it, and failed. The room was too spare, Jace in his black suit too slick, to give her senses other purchase. As he spoke she heard an edge in his voice that had not been there before.

"You are a genius in the back room. You're destined for great things. But keep on this path and one day you'll dive into that pool and we'll never find you again. You run risks. Now you hear voices. Who knows what happens next?"

"I heard what I heard."

"That's what worries me," he said. "And that's why you cannot stay."

"You're reassigning me."

He must have heard the poison in her voice, but it did not sting him. "I am developing you. You've spent your professional life up here, hiding in numbers and mythography. That ends today. You'll move down the mountain to the front office, work with Twilling's people. Receive pilgrims, make them clients. Preach to the seekers."

"And in the meantime you tell Ms. Kevarian that I've been sidelined due to mental instability. Moved to a noncritical position due to"—she had to inhale in the middle of the sentence—"a pattern of irrational behavior. And you won't be lying."

Jace didn't move. He certainly didn't nod.

"What happens to my idols while I'm away? To my clients?"

"We'll take care of them."

She pointed to his bare desk. "How much of my memory do you take when I leave?"

"None of it. No nondisclosure agreement, no memory loss. You're not leaving. You keep your memories until you're ready to come back. I don't want to disturb that beautiful brain without cause."

"How long will I be gone?"

"As long as it takes."

Not a good sentence. Not a good sign. "I'm bad with pilgrims, Jace. I'll mystify them with jargon until they run screaming. Look at my personality profile."

"The profile's a guide for growth, not a list of limits. You'll work first with pilgrims we don't need: fat old men trying to hide their souls from profligate children or twentysomething brides. Prove yourself there and you'll get more interesting work. In the meantime you'll be out of sight. And safe."

He held his hands toward her palms up, not quite wide enough to invite an embrace. Did he know he was approaching her as he would a startled animal? Claude. Gods and hells, why'd he have to bring Claude into it? She remembered fallen cutlery, overturned tables. They only threw words at each other, but once Claude stepped on a broken glass and cut his foot, had to go to the hospital. You're damaged, Jace might as well have said, or: you are damage.

"It isn't that bad, Kai. I know you. Give you a goal and you'll chase it until the sun burns out. The only mistake we've made so far is to offer you tasks you knew you could handle." He approached. She resisted the urge to draw back. He almost grasped her left shoulder, stopped in time and before her flinch, and took her right instead. "Do this for me. Please."

"I will," she said.

"Good." Relief spread across his face, plain and slow as a cloudy dawn. "Twilling knows you're coming. He's excited to have someone with your skills on board. You see. Cross-pollination's good for everyone. We're much more siloed than we should be around here."

"I'm not crazy."

"I know."

"Okay," she said, and turned to leave.

"I'm sorry." His words chased her out the door.

8

In a week Izza stole three purses, twenty wallets, one piece of wheeled luggage, a handful of religious symbols, a china cat, a hammer, two watches, and three rings. The last ring was the one that got her caught.

Rings were great for stealing—ceremonial rings especially, wedding rings or confirmation rings or university rings or pledge rings to religious orders, rings people wore for years at a time, rings that if they slipped off a finger in a cold bath the bearer would notice at once. Rings that became part of your hand, part of your dreams. Soulstuff nested in that kind of ring. Steal one and you could even pull more of the owner's soul along, if you were careful and took your time.

To get a ring like that, you needed a mark so far gone they wouldn't notice a part of their hand being cut off. Which meant opium, or dreamdust, or something else as sharp. Even the hardest of hard-up sailors didn't do those drugs in public. Private establishments catered to the rich, the kind of places with white silk covers on the cushions to show they were changed after every client, and girls and boys on call for play even if most of the customers were too far gone to get it up. Addicts with less to spend settled for cheaper, less reputable dens.

She knew a few places in East Claw, close enough to the Godsdistrikt for their customers to smell the incense and feel the heat. Knew them well enough to keep clear: dens didn't stay open long; the Watch always came to wrap them up sooner or later. Those that lasted long enough to build up clientele posted lookouts on the street and on the roofs, and they weren't kind to kids who drifted close.

The den on Palmheart occupied an old Contact-era three-story house. The roof was heavily sloped, and the widow's walk at its peak just big enough for two guys, one fat, one thin, one looking west, one east.

Guards in hophead joints didn't tend to stay too clean themselves. So Izza waited until after dark, a few roofs over, for the telltale flick of a lighter and the bright spark of a flame on the widow's walk, which gave birth to a fat smoldering ember on the end of a thick joint. The fat guard took a drag, and passed to the thin guard, who took his own. She didn't need to smell the dope to know, but she could, and did.

They started talking soon after, telling bad dirty jokes she'd heard through the doors of a hundred bars, the one about the djinn and the traveling salesman and the twelve-inch piano player, and the one about the cat that wasn't coming in but going out, and when one of them broke into a braying hoarse laugh she ran and jumped. Landed on red tile, skidded down a few feet toward the roof's edge, but didn't fall, and didn't make enough noise to be heard over the laughter.

Dangling by one hand from the gutter, she slipped down between window boards into the top floor's haze of bad dreams and sick sweet smoke. The room was big, and hot, and dark. Prone bodies lay on a labyrinth of narrow cots. Unlit pipes dangled from fingers. Rolling eyes flashed white through slitted lids. Off to her left, in the dark, a man moaned. She broke into a sweat as she began her search.

Most of these guys—and most of them were guys—didn't have the kind of jewelry she wanted. Rings too new, or the metal too cheap to hold much soul. This one with the long mustache had a nice ring, but he was too fat to pull it off. When she tried, he reared out of the dark like an albino whale and grabbed her, groaning in a language she didn't know. She slipped from his clammy grip, and continued through the labyrinth as he settled back into drug dreams.

In a corner she found a dark man with dreadlocked hair and indigo tattoos on his wrists, of suns flanked by geometric symbols. He wore a thick gold ring on his forefinger, inlaid with cursive Talbeg script in mother-of-pearl. The inscription: *Hassan, with a love constant as wind.* Ring and tattoos didn't match—the tattoos from the Southern Gleb, the ring from the north, the script a dot and slant off from the one Izza's mom had taught her.

Which by itself meant nothing. Dead men's jewelry was stolen and traded all the time. A sailor stopped in port might buy a bauble he fancied and not know what it meant. One way or another, this was the ring she wanted. Well-worn, scraped by time. Full of hardened soulstuff from hungry and desperate owners. A find.

She touched the ring. The man snorted in his sleep, snored, moaned a long, drawn-out "Yes." The ring twisted fine, but when she tried to pull it over the knuckle the band stuck. The dreaming man brushed his free hand toward her like a kitten pawing at string, fingers and wrist limp. He didn't hit her. She spent a few seconds not breathing.

A light flickered in the stairwell, and she heard footsteps. A tender or a guard, come to check on the clients. They had three floors to check, and were rising up to the second now. A few minutes, no more.

She slicked the man's finger with oil from a vial she kept in her pocket. Two drops wet against his skin, and a light touch to either side of the ring, holding his finger in place so she could guide the gold loop gently, gently over the knuckle. He was feverish, and dreams tossed through his head.

She pulled at the ring with her body and with her soul, making it theirs, this bit of gold, this shared moment in the dark. To steal a man's wallet from his front pocket you pressed against his thigh in place of the wallet's weight. To steal a man's soul, you pressed against him with your dreams and visions, so he wouldn't notice when his own lost color. Moving the ring, she remembered home fires, and her mother's smile with the one broken tooth in front, and her first breath of free ocean, and her dad's stories about the rabbit in the moon. Dreams they could share. He answered her, confused, confusing, currents and colors of dream all blended into opium brown: blood-tinted waves, a high winding wail on seashore, a girl's lips soft on his, her hands on his skin, and fire, everywhere, the smell of human meat like seared pork—

The ring came free, and she staggered back. The man groaned

in the dark, and groped blindly for something he couldn't remember having lost.

Izza stumbled, struck a cot, and the thin man within it cried out in Iskari, "No, don't, not the kitten, not the kitten, not her!" Across the dark room, a voice lower than she'd thought a human voice could be moaned like the breaking of the world.

The ring burned in her hand. She forced it into a pocket, buttoned the pocket. Tried to remember who she was, where she was. Izza. Five foot six or so. Thin girl from the Northern Gleb. Not a sailor, not a soldier, not a man, not—

"Who the hells are you?"

Shit.

She'd forgotten about the stairs.

A broad Kavekanese woman stood in the stairway door, lit by the lantern she carried. She stared at Izza with wide black eyes.

Izza held up her hands, and stepped out from the shadows. The stammer she needed wasn't hard to summon. "Cap'n Deschaine sent me. Looking for a pilot of ours gone missing. We ship out come dawn and no one's seen him since he snuck off to get high a few days back."

"They let you upstairs?"

"They had his name on the roll down at the door."

"Who let you up?"

"Fat guy, I dunno who." Most gangs had a fat guy, and most crooks had no problem blaming the fat guy when something went wrong.

"Let me see the key he gave you."

Most of these places used chits of some kind to separate the folk that paid from those that didn't. A key made sense—easy to check. Then again . . . "Didn't give me a key."

"No. Of course not." A good guess. Lucky amateur, that was all. So knocked around by stealing soul that she forgot to check the exits. Good thing Nick wasn't here, he'd never let her live this down. "Let me see the token."

She'd crossed half the room, winding through cots and past men twitching and groaning in their nightmares. Some babbled echoes of their conversation: "no key," key, "key," some token, "give name on the roll roll roll" . . .

"I set it down," she said, "over here on the sill." And moved, slowly, toward the window through which she'd come. One step at a time. Keep eye contact, and hope the woman didn't put it all together—

The woman frowned and said, "Stop right there."

Izza ran, and behind her the woman shouted, "Stop!" as loud as she could, and the hopheads writhed and echoed, "Stop!" as Izza vaulted over the windowsill, glanced down, and let herself fall.

Pinwheeling through space, stomach up in her throat, strangling a cry for the nothingth of a second before she struck the cloth awning below, feet first and toes pointed so she'd punch through rather than bouncing off. Grabbed for the awning's support rail, caught it; the structure groaned and buckled under her sudden weight, but held at least long enough for her to swing into the third-floor window and crouch, gulping air, under a sagging cot that stank of sweat and urine. The awning tumbled to the ground outside in a clash of tortured metal, and guards ran up the stairs. Five sets of booted feet, she counted. Shouting, confusion—"Get to the street!"—as she crept toward the stairwell.

Then more running, downstairs, three forms, four, and she ran after the fifth, heart in her throat, down the stairwell toward the open front door, past the wide-eyed doorman into the street, trailing the doorman's incoherent curses and cries. The guards in front of her ran left, toward the fallen awning. She ran right, turned the corner into the narrow alley that ran ridgeward toward the Godsdistrikt, and sprinted down it, cobblestones pounding beneath her feet and freedom in her heart. She glanced back over her shoulder to make sure she wasn't followed.

She ran into someone, strong and unyielding in the shadows.

A hand grabbed Izza's shoulder. She pressed into her assailant, using her momentum—kneed hard for the groin, but a hand swept her knee aside. Clawed for the eyes, but the head dodged back out of reach, and the dodge kept going, turned to a swivel of hip that swept Izza's body through the air and slammed her against the wall hard enough to knock air from her lungs. Her arms were pinned, but she could still kick, could bite, could spit into those green eyes—

"For fuck's sake, kid," Cat said. "I'm trying to help you here."

Izza stared, uncomprehending, into Cat's face.

"Come on," the woman whispered. "Let's get back home."

They walked down the alley together; Cat hardly limped at all. To her left, in a shadow, Izza noticed two slumped bodies, breathing the shallow, tortured breath of the beaten unconscious. "Sentries," Cat said, as if that explained anything.

They didn't talk more until they reached the warehouse. Cat lowered herself gingerly to the quay's edge, legs dangling over, and leaned back on her elbows to look up at the stars. Izza sat beside her. There was a bloodstain on the cuff of Cat's shirt, and no wound to go with it.

"You feel better, I guess," Izza said.

"Out of shape, is all. And my side still hurts like hell." But Cat smiled, and her teeth were white, tiger's teeth reflecting moonlight. "Thanks."

"How long have you been following me?"

"Only the last few days," Cat said. "I'm sorry, kid. I don't trust easy. And I'm trying to keep a low profile. I see you stealing enough to outfit a regiment and I want to know what's up. Penitents get you, that leads back to me."

"And who are you, anyway? I don't know anything about you. You promised to take me off this rock—"

"And I'll do it," she said. "If I last long enough. Which I won't if either of us gets caught. You keep stealing this much, and sooner or later you will."

"I won't get caught."

"You did tonight."

"I could have handled those guys in the alley."

"Maybe," she said. "Look, if you're trying to stock up for the trip, I can take care of you at least until we get to the mainland. Don't worry about tickets or any of that."

"I'm not worried about me," Izza replied. "The kids. The others. I want them to be okay when I leave."

"But you're still leaving."

She nodded.

"If you care that much, why not stay?"

"If you got on so well with your goddess, why'd you leave?"

Cat didn't answer.

"You weren't just some worshipper, mouth a prayer every once a while and wave some beads around. You were a saint. You did miracles. You fight like a holy woman."

"Fighting isn't holy."

"Why did you leave?"

"You see a lot for a kid."

"I've seen enough," Izza said, "to know what god-withdrawal looks like."

"Not many gods around here."

"I didn't grow up here."

"Where you from, then?"

"The Northern Gleb. Talbeg country."

"Shit." Cat looked up at her, eyes wide, and Izza saw behind those eyes the twist of thought she hated, that she'd run from the Old World to escape: the sudden re-evaluation, the swell of pity. "Sorry. I didn't—"

"No," Izza said. "Not . . . It's fine." And wasn't.

"When did you leave?"

"When there was nothing left to leave. When they burned my village out."

"Which they?"

"Does it matter?" Izza said, but Cat didn't look away, didn't let the subject drop. "They came at night. They dragged us to the priestess's house first, killed her family and then her. A knife across the throat, just like that. Then they took others. My folks. I guess they wanted the kids for . . . for whatever. Everyone watched. The gods screamed. I ran. We all should have run. Right? Weeks before, years, when Clock's Raiders and the One Gleb and the Khalaveri started fighting. But a whole town doesn't run together. They stand strong until they break, and then they all run in pieces."

A wagon rolled past behind them, spider-golem staggering over uneven cobblestones. Izza held the ring out on her palm. Moonlight drained the yellow from the gold. She tried to feel the fire of the sailor's soul once more, but it was gone already. She wondered if the kiss she tasted through him had been freely earned.

Cat did not speak until the street was empty again. When it was, she tested her lower lip between her teeth to feel the form of the words she wanted to say. "I" was the first, and easiest. "I was a cop, once."

"Like the Penitents."

"Like," she said, "and not. I worked for—she was a sort of goddess, I guess. She asked me to chase and destroy evil. I needed her. Because I needed her, I did things that maybe weren't evil in themselves, but close. And then, when I'd given myself up to her completely . . . she changed. Became more than she had been, and asked more of me in turn. It was hard to bear. It was scary. I had been a cop. I ended up, hells, I don't even know what I ended up. 'Saint' isn't the right word. Or 'avatar.' But close, I think. She wanted more from me than I'd ever given. And then I had to leave. Best thing for both of us. Turns out leaving's hard."

"I know what that feels like," Izza said. "Faith seems fun. So does leadership. Everyone listens to you. Then you realize that it means the bastards come for you first."

Cat laughed. "The bastards always come, sooner or later. At least a priestess knows she'll be first in line."

"Not much consolation."

"No," Cat said. "I guess not." And: "I'm sorry if you thought I was spying on you. Old habits die hard."

"I'll stop stealing," she said, threw the ring up in the air and caught it, feeling the soulstuff wound within. "With this I have enough for the kids anyway. They'll make do."

"What about the boy?"

Izza blinked. "What boy?"

"Skinny kid. Dark hair, pale skin, scar on his cheek. For a few days now he's been bringing purses to that storeroom you think I don't know about, behind the debris wall in the warehouse. Same M.O. as you—he dives into the water with the goods, surfaces empty-handed a few minutes later. What's back there is none of my business, of course. But it attracts attention."

"Scar like this?" She drew a fishhook shape on her cheek.

"Yes."

"Nick." Damn. "I'll talk to him."

"Okay," Cat said. She stood and offered Izza a hand up, which Izza didn't take. "It's not all bad," she said as they walked back into the warehouse together. "Being a priestess, I mean."

"No," Izza admitted. "But the congregation can be a pain."

9

Kai's skin tasted enough of salt, but she salted it anyway, licked her wrist, drained the shot glass, bit the lime, slammed the glass, sucked the juice, dropped the peel. Three tequilas. Four.

Slices of discarded lime piled sticky and sour on the table at Makawe's Rest. Four dead soldier shot glasses among the rind wreckage caught the light of tiki torches and table candles, and reflected a distortion of the beachside bar. A tableful of tattooed local kids close by cheered and held their hands up to be tied as the last poet left the stage: a sharp-faced Kavekanese woman who hadn't yet remade herself, bright eyed with an elegant voice, verses slipping tense and tenseless from Kathic to Archipelagese and back. Kai wondered when she planned to join the priesthood, or if. Wasn't much overlap between poetry and priestly duties, now that the gods were gone.

Closer to the stage, denim-clad Iskari expats clapped.

Across the table, Mako raised his whiskey to the level of his milk white eyes, and made a sound Kai had learned to call a laugh: rocks ground to sand, storm water beating a cliff face, works of man crumbled to dust.

"You think the Iskari understood any of that?" she asked.

Mako turned toward her unseeing. The gash of mouth in the scar tissue of his face opened to emit a voice. "Don't need understanding to love."

"Then maybe you love for the wrong reasons," she said after she finished clapping.

"Love's still love."

"Get many girls with that line?"

"Haven't had to worry about that particular problem for twenty years at least."

The Rest swirled and surged around them, a hurricane of heat even without the four tequila shots burning in her gut.

At least the ocean wind cut through the swelter of close-packed drunken bodies. The Rest had no walls, and fronted on the bay. Behind them, waves rolled against the beach, and Penitents watched the horizon, screaming inside rock shells. Drunken sun-baked tourists lounged at the statues' feet. Sand clung to wet skin, a casing, a ward.

Kai wore a pale suit, matching hat, and dark blouse. After weeks of enforced sexless hospital-gown infancy, she was herself again, in her own clothes cut to her own body—and that body hers, too, not some nurse's or doctor's to prod and poke at will. She'd stopped at a salon on the way over to tame her ragged surgeon-shaved hair to a sharper cut. She walked to the Rest under her own power, with the cane's aid, and she sat here drinking booze bought with her own soul. Gods, she'd missed this—her world, her island with its ragged and rough edges.

Glorious, but the glory wouldn't take. Maybe it had crawled down the bottom of one of these glasses, or into some other bottle behind the bar.

Bongos drummed, and a trumpet trilled, and under the white ghostlight spots a new poet staggered out onto the thrust stage: a round Iskari man dressed all in green, waistcoat, tailcoat, hat, and slacks.

"Since when do Iskari read here? Their work's staid for us, isn't it?"

Mako shook his head. "This a fat guy, dressed like a cabbage?"

"Yes. I mean. Not very fat."

"Edmond Margot. He has a bit of fire. Listen."

She listened, and he stood spread legged and inhaled, closed his eyes and dug within him, and declaimed through noise and music:

"Shout the island is our prison
Tied in promissory chains
Waiting for withheld names
Dreaming free wind

Howl, bound world with
Painted gods and wooden
Idols worshipped hungry
For lash and cuff and needle
Scream lost souls and
Writhe beneath satin
Stains and suck juice from
Skeleton fingers and
Sing"

And on and on, rapt and rigid, chest peacocked out, neck bull-frog bulged. Heaving stomach drove air through his thick throat. The music eclipsed him, supported him, crushed him, and he staggered back, eyes wide, uncertain how he'd come here, uncertain what he'd done to earn the applause, the whistles, the jeers. He woke from a bad dream to find himself on stage, naked minded, before a room of men and women cheering. Eve, the Rest's owner and stage manager, in her tight black high-necked dress, grabbed Margot's shoulders and escorted him stumbling from the light as the next poet stepped up, a sandy lip-ringed Glebland boy whose sleeve tattoos showed beneath the cuffs of his ragged tunic.

"Three mothers crying / two sons gone"

Margot's friends received him, swallowed him, applauded him, a small band of layabouts and wanderers, fat, thin, hair stringy, curly, red, black, bald, hungry.

Kai sat frozen, mouth slack, staring at Margot. She replayed the poem in her head. She hadn't made it up, the line. How did the poem run? No rhyme, and harder to memorize in Kathic than Archipelagese, but still. *Dreaming free wind / Howl, bound world with / Painted gods . . .* Her words, the words from the pool, on the tongue of this damn fat foreign bard.

"What was that?" she said.

"Margot's work, it's pretty abstract. Once an Iskari, always. But he's good. Never suffered a paper cut before he came to Kavekana, but that works for him, sort of. Some people suffer from not suffering. You want his gratitude, tie him up and thrash him with a cat-o'-nine for a while. Anyway' the scholars like it. His work. Hidden Schools called him out to give a lecture there a few months back."

"That poem, I mean. When did he write it?"

"A few months ago now," Mako said. "Give or take a week."

"I have to talk to him."

"You're drunk."

"And you're ugly." She lurched off the table, and the ground heaved beneath her. Torch flames, ghostlights, flickering tabletop candles threaded webs of light through skin and wood and meat. She drowned, and gasped for air, as the room worked its way right again. When the lights resolved to stationary points, and she no longer felt the world's spin, she sought the poet.

He stood apart from his friends at the edge of the Rest, watching the Gleblander chant his chant.

Kai groped for and found her cane, trusted its support, and ploughed into the crowd. She made slower progress than she expected. Before her fall, she would have forced her way past. Now she had to wait for waiters to cross in front of her, skirt the edge of rowdy groups that might send someone tumbling into her path or knock her cane away.

The poet did not acknowledge her approach. Up close, she could see his sweat: a slick sheen on skin, soaking his once-white shirt. His forehead shone beneath the brim of his small green hat.

"You'd be cooler if you took the hat off," she said.

He wheeled on her, spilled his drink over his hand. His eyes were round and bright, like a frightened cat's, eerie in his pale and sunburned skin.

"Hey, I'm sorry. I just wanted to say I liked your poem."

His lips worked, but no sound emerged.

"The one you read." Gods, she was too drunk for this. But the idol drowned still and forever in her head, and the scream echoed. Don't let the swaying ground dissuade you. Close your eyes and steel your spine. "Up there on the stage. That line, you know, 'Howl, bound world,' that one. Is that yours? Is it a reference to something?"

He took a step back, as if she'd threatened him.

"I didn't mean to insult you. I just heard it somewhere, before."

The edges of his eyes tightened then, and he stared, not at her, but past her, through her. Her stomach muscles clenched and she felt the old familiar terror, ten years left behind since she took holy orders and rebuilt herself: of being made, placed, pierced, identified as something she wasn't. She remembered the anger that followed, and prepared herself against it. But he only stared, bowstring tight, and said, in a voice of dust, "The poem is mine. So's the line."

"It's new? Is there something special about it? Any reference, any story?"

"Do I know you?"

"No," she said. "I just had to ask."

He shook his head, and the shake moved down to his whole body. Then he recoiled from her, shouldering off into the crowd faster than she could follow.

"Hey!" She staggered after him on three legs, one arm raised. "Hey, I was just asking!" But the crowd was thick, and a big Kavekanese in a black shirt turned to say something to a friend and struck Kai a glancing blow with his shoulder, which would have been fine, but she tripped over her own cane into a waiter, who stumbled himself but did not fall. The martini glasses he carried on his tray were not so lucky.

Neon green cocktails fountained through the air. Two landed in the sand. One landed on a table, and broke into a jade fireworks display. The last struck a tourist in the back of the head and splashed, sticky and emerald with sugar syrup and artificial coloring, down her neck and into her white blouse.

The tourist stood and cursed in Kathic. The waiter stammered an apology. And two rather large gentlemen in black shirts materialized to either side of Kai, fast as if summoned by Craftwork. "Is there a problem?"

"No problem," she said. "I'm fine."

"There's no reason to get upset," said the rather large gentleman on the left.

"I'm not upset. I'm fine, I just tripped."

Meanwhile, the waiter retreated toward the safety of the bar while the tourist pursued, stabbing the air with her finger as if she were being attacked by invisible sprites. On the stage, the Glebland poet had stopped his tirade to stare befuddled into the audience.

"You shouldn't be worried about me," she said. "Look at her."

"Ma'am, please. Remain calm."

"I just wanted to talk with that guy." Pointing to Margot, who sat now, she saw, among his ragged poet friends, pointedly ignoring her.

The rather large gentleman on the right took her arm, and she pulled it away, sharply. "Don't touch me."

Which, all things considered, was not the best course of action. The gentleman on the left now reached for her as well, and she drew back, and tightened her fingers around her walking stick. Drink and anger pounded a rapid tattoo on the drum of her heart.

"Boys. Kai." Mako's voice, behind her. Beneath the noise of crowd and argument she'd missed the tap of his approaching footsteps, and his stick. "What seems to be the trouble?"

"No trouble," said the gentleman—or boy—on the left. Both straightened slightly.

"No trouble," Kai said. "I was just making my way back to our table." And she winked at the bouncers, turned her back on them, and led Mako through the crowd.

"What was that?" the old man said when they were seated again.

"Didn't want to talk to me," she said. "Is he always an asshole?"

"He's been blocked for a while now. Lot of stress. Doesn't excuse the assholery, but then he's Iskari. Their assholes get graded on a curve."

She felt the sinking tension in her gut unwind a little. "I missed you, Mako."

"You don't miss shit. Months we haven't seen a hair of you. And you're getting dead drunk as soon as you're back, not because you're happy. What happened?"

"Who said anything happened?" She raised her hand and searched the crowd for a waiter.

"Your cane, and the fact that you almost started a fight with two bouncers three times your size."

"Hospital. Basically. And I was moved to a new job. And I don't want to talk about it."

"I've known too many men who didn't want to talk, and women, too. Not talking doesn't end any way but bad."

She shifted in the chair, and her back sang its protest. She'd felt lithe and smooth walking down to the coast from the cable car, cane tucked under her arm like a swagger stick, hands in suit pant pockets, reveling in freedom, in the round sweet scent of barbecue fires, of flowers and incense and skin. She'd knotted around herself in the intervening hours' sit. And around Mako, who she hadn't seen since Claude. "Claude and I broke up. Did I tell you?"

"Good riddance." More whiskey drained, to her and then to the Gleb poet, who delivered the final verse of a tight acrostic to the vigorous applause of a table in the third row back, either friends or structuralists. "Guy's collar's too white for you anyway."

"Hells does that mean? He's city watch. I wear ties for a living."

"Once a shipbuilder's daughter, always a shipbuilder's daughter. Those calluses don't rub off easy."

"They rub off easy enough. And his dad was a fisherman."

"Time in a Penitent breaks that out of you."

"If you say so."

Behind, on the beach, two lovers lay between the legs of a tall stone Penitent, sand covered and kissing. The idol's teeth, she remembered, had torn her lips. The island is our prison. *Howl, bound world.*

"I wanted to ask him about his poem. That's all. I heard the line somewhere."

"Likely. It's famous. Become famous, fast."

Was that it? Had she overheard the words, seen them in a

magazine perhaps, woven them into her dreams? Was Jace right? Had blood loss and panic blurred memories together? "Just wanted to talk to him, that's all."

"Mainlanders have a saying about good intentions."

"Road to hell's paved with them?"

"I've been there," he said, "and it ain't. But even wrong sayings have a point. Maybe you should take it easy."

"I came here to get drunk and pity myself. Without the second what's the point of the first?"

"You came here," Mako said. "That's the important thing. But you've been cooped up too long, and you want to do everything at once, and if you try half of that you'll break yourself so bad even the madmen up the mountain won't be able to put you back together again."

She laughed. "Blasphemer."

"I fought gods and demons with these hands." He laid them palms down on the table. His right third finger jagged at a sharp angle from the joint; his left pinkie would not lie flat. Dirt caked his nails. "I've earned blasphemy. Sleep and come back in a few days. Don't take everything so fast. If you wake up tomorrow morning with Makawe's own headache, vomiting your guts all over those nice silk sheets, you'll blame me for it and you won't come down here again for months. I'd miss you."

"My sheets are cotton."

"Don't storm the beaches, Kai. Never ends well."

"Nice. Patronizing."

"'Patronizing's' an interesting word. You think I'm acting like I'm your father, or like you're a rich idiot who needs to be told what's what about art?"

"Both, I guess." She let go of her head. "Maybe you're right." She stood with the cane's aid, and while the muscles in her side protested and pulled, she managed to hold herself up, and even took a step without falling. She left coin on the table with enough soulstuff to cover her tab. Nothing tied her here now. She did not have to lean far over to touch the old man's crooked hand. "I'll see you, Mako."

"Thanks for the drinks."

Margot stepped back onto the stage, into the burning spot. A light rain of applause fell. He removed his hat. Sweat beaded his forehead. Lips tightened, opened, a pink tip of tongue darted out to wet them. Thick hands wrung his hat brim.

I didn't ask to be here

"Neither did the rest of us," Kai said, and left.

10

Nick wasn't easy to find. Izza made the mistake of asking Ivy where he spent his time these days, which Ivy claimed not to know, though of course she did. Not weeks before Ivy would have told Izza anything she asked, would have spun fantastic tales in an attempt to please. Now she lied, and badly.

For which Izza had no one to blame but herself. Taking in Cat, announcing the end of their game of gods and goddesses, saying she'd run rather than let herself be caught for a Penitent—the kids might not know what to think, but at least they knew not to trust her. Good instincts. Not great, or else they would have run away themselves years ago, but good.

So Ivy, who Nick trusted and liked, cared for almost as for the kid sister he claimed he never had, said she hadn't seen Nick in a while, and must have put out word that Izza was looking, because after that Nick was nowhere to be found, his old haunts unhaunted, his Godsdistrikt rooftop pallet abandoned, and his cubby holes throughout East Claw cub-less.

Which might sound like it left an entire island for Izza to search, but in truth there were only so many places a kid looking to steal rich could go. A crooked alchemist who came to Kavekana to cook dreamdust had once explained the principle to Izza. You drew (and he drew, in the dust with his fingertip) a simple graph—put value on the vertical axis, and risk on the horizontal. The value-risk curve for most endeavors, criminal and otherwise, increases steadily to the right. The more comfortable you are with risk, the more value you might realize. The more value you wanted to realize, the more comfortable you had to be with risk. Kavekana (he said) was too risky for most crooks, but the combination of spendy sailors and mainlanders come for business promised high value.

The alchemist was taken for a Penitent soon after, but he left his graph behind, which had to count for something, even though Izza wasn't sure why he called the line a curve when it looked straight.

Anyway. The Godsdistrikt was low value, low risk. Few Penitents, little attention from the watch, because who cared what foreign sailors got up to so long as they didn't trouble the good people of Kavekana—those being, of course, the people of Kavekana who happened to look and talk like the ones in the Watch. Your average sailor didn't have much soulstuff, though, and tended to keep what little he had locked deep inside his own head. A few pieces of preciously guarded jewelry, a keepsake or two you could steal, a purse of coin. Not much else. Sailors watched where they put themselves.

But if you were comfortable with more risk, Penitent-wise—that is, if you were incurably stupid—you might decide to pursue a higher class of mark.

You'd stay clear of longtime wealthy residents, with their strong wards and stronger connections, but there were easily a dozen upscale resorts in West Claw and the Palm, let alone all the beaches and nightclubs and gyms where tourists and business visitors might leave their stuff unattended for the brief magic moment said stuff needed to grow wings and fly away.

Still too much territory to search.

Izza swam into the secret room in the back of the warehouse, to the altar where she'd piled her spoils. Quite a stack, there— wallets and purses and pouches and statues and jewelry. Even so, embarrassing that she hadn't noticed Nick's additions. Put it down to the shadows, or to the fact that Izza spent not an instant more than she needed back here these days. Too many bad memories. Too many corpses on the walls.

In all, Nick had added five wallets, leather and elegant and fat with soul, and three purses in questionable high-fashion taste. They held family pictures, thick wads of banknotes, Iskari and

Camlaander and Ebonwald and Coulumbite, each stamped with a priestly sigil. No clue to their origins, all documents bearing names chucked into the bay long since.

She picked up a polka-dotted velvet purse and squeezed it in frustration, feeling coins shift round and hard beneath her fingers. Coins, and something else—long, slender, pointed at one end. Izza cleared a space on the floor and dumped the purse's contents out. Coins, only coins, even in the slight starlight she could see that much. But the purse still clunked against the damp floorboards when she let it fall.

Interesting.

She probed inside the purse with her forefinger, and found a narrow pouch sewn into the lining. No button, only fabric tucked into fabric. Opening the pocket, she drew from within a skeleton key, one end all twisted teeth and the other capped by a medallion inlaid with a tinted mother-of-pearl logo: a mountain bisected by a crescent of blue ocean to form an abstract letter *A*.

In her dark room, empty but for her stolen treasure and the paintings of her dead gods, Izza swore.

The Aokane Plaza was a seashore palace cradled in Kavekana's Palm, or at least that's what its brochures claimed. Multilayered terraces and balconies draped with ghostlights and spackled by tiki torches overlooked the rolling ocean. Guests and waiters, servants and masters, flowed up and down the Plaza's many staircases, and along the ramps that connected the hotel and its beachside cabanas. Unnaturally white and gleaming, writhing with human bodies, the hotel reminded Izza of a layer cake overrun by ants and set afire.

Though the Plaza had long since lost claim to the title of Kavekana's most elegant or exclusive resort, its guests remained rich, and numerous enough that a child could drift among them if she walked fast and didn't linger. If Izza wanted to steal up-market, she'd start here. She'd discussed the issue with Nick before.

The Plaza's back rooms were a maze, miles of hallways and basements and kitchens and servants' passages, but she didn't need to worry about most of that. Nick, if he were here, wouldn't be anywhere without people he could steal from. That meant public spaces, which left her plenty of ground to cover.

She approached from the beach. Barefoot waiters in white vests and capris whisked cocktails on silver trays from cabana to cabana. On a stage by the ocean, a band of young men and women wearing old Kavekana royal garb, multicolored print kilts and shawls and feathered cloaks, drummed drums and played ukulele; a woman with a pearl circlet at her brow sang a high winnowing song in the lilting local tongue, of which Izza had never learned more than a few words. Far as Izza could tell, the song's lyrics didn't include "please," "thank you," "hide," "run," or any of the meanings of "watch" and "fence." Behind the band, Penitents stared out into the rolling waves.

A green-skinned man with a taut protruding belly lay in a cabana beside a beautiful blonde covered in scars from her hairline to the soles of her feet. They nodded their heads in half time to the trilling drumbeat. Izza stole a towel from behind their hutch and wrapped it around herself to hide her clothes. She drifted upstream past waiters and those they served. The served were the more varied of the two groups, in a way: the well-heeled of six continents and three thousand cities, of every skin color and creed and species, living and undead, skeletal or carved from stone or pink and flexible, those floppy with excess flesh, these sculpted by surgery and personal trainers into hilariously exaggerated visions of human potential. But their faces all played small changes on the same bovine physical contentment. The servers, though—locals mostly, men and women alike hired to look good in uniform— watch their faces and you'd see a greater range of attitudes. Some loved their job, some resented it, some were tired and others keen and a few hopped up on coke or joss, and that woman kneeling now to set the glasses from her tray onto a low table beside a chair on which sat a tangle of wire and thorns in the shape of a four-armed faceless man, she was three months pregnant.

Izza was taking too long. Don't linger was the best rule a thief could follow. No Nick on this beach. Check the three balconies, and get gone, out into safety and night.

On the first balcony, steam rose from a pool the color of molten emerald. Ghostlights highlighted swimmers' bodies within. Other guests lay in various stages of undress beside the pool; a three-armed skeleton angled a tanning mirror to catch the moon. No Nick here, either.

The second balcony was the ground floor: bar, reception, an empty stage, two open-air restaurants perched like Telomiri duelists across the courtyard from each other, Fabrice's and Escalier, and she imagined the maître d' of each concocting mad plots to ensnare or embarrass his rival, escalating until the hotel burned down in a cascade of envy and charred timber. More people here, three different kinds of waiters, a young woman in the hotel's gray uniform hovering with a dustpan and broom, eyeing the world reflected in the polished marble floor for the smallest flaw. Quartet of suited Iskari, you could tell by their cuffs, drinking wine with a Glebland merchant. A family in swim trunks and T-shirts, over from the New World for vacation. A few Craft-types drowning in paperwork.

No Nick.

The third balcony was the smallest, a hundred feet across at most but positioned so those seated there could see no other balcony, only the ocean a long way off and the city a long way down. Two narrow staircases led up to that level from the ground floor, each in clear view. Only an idiot would try to sneak up those stairs, or someone who thought the safest play was the play nobody saw coming.

Which was just another way of saying, idiot.

Izza picked up a slick pamphlet of hotel activities—5:42 A.M. sunrise tantra, accompanied in the brochure by a reproduced watercolor of a white woman with honey-colored hair twisted into some sort of Dhisthran exercise posture and smiling as if she enjoyed it. 8:30 complementary diving lesson, 10:00 beach golf, which who knew what that was, 11:15 crossbow skeet. Izza paced in front of the girl with the dustpan, lips pursed as if she were trying to decide between Traditional Kavekanese Woodburning and Ocean Water Polo Tricks and Tips for tomorrow afternoon, then shrugged, crumpled the pamphlet, and let it fall. The girl with the dustbin slid in behind, swept up the pamphlet, turned without a word, and retreated toward the cream-colored rear wall, and through a door Izza hadn't seen at first.

Izza followed the girl into a windowless hallway painted the off-white managers painted places where they wanted work done. The girl turned right, headed for a large trash can at the end of the hall; Izza turned left into a stairwell and sketched around a corner out of sight. She heard the door open and close again—the girl, presumably, returning to the courtyard and patrol.

No more footsteps in the service hall. Good. Towel still wrapped around herself—no sense abandoning a fitting disguise— Izza climbed two flights of stairs and reached a hallway that smelled of fire and kitchens and knives. A stenciled label opposite the stair pointed left to Level Three Restaurant, and Izza retreated to the turn in the stair as a tuxedoed waiter rushed down the hall above, cursing, a decorative white towel draped over one arm and a large domed tray teetering on the fingertips of his white-gloved hand. Another door opened, and closed; she waited a breath, climbed back to Level Three, and turned left.

She almost ran into Nick.

He wore the hotel grays, and carried a pink purse slung over his shoulder, obvious and obviously not his. He froze when he saw her, then double-took when he recognized her, face pale with the fear of the discovered. He pulled back, hands raised, warding, but too slow. Izza grabbed him by the purse strap and tugged him down the hall to the stairs.

"What are you doing here?" he hissed.

"That's my line." They rounded the turn of the stair, and, safe for a second, she shoved him against the wall, hard. "Are you crazy?"

"I'm helping." Fire and fear sparked from his eyes. "Helping us when you won't. Let me go."

"You're stealing things people will notice gone, and bringing Plaza keys straight back to the warehouse. They can trace those, Nick."

He blinked. "I didn't—"

"You almost led them to the altar. Because you didn't think this through."

"You were stocking up," he said. "I wanted to help."

She ripped the purse off his shoulder. "And you think someone who came to a restaurant with a purse won't notice their damn purse is gone? What's with you?"

"Like jumping into dreamdust dens is smart?"

"That doesn't get the Watch after you. This will." She opened the purse, dug through its silver sateen guts, found the wallet and the room key. "You really work here?"

"Yeah. They trust me to open doors and stuff."

"Trust you to be an idiot." She shoved wallet and key into his hands. "Take this. Five seconds. You run up, say you found this in the hall, saw someone running off with the purse."

"You can't—"

"Listen to me. Steal what you want, but bring nothing to the warehouse until I say."

A man's voice from the upper hall: "Nick?" And again, nearer, "Nick? You here?"

Izza gaped. "You told them your real name?"

The fire left Nick's eyes, and only the fear remained.

"Nick?" The waiter from before, dark hair and tuxedo and white gloves and towel, peered down the stairs, turned. "Who the hells is that?"

Sorry, she mouthed.

Nick nodded, and said, "Thanks."

She hit him in the face as hard as she could, and ran.

He fell, sprawled across the stairs, the wallet still in his hand. Izza vaulted over the railing, landed unsteadily one level below, and lurched down. Behind her, she heard the waiter stumble over Nick's body, curse, and shout, "Thief!"

She reached the ground floor in a blur. Probably some quick and easy exit through these service hallways, but she'd just as likely lose herself in a maze of dirty linen baskets and industrial dishwashers and boilers as find the out. Better to take the way she knew led to the street, which had the only drawback of walking her past about a dozen possible concerned bystanders, not to mention hotel staff.

Nothing for it.

She emerged from the hidden door onto the second-floor pa-
tio between Fabrice's and Escalier, purse clutched tight to her
chest. Left turn down the long hallway past reception to the entrance. Don't run. People notice when you run. Keep smooth, keep
cool, chin up, proud, a young woman who just had to get her purse
to buy some dumb thing from the hotel shop. Breathe. Walk.
Steady.

You just promised Cat you wouldn't steal anymore. Promised
her you wouldn't get caught. You promised, and here you are,
bearing a big fat neon-pink "arrest me" sign out of a luxury hotel.
Because you couldn't let an idiot take his own fall.

Nope. Bad line of thought.

She made it halfway down the hall to the front desks, a row of
them, only one staffed and that by a woman with dark circles under her eyes and a steaming mug of coffee by her hand. The recep-
tionist did not look up from her paperwork. Good. A few more
meters to the street.

Behind her a door slammed, and she heard running footsteps.
No cries, not yet, of course not. No sense alarming the guests. But
she walked faster. Reached the doormen, two towering guys in
flower-print shirts, necklaces of carved nuts, mountains of muscle
topped with that same service sector smile. She nodded to the
nearest one—don't look down, don't look down—beyond the arch
of the front gate, carriages rolled along the street, open-air wagons
bearing West Claw middle-management types on an evening bar
crawl. Did they call it a bar roll when people drove you from place
to place? A bearded partier stood to make a toast, but tripped and
spilled his beer onto the woman beside him, and everyone laughed.

Freedom.

"Stop her!" came the cry from behind.

And the doorman looked down.

Saw the purse, which by itself didn't mean anything, and the
towel, and, more important, the frayed cuffs that stuck out from
under the towel, and Izza's legs, scarred and grimed, and her ragged
sandals, which no guest of the Plaza would deign to wear.

He glanced up, smile faltering, and reached for her in slow
motion.

Izza swept off the towel, threw it in his face, and ran into traffic.

A horse neighed and reared beside her; she ducked beneath pawing hooves, and dove through the gap between the party wagon and a golem cart. Cries of "Thief" from behind and "Stop!" mixed with street noise, with the roll of wheel and the jangle of tack and the laughter of the wagon's drunks. Almost there, almost gone. An alley ahead gaped, a gullet to swallow her to safety.

Then the light struck her.

That was all, only light, no Craft to it, but the light was enough. Red and bright, like a poisoned sun. She knew this light, its color and texture, knew the sharp shadows it cast. She knew better than to look left, toward its source, but did anyway, couldn't help herself. Ruby eyes shone from the apex of a towering stone statue made in mockery of a man. A massive head swiveled to face her. Rock ground rock. And beneath that gravel-grind, she heard a woman weep.

The Penitent took a step toward Izza. Inside, its prisoner screamed.

Try to help people, and look where it gets you.

No. Don't accept this. Move, she commanded her legs, her body. Feet, fly. Don't stand here. Don't wait for them to come for you with the knives and hot irons. This isn't fate. There's no such thing. Go. Now!

Izza fled down the alley, and the Penitent followed her with earthquake strides.

11

The night wind outside the Rest cooled Kai's brow and her world stop spinning. Tourists splashed in the ocean under the Penitents' watchful gaze—tourists, or else pilgrims enjoying a night off. Islanders knew better than to swim this late. The sun watched the sea by day, but after dark monsters emerged. Mainlanders ignored local superstition and riptide warnings both to swim naked in the surf, and acted surprised when a gallowglass dragged one off to eat. Kept lifeguards in business, Kai supposed. Not to mention the men the Watch hired to dredge the harbor.

She hadn't been thrown out of the Rest, she told herself. Not quite.

It made a difference.

She knew what she had heard in the pool, in the idol's cry, in the poem. She thought she knew. Maybe the words had not come from the idol, but from her—heard in passing and projected into the idol's mouth. How much did a person read in a day and ignore? Newspaper headlines and magazine quips and menu items and shop signs and graffiti and manuals and comic books and gossip columns and upbeat slogans sponge-printed on cafe walls, not to mention conversation overheard and misheard: small talk, street corner buskers' music, and the small talk of cashiers.

Gods, but she was drunk.

She began the long climb home. Her family's house was near—the ghostlight POHALA SHIPYARDS sign flickered over a West Claw pier a half mile's walk down the shore—but she hadn't wanted to see her mother in months, and didn't now. Stupid body. Stupid spinning room. Stupid bouncers and stupid poet and stupid Mako and most of all stupid Kai.

She walked north and uphill. Her palm hurt from the cane.

Trumpets and drums receded, and the tide of natives and rum-soaked visitors ebbed to leave her alone on the sidewalk. Driverless carriages rolled past. A large roan pulled a wagon packed with drunks up the slope: head down, shoulders and flanks rippling with strength. No wasted energy in those steps. Each move a single sweep of a calligrapher's brush—only calligraphers did not have to fight to draw a line.

There were no horses on Kavekana before Iskari traders first arrived four centuries back. No need for horses, either. Kai's sister always complained of the stench of horse dung in the streets, of the animals' filth and of the laziness they invited, as if they hadn't been a part of island life for four hundred years.

As the carriage passed Kai tipped an imaginary hat to the roan. Craftwork bound and directed the horse. Did it know it was born to a life of service? Did it know how its world was made?

The horse bowed to her in turn. She stood still, and told herself she'd imagined the pointed pause, the dip of head. Anything was possible. The wagon rolled on.

Tropical night folded her in thick warmth. She sweat beneath and through her linen suit. After two blocks Palmheart crossed Epiphyte, and the shoreside party gave way to cafes and food stalls and shuttered boutiques. A woman fried coconut milk curry under a palm frond awning while her children served bowls of the stuff to lined and haggard men who played dominoes on wicker tables. A kid, maybe fifteen, juggled mangoes beside a fruit stand. Six men and two women, thickened by middle age, wearing ragged shorts and stained multicolored shirts, sat on the sidewalk in front of a closed jewelry store, passing a bottle of palm wine.

The earth shook, and Kai heard screams and fast footsteps. A dark girl in torn clothes ran onto the street from an alley. She clutched a purse to her chest, bright pink leather, obviously not hers. Wide black eyes reflected torches and streetlights both. Kai watched the girl run past, and did not move to stop her or to help. No one did. It was too late for the girl already.

A Penitent stepped onto the road, an earthquake gone for a stroll. One drunk dropped the wine bottle, and milky liquid spilled into the gutter. The Penitent stood ten feet tall, a barrel-chested almost-human carved from stone. Gem eyes burned with inner fire. The street fell silent save for the fleeing girl's footsteps, the sizzle of oil in the wok, and the Penitent's muffled sobs. Kai watched.

Light burst from stone joints. The Penitent gathered its several tons' bulk and leapt. It shrieked as it flew huge and horrible overhead, cry broken by its landing crash, three feet in front of the thief. Cobblestones splintered beneath graven feet. The girl skidded to a stop, scrambled back. A stone hand lashed out before she could flee, snared her around the waist, and lifted.

The girl's bare feet kicked at empty air. The Penitent's grip pressed her arms and the purse against her chest. She struggled to breathe. Kai heard a woman weep beneath the stone.

The Penitent turned, prisoner held in one hand, and strode off west, bearing the girl to justice, or anyway to punishment.

The cook fried on. The drunks retrieved their wine, and drank, and retold stale stories of their younger days when Kavekanese sailors had been prized from the Pax to the World Sea. Days past, but not past remembering.

Kai climbed away from drunks and dominoes and shop window mannequins.

The girl was young to be a thief. Too young, Kai hoped, for Penitence, but maybe not, if she had priors, or the victim pushed for vengeance, or the moon was in the wrong phase or the wind too heavy in the west.

Kai had jumped into the pool to save the drowning idol. To save Mara. She'd thrown herself on Ms. Kevarian's sword for the Order's sake. And in return, she had been thrust to the sidelines, even her sanity questioned. Why should she have risked herself for that girl?

Not that she could have helped, not wounded and weak, and anyway the cases weren't at all alike. The idol was her business. (Though not really.) The girl was not. (Mankind is my business, didn't someone say that once? Or else it drifted to her out of a mist of dream.) The idol was not at fault; the girl was. (What fault? She looked hungry. Could you blame a hungry person for stealing to eat?)

As she climbed, buildings receded from the road and trees advanced to compensate. Spreading palm fronds' needled shadows crosshatched streetlamp light on the sidewalk. Right foot, cane, left. Breeze blew against her neck, and leaves scraped leaves above. Bay windows shone like Penitents' eyes in a small pink house set back from the road. A backlit figure stood in one window, a shadow playing a fiddle. The music was faint and foreign, an air from northern Camlaan. Claude had said once that Camlaan fiddlers used a different mode for their songs than other Old World musicians. She had not asked him to explain, because the thought frightened her. Music, she'd always thought, was music. But if music was only a convention, if notes were games of symbol, then music could lie, like words, like numbers, like the Craft itself.

The island is our prison.

For Margot, maybe. Not for Kai. Born here, raised here, in one of the few places on the planet where she could be herself. Even if more mainlanders moved here every year. Even if traditional dress robes gave way to suits and ties. Even if only a handful of priests had remade their bodies in the pool since Kai, even if those who should know better met their transformation with silence and suspicion.

Poor fiddler. Kai left him, or her, standing at her (or his) window, playing the sad song he (or she) might not even hear as sad, and climbed on. In reverie she'd covered more distance than she thought: ten blocks left to home. She walked in triple time away from the music.

12

Edmond Margot stepped for the third time that evening into the spotlight, and tried to summon his voice.

Behind him on the stage, drums drummed low. A trumpet pealed one long, slow, high note, and sank to silence. The spotlight seared his eyes with dancing sparks. Faces hovered beyond the light, out there in the audience, watchers and waiters. He saw only suggestions of their presence: curve of cheek, jut of chin, black wells where eyes should be. In with the breath, then force it out.

Twice before he'd entered this burning light and each time recited old poems, picking at scabs and prying open scars for the crowd's amusement. Each time they applauded. A woman even came to compliment him, to mock him.

Familiar, she had been, so familiar, a vision of vanished voices risen to taunt him with unanswerable questions.

His tongue flicked out to wet his lips. The room was hot, but his sweat was cold. Fear sweat, nerve sweat. Fine vintage.

Head up. Shoulders back. You may be broken, but don't let them see you breaking. They knew his poems and liked them. Would applaud, even if he recited only his old lines from now 'til the world drowned.

Eve swayed toward him out of the shadows, all silk and slink and smile. He'd never seen her wear a low-cut dress, wondered again as ever on this island whether she really was a woman. Pressed the thought down, aside. Didn't matter. His voice mattered, his voice long lost.

Eve drew near enough to whisper through her smile. "Do you have one more in you?"

"No," he said through tight dry lips. "But I'll do it anyway."

Her nod was all the grace in the world, and when she rounded away from him to the stage's edge, he followed her body with his eyes. Fear had helped him find his voice before fear and pain honed away his lesser elements until he became a single sound. Where could he find that fear again? In the spotlight. In the heat. In standing blank minded onstage. In the sway of Eve's hip.

"Back again by popular demand," Eve announced, her voice big, one arm raised like a torchbearer, "for the third time tonight, let's hear it for Edmond Margot!"

Applause. He stepped forward, and the spotlight followed him to the edge of the stage. Eve vanished into the wings.

He opened his mouth. Opened his heart.

Nothing.

His scuffed leather shoes jutted over the edge of the stage. Below, the spotlight lit bare sand.

Inhale, deeply.

He closed his eyes.

Nothing new in his mind, nothing new in the whole vast world.

He sighed, summoned another old poem—strange that a poem written two months back could count as old already—

And screamed.

The world tilted sideways. His throat closed, strangling his cry. He hovered weightless before the stage. Images axed through his skull: a surging twisting cobbled street. A Penitent's great stone hand held him, crushing out his breath. A squat watch station in West Claw, a smeared reflection in a dark window, a girl's face that was also his. Breath ragged in his ears.

And underneath that breath, that fear . . . Underneath, he heard the voice of fire. The voice of the long nights of his soul. The voice that was not his, but spoke to him.

But tonight the voice bore no poetry, offered no divine inspiration, no holy dread. A word sliced bleeding letters into his mind-flesh.

Help.

Then he hit the ground.

Awareness returned slowly. Torches blazed. A weight pressed

against his shoulders. He realized after a second's confusion that the weight was his own head. He breathed through heavy lips and a swollen nose. Eve crouched over him, shaking him by the lapels of his coat. "Margot? Edmond? Say something." Behind her a circle of concerned faces and staring eyes limned the board roof of the Rest. He sat up so fast he hit Eve's forehead with his own. His mouth was full of sand, more sand sweat-plastered to the right side of his face. He hurt. Running one hand down his body he found new rips in the shirt, blissfully hidden by jacket and vest. Eve pointed to someone out of his field of vision and snapped a finger. A waiter thrust a glass of water into Margot's face. He took it, swished a mouthful in his mouth, spit onto the sand, coughed, and this time drank.

"Are you okay?" Eve again.

"I have to go," he said, and lurched to his feet.

She held out a hand to stop him. "You're not going anywhere."

"I will." He laughed when he realized what he was about to say. "I must find my Lady."

She reached for his arm, but he pulled back. No one else tried to stop him as he forced through the staring crowd, away from the spotlight and the man-shaped depression in the sand where he'd fallen, out into the dark, questing. Eve watched him go. He glanced back over his shoulder once, when he reached the edge of the torchlight. She stood still, a vision in black—then waved the audience back to their seats. On with the show.

Margot stumbled into the night. His ankle hurt, but still he walked, drawn like a filing to a magnet by the voice he'd lost.

13

A waist-high bamboo fence surrounded Kai's yard. Across the quarter-acre of grass and behind a row of palm trees stood her bungalow, pink walled and slope roofed, a clever investment in a criminal real estate auction; after a few years' occupancy and regular cleaning, it no longer stank of weed. A dog barked down the street. A carriage rolled past, bearing passengers to revelry and the shore.

She opened the gate and stepped inside. Wards prickled over her skin, recognizing her. She swayed up the steps and leaned against the wall as she searched her purse for her keys and unlocked the door. After a slow count of ten she pushed herself off the wall, turned the knob, and lurched into her dark living room. She swung the door shut behind her, dropped her keys in the wood bowl on the table by the entrance, set her hand on the table, sagged.

Thorns scraped her wrist. She screamed and lashed out with the cane, hitting the wall. Dizzy, and without the cane's support, she crashed back into the door. Her hand flailed for balance and struck the coatrack, which toppled onto her. She fell in an avalanche of jackets and old hats.

Lights clicked on, and the coatrack rose of its own accord. Kai blinked brilliance from her eyes. The living room resolved: white shag carpet left over from the dope-peddling former owners, ghostlights recessed into the ceiling, leather chairs and cheap tables. And Claude, standing over her, setting the coatrack on its feet. She recognized the curve of his thigh under his khaki pants, and the spread of his hips, and the swell of his forearms and his once-delicate hands, knuckles swollen by a hundred fights. He wore his uniform shirt, navy blue and short sleeved.

"What the hell." She was panting. She hoped he didn't

mistake it for desire. She wondered what she looked like, then decided she'd rather not know. Hair stuck to her face, eyes wide.

"It's just me," he said, and offered her a hand, which she ignored. "Sorry I startled you."

"I felt thorns." She found the cane where she'd dropped it, and pulled herself into a crouch. "Something grabbed my wrist."

Claude ran one hand through his cropped hair, and grinned. He had a broad face, with large front teeth. She'd loved his grin, once. She followed the direction of his eyes, and saw, on the table by the door, a dozen roses bound in purple crepe paper. "Oh, hells." A sweater remained on the floor. She bent, cursing from the pain, picked the sweater up, and hung it on the rack.

"Jace told me you'd be back tonight."

"Did he."

"I thought I'd come, you know, say hi. Welcome home."

"This is my house. You don't get to welcome me back here."

"You were hurt. I thought you could use a friendly face."

"And you think you qualify?"

"We were friends, once. I thought, even after everything . . ." He stopped. "I'm sorry. It was a bad idea." As if he'd just realized this.

She considered keeping her back to him, but felt like a punished child staring into the corner of her own living room. With the lights on, she saw more signs of his presence. His jacket, folded over the arm of the recliner he liked, the one she'd planned to sell since he moved out. A cup of coffee, a quarter full, occupied a coaster on the table. Aside from these, the table was bare, as was the rest of the living room. She knew how she'd left the place, and expected used water glasses and books facedown and splayed to hold her place, crumb-strewn plates covered in mold that would by now be halfway through the Bronze Age. Though there wasn't much bronze around Kai's living room; any prospective mold-civilizations would be out of luck. "You cleaned."

"Most of it was done already. I put bookmarks in the books. They're upstairs, by the bed."

Violation. Presumption. "Thank you." She turned a slow circle. "You get off shift early for this?"

"Something like that. My schedule's changed a little." A pendant hung around his neck; he dug it out from beneath his shirt. Ghostlight flashed off gold.

"Promotion. Nice. See how well you do when I'm not around to distract you."

"That's unfair."

"You don't live here anymore. I don't have to be fair." No malice there, or not much. She was too tired for malice. Or for manners. She sank into his armchair—no. Not his armchair, just the armchair he liked. "I saw one of your boys grab a pickpocket on the street as I was walking up here. Broke the cobblestones."

"Public works will send a zombie crew in the morning."

"Probably cause as much damage with Penitents as you stop."

"Penitents are a deterrent. They don't tire, they can't be bribed, and they're intimidating as all hells. Plus, they rehabilitate criminals. Not pretty, but it works as well as anything they use mainland."

"Did it work for you?"

A cheap blow, but it didn't seem to hurt, or else he hid it well. "You remember me when I was a kid. I was a punk. Penitence hurt, but I'm a better person now. We both are."

She ignored that. "I saw a four-ton super-powered statue chase down a hungry girl who stole a purse from some mainlander who thinks pink is a color leather should be. Isn't that overkill?"

"Best kind of kill."

"So now you're cribbing comic book one-liners."

He started for the armchair, realized she was sitting in it already, and stopped. "You don't see what's out there. Kavekana'ai's far above the docks. There's war on the street. Always some local god from the Southern Gleb who thinks he'll catch like wildfire here. Sailors bring in strong stuff from the New World. Even the drugs are getting worse: not just plants anymore, new compounds refined with Craft. I saved a kid from flying the other night. He'd taken some Rush, you know, lets you soar for a while, knocks you out for three days after. Problem is, the comedown's fast. We found two guys last week in cane fields on the north slope, broken as if they'd fallen from a height only there wasn't anywhere around to fall from. Some water rat sold it, sailed off on his ship, and left us to pick up the mess."

"What'd you do with the kid?"

"Tied him to a bed. He hovered a few inches off the surface, but a fall from that height onto a mattress wouldn't hurt." He closed his eyes. "I didn't come here to talk about work."

"Why did you come?"

"To see you."

"Here I am." She held out her arms. "All my bits fit together, at least according to the doctors."

"And to ask how you're doing."

"Fine."

"And if there's anything I can do for you."

"No." She liked that silence. Claude was the man with answers. Ask him any question, and he had a reasonable reply. That wasn't why their fights began, but it didn't help once they did.

"Four weeks," he said, wondering.

"They wanted me kept for observation."

"All on the mountain, though. They didn't move you down to Sisters?"

"They had reasons for keeping me out of the hospital. Nothing serious."

He sat on the couch. His feet rested next to hers on the carpet. Creases in the shiny black patent leather of his shoes distorted their reflection. "Kai, how can I help?"

She tried to remember how their last fight started. Her hours, maybe, or his, or else something they'd tried to do in bed, and that stupid seed grew into further foolishness until voices rose and words sharpened and a glass broke and the small house gaped empty and hungry around them. "You can leave," she said.

"You're hurt. You're tired. Jace said you pushed yourself so far there was little the doctors could do for you. I know I haven't been good to you, but I want to help and the least you can do is trust me."

"That's not how it works. And Jace shouldn't have told you whatever. I'm tired. I've had a hell of a month. And us, we're done. If you wanted to help, you shouldn't have broken into my house.

What did you expect, surprising me with roses in my living room my first day home from hospital, as if everything's okay between us?"

The clock ticked on the wall. Normally it was too quiet to hear.

"I didn't expect anything," he said. "I hope you won't push me away just because of what you think I want from you. Give me a chance to be your friend, at least."

"Leave."

The clock chimed. She didn't count the hour.

"Okay," he said, and stood. He donned his jacket, and brushed off the front of his shirt, though Kai saw no dirt there. "I'm going. You can keep the flowers."

"I will."

He opened the door. Outside, the night spread.

She sat in his chair, no, her chair, and watched the door close behind him. The fence gate swung shut, too, the latch settled, and she heard the cat's whine of the wards. The house stank of dust and stale life.

The island is our prison. Bullshit. Kavekana didn't trap anyone. People took care of that themselves.

She carried his coffee cup to the kitchen and dumped the milky dregs into the sink. She filled the mug, washed it inside and out, and left it upside down on the drying rack. The soap smell did not cut the dust, or the age, or the space. Was this what they called depression? Probably not. Drunkenness. Adulthood. She'd imagined standing here as a kid: her own house, free of family and the stink of the working harbor. Standing in skin that fit her soul. The skin felt good, and the body, but the rest of her life, she wasn't sure.

She watched her reflection in the window glass for longer than people should, and saw inside the lines and shadows everyone she had been.

She left the kitchen, turned out the lights there and in the parlor, and walked into her bedroom, where she knelt and prayed to absent gods until sleep came for her, charged with painful dreams.

14

Izza sat on her hands in the wooden chair in the bright room where the Penitent had brought her, and looked everywhere but into the cop's eyes.

"Isobel. That's your name, it says here. Isobel Sola. Not local."

Not at the cop's eyes, or his body. Bad luck to look at watchmen or Penitents. Shouldn't have glanced over her shoulder when she was running, even. They'd taken the purse. A dumb thing to worry her, but she hoped to get some soul out of this at least.

If she got out of this.

"You're from the Gleb, right?"

She shrugged.

He examined the form, most of which she'd left blank. She'd chosen the first name because Izza and Isobel were close enough that she would respond to it naturally if called. The last name she made up from whole cloth. "Parents, anyone we can call?"

Another shrug.

"If no one comes to vouch for you, I'll have to stick you in a cell until the hearing. You don't want that. I don't, either."

A cell was the first step. Once you got used to walls, easy enough for the walls to close in, to wrap you round in rock until you screamed and screamed and lost yourself. She didn't look at the cop, but she wanted to. Wondered if he had a clan scar on his wrist, or fang tracks in his arm. Had he done time inside a Penitent, or was he just a joiner? Which was worse?

He lifted a paper from the pile on his desk. Her paper. She'd never had a file before. She needed a way out, but didn't see one, so kept quiet.

"Can you talk, kid?"

She shook her head.

No need for him to know she could, anyway.

A sigh, movement: a head settling into hands. Tired cop. She might have run for it then, but a dozen others stood between her and outside, not to mention the Penitents on guard. She ran the odds in her head, and came up long.

"The woman you stole the purse from, she's deciding whether to press charges. If she does, you'll face a hearing. You're too young for community service. Just. Keep on this road, though, and you'll learn what Penitence feels like. You don't want that."

That last bit of sincerity answered her question. He'd done time. He'd changed. She tightened her grip on the chair.

"Right. Fine. Who am I talking to, anyway." He made a note on the paper, sighed, and stood. His chair legs scraped against tile. He lumbered around the desk, and set his hand on her arm. She didn't pull back, didn't resist, but she sagged into the chair, and he had to wrench her shoulder to drag her to her feet. She didn't look at him even then. The floorboards of his office were pale and straight and even.

"Come on."

She didn't. He pulled harder, and she fell out of the chair into the desk. She almost choked, but recovered her balance.

From the hall, a voice: "Mike. Someone's here for the kid."

Had Cat found her? Izza hadn't told her where she'd gone, and anyway the woman wouldn't go so near Penitents, not after their first encounter. But for a second Izza hoped.

The hand released her arm. She looked pointedly away from the cop, at the wall decorated with engraved plaques, awards for deeds of dubious virtue. In Kathic, the yellow crust on teeth was called a plaque.

"Really."

"In the receiving hall. Says she's his apprentice."

His. Not Cat, then.

"How'd he know to come here?"

"Says he has a tracking glyph on her. She snuck out yesterday."

The first cop, the hard one, examined her, slantwise, skeptical. "You have a boss looking for you?"

She nodded, once, because it was a way out.

"What you do for him? What kind of an apprentice are you?"

She mimed sweeping.

He grinned when he got the joke. "And you're sure you want to go back?"

She heard a stitch of sympathy in his voice. He could think whatever he wanted, so long as he let her go. She nodded. This time she let herself look, if not quite at him, at least near him. Three deep wrinkles cut across his forehead. A disbeliever, a raiser of eyebrows.

"Fine," he said, and led her back through the office to the bright receiving hall. She spent the walk wondering how she might tell her rescuer from the others waiting; the cop was suspicious already, and if she didn't recognize her supposed boss, or he didn't recognize her, the game was up. She walked ahead of him a few steps, fast as she dared. She remembered the route from when they brought her in: between the desks, beneath the yellowed lights and the exhausted gaze of half-dead officers propped up by bad coffee and a soured sense of duty.

The waiting room was small, well lit, pale, with metal furniture bolted to the floor. Behind a tall wood desk sat the duty officer, cap pulled low over her head. Izza recognized the hollows under her eyes, the face harder than usual for a woman of her age: a former crook, Penitent-reformed.

Few possible saviors among the room's other occupants. Two women in their forties, one in a suit, another wearing a ratty shirt blazoned with the logo of an Iskari band last famous two decades ago, both seated, both reading old magazines. A bearded man sprawled across three chairs, hands bound, a spreading stain on his crotch. A thin kid she didn't recognize, knees jutting through ripped trousers, sat balled up beside the bearded drunk. A round-bellied Iskari gentleman in a green velvet suit, threadbare at elbows and underarms, stood by the door. The green-clothed man dressed poorly for an Iskari, and formally for an islander; a visitor who'd been a long time on the island. Shifting nervously from foot to foot. Waiting.

She didn't recognize the man, but her choice was clear. Whatever he wanted, she could escape him more easily than the watch station. Probably.

She pulled out of the cop's grip, walked up to the Iskari, and held out her hand, firm, level with his stomach. He looked from the hand, to her, and she hoped he could read the determined set of her mouth. Get the message. Strong body language. Set lips. Don't act as if you think I can talk.

He accepted her hand, and shook it. "I thought I'd lost you." His palms and his face were damp. Velvet wasn't good for Kavekana's heat, or the other way around. Deep green eyes bulged in deeper sockets. His lips twitched when he wasn't talking. "You're late, Marthe."

She pointed over her shoulder with her thumb.

"You're late, and this man says you're a criminal."

Another shrug. She patted her chest, and mimed throwing her heart onto the grimy tiles.

He looked from her to the cop. "What do I owe?"

"Her name's not Marthe."

"Surely she did not write her true name on the form you gave her. Thinking no doubt that if she could protect her name, she might be able to resolve this trouble without my discovery. Apologies. She is energetic. As befits her calling."

"Most masters would let a runaway apprentice stew 'til morning."

"I am not most masters." He pinched his faded lapels, and rose up on tiptoe. "I am Edmond Margot, master bard and scion of the Cepheid Margots. And while a few evenings' jail is good poetic experience, my apprentice's time is precious at this juncture. An interruption in her exercises could lead to the loss of her improvisational seed, and with it months of work."

"Lot of mute poets out there?"

"She is not mute," Margot said. "She is merely bound to silence for the period of a year. It is a deeply held belief of my fellowship that only those who cannot speak place the proper value on words. Now." He reached inside his coat. "What security do you require for her freedom?"

The cop rapped his knuckles against the watch desk.

"A hundred thaums," the duty officer said without looking up from her ledger.

Margot paid it, though his hands trembled as he placed the coins on the desk. Izza could feel the soulstuff wound inside them: more than they asked. "Is that sufficient?"

Again, Izza risked a glance at the cop's face, and saw a war there end in defeat. She wondered if he would have felt the same whatever he chose.

"Sure. Leave your address and name with us, so we can find you when the victim decides to press charges. And if."

"Already done." He bowed. "A pleasure, as is my every encounter with the local constabulary."

"Take care of her, Margot. This town can be a dangerous place."

Was that a hint of threat in the officer's voice? A protective display? Whichever, Izza grabbed the poet's hand and pulled him after her, onto the street.

The station's were the only burning lights in an otherwise respectable cul-de-sac, the kind of place Izza wouldn't have dared visit even in daylight. Far above her comfort level on the risk-value curve. People around here had souls, but they didn't come free or easy. You could grab a drunk's or gambler's soulstuff no problem: their spirits flowed outside their skin. Artists were the same way, and musicians, and priests. Three months back and a lifetime ago she'd skimmed ten thaums off a Kosite who'd stopped to watch two kids fight over a pineapple in the mud. Conditions like that made for great graft: empathy roused the mark's soul, easy to nab a corner without their noticing. That's why she set up the fight in the first place. Ivy and Nick got a cut, of course, to make up for their bruises and dirty clothes. They all split the pineapple after.

Margot walked beside her with the quick high step of a man getting away with something. She walked faster when she saw that, because if the cops did, they'd give chase. Her savior, it seemed, was not used to this kind of thing.

They cleared a few blocks from the station, and turned downhill toward shore. The street shrank, and packed earth replaced cobblestones; white plaster buildings sprouted awnings, decks, and tables barricaded by citronella torches. Far enough. She slowed. So did he.

"You're not mute," he said. "Are you?"

She reached into her mouth, and produced a thin gold disk from beneath her tongue. "No. Just hiding." She held the disk out for his inspection, firmly gripped between thumb and forefinger.

He touched the disk, and his eyes widened. "A lot of soul here."

"People put more of themselves in the things they own than they think." She vanished the coin into a hidden pocket. "Memories." She touched the sleeve of his jacket. "I could get a few thaums out of this, I bet."

"They said you stole a woman's purse. You stole . . ." He groped in the air in front of him, actually groped for the word with his fingers. She'd never seen a person do that before. "You stole the idea of her purse. Her connection to her purse." He laughed. The laugh was the only part of him that didn't sound nervous. Big bellied, joyful. She looked up and down the street, wondering who might be listening. The laugh ended, and he wiped tears from his eyes. This too she'd never seen. Most people she knew had little use for tears. Especially the kids.

"Who are you? How did you find me? And what do you want?"

He removed his spectacles and polished them on the lapel of his coat.

"If you get weird," she said, "I'll leave."

He replaced his spectacles. "May I ask you a question?"

"No."

"I saw you," he said. He held out his hand. She stepped back. "I saw you held by the Watch, in that station. A vision, clear as mine used to be. I came to find you. I'm wondering. I don't . . . I don't know how to say this. I'm looking for the Blue Lady. I've lost her. Can you help me find her again?"

Izza stared from his palm to his bulging green eyes, and back again to the hand.

The Lady. How did he know that name? How could he have known?

Didn't matter. In the end, this was just another cry for help.

You can't leave. Nick stood in the broken warehouse of her mind.

Margot reached for her.

She ran.

"No!"

She was fast, and young, and though a Penitent might catch her on an open stretch no fat Iskari poet could do the same. She crested the fire escape, scampered onto the roof, and threw a handful of gravel onto the roof of the next house over so he'd think she'd run farther. Then she lay sprawled, and listened.

"I miss her, too!" he shouted from the street, not after her so much as at the stars. His voice was ragged with fear and longing. "I need her!" Footsteps on concrete. "Help me." Fainter now, and distant. His back turned, given up.

Soundless, she stood. Margot shuffled down dockside streets, green dyed black by night. The moon hung low in the west, a sliver sharp as a smile. She followed him.

Across the street, blind eyes watched them go.

15

Izza returned to the warehouse late, tired, scared, and found Cat seated in the center of the floor, legs crossed so each foot rested on the opposite thigh, hands palms up on her knees. Cat's green eyes reflected the thin light that filtered through the broken warehouse roof.

"I found Nick," Izza said. Her voice shook. She steadied it. "I told him off."

"Thank you," Cat said. "Must not have been easy."

Izza nodded. She stood by the hole, and did not enter the warehouse.

"You want to talk?"

But the words hung on empty air. Izza was gone already. She climbed to the rooftops, and crossed a few blocks over to bed.

The next night she brought Cat food and water, and the next and the next after that, but each time she said "you're welcome" when Cat said "thank you," and left.

On the fourth night, when she entered the warehouse, she heard footsteps behind her. She turned fast, felt the food she'd brought slosh in the wicker basket. Cat crouched in the hole they used for a door, blocking Izza's avenue of escape. "Hey," she said. "Are you okay?"

"Get out of the way."

"You've been on edge. If we're watching out for one another—"

"I never asked you to watch out for me."

"What happened that night, with Nick?"

Izza walked to Cat's bedroll, set down the basket and the water jug, and turned back. "I took care of it," Izza said. She wanted to sound blunt, badass, but she knew she didn't.

"Something scared you. You want to protect yourself. I get that. So do I. I need to know if we're in trouble."

"If you're in trouble, you mean."

"If you're in trouble, so am I."

"We're fine." But she was tired, and alone, and Cat remained in front of the exit, not threatening, just there. The woman had saved her—they'd saved each other. She deserved to know. "When I found Nick, he was about to get caught. Basically. I tried to keep him safe. Ended up running from a Penitent."

Cat stepped into a shaft of moonlight. If Izza wanted, she could sprint around the other woman and out. She didn't. "You got away." Cat said it like a fact, but there was a question hidden.

"No. I got caught. Don't worry, we're fine, nobody knows about you. Someone saved me. Bailed me out. I didn't—I didn't even know him."

"A kid?"

"No. A man in a bad green suit."

"What's his angle?"

"I don't know," Izza said. "He asked me about the Blue Lady, that was all. And he looked at me like they do."

"Like the kids."

She nodded. "Like the kids."

"The Blue Lady, that's the story you tell the children."

"More than a story," Izza said. "She's real. Or she was. But she was ours. That guy doesn't know her. Couldn't." She was pacing, and she hated pacing. Her hands hovered in front of her, palms up, cupped as if to catch rain. When she noticed she stuffed them in her pockets.

"But he asked about her anyway."

"He did."

"What did you say?"

"I ran."

"Okay."

"Hells, do you mean 'okay?'" She wheeled Cat, but she did not flinch. "Why should I let another person come to me for help? Help people and you get caught. They stick you in a Penitent forever, if you're lucky. If not, you just die."

A rat scampered over a box in the shadows. Beneath the warehouse, Izza heard the waves.

"You're a good person," Cat said.

"You say that as if it's a problem."

"It makes what you're trying to do harder."

"What do you think I'm trying to do?"

"Survive," she said.

"I've survived this far."

"But it's not easy for you. You want to help people, even strangers"—and she tapped her own chest, below the collarbone—"of debatable character. But that way of life means sacrifice. You don't belong to yourself. You live in, you know, connections. Duty." She broke off, shook her head. "Listen to me. As if I know what I'm talking about. I'm the wrong woman to offer advice. Life sucks, especially for good people."

"I knew that already," Izza said.

"Sure." Cat sat beside Izza on the bedroll. "It's not like the world comes down to one neat choice—help myself or help other folks. Survival and duty. More like, every day we make a hundred little choices, and sometimes they contradict. Hells." She lay back, arms crossed behind her head, and stared up at the ceiling. "Now you see why I suck at being a priest." She sniffed. "Food smells good."

"Plantain," Izza said. "With chicken."

"Thank you."

"Have you ever had one of those clear choices? Between duty and survival?"

"Yeah. I guess."

"What did you choose?"

Cat didn't speak for a long time. At last, she shrugged. "I came here."

16

Cat took long walks every morning around sunrise. Izza followed her for the first time a few weeks after the affair of the purse, the Penitent, and the poet. Let the tables turn for once. She hung back a block, hiding in crowds and behind rubbish bins, and watched.

Cat strolled south along Dockside, warehouses to the left and wharfs to the right. Tongues and odors mixed on the air: Iskari and motor oil, sweat and leather, Camlaander and Archipelagese and some Shining Empire dialect like silk-muffled cymbals. Oxen strained each step to pull cargo-piled wagons. Old fishermen perched on the edges of docks, still points amid the surge of traffic. Thin long bamboo fishing poles bent under their own weight, and the line's, and bait's.

No fish yet.

Cat moved stiff and sore. How much of that was injury and how much withdrawal, Izza could not say. Pieces of both, likely so intertwined Cat herself could not judge. The woman kept her hands in her pockets, her head down. She stopped every few blocks to sight the distance to Kavekana'ai with her thumb, then knelt and scribbled figures on the sidewalk with a piece of chalk. Izza couldn't make the figures out; every time Cat moved on, she erased the marks with a swipe of shoe or palm. Only an illegible smudge remained.

Once, Cat bent to mark up a loading dock, but a drover chased her off before she could erase her writing. She apologized, crossed the street, and walked on. Izza ran to the ramp after the drover's cart passed, and knelt to read. Five men pushed squeaking wheelbarrows down the sidewalk past her. She had not expected to understand the language Cat left behind, but she couldn't even place the script. Sharp lines and angles, letters made for chisel and knife, and beneath it all a great smiling mouth.

"Following me for a reason," Cat said behind her, "or just bored?"

Izza spun and rose, weight on the balls of her feet, ready to fight or flee.

Cat stood well out of reach, arms crossed, grinning a slight self-satisfied grin.

"Don't worry about it. Come on." She nodded south. "Walk with me." Before they left, she erased the signs.

They passed old folk seated behind carpets spread with baubles of almost-silver and not-quite-gold, sculptures of imitation lapis and real handwoven grass. The farther south they walked, the wider the streets grew. Steel and glass and poured concrete displaced stone and brick and plaster. The ships moored at dock changed, too. Fewer sails, and less wood; more metal, more towers glimmering with sorcery. Cranes swung to load and unload. Gears ground and the smell of spent lightning overlaid that of smoke and sea. The people here did not ramble, but moved from point to point, or in circles, like gears themselves. Zombies guarded the gates of chain-link fences. Cat paused every few blocks to make and erase her notes.

"What's that for?" Izza asked.

"For safety," Cat said. "And for the future."

"I thought you were just trying to draw me in."

"That too." She cracked her neck, and then her knuckles.

"Looks like a religious symbol."

"It is, kind of. You know how gods aren't allowed on the island? They're nervous about contamination up there on Kavekana'ai, want to keep other deities as far away as possible. Customs block even a trace of joss."

"Sure."

"I still smell of old goddess. That's why I was in trouble the night we met. I'd snuck on a ship, but customs found me; I jumped ship and swam to shore, but the Penitents caught my scent. I don't want that to happen again, so I leave marks and holy symbols, spreading the scent around." She threw the chalk up in the air and caught it. "Classic misdirection. So what did you track me down to ask?"

"Am I that obvious?"

"Pretty much."

They passed a fenced-in yard where Penitents marched between shipping containers, opening one after another for inspection while nervous men with clipboards watched. "What happens when a goddess dies?"

Cat's stride caught. She turned back to Izza. "Hell of a question."

"You know more about gods than anyone I trust."

Cat leaned back against a warehouse wall to watch the customs Penitents work. "Same thing that happens to anyone else. She goes away."

"To her worshippers, I mean. If a goddess dies, what happens to her people? They were connected, through her. Does that connection last?"

In the customs yard a Penitent broke open a crate. Wood splintered, and packing cloths fell away to reveal a statue of a four-armed Dhisthran goddess. A clipboard man shouted in protest and produced a sheaf of documents, which the Penitent ignored. "Sometimes," Cat said. The word sounded hollow. "When gods die they leave bodies behind. Those bodies tie faithful together. The bond sticks. Its meaning changes. Weakens, over time. Like when you lose a friend: you're still tied to everyone else who knew them. Sometimes the bond helps. Sometimes it makes the whole thing worse. For priests and the like, most of the time it's worse. They're tighter bound. They know how much they've lost."

The Penitent lifted the goddess statue and carried it to a white wagon packed with religious contraband: reams of printed leaflets, piled prayer beads, heaped ebon effigies. The clipboard man tried to pull the goddess from the wagon, but he wasn't strong enough to lift her. The wagon rolled away toward impound.

Cat made her marks on the wall, chalk scratches and the eyeless smile, and erased them once more. Silver dust stuck to her palm. "I'm done. Let's go."

They left the clipboard man staring after his cargo, or his goddess—Izza couldn't tell which.

17

Kai lay bound on an iron bed in the dark.

Leather cuffs cased her wrists and ankles, held her rigid to the rails at the bed's foot and sides. A harness tied her shoulders to the frame. She could not move up or down, left or right. Her attempts to rise twitched her on the rough cotton sheets, like a live moth pinned through the wing. She stopped. Breath rasped in her throat.

The ceiling hung above her, unfinished stone painted black by shadows.

She heard others. The sound she'd taken at first for the rush of waves was in fact breath—the breath of several hundred breathers, soft, harsh, rapid, slow, pained. Past the iron rails lay another bed, a man tied atop it, and beyond that bed another and another still. Thousands maybe, too many to count, arrayed in a grid. Transparent tubes ran from Kai's wrists and stomach and nose to trail along the ground. Similar tubes sprouted from each prisoner. Dangling IV bags fed drugs into immobile arms. The room was so large she could not see its walls.

Her heart beat panic. She lay still, and felt no pain. Intentional. Pain was anathema to this place. They wanted her quiet, asleep.

Then she heard, beneath the breath, the whispers. At first she thought them patterns like those the mind imposed on any chaos: song in the surf, a voice from the crackle of a burning bush. But as she lay trapped she heard the words repeated.

"Help us."

"Hear us."

"Save us."

She wanted more than anything to answer them, but a mask

bound up her mouth. The most she could manage was a faint moan through closed lips.

She yanked again at her manacles, twisted her hands inside them. Leather chafed and cut. The left cuff was looser than the right. Cupping her thumb into the nest of her four fingers, she pulled. The meat of her thumb caught, and beneath that meat the angular protrusion of the joint.

She pulled harder.

The pop as her thumb joint gave echoed through the room, or else only in the confines of her head. She strangled her own cry. She wanted to be sick, and could not. The tubes would not let her.

With four good fingers she tore at the buckles of her mask. Metal bit her fingertips, but at last the buckles gave, and she gasped fresh air free of leather and dried spit. "Help!" Her first shout cracked midway through and fell, a broken bird. "Help!" The second had wings. "I'm here!" No answer but echoes. The whispers stopped. "Let me go!"

Footsteps struck stone. She craned her neck up and saw a woman drift down the aisle between beds, white coated, hair up in a bun.

Kai clawed at the harness that bound her shoulders, but found no buckles to open. Nor could she pull her right wrist free.

The footsteps neared, and stopped. The woman loomed over Kai like a mountain. Her face seemed familiar. A mother's face.

She caught Kai's wrist. Kai fought, but was too weak, too slow. The woman held her without effort.

"I'm sorry," the woman said. Kai realized she was crying.

The needle was sharp. She barely felt it slide into her arm.

"Gods and demons." Mara held her coffee mug with both hands, but still it shook. She sipped, and stared out the restaurant window over the ocean. "And how long have you had these dreams?"

"Since I got home," Kai said. They sat in the main dining room of the Grande Flambeau, all white, pine, and linen, the kind of place rich pilgrims ate. A skeleton in a hooded cloak read a newspaper by the gilded ornamental fireplace. Two bankers, a pale-skinned Iskari woman and a shorter man, probably Quechal, argued about interest rates at the next table over. Cotton light filled the air: everything here reflected. Kai sank into the opulence, into the silk tablecloths and cushions. The bay beyond the window glimmered. This at least was not a dream. "Maybe longer. I first remembered the nightmare a few days after I came down off the mountain, but it felt familiar then."

"I'm sorry I asked." Mara set the coffee down and forked a bite of omelet.

"Don't worry about it. Dreams are dreams." Kai had cleaned her own plate before she began the story. She regarded her reflection in the white ceramic, then speared one of Mara's home fries. "Probably a holdover from the hospital. You ever wonder if anesthetic stops you from feeling pain, or just makes you forget it after?"

She shuddered. "I will now. Order more if you're still hungry. I'm paying."

"We'll split the check."

"This is the first time I've seen you in weeks. Please. Eat. You need to heal."

"I'm fine." Kai half-turned in her seat so Mara could see her back, and slid her shoulder out of the wide neck of her blouse to show the scars there. "See? All better."

"People are looking."

She laughed, but fixed her blouse, and brushed her hair back into place. Weeks and she still wasn't used to its new shorter length.

"You still need the cane, though."

"Thanks for the reminder." Kai finished her coffee.

"I didn't mean—"

"It's okay."

It wasn't, but she had to say something. Even that didn't break the silence.

"It's good to see you," Kai added at last. "I miss the old office. Harder to make friends with Twilling's people. I don't have much in common with them. They're fine, just, you know, sales types. A locker-room culture. Reminds me of the shipyard."

"How's the work?"

"Weird. We memorize catechisms about pilgrims and prospects, wants and needs, expectation and return on investment. Endless training sessions where we trade off the roles of pilgrim and priest. I don't think anyone has even mentioned faith, or rapture, or responsibility. Prayers, sacrifices, litanies, all the work we do up the mountain—it's by-product to them."

"Are you surprised? Pilgrims want security, anonymity, ROI. Worship is our job."

"I didn't mind that arrangement when I was the one worshipping. But I feel like I'm going crazy without something to believe in. I miss my idols; I miss my prayers. I miss building things."

"You've been stuck in training for weeks. Once you're out, the work will get interesting."

"Let's face it. I'm great in the pool, or behind an altar. I'm no good at interpersonal stuff."

"I wouldn't say that."

"What would you say?"

"You're fine at interpersonal whatever. You just happen to be a bit of a jerk."

Kai wadded up a napkin and threw it at her. Mara laughed, too loud for the room. A waiter glanced their way, and Mara covered her mouth and faked a cough.

"Maybe you're thinking about this wrong," she said. "None of what we do is possible without pilgrims. The sales stuff brings pilgrims here—for them, our theological work is a means to an end. In a way you're more central to the business now than you ever were up top." Mara raised her hand, and called for the check.

"We'll test that soon enough. I have my first meeting with a pilgrim today."

"On your own?"

"Twilling thinks I'm ready." She nodded north, to Kavekana'ai. "How's the Grimwald case? Once that's over, Jace has one less excuse to keep me here in the outer darkness."

The waiter brought the check. Kai reached for it, but Mara reached faster, and paid with a signature and a small heap of soul. "I don't know, Kai."

"Not good, then."

"Not good. Their Craftswoman, Kevarian, she keeps digging for more information about Seven Alpha. Nothing's enough. I don't even know what she's looking for. Our Craftsmen can't stop her. I've gone in for three of those interrogation sessions now. Like needles driven into my brain. I tell her the whole story every time, but she doesn't stop." She folded her hands and looked out to the skyspires that hovered above the waves, miles distant. "You asked me, back on the balcony, if I'd ever heard a voice in the pool."

A little electric chill feathered up Kai's arms—a ghost's unkind caress. "I did."

"And I asked you if you had. And you never said."

"I didn't." Mara waited. At last, Kai surrendered. "Fine. I heard something, I think, just before the idol died. Like a voice in my ear. 'Howl, bound world.' That's it. I found the line later, in a poem, but I don't know where it came from."

"I've never heard those words before. Haven't heard anything inside the pool."

"Then why did you ask?"

"I don't know why Kevarian's pressing me so hard; I thought it might be connected to your question, but . . ." She shrugged. "You're sure of what you heard?"

"I passed out a minute later, and spent the next two weeks on about nine forms of opiate, and I've had this recurring dream about being strapped to a table, so: maybe?"

Mara laughed, and looked guilty after. "I miss you."

Kai heard the silence between them. "What's wrong?"

"Nothing," Mara said. "Nothing at all." She looked down. "I've made partner. I thought you should know."

Waves peaked into whitecaps. Sea breeze blew through the open window. Kai smelled salt and ozone: wards on the window burned away the scents of oil and dead fish. "That's great," she said when she found her voice. "That's great. You deserve it."

"I don't. I mean, I didn't expect it. A surprise. Jace told me three days ago."

"At least I feel better about you picking up breakfast." She forced a laugh. "You get a bigger office? Minions to do your work for you?"

"Maybe. They're working on the details. The salary bump's standard. Profit-sharing."

"I wouldn't share the prophets if I were you. You'll need them to stay ahead of the market." She tried to lighten her tone, and knew she was failing.

"That's a horrible joke."

"I know."

Mara took Kai's hand. Kai's hand was larger, but the other woman's fingers enclosed it like the wires of a cage. "It should have been you."

Damn right. "You took Seven Alpha on the chin, and came out swinging. You deserve this."

"You don't need to say that. You've tried to save my job twice, and now you're sent down here, square one, and I get the promotion."

"I'm happy for you." Too sharp. "They made the right decision." Kai placed her free hand on the back of Mara's, and squeezed. "Enjoy this. Don't waste time worrying about me. I'll take care of myself."

"Can you?"

"I never should have told you that damn dream."

"This all feels wrong," Mara said. "I don't know why."

"You'll be fine."

"Promise?"

She grinned. "Trust me."

Mara leaned back in her chair, rested her front knuckle on her chin. She sat so still Kai thought she'd turned to stone. "Sure." She stood, adjusted her jacket, and shouldered her purse. Together they walked out into the morning heat. Beyond the Flambeau's wards, the dockside smell returned. Clouds crouched low in the southwest, windward. Storms this evening. Mara hugged her again before she left.

"Take care of yourself," Kai said as they parted. Mara nodded, and turned, and walked briskly away. Kai watched her go, then walked in the opposite direction, though she should have taken the same road. She made it a block and a half before the anger building in her stomach seized control, and stopped her. She looked south, to the sea, and north, to the mountain looming overhead, and swore.

18

Kai took a stroll after breakfast to calm down, but the exercise didn't help. She moved with a quick heavy step, hands stuffed deep in her pockets, eyes skyward. As a kid, she'd learned to watch the ground. Though her mother and their staff kept the docks clean, tools and ropes and loops of wire had a way of jutting out to catch unwary ankles. Looking into the open sky was dangerous.

After a half hour's march anger had melted her thoughts from coherent sentences to puddles of emotion. Mara's pity. Jace's fear. Claude's calm concern. She stomped past the shipyards, realized she'd gone too far, turned, and stomped past again in the other direction. She bought herself another coffee from a food cart. By the time she reached the Order's office building, a glass-walled tower in the Palm, caffeine buzzed through her blood and burned behind her eyeballs. Perfect attitude for work. Easier to solve problems when you could direct the full weight of your messed-up life against them.

She realized her mistake when she reached the conference room and found a human being waiting for her, rather than a set of theological enigmas.

Kai stopped at the door. The pilgrim was a curvy Quechal woman, five six or so, skin darker than Kai's, hair short and curled. She wore a pinstriped suit and a bolo tie, and if she noticed Kai's mood, she did not let on. She swept forward, beaming, hand extended straight and sure as a ship's prow. A silver wire bracelet gleamed on her left wrist. "Miss Pohala? I'm Teo Batan. Thank you so much for taking this meeting."

Kai took the woman's hand by defensive reflex. Her grip was firm, her smile the kind of genuine only naifs or consummate professionals could manage. Kai suspected she was the latter. "Nice to meet you, Ms. Batan."

"Call me Teo, please."

"Kai," she said, again by reflex. She ushered Teo to a chair, but the Quechal woman shook her head.

"Do you mind if I stand? I've spent the last three days shipboard in a cabin the size of a doghouse. Feels good to stretch the legs." She rose onto her toes, settled back to her heels, and swept her arms through the air.

"Fine by me." Kai walked around the table, so the wood lay between them at least. She opened the project folder and fanned through pages of information she'd memorized already. She looked across at Teo, who looked back. Once more Kai felt that foreign frission, the fear of being spotted. Old Quechal society had little room for people born in wrong-sexed bodies; they'd kicked out their priests and pantheon at the end of the God Wars, but ancient attitudes lingered. The subject wouldn't come up, no reason for it, but the extra tickle of tension tightened Kai's nerves, which needed no more tightening. She took a breath and tried to think about water, or anything else. The first step of a sale, Twilling taught, was identification, connecting with the prospect. She'd done that already, or Teo had. Needs assessment came next. "Why do you want to build an idol, Teo?"

"I don't," the other woman said.

Kai closed the folder. "I guess we're done, then."

"Sorry. I didn't mean to be flip, just honest. I represent a sort of Concern called the Two Serpents Group, and we're debating whether to work with your Order. I've come to investigate, and advise my board."

No wonder Twilling gave Kai this assignment. Scut work. "Long way to come for an informational interview."

"Consider my three days of seasickness and muscle cramps a compliment to your Order's reputation."

"You didn't have to come all this way. We could have met over nightmare telegraph."

"I never liked nightmares. Not very personal. I mean, in a way they're personal as you can get, direct mind-to-mind contact and all, but they're not, you know, real. I'm an old-fashioned gal. I like to see people face-to-face. Get out of the office once in a while. Hence my presence here. I was in Alt Coulumb for a conference, which made this trip a natural addition. We've been debating this move for a year at least, usual analysis-paralysis dance. Good arguments on both sides, and whenever time comes to make a final decision, more pressing business presents itself."

"What side are you on?"

"The against side," she said. "I don't like gods."

"Our idols aren't gods."

"I don't like anything that looks like a god. But I'm prepared to be convinced." Teo leaned back against the windowsill, sun behind her. The light stung Kai's eyes.

"You're looking for a reason to reject us."

Teo shook her head. "I have plenty of reasons. Give me more and I'll take them, sure, but I'm looking for a reason to work with you."

Kai crossed her arms. This was why she hated humanity. Idols were clear. Such and thus a rate of return. This contract, with that consideration. Humans hid their goals within a mess of flesh and lies. Teo could be telling the truth, or not, or saying things she thought were true but were in fact lies she'd sold herself. People cherished lies. Kai herself had believed she was in love for years.

Human beings. Liars all, and surprisingly it worked. She'd heard that the Badlands east of Dresediel Lex harbored tribes of scorpions grown large and sentient, which skittered, hunting, across the desert. She wondered if they were any easier to handle.

"Perhaps," she said, "you could tell me something about your Concern."

Teo nodded. "We're . . . a little different than most you see through here."

"Everyone says that."

"I expect they do." She laced her fingers. "We spend soulstuff. We don't make it."

"Good luck with that."

"See what I mean?" Teo grinned on a slant, like Mara. She'd told this tale before, and met the same reaction often enough to find humor there. "We form peaceful, mutually beneficial agreements between gods and Deathless Kings."

"Is that even possible? Gods and Deathless Kings don't tend to see eye to eye."

"The God Wars were a long time ago," she said. "These days, gods and human Craftsmen have plenty of common interests, which lets us find win-win scenarios."

"For example?"

"We do a lot of restoration," Teo said. "Where the God Wars scarred the earth, when a Deathless King's golem manufactory infests a mountain range with demons, we step in to solve the problem."

"I'm surprised the Deathless Kings care about cleaning up after themselves."

"You'd be surprised how interested a Deathless King—or Queen—can be in the environment if you frame the problem right. My business partner explains all this with a high-handed pitch, lots of appeal to human destiny and the future of"—she waved vaguely beside her ear—"whatever. For me, it's simple: without people you have no power; without a planet you have no people. Deathless Kings need something to rule. We preserve the something."

"And they pay you for that."

"They back us. Cover expenses. Keep us inspired, though not as richly as I'd like. I came out of sales and contract management, commission-driven roles for the most part. I'd be lying if I said I didn't miss that nice fat gob of enlightenment every quarter. But damn if this isn't more fulfilling, day-to-day."

"And you've been operating for?"

"About three years now. Founded four years ago, but it took us a while to get rolling. You know the drill. Paperwork, demons, more paperwork because of the demons."

"You've mostly worked in Northern Kath, it says here."

"So far. We're looking to expand to the Old World, though. The Shining Empire first, natural since they're closer to DL, but also Koschei's kingdom and the Northern Gleb." She paced the room, hands in pockets. A ship must have felt like death to this woman.

She liked to move. "That leaves us in an odd position. Most of our board members are serious God Wars vets—Craftsmen. To say they don't like gods puts it mildly. Operating on the ground in the Old World means sacrificing to local deities, and they want to avoid that. And please understand, when I say 'want to avoid' I'm being professionally euphemistic, the actual terms our sponsors used were more . . ." She trailed off.

"Flowery?" Kai suggested.

"'Bloody,' I think, is more fitting."

Okay. Needs assessed, offer a solution. "Well, Kavekana is well positioned to help with sacrifice planning. The maintenance fee for your idol supports priests up the mountain"— and she actually managed to say that without a self-pitying wince, not exactly a victory worthy of triumphant song but not bad, either—"who worship the idol in your stead. The same priests help construct and manage the idol's investments, and ensure grace is dispensed where and when you need it."

"That's just what the pro- faction on the board says."

"You're not convinced."

"Well, here's the thing. You know how I said I don't like gods?"

"Sure."

"My sponsors are worse. And when I say 'worse'—"

"Another professional euphemism?"

"Basically. I've had a few bad experiences. Most of our sponsors, they have a history. The King in Red broke the Quechal gods on his altar, and killed the moon in single combat; Ilyana Rakesblight and the Blade Queen seared the sky over Kho Katang. You don't even want to know the outline of half the stories I've heard about Belladonna Albrecht."

"What are you saying?"

"I'm saying my bosses want to be sure they aren't supporting gods when they deposit their soulstuff here."

Was that a lure to her anger, or an honest question? If this woman wanted to sabotage her board's plans to build an idol on Kavekana, she would see a fight with Kai as a win. "Our idols are not gods, Ms. Batan."

"You have priests, and altars, and prayers. What's different?"

Kai closed her eyes, and breathed her anger away. Unfortunately, it was still there when she opened her eyes again. "Do you know anything about Kavekana's history?"

"A bit, from the brochures."

"Our gods rowed off to fight your sponsors in the Wars," Kai said. "The greatest warriors and priests of the Archipelago went with them. They never came back. But people stayed, and kept faith. The priests of Kavekana took that faith and made new images, idols to watch over us with the gods gone. They weren't alive, these idols, not like the gods were—they couldn't speak, or guide, or love, or correct. Didn't have the history, the complexity. But they helped, and later we learned that mainlanders found them useful."

"That doesn't answer my question," Teo said.

"No one who has seen a real god would confuse the idols we build with one."

She nodded, still skeptical. "I'm not used to this sort of thing, to be honest. I'm no Craftswoman, nor, obviously, a theologian Applied or otherwise. We don't have much truck with gods and spirits and idols and the like back home in Dresediel Lex. At least, we don't if everything goes according to plan. If it's a question of seeing, could I see these idols of yours myself? The whole Two Serpents board knows how I feel about gods; if I go back and tell them there's no trouble, they'll believe me."

So close, Kai thought. She could hear Teo teeter on the brink, changing her mind, ready to work with her. It hurt to say, "I'm sorry."

"Why not?"

"Privacy. We have to protect our pilgrims."

"If I can convince my board to work with you," Teo said, "we might be talking about a big investment here. Could you make an exception?"

Kai shook her head. "There are too many secrets in the pool. I can tell you about idols we've built. I can describe common structures of faith and myth. But I can't show you specifics. Gods and Deathless Kings the world over would kill children for a chance at the knowledge you just asked me to give you. We host idols worth millions of souls, and we take our pilgrims' privacy very seriously." She trailed off, remembering Seven Alpha. Not, for once, the idol's death, not the words, but what came after. The room of glass and edges. Ms. Kevarian's questions, probing, piercing, endless. "Very seriously," she repeated.

"I get it," Teo said. "I can keep secrets. I'll sign a nondisclosure agreement if you want—you can lock my memories of your idols away except when I'm in the same room as Two Serpents board members."

"All of whom are major players on the soul-markets themselves. I'm sorry. I can put you in touch with other pilgrims who have volunteered to discuss their experiences. Their successes." She keeps digging, Mara had said. I don't even know what she's looking for. The Grimwalds had signed off on the Shining Empire trade. They knew the risks—might they have known the trade would go south? Did they approve it expecting their idol to fail?

"I'm sorry," Teo said. "That would help, but I don't think it will push us over the line. I hope you appreciate my position."

Kai was barely listening anymore.

I seek the truth. Ms. Kevarian's own words, in their meeting, in the nightmare.

What truth?

Teo continued: "I don't mean to be difficult. But if we're to work together, I have to see."

"I understand," Kai said. "I'm sorry you traveled so far, for so little." She closed the folder, and walked out of the conference room.

She felt Teo's eyes follow her. She ignored them.

19

"What do you know about poets?" Izza asked that afternoon, as Cat did handstand push-ups on a stretch of bare floor.

The woman's back and shoulders rippled with muscle; her toes pointed straight at the sky and the sagging roof. Six weeks give or take since her injury, one of those shaking from withdrawal, and already so strong. As if pain hurt her differently from normal people. "Lots of questions today."

"Just curious."

"Poets in general or"—Cat growled as she pressed herself back up into handstand posture—"specific?"

"I've been thinking about the man who saved me from the watch," Izza said. "He was a poet. Or he said he was."

"Saving"—through clenched teeth as she descended into another rep—"isn't a poetish"—and up again—"thing to do." She paused for breath this time in her handstand, but her arms did not shake.

"He called himself a bard," Izza said, remembering the coat proudly worn and the pedigree proudly proclaimed. "What's that mean?"

"Could mean a lot of things." Cat bent her legs, set the balls of her feet on the floor, and stood, swooping her arms up and back like wings. She grabbed a jug of water and drank half in three long swigs. "'Bard's' one of those words, like 'cop,' that shift depending on who says it. Iskari have this old bardic tradition, dates back to the Devirajic Age, you know, courtly love and all that. Truth and honor and beauty and ladies' handkerchiefs. Then there are Camlaan bards. Tale-twisting, curse-spreading, cheats at cards and politics and marriage. Back in Alt Coulumb most of the bards have some kind of relationship with the Crier's Guild, spreading the day's news, so they end up kind of like spies, or reporters I guess. They hear news, pass it along. You know where this guy's from?"

"Iskar."

Cat set down the jug. Water sloshed inside. She sat still. When she spoke again, she sounded more serious. "Do you know his name?"

"Margot, he said. Edmond Margot."

"An Iskari poet named Edmond Margot." Her face and voice had closed like doors.

"You know him?"

"I've read his work." She crossed her arms over her knees and frowned. "And he knows about this Blue Lady of yours?"

"He claimed to."

"Would anyone have told him?"

Izza shook her head. "Nobody I know. The Blue Lady was our story. Secret."

"Mind if I ask you a question? It's a little personal."

"Go ahead."

"Tell me about the Blue Lady."

"You heard the stories I told Ivy and the others," Izza said.

"Stories, yes. I'm more interested in a description."

Izza wandered around the warehouse, looking for something to kick. She found a suitable rock and with one sweep of her sandal sent it skittering off among broken crates to shock a fat scuttling beetle from its den. "A description."

"A few details, that's all. What she's like."

"What she was like."

Cat blinked. "That's right. You mentioned that she was gone."

"She died. Happens to gods a lot around here."

For some reason that seemed to set Cat at ease. "She wasn't the first."

"No. But she was nice. And I told her stories, so she was more mine than the rest."

"Keep going."

The beetle retreated into the shadow of a piece of broken masonry. Izza knelt, grabbed another stone, and judged the distance. "She was a bird, and a shadow, and a friend." She tossed the stone in the air and caught it twice, testing weight. "The noise to make a rich man look the other way while you reach for his pocket. The hand that catches you when your grip slips and you're about to fall. Speed and silence." She threw the rock as hard as she could. Crack. The beetle's guts smeared black through the dust. "You wouldn't have liked her very much, I guess."

"A goddess of thieves," Cat said, as if the thought was funny.

"I don't know about thieves. She was ours."

Cat nodded. "My goddess back onshore, she was moonlight and order and water and stone. A lantern in dark places." For the first time, she didn't sound angry at her old life. Sad, instead, and distant.

"I guess they wouldn't have got along."

"No," she said, though she didn't sound as if she saw the humor. "There is one thing about bards you should know."

"What's that?"

"They attract stories. They're sensitive to them, pick them up out of the air, out of dreams. If Margot knows about the Blue Lady, it doesn't mean much more than that he's good at his job."

"He doesn't just know the story," Izza said. "He believes it. He thought the Blue Lady led him to me, even though she's dead. That's why I asked you what happens when gods die."

Light glistened off the sweat that slicked Cat's arms and face, outlined contours of muscle. Izza remembered her as a silver statue, breaking Penitents bare-handed.

"What's wrong?"

"I don't know," Cat said. "If I were you, I would keep away from this guy. Dead gods are trouble, and so are men who're mad for them."

"He could help the kids after I'm gone. They can take care of themselves mostly, but it's always nice to have a friend. Besides, I feel like I owe him something. He got me out of jail, and I ran because I was scared."

"You don't owe him."

"What does it matter to you?"

She laughed, hollowly, into the floor, and shook her head. "That's a good question."

Izza felt something sharp and small break inside her.

Cat looked up. "I care about you, kid. I won't say I know what you've been through, but I understand why you want to get away from this life. I want to help you before you hurt yourself, or someone else does the hurting for you. You need to let all this go. The island, your kids, the Blue Lady, the poet. They can take care of themselves."

"You're scared," Izza said.

"Yes."

"Don't worry." Izza did not bother keeping the scorn from her voice. "I'll make sure no one finds you."

And she left, before Cat could say anything more.

20

The rest of the day Kai pretended to be productive: reviewing intake forms and trade requests, directing each to the relevant priest. Her thoughts throbbed with conspiracy. When time came to write up her meeting with Teo, she scrawled "theological differences" in the form's comment box and stuck it amid the others, hoping it would be overlooked. She had more important things to do than a postmortem with Twilling.

At sundown she strolled down Epiphyte, east first, then south, to Makawe's Rest. The club wouldn't open for hours; poets slept late on weekdays. The stage stood empty, and the tables with up-ended chairs looked like pictures she'd seen of Shining Empire tombs. Penitents watched the water, their prisoners asleep. She heard no screams.

Mako stood on the beach between two Penitents, hitting golf balls into the ocean. He'd spread a carpet of fake grass at his feet, stood the clubs in the sand beside him, and placed a tee upright on the carpet. Kai watched him swing three times, and miss. His fourth swing connected, and the ball arced twenty degrees to the swing's right. Kai squinted, and thought she saw a splash fifty yards out on the still blue bay.

She shouted from up the beach, reluctant to approach. "If Eve catches you doing that, she'll tan your hide."

"A man's still allowed to play golf on this island."

"You could hurt someone."

"This time of day? Anyone who works for a living's back in port, and anyone who doesn't could use a golf ball to the head once in a while."

"Wait until they stick you in a Penitent for killing a tourist."

He groped into his golf bag, found a ball, and knelt to the

mat. He placed the ball on the tee, but as he stood, it fell. With an exaggerated sigh he knelt again, replaced it, and rose slowly to his feet. The ball rocked left and right, but stayed. "Nothing they could do to me someone else hasn't done already."

She approached, keeping well clear of his arc of fire. She stopped beside the Penitent to his left, sat down, and leaned against its calf. The stone was warm. "I hear it hurts the mind more than the body. These things make you move the way they want, think the way they think. And the way they think isn't human."

Mako swung, and missed the ball by a foot. He frowned. "Lots of things force folk to think in ways that aren't human. Try joining an army someday, if there's ever a war for you to fight. Hells, I bet you thought at least five inhuman thoughts before work this morning." Another swing, another miss. The club slipped in the old man's hands, and Kai flinched. Mako reset his grip. Sunset transformed his face, scarred and cragged and wrinkled, into a landscape of flame. Not for the first time, she wanted to ask what he'd done in the war. Not for the first time, she decided against it. "You shouldn't be here yet," he said. "What's brought you?"

"You expected me?"

"Always do."

"You're often disappointed, then."

He swung. The golf ball tipped off the tee, and rolled to rest in sand.

"It's by your feet."

"I know where it is." He knelt again, and patted about his knees until he found the ball.

"I can't believe Eve lets you keep those clubs."

"She doesn't know I have them."

"Somehow I doubt that."

"Doubt what you like." Back on the tee, and standing. He adjusted his feet.

"A little to the right."

He grunted, and bent from the waist, wagging the club. "What's up?"

"I'm in a fix."

"Must be hard for you."

"No harder than for a blind man to golf."

"Great thing about the ocean," he said, "is that it's one big hole. Easy to hit." He draped the club across his shoulders, hooking his wrists over its either end. He twisted his torso sharply left and right, and his back popped like festival fireworks.

"Oh my god."

"Yes?"

"You should get that checked."

"Eve sends me to a masseuse every other week. Says it's the least she can do for all the pain I cause her."

"I don't think a massage counts as revenge."

"You haven't been with my masseuse." He laughed, and coughed, and spit. His spit landed with a solid fleshy sound in the sand, startling up a seven-legged sand-colored beetle that reared, bared sickle mandibles in protest, then scurried away. "She's from those jungles south of the Shining Empire. Girls there are born with chisels for fingers and pistons for arms. Every other Thirdday she avenges each acre of forest I burned in the God Wars."

"She know you talk about her this way?"

"Hells, I talk about her this way to her face. She only really opens up on the back when she wants to hurt me."

"You're a horrible human being."

"Never have been any good at it." He thrust his hips forward and bent back. His shirt rode up, revealing stomach roped with scars. "And yet you come to me for advice, so what does that make you?"

"A horrible human being," Kai said with a sigh.

"What's the problem?"

She pressed her fingers into the sand, past the warm top layer, into the damp cool beneath. The beetle marched past, and saluted her with its mandibles. She flicked it, and it hissed at her. "You know Jace sent me away from the mountain."

"You may have mentioned it a few hundred times or so when you were drinking."

"He wanted to appease some clients who are suing us because

their idol died. They don't have a chance—but they keep prying anyway. I think they're looking for something."

"Like what?"

She heaped the sand beside her into a fortress, and carved a moat around its walls. "The idol that died was tied to a lot of others. If the Craftswoman gets those records, she might be able to learn about our other clients—who they are, how they spend their souls. And if that happens, we could all be in trouble."

"Is that possible?"

"Maybe."

"So tell your boss."

"Who will call me obsessed and maybe he's right. I might be making things up to compensate for being reassigned. Seeing conspiracies everywhere. I don't want to be the girl who cried kraken."

He adjusted his grip on the club, and held it out to her. "Are my *V*'s pointing in the right direction?"

"I don't even know what that means."

"Just say yes or no. You have a fifty-fifty shot at being right. Better than most coaches in my experience."

"No."

"That's what I thought." He shifted his hands, and turned back to the artificial green.

She demolished the fortress she'd built, and filled the moat with its sand. "I should trust Jace to deal with this."

The club rose without tremor or hesitation. The old man's body was a perfect line. Then the club fell.

A sharp clean crack echoed across the beach and back again. The ball flew out, and up, and straight, until it disappeared into the sunset-singed sky. Mako nodded. "That look as good as it felt?"

"Yes."

He fished for another ball. "Find what's wrong with the foundation, then fix it."

"You think I won't be able to move forward until I settle this question."

"I was talking about my swing," he said, fishing for another ball. "But why not?"

She stood, slapped sand off her skirt, and leveled her fortress's ruins with her shoe. "Guess I better get to work."

"What's your plan?" Mako asked.

No one remained to answer him. He shrugged, raised his club, and swung again, missing.

21

That evening Izza crept to the Godsdistrikt, where she panhandled for scraps of soul and watched an itinerant players' opera. The performers were boat people, island-hoppers of the Archipelago, who lashed watertight barrels of props and costumes to the outriggers of their canoes. They sang while they paddled. Their proud voices rang out over the ocean as they approached on the morning tide.

No performance could match that pure dawn cant. Hearing them across the water, if Izza shut her eyes she could imagine they were not players at all but Makawe home from the wars, bearing treasure in crystal boats. Izza wasn't Kavekanese of course, but she'd always liked the prophecy of the gods' return and the paradise to follow.

More, anyway, than she liked this opera. Hard to pin down why. At first she thought she didn't believe the abandoned bride would really wait three years for her husband to return. Later, watching from a fire escape above the crowd, face pressed between iron rails, she decided that, no, people believed crazier things every day. The problem was the last act, when the bride received a letter announcing that her husband was dead or remarried or something—Izza didn't know enough Descended Telomeri, especially when sung at high volume with poor intonation, to follow the fine points of the plot—and committed suicide. Izza bought the suicide. The bride's acceptance of the letter was a stretch. A real person would put more work into self-deception.

But the singers sang beautifully despite the occasional dropped consonant. After the bride plunged her knife into her neck and the orchestra crescendoed its last crescendo, Izza only stole a little from the hat they passed around for donations.

The sun had long since sunk. Godsdistrikt lights burned a million shades of red, and mainlanders milled down narrow streets seeking food, drink, and sex from businesses happy to oblige. Izza bargained for her dinner with a kabob stand owner: an hour's work passing out glyphed placards to pedestrians, each placard stamped with a crude picture of a meat skewer and a subtle charm to guide its bearer to the owner's stall. She ate the kabobs she earned for her work on a rooftop near a thronged intersection where smuggler priests promised pieces of cut-rate heaven to passersby.

When she finished the kabobs the priests were still chanting discount salvation, with no more takers. Some nights she could watch them for hours, but now she was only killing time. She wiped her hands clean on her pant leg, left the skewers piled on the red tiles, and crossed roofs north to the poet's house.

22

Kai watched bubbles of light bob down and up the mountain. Evening cable cars descended the slopes of Kavekana'ai, burdened by priests and shamans, acolytes and overseers all homeward bound. The night shift arrived before the day shift clocked out: functionaries passed functions to their counterparts, so the idols would not be left untended.

She shouldn't do this. Better to take Jace's broad hint and see a shrink. The psychological underpinnings of her theory were so obvious even she could see them: anger at Mara's promotion turning to denial of reality, to rationalization, to the spinning of elaborate stories about how the world went wrong. Kevarian had motive enough without any need for conspiracy. The Craftswoman wanted to win her case. This whole exercise was one more piece of proof that Jace was right, that Kai was cracking.

But it wouldn't hurt to sneak back into the mountain, to take a final look at Seven Alpha's death, see what dirt Kevarian might find if she went looking. Wouldn't hurt, so long as no one caught her.

And besides, while she was here she could investigate the poem.

Jace had banned Kai from the pool, but she didn't need to dive. The mountain's library held a wealth of information about Seven Alpha's death. With luck, Kai could enter the library, do the research, and leave without Jace hearing of her visit.

At night she faced a smaller staff, and fewer chances of detection, but she still didn't want her name on security logs, which ruled out the cable car. She'd have to take the stairs.

Kai returned home, spent a half hour cleaning to settle her mind, and changed out of her heels into walking shoes. She wished she could have dressed for the climb, but though the Order wasn't as white-shoe as mainland Craft firms, walking its halls in gym clothes would attract notice. So she donned her lightest linen suit and a black shirt, slid her purse over her shoulder, and set out to break the rules.

She entered the forest a half mile from her apartment via an unmarked dirt path overgrown by roots and thick foliage. Soon the forest writhed around her, come to life. If she glanced back over her shoulder she would not see the road or distant streetlights. She did not look back. Hidden wards had welcomed her onto secret ways.

Before the cable car, before pilgrims traveled from around the globe to Kavekana, before the gods sailed off to fight the world's wars, priests had only climbed the mountain on holy days: a journey of fear and trembling that began with this walk down a narrow dirt path through dense forest that smelled of motherhood and rot.

Trees and heavy air pressed close. Swelling silence overcame insect song. A bird cried. Another screamed. Soon she lost her bearings in the wood.

After a long wander, she found a path to her right blocked by thorny vines. She turned that way and the vines writhed tighter, snakelike. Thorns dripped dew and poison.

She walked into the vines, passed through tearing thorns, and found herself at the foot of a moonlit slope. Shallow steps switchbacked three thousand feet up the mountainside to the balconies and overlooks that ringed Kavekana'ai.

She took the climb slowly. As a novice, she'd sprinted up the stairs until her legs jellied and she almost tumbled off into space. Older now, and injured, she broke her climb into twenty-minute increments counted on her pocket watch, with five minutes' rest between each. Her blood sang, and her legs burned, and her wounds, too, a sharper wire-pain compared to the muscles' fire. The fat moon laughed overhead, outshining stars and the burning city below.

She prayed as she climbed. With no idols to care for, she prayed to the old and absent gods, who'd run off to the God Wars and not returned: Makawe, Heva, Maru, Aokane, all the rest. Mako had gone with them, fought his youth away in foreign lands. Last human survivor of the Wars on Kavekana, but even he was not immortal. Soon his strength would fade. The Rest would lose its heart.

The old gods' songs had good rhythms, and she sang them to keep her pace. Makawe's journeys below the world, seeking fire from the older powers of the depths. Heva comforting the first humans as they scraped, lost and cold, at the mud in which their souls were trapped. The war between Maru and his siblings. She climbed the long stair until the moon hung full overhead.

When she reached the lowest balcony of Kavekana'ai and found it vacant, she sagged against the railing, breathing hard. She wasn't in mountain-climbing shape anymore. Her leg had ached during the climb, but she only used her cane for the last few hundred feet. Should have used it the whole way. She'd regret all this tomorrow, or later tonight.

A delta of sweat ran from her collar down her shirt to her stomach. As her heart calmed, the chill of wind and heights raised goose bumps on her arms. She wrapped herself tight in her jacket. The thin fabric did little to cut the wind, but little was better than nothing.

Kai stepped forward, and stumbled. Her leg gave way. She cursed, caught herself, and stood still again, listening to the wind and the silence of the slope, wondering who might have heard. Leaning on the cane, she tried again to walk, and this time held her balance. Three-legged, she proceeded to the wall, and stepped inside.

The stone accepted her. She knew its secret name, and it knew hers. This mountain was formed when gods and humans first rose from the earth. Men and mountain were made of the same stuff. For those who knew its secrets, the stone itself was a gate, and this gate had not been closed to her. Yet.

She stepped out of the stone into a semicircular chamber, brightly ghostlit, walls painted flat beige. Decades ago they'd been rough-hewn rock, lit by flickering candles, but occult design customs didn't mesh with the demands of a modern office. In the seventies Jace's predecessor had hired Graefax Tepes Ross, design consultants to the Dread Empire and to the Deathless Kings of the New World, to modernize the Order's look. Kai thought she would have preferred it the old way.

Tunnels branched from the chamber. Kai turned left: up, and in.

She passed two junior priests arguing Iskari theology. "They want to reduce sacrifice flight domestically, which makes it a policy goal when negotiating treaties abroad. Which means us. You don't seem to understand our position."

"No, I do. The thing is we can't afford to recognize their rules. Preparing to satisfy reporting requirements is tantamount to honoring those requirements. If you think—"

"You're not even *listening* to me."

"I'd listen if you—"

Kai walked on, and their argument receded into insignificance.

She reached the office levels and kept climbing, two more floors and right, down a hall paneled in cherrywood, through a glass door, to the library.

A golem sat behind the front desk, bucket of coffee clutched in a clawed metal hand. Servos spun as it raised the coffee to its mouth-port. Lenses in its eyes realigned with delicate clicks. Kai walked past the desk to the windows at the library's far wall, which opened on to the caldera. Other office windows glowed across the pit, human constellations echoing the stars in the alien sky above and the pool below.

No sense lingering, but how could she resist one glance, possibly her last, on the star-studded space at the caldera floor where by all rights lava should have bubbled, one glance at the hole where she'd rebuilt herself, the womb that birthed her people? A few figures stood there on the beach at the end of everything, heads bent in prayer. Her shoulders ached, and her heart too, to swim again through the black, to breathe the uncreated, once more to weld soul and dogma into living form.

Not now. Maybe never again.

She turned, and ran into a wall of Gavin.

He stood behind her, lumbering and tall as ever. He clutched a bag of scrolls to his chest, and he wore a polo shirt and slacks and a shocked expression. His lips tried three times to form her name before it came out once: "Kai! What are you doing here?"

She would have winced anywhere, but most especially in the library at night. The carrels and long tables were almost empty—a handful of acolytes leafing through old contracts and Craft journals—which made the silence, and their anger when it broke, more profound. Still, she couldn't begrudge his wide smile, so glad to see her.

"Gav. Keep your voice down." She laid a finger beside her lips.

"Sorry," he whispered. "You've been gone awhile, is all. How have you been? We miss you."

"I miss you, too, Gav." She hugged him around the scrolls. He was large and warm and soft.

"Did you come to visit? I'll get some of the guys. I think Cal has a flask at his desk, I mean, it's not good booze I think and it's not much, but we should celebrate." Gavin wasn't a drinker, and the word "booze" sounded strangely affected in his mouth.

"I'm sorry, I can't. Wish I could." Clicks and spinning gears: the golem librarian turned toward them and the apertures of its eyes irised tight. Still holding Gavin by the shoulder, Kai walked him out past the desk, into the hall where at least the wooden panels would dull their voices. He followed, easily steered, like a two-hulled catamaran in a strong breeze. Easily steered, and just as easily tipped. "I can't stay long."

"I thought you were still recovering. Working with pilgrims."

So "recovery" was how Jace sold her exile to the team. "I need information to seal the deal for this one pilgrim. I don't want to promise the world only to learn we can't deliver."

He nodded slowly. "That happened to me a while back. Someone thought we could make an idol who'd just resurrect things for fun." He chuckled. "Hard commitment to back out of. But, I mean, here, let me tell the guys, and when you're done you can come down to the pool and we'll all hang out. Only the night crew's here now, and it's slow." He pressed the scrolls closer to his chest. "I wanted to catch up on my reading."

She should have used that excuse, rather than concocting something about pilgrims. "I'd love to. Just . . ." I'm not supposed to be here at all, and every second I stay is a risk I shouldn't take? It would hurt too much to sit with friends and talk as if nothing happened? Both were true, and neither would help. "I'm recovering. I don't want to push it. Maybe you could all come down the mountain and hang out with me. I'd like that."

He breathed in through his mouth, stuck out his jaw, and nodded. "Sure. I can see that. Most of the guys don't go anywhere except the mountain and their own apartments, but I think I can swing something." His eyes widened. "I mean, are you okay? I'm sorry, I wasn't thinking. Is there anything I can do for you? Should you even be up here without help?"

Damn. "I'm fine, Gav. I only need a couple files." She grinned winningly as she could manage, and hoped she didn't look too tired. If Gavin's misplaced sense of chivalry engaged, she wouldn't be rid of him for hours. "I can do this myself. Just a little research, is all." She touched his bag of scrolls. "Go on. You have work."

"Okay," he said, still skeptical. "It's good to see you again, Kai."

"Good to see you, man. It won't be so long next time."

He nodded, once, smiled, and lumbered away down the corridor. She watched him go until he turned left and disappeared. Letting out the long breath she hadn't realized she was holding, she sagged against the wall and stayed there until her heart calmed again. Fear chilled her brow and neck. She didn't like being afraid of Gavin.

She tugged her clothes straight and returned to the library. The golem glared at her, and refilled its mug of coffee from a percolator in its chest, but did not stop her or ask her business. This time she ignored the window and the view, stepping softly so as not to attract more attention. None of the library's denizens looked up from their books as she passed. Pages turned, scrolls rolled. A young woman coughed. A teenage acolyte's leg twitched up and down like a sewing needle as he read. *He*, Kai thought, noting the military hair and the loose shirt and the other signs that the acolyte with the restless leg was waiting for initiation, waiting for the pool, waiting to remake himself into himself.

She smiled, and wanted to say something to him, but she'd stood out too much already. Get the data, and get out. That was all she could afford now.

She counted four doors, five, on the outer wall: small, curved, and paneled to match the walls' wood, marked over the jamb with names on bronze tags. Once, every senior priest had her own niche, but office space had grown too crowded for such luxury. Kai passed her own door without hesitation and continued an eighth-rotation around the caldera until she reached the door bearing Mara's name.

She stepped through into a tunnel of volcanic stone. Cloying warm air bore a sulfur stench and hints of ozone. Ghostlight tubes painted everything pale purple-green: the worn smooth path down the center of the hall, the petroglyphs, the thick brass pipes gleaming with silver Craftwork. Her footsteps and her cane's taps joined the pipes' weird symphony: the clink and groan of heating and cooling metal, the rush of hydraulic surf.

The tunnel opened into a cave cramped with machines and carved wooden totems wound with wire. Kai stepped onto the grate that served for a floor, and did not look down; beneath, the cavern plummeted to a pinprick of perspective, its walls lined with scrolls. A central pylon plumbed the pit's depth, and bejeweled pneumatic spindles rose and descended that pylon, sparks arcing from their tips to the scrolls. All the history of Mara's idols lay here, entombed.

And Mara was here, too.

Kai had not expected that.

An iron stair rose to a catwalk that ran below five niches in the rock wall. Mara stood in the center niche, head back, eyes closed, body rigid, rimmed by metal thorns. Wires pressed against her wrists, snared her neck, snaked along her legs. One thorn hovered above the vein at each elbow, tipped not with metal but with a spine of light.

This arcane contraption was one more cost of doing priestly business in a Craftsman's age. No single human being could comprehend the millions of points of data that made up an idol: bargains, transactions, contracts, records of prayers received, heard, fulfilled. Old-fashioned gods handled most operations themselves. "Makawe hears all prayers," the old saying went, "and laughs at them." The idols Kai and her comrades built could handle basic functions on their own, but priests had to make harder choices for their idols. Theologically risky, of course, which was why they asked Craftsmen for help—Craftsmen had a history of stretching theology's borders, or else ignoring them altogether.

Kai had not expected Mara to be working late. Fresh off a promotion, elevated to the highest levels of the priesthood, why would she spend her evening on low-level prayer management? The Order paid acolytes to do this sort of thing. But there was no sense trying to justify away an unfortunate reality. Maybe Mara had a high-stakes audit coming. Maybe she was reviewing her archives for inspiration. Whatever the reason, she might notice Kai entering the system. Best to leave and wait for another chance.

If she had another chance. Mara might be here the next time, anyway. Or Jace might cancel her clearance, or Gavin let word of her visit slip. To wait was to lose. She could still learn what she needed, if she moved fast, and subtly.

This was a bad idea, she thought as she climbed the stairs and leaned back into the niche farthest to Mara's right. Machines woke about her. Dormant Craftwork smelled her blood and burned with hunger. The system's demons knew their feast approached. Oh yes. A very bad idea.

Leaning back in the niche, Kai stared at the opposite wall, at the painting of a starlit beach on West Claw, white sands and spreading calm water. A suggestion of sunset lit the horizon. She forgot whether the painting was Jace's idea or if it sprang in full tacky glory from the forehead of a Graefax Tepes Ross consultant. Each carrel had one, always the same scene. The intent was to calm priests amid this unholy system of metal and wires. We promise to make the process of ripping your spirit out of your flesh as painless and routine as possible. In her early days with the

Order, Kai had wondered at the choice of scene, until she realized that the rush of arcane fluid through hydraulic pipes was supposed to provide an audio component to the painting, a sound of surf. Better to have chosen a foreign image. An alpine meadow, maybe, like the ones in old mystery play musicals: priestesses capering among goats, singing swollen songs to their living mountains. Kai had grown up with surf, and sand, and the painting felt like a fake smile from a trusted friend.

She swung counterweighted metal claws into position. Gears ground in hidden mechanisms. Metal fingers settled against her temples, her ankles, her waist, her neck. The cavern air was warm, but the metal cold. She shivered in her linen suit. Wires and needles waited within those arms, cold tendrils coiled under tension. She looked up at the ceiling, raw unfinished hungry black. "I offer myself," she whispered. The machine heard her. The claws at her arms extended thin points of lightning that tickled the inside of her elbows, sought and found the veins there. The hairs on her arms snapped to attention. She was the core of a thrumming beast. All she had to do was straighten her arms, and plunge the lightning needles in.

She clenched her teeth, and punched her arms straight, and fell into the open mouth above.

23

Falling, again, and always. Kai's eyes sang. Broken glass was the world and gleaming, every moment and memory a cutting edge. Assembling those shards into a mosaic hurt.

Teeth ground teeth, a vibration in her skull. That was reality, distant, fading, gone.

She hung inside the gaping mouth, in the blackness charged with idols. They formed a perfect sphere with Kai at the center, frozen skeletons of many-colored lightning. Some she recognized, forms she'd helped Mara shape. Fish-men, kings of ocean and stream. Great burning bull-beasts who ate children and dispensed prophecy. Winged serpents who bore planets in their talons. Others she did not know, older projects, even a few quaint ancestor spirits. She found Seven Alpha at once: winged woman, legs bent backward, floating dead and dull in the black. An echo of her former glory, echo even of the frightened, drowning creature Kai had tried to save. Patches of her had been torn open, lines of breast and stomach. One wing hung crooked, pinions shorn. The ray-trace suggestions of her eyes seemed closed.

Kai approached, and heard voices.

"I don't know how many other ways I can say it." Mara, tired. Drawn drum-tight. Nervous. "An individual idol has too few believers to support more than a handful of basic functions."

"That much I understand." The second voice she also knew, cold, precise, clipped. Pinstriped suits, and an arched eyebrow. Ms. Kevarian. Kai froze in simulated space. The Craftswoman could walk through nightmares, and this was a sort of nightmare. Her body might be on the other side of the world. The how wasn't so important as the fact of her presence. If Mara didn't notice Kai, the

Craftswoman would. "Which means the idol's behaviors are automatic, and circumscribed."

"That's the theory." Kai heard the slight hitch in Mara's voice. She didn't like this conversation.

"Then, if your records system works, any discrepancy in the accounts must result either from malice or negligence. Which is it?"

Space and size were malleable in this imitation realm. Kai became small and swift, and gnat-sized swam toward the skyscraper of dead Seven Alpha, toward vast and broken wings and the gaping seas of her wounds. So close to discovery. Kai's throat constricted. Damn it, she didn't even have an endocrine system here. Shouldn't that soften the fear a little? Control yourself. Do what you came to do, and leave.

"This is a complicated situation," Mara said.

"Truth is truth, Ms. Ceyla. People make it complicated."

Kai slipped between two lines of Seven Alpha's body and hovered. Mara sat huge and cross-legged on the idol's spreading back, between the roots of her wings. Ms. Kevarian paced in front of her, along the idol's spine, her footsteps sharp, as if she strode on stone.

They hadn't noticed her yet. Good.

Kai turned back time, and felt the idol wake around her: a shudder in the lines, a memory of breath. Mara and Ms. Kevarian vanished, phantoms of the abandoned present. Kai sank back past the idol's death, her flail for almost-survival. Months rewound in minutes.

She changed her perspective: the wires of Seven Alpha's body faded, replaced by a web extending from the pumps of the idol's artificial heart. Each wire was a deal, a contract, appended with relevant names and account numbers in angular glyphs. She spun time on its axis and slid forward again, looking for some gold, for Kevarian might be hunting some treasure for the Order to protect. Over time, Seven Alpha bound herself to more Kavekana idols as Mara diversified her investments. Kai wouldn't have made so many bonds—hundreds, it looked like, and multiplying fast—but it happened sometimes.

If Ms. Kevarian wanted to map the idol network, this would be a good place to start: before Seven Alpha's death. Kai altered the artificial dreamscape to clear away all information Kevarian had not requested.

Night fell, infinite and everlasting.

Not this far back, then. So what did Ms. Kevarian want to see?

She advanced until Seven Alpha took shape again in the darkness, shining, smiling, divine, all assets invested in a massive bid on Shining Empire debt. Risky move. Kai had never pegged Mara for such a gambler. She hung back even from the office ullamal bracket, bet only a few thaums at a time. But bad gamblers took big risks. Seven Alpha borrowed, and bought. The investment's value fell, and the idol collapsed. Kai watched Seven Alpha die in slow motion. The brilliant heart corroded. Claws caught nothing. That last single desperate surge, grasping for an invisible rope—Kai's offer.

Then, death.

Kai hovered alone in the artificial past. She watched the death again, and again, and heard no strange words, saw no hidden truth. *Howl, bound world* was an invention of her drug-addled mind, a line from Edmond Margot's diseased brain passed along to her by a strange and untraced course.

The idol died. That was it. That was all.

What else did she expect? Mara took a stupid risk. The idol suffered. Kai took a second stupid risk to save her, to save them both, and that didn't work out, either.

Sometimes gambles don't work out.

Sometimes people die.

She thought about her father, and the old gods.

Ms. Kevarian had not found any information that might expose the Order's other clients. Either she hadn't asked for it, or she had and Jace blocked her. So much for Kai's cavalry charge. So much for discovering, in the depths of disgrace, a secret threat to island and Order. So much for Jace welcoming her back as savior. Arrogance, vanity, to think that she, by herself, could uncover a threat Jace and Mara and Gavin and all the others missed.

She did not return to the present. Why risk discovery again?

The illusion slipped, and she fell back to her own body, pierced and sore. Air cut her lungs. The beach painting mocked from the far wall. Fake surf rushed and retreated.

Wires slithered like serpents and unwound from her neck, arms, legs. Claws unclenched. Lightning thorns withdrew. Shaking, she pushed the machines away, and on the third try grabbed her cane. She trusted it, and stepped out of the niche into the cavern.

The empty cavern.

Mara was gone.

Her conversation with the Craftswoman had sounded serious, midpoint of another long interview like Kai's—hours ahead yet, the kind of drawn-out meeting no one quite knows how to end. Kai'd expected to leave long before Mara woke.

Don't panic, she told herself. She might not have seen you. Conversations with Craftswomen took a toll on the mind. Maybe she staggered from her niche, down the stairs and out, without a backward glance. Yes. And maybe tomorrow morning Makawe would return from the Wars on a treasure-brimming boat, to usher in a new age.

Best not to depend on either.

Mara had probably left to find guards, or Jace, rather than confront Kai herself. A few minutes' grace, then. With luck, Kai could escape down the mountain, deny the entire thing. Her word against Mara's. Who would Jace believe: the woman he'd just promoted, or the one he transferred for mental health reasons?

She walked faster.

No one tried to stop her as she left Mara's carrel; the library remained quiet. Plush green carpet consumed her footfalls, and the taps of her cane. The night owls didn't look up as she passed. The librarian golem did, though. As Kai neared the door, it extended a talon to stop her. "Excuse me." It had a voice of blades and wind. "I must inspect your bag."

She almost ran, but couldn't beat the golem on foot; she'd seen it reshelving books, quick as a blink. So she stopped, and opened her purse. Jointed metal fingers split into thin manipulators, and crawled through the jumble of wallet, medicine, notebooks, cosmetics. Kai blinked. Notebooks? She carried a small notepad for jotting down dreams and shopping lists, wire-bound with a thick green cover. But her bag held two: hers, worn green, and a newer volume covered in red leather and bound with a ribbon. The librarian golem returned the bag without comment and nodded once, a tickling of gears. Its eyes followed her as she left.

She kept her pace slow until she was out of sight. She wanted to tear the red notebook from her bag and read, but there wasn't time. Her watch showed half an hour gone since she'd entered the niche.

Down she ran through echoing halls into the mountain's beige depths, down until she reached the entrance she had used, and stepped out through rock onto the moonlit balcony. Slope wind blew cool beneath a black velvet sky. From this height the island's green was a brief skirt before the spreading legs of the sea.

"I didn't expect to see you here so soon," Jace said from the balcony's edge.

Every part of her stopped at once, and restarted slowly. He leaned against the banister, a sliver of shadow in gray turtleneck and navy slacks, thumbs hooked through his belt loops. She tried to walk toward him, calm and measured, but her knee buckled and she had to catch herself with her cane. "I had work to do."

"Work up the mountain?"

"A pilgrim asked me some questions today. I needed an answer."

"No answer you find here will help a pilgrim decide whether to invest. Some need us; some don't. The ones that do, you only have to guide them. The ones that don't, nothing you do will change their minds."

She forced herself to look him in the eye. The hollows of his face were deep wells in the moonlight.

"Why are you really here?" he asked.

Someone else could have lied to him. Not Kai, not now. "I thought we were in danger. I thought Ms. Kevarian and her clients might be trying to learn about other idols—to use their suit as a pretext to map the pool, to learn our secrets."

"You climbed the mountain, and snuck into the library. And what did you find?"

"Nothing," she said. "They haven't pushed discovery that far back."

"They tried," Jace said. "We stopped them."

"Then Kevarian does want to map the pool."

"Kevarian wants every scrap of information she can pull from us. Everything she doesn't yet know is a potential weapon in her case."

"They have a plan," she said. "There's something deeper at work here."

"Even if there was, discovering it is not your responsibility."

"I am a priest. I have a duty to the gods. The idols. The island."

"And I sent you away." The calm facade slipped, and beneath she saw his anger and his fear. "For your own good, for our good. If Kevarian heard you snuck in to investigate Seven Alpha, she could argue that you lied in your deposition. That you think we could have saved the idol. One lie blows the case open."

"I thought we were in trouble. Was I supposed to stand by and do nothing?"

"Yes. Let us deal with the mess. Let go. Accept that good intentions don't count."

He stopped. The night closed around them both. In their anger they had grown large, but silence made them specks on the mountain under a spreading sky.

He walked to her, and around her, shoulders slumped. Kai tensed as he passed behind her back. When he emerged, he seemed smaller, like a comet part-melted by its orbit.

"Go on," Kai said. "Might as well get all this out in the open."

He removed his glasses, and rubbed his temples between the thumb and fingers of one hand. "Kai, why did you join the priesthood?"

"Does it matter?"

"It's an honest question."

"With an obvious answer."

"You didn't need to stay with us after your initiation, after your change. Could have chosen any line of business on the island or off it."

"I wanted this since I was a child."

"Why?"

The moon was full, and the rabbit-shadow inside dark. "My folks work with ships. Mom, Dad, they realized back before I was born that the boom market for Kavekana sailors wouldn't last. We're a small island in a big world. We wouldn't always be the cheapest source of labor, or the best." She struck the balcony stone with her cane. "That left the Order on the one hand, and on the other, waiting tables for cruise-boat tourists looking to guzzle a Mai Tai or seven."

"Why not leave?"

"This is my home," she said. "I don't know what would have happened to me if I'd been born in Dresediel Lex, or Dhisthra, or the Shining Empire. This is where I became myself." His bowed head, his careful soft voice, unnerved her. She'd expected the shouting match, not whatever this had become. "Why did you join, Jace?"

"Same reason, " he said, "different decade. I wanted to help my home. The gods didn't come back from the Wars, and we had to keep the island together. Who knows what Kavekana might have become if we let history take its course? If we gave up after the gods left? No idols, no pilgrims, no Penitents. It might have been better."

"No."

"How do you know?"

"Look at Dresediel Lex, ruled by hungry skeleton kings. Look at crumbling Alt Selene. Would you rather we be the butcher of a continent, like Shikaw, or a mechanical wasteland like King Clock's country? Or I guess we could have sold ourselves to the Iskari, or to Camlaan. Played host to military bases and squid cathedrals. They're worse than tourists, I hear." She nodded down the slope, to the lights of the bayside city. "This way, we stay ourselves."

"Do we?" Jace stretched out his hand for her shoulder. She hesitated, then stepped closer so he could reach it. He was old, but his grip was firm. "You want to help Kavekana," he said, "but what Kavekana? You have a vision, a dream of a place that's not here anymore. I sent you away to save us, but also to learn. You don't appreciate what we mean to our pilgrims, how we fit into the world. As long as you don't know that, I can't trust you." He released her shoulder. "Do you understand?"

Jace was bent around a point a few inches above his heart. Craftsmen said that mass, energy, spirit, warped the world like weights on a rubber sheet, making straight lines curved. Younger, Jace had stood straight, a grand architect shaping idols. He'd lived a thousand years since then. Even light bent, in the spaces where he walked. "I think so."

"I don't like sending you away. But I will, to protect us, and you."

"You can't protect me from myself."

"I can. I have. As of this midnight, the mountain's locked against you. The rock won't let you pass, nor the forest. The halls will turn your footsteps, the golems and glyphs bar your way. You'll lose yourself if you try to climb the stair."

"Forever?"

"For now."

"This isn't fair," she said. "It isn't right."

"No," he said. "But gods and priests are rarely fair, and seldom right."

She said nothing.

"I love you, Kai. I wouldn't do this if I didn't have to."

"Do you expect thanks?"

"No," he said. "We'll go together to the cable car. I won't make you walk down alone, like a novice or a thief." He paused at the rock, and turned. "I asked the watch for someone to escort you home. They sent Claude. He's waiting. I could send him back, keep you here until another watchman comes."

Beneath them, the city shone. Water lapped the shore.

"No," she said. "That's fine."

24

The poet lived in a walk-up apartment on the second floor of a two-story stucco house. Bed linen hung drying over the balcony. Palm trees grew in neat rows to the house's either side, and more in the narrow yard behind, near the alley wall. Izza climbed that wall, jumped to a palm tree, and kicked a coconut crab off the trunk when it snapped a massive claw at her heel. The crab was large, and landed heavily, but it raised itself on spindly legs and lumbered off. From her perch, she watched.

Edmond Margot sat by his window. Candlelight glinted off his bald patch. She couldn't see the details of his room, the packed bookcase and the bare china cabinet, the worn rug and the bed with no blanket but a sleeping pouch sewn out of a doubled cotton sheet. She didn't need to see these things; she'd surveyed his apartment earlier, looking without success for hidden weapons or the remains of kids abducted, tortured, butchered. The room made him seem unbalanced, a good sign: the worst predators she'd known were the ones that put the most effort into seeming normal. Still, even poor predators had teeth.

The wraparound balcony ran beneath the window where Margot sat writing. Long jump, but this way she wouldn't be seen from the street.

So she jumped, caught the railing, and pulled herself up and over, light as falling leaves. The poet, though, was less focused than she'd thought. His shoulders twitched, and he looked up. His eyebrows rose, mazing his high forehead with furrows.

Before he could speak, she set a finger to her lips. He closed his mouth. Izza thanked whoever was responsible that she was a girl, and skinny. She might be a threat, but she didn't look it. If she'd been larger, or a boy, Margot might have cried for help before he recognized her.

"Pick up your pen," she said.

"What?"

"Your pen," she repeated.

He looked down. In surprise he'd let the pen droop to paper, and a pool of green ink had welled around the tip. He wiped the pen and slid it into a metal stand. "Thank you."

"Do you know me?"

He nodded. "From dreams. And"—hasty, remembering their last meeting—"the police station. The girl whose name isn't Marthe."

"That's right."

"You sought me."

"You're not hard to find."

"Artists learn not to be. Obscurity is our mortal enemy. I've seen minstrels in Palatine stand between lanes of traffic, holding their sonnets overhead." He mimed in miniature, hands not higher than his eyes. "Painted on pine boards, you know. Dripping. Atrocious calligraphy. The word 'God' ends up indistinguishable from 'gad.'"

"Good poems?"

"Not as a rule."

She leaned back against the balcony. "How did you find me at the watch station?"

"Visions," he said, and covered his mouth, and coughed. "As I said."

"Visions of the Blue Lady?"

Drunks stumbled down the alley behind her, singing sea shanties off-key. Margot's eyes were the same shade as the ink spilled from his pen. Fear showed in the green, under light. "I hadn't dreamed of her for weeks. You understand? Find the love of your life. Fear her at first. Welcome her into your mind, your work. And one morning, wake to find you've lost her for good. You cannot even dream her anymore. Watch your fame grow in her absence as you struggle to mate dead words on dry paper.

Then, when you stand drunk in a spotlight reciting stale work, you see a vision, strong and clear as yours used to be—a girl, in danger."

"You saw her." Izza had not meant to whisper. "That night."

"I didn't," he said. "I saw you. I knew where you were, and I tried to help. I thought you could lead me to her again."

She'd felt nothing since the Lady died. No presence, no dreams. But Cat said ties still bound the faithful, even once their gods were gone. If so, she'd never be free, no matter how far she ran. Unless she gave the Lady up forever.

"Please," Margot said. "Tell me about the Blue Lady. I miss her. Where did she go?"

She wanted to tell him everything: tell him about the Lady wreathed in fire who blessed the hungry with her kiss, who fought Smiling Jack to save the souls of Kavekana's children. She wanted to tell him how she had healed Izza from the depths of a searing fever. The Lady set a cool hand on her brow, whispered a promise in her ear. Day broke when Izza thought she would never see another dawn.

But when she opened her mouth, those words wouldn't fit through, because they were bigger than mere sound, like islands weren't just the part above the water but the parts below it, too, mountains rising miles over seabed.

In the end all Izza could say was, "She died." She owed him that at least.

He did not flinch. Did not cry. Did not move except to ask: "How?"

She knew that look, the hunger behind it. Margot needed her, surely as the children did, and that need would not fade no matter how many answers she gave him. Izza would remain priestess of a dead goddess, clutching the jagged edges of a broken dream, until she broke.

Cat's voice: *You have to choose.*

"The same way as anybody else," she said, and leapt away into the deepening night of her failure.

25

Kai rode down the mountain with Claude. The cable car was clean, well lit, and empty but for them. Reflections chased her from the glass. She did not speak, and neither did Claude. He watched her, not the reflections or the slope. His hands rested on his knees. He rarely crossed his legs, or his arms, or his beliefs. His fingers drummed against his thighs. He saw her looking, and stopped.

They slid past a stanchion. Pulleys and rollers realigned. The car swayed, and continued down into the canopy of trees.

Claude followed her out of the empty station. Cable cars didn't generally run this late. Jace must have started them again for her. Another allowance. She ran her hand over a painted rail, descended three steps to the vacant street, and walked along the sidewalk from the puddle of one streetlamp's light to the next.

Claude kept pace three meters back, his steps slower than hers to account for his longer legs. Her faithful follower, backup, and minder. The Zurish gods Dread Koschei had supplanted, those lords of gold and raven hair who once ruled the steppe, they used to send priests (she had read) to accompany every warrior and diplomat, tradesman and spy and scholar who traveled abroad. Theological officers, the priests called themselves, haunting those they escorted, noting their every failure.

She wasn't being fair to him. *Gods and rarely priests are fair, and seldom right.* Screw that.

"Why are you walking so far back?" she said, and stopped.

"Jace sent word through the Penitents that they needed someone to escort a priest home. He didn't say why." She stood at the edge of one streetlight circle, staring out into shadow; he stood at the circle's other pole, staring in, at her. His gaze burned her neck. "He didn't say you."

"Or you wouldn't have come."

"Of course not. You don't want to see me. It was hard to accept for a while. Still is hard. But this is for the best, for both of us."

"Then why walk so far back?"

"I like the view." He heard how that sounded. "No, that's not. I mean. It's hard to walk next to you."

"When have we ever done things the easy way?" She glanced over her shoulder. Streetlight blanched him, and made him seem small. "Come on. Walk with me at least. We don't need to talk. But you freak me out, trailing back there like a Dhisthran bride."

"I won't jump onto your pyre," he said, approaching slowly, as if she were a scared monkey.

"That's a weight off my shoulders." Being with him was easy. They knew each other's jokes, even the bad ones, and the weak points in their walls. That was why their fights were so harsh.

They walked together, neither looking at the other. "Why did they need someone to come get you?" he asked after a while.

"Off-limits. Sorry."

"You can tell me."

"I can't," she said, "actually. Rules."

"Okay."

They continued down.

"Jace asked if I minded that it was you," she said. "He offered to send you home."

"And you said no."

"We're adults."

"We're sort of adults," he agreed. "It's like we're tied together. I mean." He fell silent.

"Bound in promissory chains," she said. The words floated up from the pit of her mind, from Margot swaying on the stage.

"What's that?"

"A poem."

"Poetry," he said, as if that one word encapsulated every-

thing unsatisfactory in the world. Dry fallen fronds scraped together behind them. Pebbles rolled on the road. But there was no
wind, and the road was empty. "You ever go back to the Rest?"

"Sometimes."

"You're limping."

"Busy night," she said.

"Do you want a shoulder?"

"I have two."

"That's not what I meant."

"I know what you meant. The answer's no."

"Okay," he said. In the silence, she took inventory of her
wounds. Bones broken and harshly healed, flesh welded back to
flesh, nerves rewired, soul rebuilt. All the physical traces of her
fall.

They reached her house ten minutes later. She opened the
front gate. He followed her up the footpath to the porch. He had
to duck beneath the vines that trailed from the overhang. Loose
dead ivy leaves stuck in his hair. He waited, quiet, eyes averted,
hands in pockets. Muscles stood out on either side of his clenched
jaw, like they did when he had something to say and was trying
not to say it.

Kai searched her purse for her keys, found them, kept searching. She closed her eyes and leaned against the door.

She thought of the red notebook in her bag, but all she felt
was tired. One more conspiracy, one more chance to jump in and
try to save the world. Always throwing herself at other people's
problems. Sickening, and a sign of sickness. Stand aside. Let go.
Accept.

"Are you okay?"

She took the key from her purse, slid it into the lock, turned
the knob sharply as if breaking a kitten's neck. The house received
her, warm and empty, walls and furniture and the drug dealers'
bad shag carpet. She should get a pet. A dog, maybe. A big, noble
dog. One of those with floppy ears. Strong across the shoulders.
Happy to see her.

"Would you like to come inside," she said. It wasn't a question.

For a sentence to be a question, you had to care about the other person's answer.

He stood at uneasy equilibrium, not quite balanced, not quite falling. She prepared for him to ask—are you sure. Is this what you really want. You're upset. Whatever happened to you tonight, it set you off, and it wouldn't be right of me to take advantage. Prescient, telepathic, she saw him form all those answers, all those ways to say no and make her feel a fool for asking.

She dreaded his voice. Even if he said yes, she thought, she'd close the door in his face.

He stepped inside. He took her in his arms. They kissed like crashing rocks. Their teeth touched. He smelled of sweat and scorn and so did she. They broke, separated, saw each other: her dead eyes reflected in his own. She closed the door. The latch clicked. She left her cane propped against the wall and with the wall's help walked to the stairs, pulling him behind her, up to the bedroom they had last shared months ago, the bedroom hung with charcoal drawings and dark curtains. A spider crawled across her down comforter. She swept it away with the back of her hand.

His jacket fell to the floor behind him. As she watched he pulled his polo shirt off over his head. She hadn't turned the lights on, and he did not, either. Scars crossed his chest and arms, where the Penitents once and forever broke him.

They seldom talked about his crime: he was a tough poor kid, and he ran with a dangerous crowd, and one day a fight turned bad, and a boy died. He wasn't part of the fight, but he didn't stop his friends, either. Only watched. The court judged him old enough to serve, and threw him into a Penitent. When he emerged, his body was a molded weapon, his mind a made thing. When they met again at the Rest three years back, she barely recognized the boy she'd known. He barely recognized her.

He'd gained weight since she last saw him naked. Muscle, mostly. She bit her lip, hard, and clenched her hands into fists. Nails dug half moons into her palms. Blood tasted copper. He stepped forward. She hadn't yet removed her jacket.

Her life was bounded by mistakes. Trying to save the idol was not her first, and she'd made others since. So Jace told her, and Mara, and even Gavin by his eyes and his hesitation. This was a mistake, she knew. He had always been a mistake, her greatest.

She let her jacket fall, and made him.

26

Hours later Kai still ached. She lay hung over on her own bed, alone despite the swell of sleeping flesh beside her. She wanted a cigarette. She'd never smoked. She padded downstairs and sat on her couch in her dressing gown. Her purse lay by the door, discarded in that rush of anything but passion. Hatred, maybe. Disgust—but with whom? She limped to the door, grabbed the purse, returned to the couch, and sat again, purse on the table before her, lump of leather tangled in its own strap.

She clawed inside, past wallet and keys and comb and lipstick and gloves and bandages. The red notebook looked gray as everything else in the dim light of streetlamps through her windows.

She untied the ribbon and opened the book. Its stiff spine cracked, and the pages clung together. Most were blank. Sketches covered several near the beginning, the outlines of a goat-legged woman with horns and spreading wings. Despite the artist's poor draftsmanship Kai could tell she was supposed to be beautiful. On later pages the drawings degenerated into flowcharts and diagrams, arrows connecting labeled circles. Names, some she recognized, most she didn't, none human. Concerns, gods, idols. Lists of numbers. Accounts, maybe, or thaums transferred, or the addresses of certain dreams.

Aside from the diagrams and the lists, the book was blank. No memories inscribed here. No explanations. No name, either. Good practice. The notes here could cost a lot of people their jobs.

Not as many, though, as the five loose and folded sheets that fluttered out from the notebook when Kai fanned its pages. The sheets were vellum, not paper, which told her everything. On Kavekana, only the Order used such expensive material for book-keeping, and then only for Craft-readable records. These pages had been sliced neatly from a ledger, and she recognized the format: a list of true names, and beside each, columns of numbers. Someone had cut these sheets from an idol's records, no question. The script was right, and the watermark, and the silvery Craftwork glyphs that headed each column of the table.

As for which idol, she did not need to wonder. Each page, at its bottom, was stamped with a long number that ended with a dash and the symbols "7A."

Most of the names on these pages were cryptic, like those earlier in the book, but one she recognized. A few thousand thaums of grace had been dispensed to Edmond Margot.

Kai read the ledger pages twice, but the name remained.

Howl, bound world.

She folded the parchment again, returned the pages to the notebook, and tied the book with its ribbon. She moved to the kitchen and found a glass, and whiskey, and ice cubes from the icebox. The ice clinked in the glass. The shadow of glass and ice lay long on the counter, sparked in its middle with focused light. Kai threw the ice into the sink, and turned on the water. The ice pitted, shrank, vanished. She turned off the water, poured herself a finger of whiskey, threw back the whiskey, washed the glass, and returned bottle and glass to their cabinets and the notebook to her purse. She stood alone in the living room and listened to the night. Wind, insects, a whooping bird she could not name.

Margot was a poor poet, no follower of the Grimwalds, no mainlander hoodlum. But if these records were correct, he had drawn power from the Grimwalds' idol.

Any discrepancy must result either from negligence, or from malice.

Back in the database nightmare, Ms. Kevarian had accused Mara of manipulating records. Another baseless accusation, Kai had thought. More intimidation.

But here, in Kai's purse, were vellum pages cut from the Order's own ledgers. A handful of people could access the ledgers in person—and of that handful, Mara was the most likely culprit.

Why would she hide the pages with Kai, then turn her in to Jace? Unless Mara hoped Jace might search Kai and find the papers. Unless she planned to frame Kai for the cover-up.

Mara was her friend. Mara had come to her this morning, to apologize.

To apologize for what?

Kai could go to Jace with this theory, about Mara trying to frame her—for what exactly? What was Mara trying to hide? Margot, perhaps, but what did Margot have to do with anything? He was an awkward poet with a three-month-old case of writer's block.

And his words called out to Kai through Seven Alpha when she died.

Three months ago.

Idols, gods, and muses. Was it possible?

The living room seemed darker. Whiskey fuzzed her nerves, and shadows spun laughing in the corners of her living room.

Couldn't tell Jace, not yet, not after their fight on the mountain. She could not go to him without proof. Kai needed to learn the whole story first. Then, act.

Now, though, she needed sleep. If she could find it.

Kai walked to the stairs, almost climbed them, turned back, and tucked her purse under the couch.

Claude lay in bed. He breathed heavily through his nose, choked every few breaths from the weight of his neck and his chest. He'd spun the bedclothes around him into a cocoon. She wondered what butterfly might emerge, and decided not to wait and find out.

She prodded his shoulder until he snorted and flailed at her with one arm, an easy dodge. "Behold the great watchman, forever on guard against danger."

He blinked sleep from his eyes. When he looked at her, though, his eyes held something else, something he could not blink out. She wondered if he would call it love. "You're not danger."

"Time for you to leave."

"Other guests?"

"Me, myself, and I. Scoot. I'll have a hard enough time explaining tonight to myself come morning without you around."

"I'm sorry."

"You're sorry for a lot of things."

He stretched on the bed, a rigid rod, eyes screwed shut. When he opened them again they just looked tired. He sat up, and stood, and after a minute's padding around the bedroom found his pants, shoes, and shirt. "My socks are here somewhere."

"I'll mail them to you."

"There's no need for this."

"No. But I want you gone anyway."

He pulled on his shoes without the socks, slid the shirt over his head, and walked downstairs. Heavy footsteps vibrated up and down the steps, through the floor.

She followed, and watched him fumble with the latch. "Thank you," she said when he got the door open.

"I hope that helped," he said. "I hope. We need to stop doing this to ourselves."

"Thank you," she repeated. Her voice was harder and less kind.

He shut the door and left. She waited until he wouldn't hear to lock the door behind him, then limped back up the stairs to her room. Shutter-slat shadows striped the ceiling above her bed. She must have slept, but she remembered only those shadows fading as morning neared.

27

Kai walked three circles around Makawe's Rest in the pre-dawn mist, but saw no sign of Mako. Late night for him, then. New poets, perhaps, or a lover, maybe both. Eve would be furious either way.

She found a few stones in the morning surf, returned to the bar, and threw the stones up against the ceiling as hard as she could, one by one. They left white marks on the heavy boards. When she exhausted her ammunition without provoking a response, she collected the fallen rocks and tried again. Four volleys later she heard a foul groan and a scramble of limbs against wood. A hatch in the ceiling opened and Mako's face appeared, surrounded by a gray seaweed tangle of hair. "Get outta here, we're closed."

"Shame," Kai replied, hefting another rock. "Even closed for conversation?"

"Kai! This is a bad time."

"I need to talk. Who is it you have up there that you can't bother later?"

"Bothering's what the kids call it these days?" He cackled, or coughed. Kai wasn't sure which. "Not a who. A what. Dreams."

"What kind of dreams?"

"War dreams."

"Figure I just did you a favor, pulling you out of nightmares."

"These aren't nightmares."

"I've never heard of good war dreams."

"You've never seen a war. Don't talk as if you know." He beat a tattoo on the hatch with his fingers. "What are you here for?"

"We need to talk. In private."

He spit, and the spit splashed into the dust on the floor beside her. "I'll be down." His head disappeared, and Kai watched the hole, wondering if he'd stumbled back to bed.

Wood groaned; metal screeched. A ladder appeared in the hatch, tipped down, and fell, unfolding. Metal feet clapped against the stone floor. Mako descended the ladder like a drunken spider, feeling each step with his toes. She spotted him with her hands. He hadn't fallen yet, not in all the years she'd known him, but he was an old man, getting older.

"You ever think about taking a room on the ground floor? Or moving out of the Rest?"

He stepped off the ladder, touched a glyph on its side, and nodded in satisfaction as the ladder shuddered and rose, retreating back into the ceiling hatch. "Eve would kill me. You have any idea how much she spent putting that thing in?"

"More than you're worth."

"Hah." A dirty brown earthworm scrunched over Mako's bare foot. He plucked it up and threw it underhanded onto the sand. "Maybe so. To what do I owe the pleasure of your interruption?"

"I'd like your advice. In private." She glanced down the beach toward the Penitents standing guard. They weren't looking her way, but they listened well.

"I know a spot." He groped, found the corner of a table, and used the graffiti carved there to orient himself toward the bar. From beneath the locked liquor shelf, he retrieved his crooked stick, leather handled and brass shod. "Follow me." She walked with one hand around his arm, the other on her own cane. His skin felt dry and loose beneath her palm. He'd been larger, once.

Mako guided them away from the beach, north three blocks, and west down an alley of shuttered laundries and closed convenience stores, most long since taken over as outbuildings for the great gleaming coastal hotels.

"Are you sure this is the right place?" Kai asked.

"Another block down, at the corner, on the left."

There, true to Mako's word, they found a small diner, a grimy place with plush booths upholstered in green fake leather. When Kai opened the door a smell of cigarettes and bacon wafted out; stepping inside, she noticed the lack of ashtrays and the NO

SMOKING sign. Behind the counter, a round cook slid plates through a slit window and called an order number. No one looked up.

Mako lowered himself into an empty booth. His bent knees cracked and popped, and when he sat they pressed against the underside of the table. Kai ordered a cup of coffee and dry toast when the waitress came. Mako ordered coffee, too, black.

"This," he said after the waitress left, "was the first place I ate when I came home from the Wars."

How to answer that? "Because you knew it?"

"No. Any place I knew would remind me how much the island changed since I left." He rapped his forehead with a knuckle. "Or how much I had. I wanted somewhere it wouldn't feel strange to be a stranger." The waitress returned with coffees. Mako drank all his in a gulp, then grabbed Kai's, drank half, and set the mug back down in front of her. Steam rose from the black liquid. "Course, even someplace new gets the old familiar stain in time."

She grabbed her coffee in both hands. Still too hot for her to drink, but safe at least from further theft. "Why come back, if it hurt you to be here?"

"Firstways, didn't know it would hurt so much. Secondways, you can't escape yourself, and you're the only thing that hurts you in the long run."

"That and rocks."

He laughed. "And rocks. And knives and swords. Lighting, thorn, paper cuts, fire, acid, teeth, claws, ice, drowning. Well. Drowning only sort of hurts." He banged his empty mug on the table, and the waitress looked over. Her sallow, up-all-night expression made her seem ten minutes' hassle short of serial murder, and with Mako she was counting down the seconds. "What do you want from me, Kai?"

She removed the red book from her purse, and untied the binding ribbon. The vellum sheets crackled when she unfolded them. For the hundredth time this morning she read the list of names, hoping they had changed. No such luck. "What can you tell me," she said, "about Edmond Margot?"

"You talked with him at the open reading a few weeks back."

"I talked with him. But I don't know him, and you do, and I'm buying breakfast."

"He came to the island a few seasons ago, after the rains. Lives alone. No lovers Eve's figured. Good voice. Reminds me of some Iskari I knew back in the Wars. Ones as fought in the deltas, or in Southern Kath, when they came back from the jungle they were only echoes of what they'd been up-country."

"He was a soldier?"

"No. He had that same aftermath feel though, an echo looking for the noise that made it. He found the noise here." Mako grunted thanks as the waitress filled his coffee. She rolled her eyes and strutted off.

"What do you mean, found the noise?"

"He showed up at the Rest for the first time back after the rains, you know, with a sheaf full of poems, made a righteous thud when he set it down on the bar. Asked for, what'd he say, the right to perform. So I listened to some samples and I said no."

"I didn't think he was that bad."

"You didn't hear him then. His work had skin, but no bone, no marrow. All art, no." He groped across the table, found Kai's arm, squeezed hard. She grimaced and slapped his hand away. "You see."

"And you told him no."

"I'm not cruel. I told him start on the open stage, nobody likes some big shot they've never heard of coming in from abroad as if he's gods' gift to poesy. Perform with the others, quality will out, and they'll clamor for Eve to give you a show."

"That's not cruel?"

"Maybe I was a little mean." Mako scratched his head, and a moth flew out from his hair. "Anyway, he needed himself taken down a peg. Not his fault. Iskari don't have natural rhythm. Comes from all the squid-goddery, you know. Worship something that doesn't eat, sleep, screw like you do, do that for a few thousand years, and see if you don't lose your rhythm. Even in bed they work funny: all straps and ties and games."

Kai's hand hurt where he'd grabbed her. The waitress brought her toast, cold, and topped up her coffee. The toast crumbled in her mouth as if baked with sand instead of flour. "Margot didn't do well on the open stage, is what you're saying."

"First night, he was up against some Gleb boys, and a pair from Alt Selene that throw their lines back at each other. He stumbled through a sestina and got a weak hand off the stage. Come back next week, I said. And he did. Surprised the hells out of me. You know what happened then?"

"Same thing?"

He nodded. "Same thing. He barely got words out of his mouth that time. Doggerel about flowers or some shit like that. Even worse reaction from the crowd, but he grinned like an idiot at the end, as if he knew he'd gone bad along the way, and having some-one tell him so was the highest order of compliment. Next week, same poor show, bigger smiles. The boys got fresh with him. You ever meet Cabe and them?"

"No."

"Big fellows, work down dockside. Old-style Kavekana boys. You know."

Kai knew.

"Time was, they'd all be off on a ship hauling rock or salt pork or oil or whatever cross the ocean, with a captain's whip over their heads. Which would have been good for them."

"Because beatings make better men."

"Hells no. Just that bad times pull folk together. Mad captain, he builds a crew. Ocean does, too. And age—age's harsher than a whip. Point is, if you're a young man and you have nothing harder than a clock to fight against, 'fore long you make up things to do with your time. And one of those might be, you know, find a poet you don't like and jump him in an alley while he's drunk and tak-ing a piss, and beat him until there's a stain on his pants and he bleeds from the nose and mouth."

"Gods."

He raised his hands. "Well, yeah. I mean. I saw what was going to happen, too late, when Eve told me Cabe'd settled up their bill early. I walked out after, to stop them."

"You?" She tried to keep the surprise from her voice.

"They aren't bad kids, understand. Bored. Young. Angry. They wouldn't jump an old vet." He slapped his sagging left bicep with his right hand.

"Awful lot of trust to put in thugs."

"Nobody's a thug from birth. So out back I went, and found them."

"How bad was he?"

"They were all bad."

"You mean Margot fought."

"No. Margot was beat up proper. Face swollen, lips busted. The kids, though, they were cringing. Scared. Most unconscious. One awake and babbling. I say pain can make a man: those boys got scars that night they'll wear with pride one day, once the fear fades enough to let pride back in. That's the last mugging they'll ever try."

"Margot beat them up?"

"Margot didn't do nothing. No blood on his hands, nor under his nails, neither. When he came round, though, I heard rapture in his voice. Like I hadn't since the war, you understand? Like he'd found something he never knew was lost. He thanked me. I took him back, cleaned him up with cheap rum, and he didn't flinch when I poured it on his cuts. The Penitents came by to see if he could name his attackers, and he said no. So they left, and he left, and I thought that was the end."

"But he came back."

"He did. The next week, at the reading, he spoke thunder words with a hurricane voice. When he was done they screamed for more. Eve dragged him into the light. He had other poems he hadn't finished yet; he said them, and the crowd roared. The next week we gave him his own gig, and he killed again. Two weeks later, folk came in raincloud masses."

"And I missed all this."

"That's what you get working so hard, as if that'd save you from what soured twixt you and Claude." He wound his broken fingers together, then unwound them as if scattering water drops on the table.

"Thanks for the editorial," she said. "I saw Margot a few weeks back. He was good. I wouldn't say genius."

"I'm talking then, and you're talking now. He's had a bad run the last couple months. A curse broke. The voice took him up, and he wrote in its grip for two seasons, and it set him down as fast. Hurts, but hell, six months is more than most folks get out of love. I've known men who chased the line for decades after one night's grasp of what Edmond Margot held for half a year. He doesn't need your pity."

Six months. Kai frowned. "This started, what, eight months back?"

"I can count. And I can feel the seasons change." He opened his mouth wide, baring yellowed teeth. The point of his left incisor was missing, snapped off, casualty of some God Wars fight. "Eight months it was."

"Where does he live?"

"Why do you care?" He drank his coffee again in one long gulp, wiped his mouth with the back of his wrist, and sighed, heavy and wet and sated.

"I want to talk to Mister Margot," she said, "about faith."

28

The poet's street looked no nicer by morning. Same stupid row houses, same slumping newsstand on the corner, same pox of printed tulips on every window's curtains.

Izza sat against the wall south of the newsstand, hands cupped in her lap. Once in a while she glanced up and down the road with the unfixed, vaguely hopeful expression she wore when begging. Traffic was light, but she got a sliver or two of soul before Cat bought a paper and sat down beside her, cross-legged, paging to the funnies.

"We don't have these where I'm from," Cat said. "Surprises a lot of folks when they visit Alt Coulumb. You'd think, big city, big papers, but it ain't necessarily so." Her accent slipped into a drawl at the last, as if she were quoting something.

"You're spoiling my act."

"You're not here for the act, kid." Cat turned the page. "I like this one."

Izza looked. "It's not funny."

"No, it is. It's funny because their dog, see, it's really big, so it eats more than the rest of the family."

"That's not funny."

Cat chuckled. "Guess not." She set down the comics and picked up another section. "Looks like Zolin's out the next couple of games for giving Kasadoc a concussion. Unnecessary violence, which what that means in a game of ullamal I do not know. Also the Oxulhat police seem to have found three kilos' worth of dream-dust in her luggage. Doesn't look good for the Sea Lords. Gods, I love sports. All the excitement of real news, only it doesn't matter so you don't have to worry about it."

"What are you doing here?"

"Getting a grip on current events. What are you doing here?"

"Begging."

"On this sleepy street? Houses that way, apartments that way, residential for three blocks on both sides. And this part of town isn't exactly high-rent. Most of the folks who live here leave for work before sunrise. Not a choice spot."

"I remember a month ago," Izza said, but Cat interrupted her.

"When I was flat on my back unconscious. Good times."

"When you couldn't find your way around this island to save your life."

"I can learn, you know. Give a girl some credit."

"You're not here for the paper."

"Well," she said. "You're not here to beg."

"You warned me to stay away from Margot last night."

"And you stormed out and didn't come back to the warehouse afterward. I had to venture out to scrounge up my own supper." She laughed. "I figured I struck a chord. Which meant you were as likely to be here as anywhere else."

"I spoke to him," Izza said. "He recognized me. He asked about the Blue Lady. I told him the truth."

Cat nodded, that nod people gave when they had something to say but didn't want to say it yet. "And?"

"He wanted more, just like the kids. And I still want to get out of here." She shot a hopeful glance at a passerby, a bearded man wearing boxer shorts, a bathrobe, sandals, and dark glasses. The man dug into his robe pocket, withdrew a folded slip of paper, and dropped it into her cupped hands. Izza said, "Thank you," waited until he moved on, and looked at what he'd left: an expired library card.

The man waved to Izza from the corner, grinning. She flipped him off in return.

"What did you do when he asked?"

Izza tore the library card into thin strips. "I left him."

"You're here," Cat said, "because you don't know if you made the right choice."

Izza waited for the man to leave before she replied. "That's part of it."

"What's the rest?"

"I told you Margot's name, yesterday, while we talked. I never gave you his address."

Cat folded the sports section and laid it on top of the funnies. "Plenty of possible explanations for that."

"You recognized his name. You know where he lives. What's going on here that I don't know?"

"Begging's the wrong line of work for you. Should have been a cop. Or a spy."

"I never had a chance to choose."

Cat leaned back against the wall. Her skull met brick with a heavy sound. She closed her eyes, laced her fingers together, and squeezed. "Look. I came here because the local priests don't let other powers near Kavekana'ai. If you're on the run from gods and Deathless Kings, this is a great place to hide. That suited me fine: I could lie low, get clean, and leave. Thing is, my old . . . well. My people back onshore have a, let's call it a professional interest in this island. There's not much crime here by mainlander standards because of the Penitents, but the lack of gods and extradition treaties makes Kavekana a spa for all the better kinds of criminal. Those guys who live out on West Claw, puttering around in sandals and flower print shirts, drinking rum punch and playing bad golf—you ever wonder how they got the soulstuff to support that lifestyle?"

"What does that have to do with Margot?"

"He attracted our attention, back onshore. A bard like him, a nobody, a third-rate scrivener, moves to this island of all places and suddenly produces top-flight work. Inspired stuff. That's a surprise, and surprises are suspicious. I recognized his name when you said it."

"And remembered his address."

"I'm good at my job."

"It doesn't make sense," Izza said. "He writes a few poems, and gets the gods' attention?"

"Like I said. It's hard for mainlanders to learn what happens here. The local priests are thorough, not to mention the Penitents, for proof of which see my ribs and shoulder. So we used to flag anything unusual that happened here, stuff that wouldn't attract attention anywhere else. Even money was on him being an Iskari spy."

"He's a poet."

"Means nothing. Deathless Kings built a whole literary magazine in Chartegnon back during the God Wars as an intel front."

"No," Izza said. "I mean, you haven't seen his room. I have. He's a poet. And a hungry one."

"If you say so." Cat stood, and Izza had to squint against the brightness of the sky behind her. This would be a hot day. "Yesterday you said I was afraid. You're right. I'm hiding. I don't want the kind of attention this guy attracts, and you don't, either. If I were you, I'd draw the line here. I would have drawn it earlier."

"I owe him," Izza said. "I tried to pay it off yesterday, but I only made things worse."

"I know the feeling. Just think about what your debts might cost you." Her face twisted as if she'd just swallowed something foul. "I hate the way I sound. This cloak-and-dagger crap. One more reason to get out of the gods' game while you can, kid."

"I'll think about it."

"Being so close to this guy makes my skin crawl. Shouldn't have come here. Wouldn't have, but for you."

"Thanks," Izza said.

Cat glanced up and down the empty street. "I'll see you back at home. Think about what I said, please. And watch out."

"Okay."

"You can keep the newspaper." Cat looked as if she were about to say something more, then shook her head, hooked her thumbs through her belt loops, and walked away, shoulders slumped. She glanced back before she turned the corner. Izza thought she saw a flash of teeth between the woman's lips—the hint of a smile, maybe, at the fact Izza was still watching. Or else a trick of distance and light.

She was too far away to say for certain.

The sun rose, and the day began to burn.

29

The address Mako gave led Kai to a quiet, poor part of the island: rows of tree-divided houses, stucco with highlights in pastel. A Glebland beggar girl crouched at the street corner; she watched Kai with shocking black eyes, and held out an empty hand. Kai dropped a coin into the girl's palm, invested with a trace of soul, and walked on feeling lighter.

That lightness faded as she climbed the stairs to Margot's apartment. Blank windows watched her from across the street. The sky hung close and blue above, as if only palm fronds supported it, and those might any moment give way and let the heavens crash. When she reached the second floor, the railing's dust had stained her fingers black.

Knocking on the purple door yielded no answer. She tried again, louder. Still nothing. Wiped a patch of the door clean of storm scum and pressed her ear to the wood: heavy, slow breathing inside. Margot, asleep.

She should leave. Go to work, and try to corner him later at the Rest, if not tonight then tomorrow or the day after. But the Rest was a public place, and she couldn't ask him the questions she wanted in public. Might not even be able to ask them in the privacy of his room. Besides, she was fed up with waiting. She struck the door, leaving dirty handprints on the bright purple paint. "M. Margot? Are you in there?"

A groan, a grunt, a cry, a scream. Thrashing amid sheets. The sound of flesh and bone striking a wall. Cursing in Iskari. Kai's Iskari was rusty, but she thought most of the things he was saying weren't physically possible, at least for unmodified humans. "M. Margot?"

"Go away."

"Mako sent me." A little lie, but Mako would forgive her. "My name is Kai Pohala. We met a few weeks back, at the Rest."

The door shuddered, and opened a few inches, jerked short by the chain. Margot stared through the gap, one green eye bloodshot, swollen lips pursed. He had the crushed-flower look of a man hung over. "I remember you," he said. "Go away."

"I want to talk about your poems."

"You accused me of stealing."

"I think you're in danger."

He slammed the door. She blinked from the wind of its closing.

"Margot." She pounded on the door again. "I won't leave."

He moaned from the other side. "Enjoy the balcony. Gets hot in the sun. Be careful about the flies. Their bites itch."

"You treat all your fans this way?"

"You're not a fan. You look like a Craftswoman." Scorn on that last word. Typical poet. Typical Iskari.

"*Howl, bound world,*" she said. "Margot, I know where you got those words."

"Go away."

"You're in danger," she said. "You're caught in something bigger than you know."

"Leave me alone."

"I know why you've stopped dreaming."

The door jerked open again, and again the eye appeared.

"I just want to talk."

"About poems."

"About poems," she said, and nodded.

He closed the door, softer. The chain rattled, and this time the door swung all the way open. "Come inside."

Margot's small room was bedchamber, study, and kitchenette combined. His desk, bed, sea chest, and chair occupied most of the floor space, and clutter consumed the rest. Stacked books and newspapers supported mugs of tepid tea. Clothes wadded and piled on the cheap carpet. His few possessions were spread in a thin film over every surface save the desk, which was bare but for leather mat, inkpot, and pen stand in which two pens stood straight. "Apologies for the mess," Margot said. The man himself looked even sloppier than his room. A red-burned scalp showed through failing mousy hair. He wore a billowing white shirt and green velvet slacks, poorly mended and shiny with age. Toes jutted through the straps of his leather sandals; the hem of his open bathrobe swept against his calves. He swayed, he paced, he turned, never quite looking at her. "I rarely host visitors."

"More than usual, recently?"

"No." Too fast for an honest answer, but she didn't want to press him on this, when she had to press him on so much else.

"M. Margot," Kai said. "You were wrong, before, when you called me a Craftswoman. I am a priest."

"Of what god?"

"Of no gods," she said. "I'm a priest of Kavekana'ai."

"I know your Order," Margot said, "by reputation. Purveyors of false faith and strained promises."

"We're not so bad once you get to know us," she said. "I think you're in trouble. I think I can help you. But I need to hear your story first."

Margot turned and fixed her with a bright, hungry stare. Again, she remembered her mother's advice about drowning men. He began to pace again, hands stuffed in the pockets of his ratty robe. He didn't try to kick her out, though. A good sign.

"You're blocked," she said. "You haven't written new poems in months."

He nodded.

"Why?"

"What do you want me to say?"

"The truth."

He chuckled, meanly. "Never ask a poet to tell you the truth. We have ten different ways to describe a drink of water, and each is true and all lie." With his toe he nudged a crumpled shirt on the dirty carpet. "This room says all you need to know."

"You can think of ten ways to describe a glass of water. I can think of ten paths a man could take to this room. Which one's yours?"

He lifted the shirt and tossed it in a hamper. The circle of revealed white carpet glared up at them like a glaucomic eye. "My path's the one walked by a man who lived a good life in southern Iskar, a minor functionary in the troubadour's guild, who wrote poems in his free hours and shuffled paper the rest of the day. Wine with friends on Sixthday and snatches of verse in university magazines, that was me. Couplets written in the odd hours between sleep and waking. I had a wife, until she ran off with a marine from Telomere. I took leave of my office and came to Kavekana, to live in solitude and write. I meant to go home a few weeks later. I would have gone home."

"But you found something."

"Words took fire in my brain."

"More than words."

He nodded. "My Lady. My queen. My muse."

Kai felt as if a trickle of cold water had been poured down the inside of her spine. "Tell me."

"In the first few weeks after I came here, I felt something scrape at the glass of my mind. Panic, I thought. You know that I was." He swallowed. "Attacked. Mako may have told you."

"Yes."

"That night, when they beat me, the panic broke through the glass. Something crawled out of the hole it made. Blades tore from my lips. I do not mean that as metaphor. Glass and steel spines, a creature of solid light. That night, when I slept, I dreamed of green fire. A . . . a green man with a skull's face and claws like a bear, only not. We embraced. It is strange to say. And the words came."

"Not so strange." A man. Interesting. "You said this muse was a lady."

"The man was first. The Lady, later."

"And after the attack, your work took off."

"Yes." He nodded. "The work had never seized me that way before. A whole-body trembling, a terror. I lived that scream. And then one night it stopped."

"Stopped," she echoed. "About eight weeks ago."

"Yes." He stopped, facing the off-white wall. "How did you know?"

She slipped the folded vellum out of the notebook, and held it between them, though he was not looking. "Three months back, on the twenty-ninth, an idol died up the mountain. I tried to save her, but I failed. When she died, I heard a line from your poem. *Howl, bound world.* Just that. Our idols don't speak; they have no minds. Those words have haunted me ever since. That's why I came up to you that night. That's why I asked you for your sources."

"Could have come from anywhere. That poem's popular. They ran it in the *Journal.*"

"That's what I thought, at first. I convinced myself I imagined the whole thing. But we keep track of our idols. Every gift they grant, every bit of grace they bestow, is written in our library. I found this list of gifts issued by the dead idol. Your name appears again and again. But you're no pilgrim of ours."

He turned from the wall to face her. "I don't understand."

Somehow she found the strength not to look away. "What do you know about idols, M. Margot?"

He swallowed. "They are . . . repositories. Holes where one hides soulstuff from gods and kings."

"I think when you were attacked, you needed help so bad you somehow broke through into the pool, into the space where our idols live. I don't know how, yet, but you took soulstuff from them. You prayed, and your Lady answered those prayers. Your poems caught fire, and some of them bled back along the bond into your Lady, and lingered inside her. Until one day she died. Now you have a reputation you can't sustain without more poems. Meanwhile, our vaults have been pilfered, our pilgrims robbed. On paper, it looks like you were stealing from the Grimwalds, a family of, let's call them legitimate businessmen. People who are very jealous of their property."

"I didn't steal anything. I wrote."

"Great writers steal," she said. "Didn't someone say that once?"

"What happened was a consummation."

"Maybe. Look. I bet the priests up the mountain have been hunting everywhere for Edmond Margot—but they're looking for a thief, not a poet. You're lucky my friends aren't literary types."

He didn't seem to get the joke. Kai continued. "It gets worse. The Grimwalds have a Craftswoman working for them, and she's already suspicious. She's combing through our records, and when she learns the truth, she'll come after us both—the Order in public, and you, too, if your luck holds."

"And if it doesn't?"

"She'll come for you in private. I doubt her clients would use anything flashy. Knives are cheap. Efficient. Hard to trace."

"I didn't mean to take anything."

"Intent doesn't matter, it's the fact of the taking. What you did should be impossible. If others can follow in your footsteps— the pool holds tens of millions of souls. If you knew what you had tapped into, you could be the richest man in the world today. Hells, I doubt the Grimwalds will even kill you. Their smartest play is to take you apart and learn how you wormed past our defenses."

"Let me see that." He reached for the vellum, but she pulled it away.

"No."

"You expect me to believe you on the strength of evidence you refuse to show me?"

"I'm not supposed to have these papers. If you see what's here, you could end up in even more trouble."

"If you're not supposed to have them—"

"That's not important. If you come with me, I can protect you." She'd think of something, anyway.

"Protect me," he repeated. "You don't want to return my muses. You want to stop me from finding them again. Your people will keep me in a cell. Deny me pen and ink until you can plug up the wellspring of my art."

"You'll be safe."

He shook his head. "You offer me a cage, and say this cage will protect me from wolves I have never seen."

"You don't see these wolves. That's my point. You're walking down the street and all of a sudden you die. These people can destroy you."

"Manuscripts don't burn," he said.

"Maybe not. But poets do."

He looked at her as if she stood a great distance away, rather than a few feet. A ridiculous man, nothing about him noble or grand. Fool who traveled a foolish distance for foolish reasons, hungry for a foolish death. She wanted to help him climb from the hole he'd dug himself. She wished she didn't feel as if she were the one in the hole, and he the one outside. "Will you force me to accept your help?"

"You mean am I going to wrestle you to the ground and drag you up the mountain if you say no?"

"Yes."

She closed her eyes, and breathed, and reviewed the extent of her injuries, of her weakness. "No. I'll get someone to do that for me."

"Someone who will understand where you found the slip of paper you aren't supposed to have?"

She crossed her arms.

It took a long time for him to speak his next words. "I will not go with you."

"You don't believe me."

"I believe you," he said. "As much as I've ever believed anything."

"This is for your own good."

"I came to Kavekana for my own good," he said. "I thought I knew what I needed, and I had to go to the edge of death to learn that I knew nothing. If you're right, if my need is the gateway into your idols' world, perhaps I'll meet my Lady again when your gremlins come to kill me."

"Your Lady's dead, Margot. She never lived, not the way you think. You invented a muse, and made believe it loved you."

He pulled his hands from his pockets, and set them on his hips. Gallantry, Kai thought, always looked ridiculous. "Her love was not a lie. She spoke to me. And I will wait for her. Call your people, if you can. Imprison me. But I will not walk into your cage of my own will. Now." He pointed to the door. "Please, leave."

She slammed the door behind herself so hard the trees by the balcony shook. Her chest hurt.

She waited, hoping he'd open the door and apologize, say he'd seen reason and would follow where she led. When he didn't, she retreated down the steps and into the city. She was already late for work.

30

Izza watched the woman enter Margot's house, and waited. Island time flowed like cold honey. She walked the coin through her fingers and felt the soulstuff there. No surprise the woman had convinced Margot to let her in. He was all arm, and easy to twist.

Izza didn't trust her. Looked local, but walked foreign: back too straight, chin high, shoulders square like she had something to prove. Some of that might be from her injury—she used a cane. But the rest spelled priest, and trouble.

I don't want the kind of attention this guy attracts, Cat had said. And you don't, either.

But if Margot was in trouble, so was Izza.

She bit the coin and inhaled its soulstuff. Most folk didn't bother to taste souls, just sucked them down quick, hungry for that rush of life. Linger on a thaum or two, though, and you could feel the other spirit bitter on your tongue. Regret, here. Anger. Fear. More fear than she expected. Fear was trouble.

Izza crossed the road and climbed the stairs. When she reached Margot's floor, she crouched low, crawled to the rear balcony, and waited beneath the open window. The curtains were closed, but she didn't want to risk a flicker of shadow or skin betraying her.

Kneeling, she listened. The priest kept her voice down, but Izza heard the important words. "Theft." "Idols." "Muse. The priest thought Margot had stolen from her, thought he was in danger. Promised him protection, which sounded like jail to Izza. And when he refused to go with her, she threatened him, and left.

That last happened so fast Izza had no time to hide, or even to slip off the balcony down to the yard. The priest stood a few feet away, out of sight around the corner, close and quiet. Izza could hear the softest shift of shoe on stone. She withdrew deep into herself. Breathed so slowly a flower petal set under her nose would not have fluttered.

The priest swore. Izza wondered what her soul would taste like now.

Heels descended the stairs, sharp taps like the wood blocks in a Shining Empire orchestra. This woman didn't seem the type to let go when frustrated, or back off when afraid. She'd return. Or she would send the watch, the Penitents, who asked questions and got answers and didn't so much care how much pain they inflicted between the two.

If the Penitents snapped him up, then they would come for her next. And then they'd find Cat.

Which meant Izza had business with a priest today.

31

Kai left the poet's house walking fast, but her leg soon revolted, forcing her to slow and lean heavier on her cane. The stroll should have been pleasant: a brisk cool trade wind blew off the morning's heat and the harbor's soft stink, leaving only salt and sun and space. But her talk with Margot festered in her mind.

Idiot. Fool. Romantic. She didn't know whether she meant her, or him.

Margot couldn't be left free. If he'd done what she thought—and all the evidence, including his own story, pointed in that direction—he was a threat: Not the man himself, but the possibility he represented. He had broken the island's security somehow. What he did unconsciously, others could learn to replicate. If clients knew the pool was no longer safe, they would desert the Order in droves, and without the Order, the island would wither. Kavekana had no military, few resources. Without pilgrims and Deathless Kings, Kai's home was a coconut lying in the sand, waiting for someone to break it open.

She could, should, tell Jace everything she knew, but after their argument last night, she doubted he would listen to anything short of an airtight story. He thought Kai was paranoid, desperate to the point of hallucination; that might cause him to miss a real danger. And Kai still had too many questions, about Mara, about Ms. Kevarian, about Seven Alpha herself.

Thinking about the problem all at once would get her nowhere. Break it down.

Start with simple, easy knowns: Margot was a thief. He should be in custody, for his own protection and the island's. Take care of that first. Next, find Mara, confront her, learn the rest of the story. Then go to Jace.

She needed muscle. Fortunately, she knew where to get it.

Her schedule this afternoon was all but empty. She'd claim a doctor's appointment, and take care of Margot fast. Every minute spent was a minute wasted.

She reached the Order's building, brushed through glass doors into the lobby, and tried and failed to catch the lift. She pressed the up button, crossed her arms, and waited, frowning at her reflection.

"Kai?"

A touch on her shoulder. She tried to turn, but her leg betrayed her and she tripped. A strong hand caught her arm before she fell.

"I'm sorry," Teo Batan said. "I called your name, and you didn't hear me." The Quechal woman looked rested, happy, and innocent. She braced Kai's weight and helped her right herself. "I thought we got off on the wrong foot yesterday." Was that only yesterday? "Are you okay?"

Kai checked her skirt, her blouse, her hair, all in place. "I'm fine. Ms. Batan."

"Teo."

"Teo. I didn't expect to see you again."

"Surprise." And again she deployed that wide, easy saleswoman's smile, the smile of a person who'd practiced being personable. "I thought about what you said, and I'd like to keep talking. I don't blame you for bristling at me. I'm curious. I pry into things that don't bear prying. Stubborn. That's what my girlfriend says."

"Ah," Kai said, and to cover surprise, "I'm sorry. I wasn't offended."

"Great." She was growing to hate that grin. "What's the next step?"

Faint chimes rang as the elevator descended. "I think my next step is to recommend you to another priest."

"Why not you?"

Because I have more on my mind today than some mainlander pilgrim who wants to save her boss's soul. "I don't think I'm the best guide for your pilgrimage. For this to work, we must be partners. I need to know your inner needs. I spoiled our first meeting for reasons that have nothing to do with you. I hope you'll accept my apology." Four bells. Lifts arrived too fast, except when you wanted them to. "But don't worry. I'll find someone more compatible."

"You fought back when I pushed you. Stood up for yourself. That makes us compatible in my book."

Finally the doors rolled open, and Kai escaped into the lift. She spread her arms to stop Teo from following. "I have enough battles to fight already. I'm sorry. I will find someone to help you. Someone else."

The doors shut on Teo's answer. Kai leaned against them, and found them cold.

32

Kai trained all morning: chanted the acronym litanies once more, recited the steps to a relationship sale, joined yet another role-playing exercise. ("What are you looking for from a god?" The putative pilgrim hems and haws and finally says: "I'm worried about my children's future. We live in unstable times. I want to know they'll be taken care of when I'm gone." "I hear that you're interested in security and grace. Is that right?" "I suppose." "I think we can help. I'll describe some myths for you. Listen, and at the end you can tell me which ones most resonated with your situation. Which spoke to you. How does that sound?") She emerged less settled than before.

Eleven was late enough to clock out for lunch, so she left a note on her cubicle desk, donned her coat, took her cane, and descended to the street. She squinted against the sun, and began to sweat. Back before the Wars, Kavekana had been an island of loose light clothing, bright patterns, and bare skin, even for priests and high officials. Not for the first time, Kai wished it had remained so. Wool suits weren't designed for tropical heat.

She walked north two blocks to Epiphyte, then west, circling the bay. Across the water East Claw sprawled, its hills a warren of warehouses, flophouses, and docks.

West Claw's streets, by contrast, ran straight and broad between boxy pastel houses. Pale Iskari and Camlaanders strolled along the sidewalks here, tourists and expats wearing straw hats, loose shirts, and shorts that bared skinny sunburned legs. Hotels rose near the shore, fewer facing the bay than on West Claw's sunset side, but hotels nonetheless, with white verandas and stretches of private beach and rooftop decks and pools warmed by Craft and sun.

Kai hadn't come this way since her injury, and she was shocked as always by how fast the commercial landscape shifted. Locals owned half the stores here, but the rest belonged to mainlander émigrés, who came to Kavekana as pilgrims only to find they liked island life better than the rule of gods and Deathless Kings. They opened shops to pass the time on an island that ignored time's passage, and these flourished and died quickly as jungle flowers, devoured by the earth.

On this corner, a wizened man from northeast Telomere used to run a map store—though Kai could only charitably call it a store, since she'd never seen a customer inside. The maps he stocked were ancient, of Kathic lands before the Quechal wars split them in two, pre–God Wars charts of island empires long since sunk or broken, yellowed cracking parchments pressed between thin glass sheets, worlds lost to time and touch. She'd planned to take one of his maps home someday, hang it in her living room, close the curtains, and sip wine and ponder a vanished world. Now the shop itself was gone, replaced by a store that sold tart frozen yogurt with berries and crumbled sweet crackers on top. Kai bought a yogurt, turned right, and climbed the ridge.

Buildings thinned a few blocks north of Epiphyte, and soon gave way to a slope of mown green grass. The families that once lived here departed decades past and left their homes to rot. Only the grass grew now, tended by the same Concern that trimmed the golf courses on Kavekana's leeward northern shore. Old houses' decaying remains rose amid the green: mossy wooden hillocks with stone foundations, skeletons of discarded lives.

No one had forced these people to move, nor did the law stop locals or mainlanders from building on the slope. The Penitents' screams were more effective than any rule.

At the base of the ridge Kai couldn't quite distinguish the screams from the wind. Climbing, she heard them better, moans and cracks and high faint whistles like the complaints of a forest in a storm. Soon they were too loud, too clear, to be anything but human voices in dissonant chorus, and in pain.

About that time, she saw the Penitents.

They stood at the crest of the ridge, half facing east, the other

half west. Sunlight glinted off jewel eyes and sank into the rock
of their faces, chests, arms, three-fingered hands. They scowled,
gray sexless sentinels waiting for gods who never would return.
The newly Penitent guarded the ridge for weeks as stone voices
worked on their ears and stone wheels ground their bones, preparing them for duty. The first Penitents had been hewn from
living rock here. The story ran that Makawe shaped them to
guard for his return. The truth was more complex: Makawe
carved a handful first, and after the wars the Order hired Craftsmen to copy and refine those models, make them bigger, stronger, faster.

Penitents jutted from the ridge like jagged teeth from a green
jaw.

Kai climbed. She was not the only one who walked this road—
watchmen and watchwomen and Penitents passed alongside her—
but still she felt alone.

Claude had described Penitence like this: The statue directed
your mind. You saw what it believed you should see. You did what
it believed you should do, until your will and the statue's merged.
Then, at last, it let you go.

She shuddered, and pressed on.

Watch houses squatted below the ridgeline: low structures
with angled roofs, thick walls, and tall black-tinted windows. Kai's
path led to the largest building, which was dug back into the hill.
Posted signs warned of dire fates for trespassers. A carved slab
above the door read: West Claw Station House.

Watchmen did not tend to be creative with their names.
Penitence broke creativity out of them.

Kai entered a dark lobby lined with dark plaques and dark
furniture, and told the duty officer she wanted to see Claude. The
officer looked up at her, blank, and Kai searched the woman's haggard face for a sneer. She saw none, but that didn't mean much. A
sergeant dispatched into the station house returned a few clock-
ticked minutes later. "Follow me, ma'am."

He ushered her down one long windowless hall, and, turning
right, down another. Black wood doors punctuated the hall at reg-

ular intervals; none bore name or number or any markings she could see.

The sergeant stopped at a door like all the rest, stood aside, and waved her in. She stared into the matte, into her own shadow, and knocked.

Claude opened the door. He did not seem surprised to see her—though, of course, the sergeant would have warned him. Kai hadn't given her name, but his coworkers knew her face. That had been a good thing, once. He closed the door once she stepped inside.

"New office," she said.

"Yes. You remember I was promoted." He walked back to his desk.

"It suits you." Odd thing to say about an office, but the room did fit him, neither too large, as her living room seemed, nor too small, as his last office was, straining at his shoulders like an ill-tailored suit. The far wall was made of glass, and outside, on the ridge, Penitents watched the sea for their absent gods' return.

Like Jace, Claude kept his office simple. Low three-shelved bookcase against one wall, empty save for five thick binders. Coat stand bearing two watchman's jackets and two gray hats of identical make, one old and water stained, the other its crisp replacement. His desk, one corner occupied by a wire "in" box with a small stack of paper, and a wire "out" box with a larger stack. On the desk lay a plate of barbecue beef, cold, and a hardcover book, open. Claude retreated to the desk, and closed the book.

"Velasquez?"

He laughed. "No."

"One of your God Wars adventure novels, though."

"Cawleigh. Velasquez has dragons, pyrotechnics. This is kingship, politics, murder. Awful lot of murder. Especially at parties for some reason." He held up the book so she could see the cover: brown leather embossed with a basket-hilted rapier, point down, flashed in silver. "But there's a point to it, I think. Not a moral, but a reason to keep reading. You'd like it."

"I always liked your books."

"I mean, I wouldn't recommend these editions, too expensive, but in Camlaan and Alt Selene they print flimsies, paperbound, fall apart after a read or two, but cheap." He blinked. "Wait. You hate these books. I gave you Velasquez's *Burning City*, and you panned the dialogue, the descriptions, the politics, the characters. You loathed it cover to cover."

"I didn't like Velasquez," she said. "Doesn't sound like I'll like this Cawleigh guy, either, but if you think he's good, I'll try him."

"Her, actually."

"Excuse me?"

"He's a she. Terry Cawleigh." He held the leather volume with both hands, and squeezed, as if testing a fruit for ripeness. He smiled, briefly, and returned the book to the shelf. Its leather spine seemed out of place beside the binders with their steel rings and uneven pages. "Why say you like my books when you don't?"

She leaned against the room's other seat, a sturdy old armchair of stuffed leather. She thought she remembered it from Claude's father's house, years ago. "Did you move this up from your dad's place?"

"After he moved into the home."

After the breakup. "How'd that go?"

"As well as you can expect. He's sad to be gone, happy to be surrounded by a bunch of folks old enough to know how to play cards. And his son visits sometimes. So there's that."

"I don't like the books," she admitted.

"That's what I thought."

"I liked that you like them."

He turned his back on the bookshelf, but didn't look at her. Didn't look at anything.

"I used to come home late," Kai said, "and see lights flicker in my living room, and I'd know you were there, reading by candle. I'd walk to the door, and if you forgot to pull the curtains I could see you through the window, on the couch. Once I found you on the carpet with your feet resting on the cushions, holding the book open over your face." His shoulders twitched, but he made no sound. "You smile as you read, you know that? Lost in those books. Velasquez, LeClerc, Probst, Evander. Lost, and happy. I tried to read Velasquez because I wanted to see what made you smile like that. I watched you, happy, as I stood on the porch, in the dark. I knew once I walked in the door that smile would break, and I'd be the reason."

"You weren't," he said, of course.

"Oh, I know," she lied.

"I was messed up," he said. "I'm still messed up. And hells, you remember what I was like before the Penitents. There are nine kinds of evil inside my head. None of that's your fault."

"Still. It was nice to see that you could be happy, once in a while. After we split, when I came home late, I'd imagine you on the couch. As if the light was still on. It was on somewhere, I guess, just not near me."

"It wasn't."

"Wasn't?"

"The light. Wasn't on. I couldn't read for a long time after we broke up. Whenever I opened a book the words swam."

One corner of her mouth quirked up, then down. "I sort of wish you hadn't told me that."

"I wish a lot of things."

"I'm sorry about last night," she said. More words rose to her tongue unbidden, and she closed her mouth to keep them in.

"You didn't come here to apologize."

"No."

"This is a business call." That sentence should have been a question, but his voice didn't rise at the end. He sat back behind the desk, frowned at his half-eaten lunch, and slid it aside.

"Yes." She'd rehearsed many versions of this conversation, but the strange start had skewed her. "I need to report something. Anonymously."

"Coming to me is hardly anonymous."

"No. But it's my best alternative."

"Why not go to another officer?"

"Come on, Claude. We dated for years. Bitter separation. Do you think there's a watchman on the force who doesn't know my name by now? I could feel their contempt from the bottom of the ridge. I doubt any of them like me, or trust me, which means I can't trust them. Which leaves you."

"Or a Penitent."

"I'm in a delicate situation, and the Penitents are a blunt instrument. I'd rather talk to someone with a mind of his own."

"Penitents have minds."

"They possess minds. It's not the same thing."

He balled his hands into a mound of bone, skin, and muscle. "The more you talk, the less this sounds like an anonymous tip, and the more like you coming to your ex-boyfriend for a favor."

She nodded.

"I can only do so much for you. I only want to do so much for you."

"I need someone I can trust. That's all."

"Tell me what's happened, and I'll say whether I can help."

"Can you keep this private?"

"The door's closed," he said. "Those windows are double layered with empty space in the middle. The walls here are thick. No one will hear us."

"And you won't tell anyone what I've told you here?"

"If you ask me to do anything official, I have to tell someone."

"But you won't say the information came from me."

He clenched his jaw, and relaxed. "Not unless I have to."

"I need more of a promise than that."

"I can't give it."

She exhaled. "Okay."

"Are you sure you want to say whatever this is? Once you tell me something, you can't untell it. I'm not in the job of ignoring crimes. They break that into us, too."

She remembered Edmond Margot's desperate eyes. "I'm sure."

"What's happened?"

"A theft," she said.

He blinked. "I thought you said this wasn't Penitent material."

"It's not a normal theft."

"I'm sure," he said. "What's been stolen?"

"Souls. From an idol."

Outside, the Penitents' shadows shrank as the sun reached noon. "Interesting."

"No one has ever drawn power from our idols without permission. It should be impossible. The pool is one of the most heavily warded places on the planet. The caldera of Kavekana'ai doesn't even exist in this world anymore: fly over it and you'll see only solid lava."

"But someone's stolen from you."

"A poet. An Iskari named Edmond Margot."

"How?"

"I don't know how. Margot himself didn't know he was a thief until this morning."

"He stole accidentally? What does that even mean?"

"He went looking for inspiration, and in a moment of terror or genius or both he found an idol. He thought she was a muse, and he used her power to write poems. Took a crime and turned it into art."

"And you want me to arrest him for this."

"He's in danger. The pilgrims he stole from are the kind of people who wander into your village and look around and say, This is an awfully nice entire population you have here, it'd be a shame if something were to, you know, happen to it. If they learn what Margot's done, they'll kill him. Or worse, study him to find how he broke into the pool. We need him alive, and in custody, so we can stop anyone else from following suit."

"This sounds like priestly business."

"It is."

"Then why are you here, not up the mountain?"

She sighed. Always to the point with Claude. "Because Jace kicked me out. I'm going to tell him, but I need more answers first, and answers take time. Meanwhile, we can't leave this guy walking around."

"Are you sure Jace doesn't know already?"

"If the priests knew, Margot wouldn't be free. If the people he stole from knew, he'd be dead, or worse."

"And how did you learn this?"

"I found some papers I wasn't supposed to find. I recognized Margot's name, and here we are."

"Okay." He spread his hands on the desk. "What's the hurry?"

"The idol he stole from died awhile back. Its pilgrims hired a Craftswoman to resurrect it, and this woman knows her business. If she doesn't know about Margot already, she will soon. She was close on the trail last night."

"Let me see your evidence."

"I can't. My having these papers is a breach of about five ethical guidelines."

"As bad as letting this guy get killed? Or his theft going public?"

"A second mistake won't fix the first."

"Kai," he said, and repeated, "Kai," as if saying her name twice might make her bend. "You understand, you're asking me to grab someone off the street—"

"Out of his home, probably. He doesn't leave much."

"You want me to invade someone's home, lock him up, for the good of an Order that wants nothing to do with you. All because of evidence you can't show me, which you're not even supposed to have."

"I haven't done anything wrong," she said, and thought, Technically.

"I can't hold people for no reason. If my superiors asked why is this man in jail, and I said theft, and they said what of, and I said soulstuff from the priests, and they asked your bosses about it and they deny anything is missing, and then they ask who gave you this information, and I say that I promised my source anonymity, what do you think would happen?"

"Nothing good," she said.

"Nothing good. They'd let him go, and it might be my head that I grabbed him. Or another few months in a Penitent, and"—he laughed, bitterly—"I can't really afford to clear my schedule at this point. Aside from the excruciating pain, which is also a factor."

She sat watching him, watching her.

"I'm sorry," he said after a while.

She opened her purse, and opened the red book, and passed the vellum sheets to him. "Read these. I'll wait."

He accepted them, scanned. "Who are these other names? Some of them show up as much as your guy: Arthur Nicodemo Cuthbert. Jalai'iz. Whatever kind of name that is."

"It's Talberg. And Margot's the only one I recognize. The others probably work for the pilgrims."

"That's a weak argument, Kai. They all could be in danger."

"Maybe. But I know Margot is. And his theft was a miracle; there can't be others like him out there. If it was that easy to break into the pool we'd know by now."

"You won't let me keep the list? Or copy it?"

"The more you know, the more screwed we are if word gets out. A Craftswoman can flense the truth from your mind."

Claude folded the parchment again, and passed it back to her. He was not smiling now. She wanted to squirm, wanted to stand, and knew Penitent-trained officers, and Claude, well enough to stay still. Movement made you look weak, to them.

"This is important," she said. "Margot is a danger to the Order. Without the Order, the island folds. We'll be one more tourist destination. And once that happens, wouldn't Iskar love to snap us up? Nice excuse to expand their Archipelagic presence." Unfair, she knew. The Penitents' first rule: defend Kavekana. They broke that into their prisoners. But she needed Claude's help, even if she had to call on his training to convince him. "Will you help us?"

"I will," he said at last.

She didn't let her expression change. "Good."

"I'll arrest this man. No idea how long I can hold him once he calls for a Craftsman, or his embassy. But it's a start."

"A start is all I need. Keep him safe while I go to Jace."

The desk separated them, and space, and time. They lay between themselves, turning on a sodden bed.

"I need to finish my lunch," he said.

She stood. "You'll take care of this today?"

"As soon as I can. Whatever gods are watching, I hope they help us both."

"Let's keep gods out of it."

She closed the door behind her, and retraced her steps through the silent halls. At the front desk she signed the logbook and left, out into the green and the sun and the screams.

33

Izza followed the priest to an office building by the bay. The woman didn't notice. People who wore suits didn't tend to notice Izza. To them, all street kids looked more or less alike.

So she paced the woman down alleys, across rooftops, over fire escapes, and along the sidewalk, then waited outside her office, singing snatches of opera for passersby. Busking attracted attention, but this was a posh area, buildings all metal and glass, full of merchants and Craftsmen and clients of the Order, and she'd be hustled along in a hurry for loitering. After two hours her voice tired, her stomach growled, and she stole an orange from a fruit stand across the street.

She was hiding behind a trash bin eating when the priest walked past the alley mouth. Izza abandoned the orange rind and trailed her through the drifting noonday crowd, under striped awnings, down into West Claw—familiar territory. Kavekana's richer immigrants were generous if you caught them in the right mood. Hard to stay for long, though. Shopkeeps watched their storefronts here, and chased even buskers off. No singers on these streets, and their parks never heard a lick of opera.

When the priest turned onto Stockton, Izza followed, grim, up Penitent Ridge. She climbed a decaying, abandoned house and lay on the broken tile roof, sun warmed as a lizard, while her quarry entered the watch station. Time passed. The sun peaked, descended.

Perhaps the Watch had taken the woman prisoner. Stuck her in a Penitent.

No such luck. The priest emerged after the better part of an hour, limping and leaning on her cane, and descended the ridge without a backward glance. Izza saw her face, briefly, when she passed below. Tired, drained, determined. She'd done what she came to do.

The priest returned to her office, and Izza stopped in the alley opposite to think. This was bad. If the Watch came for Margot, it would hunt her next.

She might be too late already. Watchmen moved fast. But she didn't want to lose track of her quarry. If the priest hurt Margot, Izza would have to find her, and stop her.

She needed help.

34

Kai returned a half hour late from her lunch break, and smiling. Officemates noticed the change, and smiled back; she stopped for the first time in weeks to chat about the weather, about Sherry's granddaughters and the outcome of the ullamal championships in Dresediel Lex now that Zolin was benched. Whatever that meant.

Claude would have Margot in custody by nightfall. Now, she had to figure out how to loop the Order in. How to approach Jace. Which meant deciding what to do about Mara.

After she ran out of small talk, Kai poured herself a cup of rancid coffee from the office kitchen, and retreated to her cubicle. The coffee tasted about as good as the harbor smelled on a hot still day. She'd have stood at the window to watch the ocean while she thought, but some infuriatingly personable officemate might have tried to trap her in conversation. Kai's burst of post-lunch cheer (not that she'd actually eaten lunch, her stomach growled to remind her) had used up her patience and charity. She needed to think.

Kai walked to one of the cupboard-sized shared offices reserved for the writing of reports and the working of complex math. She closed the door, removed her shoes, sat cross-legged on the desk, shut her eyes, and descended into memory.

Seven Alpha took form around her: lightning skeleton, suggestion of volume in nothingness. Her mind retained Mara's archives as a waking dream. Easy. Memory was important in the Order's business of secrets and sacrifices. As an apprentice she'd memorized lists of random numbers, built palaces and cities in her mind, invented whole pantheons, and subjected them to private ragnaroks. Her recollection of Seven Alpha was not perfect, but close enough to serve.

Sliding through time, she searched her dream for the transfers to Margot. One should have been dispensed from the throat chakra, and another here, from the third eye, at six o'clock on a Thirdday morning. Nothing.

This much she expected. Someone, probably Mara, had wiped away all trace of Margot's theft. The papers Kai had found were the last remaining evidence. She would have called them forgeries but for the perfect watermark, the glyphs, the texture of the ink, the slick fused sheen of records often read by Craft. And, of course, for Margot.

Assume Mara cut the evidence from the original files, leaving a few slips of vellum. Why? To hide the transfers from Ms. Kevarian. But Kevarian found her out anyway—or got the scent. Discrepancies, the Craftswoman had said in last night's nightmare. A kind version of: you're lying.

So Mara woke to find Kai in her crèche, and seized the chance to blame her friend for the whole thing.

Possible. Kai couldn't believe that was Mara's plan all along. She might have given Kai the papers in desperation. Or as a plea for help.

Too many questions. Too many secrets.

Let's assume for the sake of argument (Kai thought) that these records scare Mara as much as they scare me. Mara isn't evil. If I find her, I can convince her to go to Jace, get this fixed before Kevarian finds out. I've done the heavy lifting, tracked down Margot, put him in custody. There's no need for me to be part of the story, even. Mara can present the problem and the solution to Jace at once. Get another promotion.

Which rankled, but this was bigger than Kai's ambition, bigger than her need to be a hero.

Settled.

Kai opened her eyes. She was not alone.

Twilling stood by the open office door, white robe and prayer beads bowed out by the swell of his stomach. Kai had met her boss a handful of times since she came to the front office: a former prodigy of the pool, long since descended to pilgrim relations, where he became manager of this distasteful cube farm and master of its training binders and role-playing exercises and arcane acronyms. "Thinking?" His pitch rose all through the word, rather than just at the end. "Or napping?"

"Thinking," she said. "I wanted to review this morning's exercises."

"Kai, I thought I'd drop by to tell you how much we appreciate your work." Twilling sounded genuine and superficial at once, as if he had read books about empathizing with employees and almost understood them. "Working with pilgrims is different, I know, than working in the pool. But it's so rewarding. But once you're up to speed, your expertise will help you identify pain points, and build solutions, better than any candidate we've had in years."

She repressed an urge to wince at the jargon. "I've learned a lot in the past few weeks. I'm growing every day." Use their language. It's easy if you just imagine you're speaking Iskari. "Can I ask you a question, Twilling?"

He beamed. "Of course."

"You remade yourself, like I did." Not polite, but not a secret, either. "Why did you come down here afterward?"

"Why settle for working with clients when I could have had such a bright career up the mountain, you mean?" He laughed, and let the laugh die, and when he spoke next his voice had lost the forced edge of managerial cheer. "Priests stand between worlds. When I was young I thought that meant building idols, praying to them; after a while, I realized that no matter how I prayed, the idols didn't answer. I was worshipping my own reflection. Not healthy. In this role I stand between Kavekana and the mainland— and the mainland talks back. Every day I wrestle with gods, like the desert prophets of ancient Sind."

"But everything happens up the mountain."

"Everything," Twilling said, "and nothing. The gods' power used to flow down from Kavekana'ai, out over the waves. Now, power flows in the opposite direction. Speaking of which." He spun the chair out from the desk and sat in a flaring of robes. "I hoped to talk to you about the Quechal pilgrim, Ms. Batan. How have you found working with her?"

Kai stood and adjusted her clothes to cover the delay while she framed her response. "I think she needs a more experienced guide. We're not compatible."

"Is that her fault, or yours?" He said it with a smile so she couldn't snap back. "She's ripe, Kai, ripe. I spoke with her during the intake process. She needs what we offer. You've rejected her twice now, and still she returns. The woman has a true need."

"You've been talking with her behind my back."

"We watch all new pilgrims, to ensure the quality of our service."

Damn. "She doesn't like me."

"You don't like her. I understand. This process would not be a trial of your faith and skill otherwise. And it is meant as a trial."

She needed out of this conversation, not to mention this department.

"If you want to progress among us," Twilling said, gentler, "you will need to work with pilgrims. Understand them. Develop them. Consider their needs, and how they may be guided. I know you're reluctant, but she is a fine young woman. An ideal first project."

"She complained to you," Kai said.

"Not at all. She asked if I could assign her another guide. I said you were an excellent fit, and that I'd encourage you to speak with her again. She has nothing but praise for you."

This was a distraction. She had so much else to worry about. Dying idols. Secret notebooks. Mara. Claude. "Okay."

"Good, good, good. Thank you. Thank you." Twilling bobbed his head twice more. If he heard her skepticism, he didn't mention it. "Jace dropped by to ask me how you were doing, you know."

"What did you tell him?"

"I told him you were wonderful. Performing far above expectation."

"Thanks."

"I'll leave it to you to arrange your next meeting with Ms. Batan. Go with the gods." He smiled, and swept out of the room. His words hung on the air after he left, faint but sharp.

"Go with the gods," she said.

35

Izza found Nick curled up under a cleaning cart near a park two blocks away. Groundskeepers had piled the cart with fallen palm fronds, then retired to a nearby cafe for drinks. Nick slept in the shade between the wheels, hands behind his head, dirty shirt pulled up to reveal his thin stomach. Save for the scar his face was smooth and soft, the way mainlanders painted kings asleep or saints dead. She climbed under the truck and punched him in the ribs.

He darted up, and she winced when his forehead struck the underside of the wagon. Nick awake resembled no king or saint Izza'd ever heard of. He cursed.

"Language."

Confusion vanished when he heard her voice. "Izza." He lay back on the cobblestones, and the top of his head grazed the cart's undercarriage.

"That all you have to say?"

"I knew you made it out of the Plaza. I heard, from Ivy."

"Ivy has a big mouth," Izza said. "You're welcome, by the way."

"Thanks," he said. "It was you who almost got me caught in the first place."

"You would have been caught sooner or later. I saved you."

"They fired me in the end anyway. Sleeping on the job." He shrugged. "I thought you were leaving. For good, you said."

"I have to take care of a few things first."

"What kind of things?" That question had an intensity she didn't like.

"The Blue Lady," she said.

"She's dead."

"Maybe."

"What does that mean?"

"I'm not sure," she said. "I need your help. I need you to follow a priest for me."

"Why?"

"I want to know where she sleeps." She pressed her hands against the cart, hard, until her arms shook and her fingertips and knuckles turned white. "And what kind of wards she has. What protections."

"Some favor," he said. "I didn't mean why do you want her followed. I meant why should I help."

She rolled onto her side, and looked at him.

"Because no matter how you try to talk it off, you know I saved your ass back in the Plaza. Because they almost stuck me in a Penitent that night, and now the guy who rescued me is in trouble. Because we're the Lady's children, and there's nobody to help us but us."

"Fair enough," he said.

They rolled out from under the wagon and dusted themselves off on the street. Angry drunken shouts from the cafe heralded the groundskeepers' return, and they fled uphill into the Palm, lost their pursuers in an open-air market mess of food trucks and jewelry stalls.

Together they climbed a shopping center across from the priest's office. Izza searched the mirror-pool windows opposite for the woman's face, while Nick stuck his head over the building's edge and spit down into the clogged river of afternoon traffic. Whenever someone looked up, he ducked back onto the roof, chortling. She thumped him on the skull, and he stopped, for a while.

Izza spotted the priest before Nick grew bored enough to move on to a newer and dumber game. A lucky glimpse: the woman leaning against a windowsill and watching the clouds as if they held a secret. "That's her."

"The one with the lips?"

"I guess she has lips. That one there."

"I see her."

"I want you to follow her."

"Okay."

"Don't steal her wallet or anything. Don't get cute, or close enough she'll see."

"I've done this before."

"Just follow her home. I'll meet you in the Grieve at nine."

"Sometimes these folks don't go home. They drink, or stay in the office all night."

"Keep after her, then—if I miss you at nine we'll meet again at dawn. If that doesn't work, leave a note in the warehouse."

"Your friend'll chase me out."

"Cat? Tell her you're looking for me."

"Why not follow this woman yourself?"

"Have other things to do."

"Will this be dangerous?"

"Is thieving dangerous?"

"Not unless you're caught."

"Right."

He watched the priest, silent, for a while. "I wish the Blue Lady was here, is all."

"I know."

"I miss her."

"Me too," Izza said.

"Okay." Closed eyes, a breath, a whispered prayer. "Okay. What'd this woman do to you, anyway?"

"Nothing," Izza said. "Yet. And I hope it stays that way."

She left him lying there, chin resting on folded fingers. Thin puckered lines showed pale against sun-browned skin through the ripped cloth of his shirt. She'd never asked about those scars.

Izza climbed down the dizzying height, from fire escape to drainpipe to garbage bin, to crouch in the alley and watch the sanctioned world walk past. Somber suits, linen dresses, suitcases, and bags: soulstuff condensed into physical form, life made concrete. She thought of the crabs she hunted in the surf, seaborne insects who built heavy shells around themselves. You could grab them by those shells, lift and throw, and watch the splash.

She slipped back east to the poet's house. The afternoon streets in East Claw belonged to working men and women. Construction workers, shirtless, climbed bamboo frames, tool harnesses slung over broad shoulders. Teamsters drove wagons piled with grain sacks and bales of cloth and packaged goods across town to West Claw shops. Wood strained and leather creaked. A drover wiped her forehead on her sleeve, then swatted an errant cow with a goad. A road crew hauled up broken cobblestones, cemented new ones into place. Laundries flew a war's worth of surrender flags from clotheslines. Shining Empire sailors toasted one another with sorghum liquor at a sidewalk table outside an Imperial restaurant. An old Kavekana drunk crouched alone on a corner, and watched her with milky eyes. She walked faster.

Margot's street was deserted. She knocked on his door, but no one answered. She walked around the balcony and peered in the window. Room a mess, bed made, poet absent. Off for an afternoon stroll. If the watch had seized him already, they would have left signs. The door wouldn't be locked, for one thing, or on its hinges. Watchmen didn't like obstacles, and Penitents were a universal key.

She'd trailed the poet often in the three weeks since her rescue, and knew his daily routine and where he went on walks. After an hour's hunt she found him southbound on Dockside—easy to spot, clad as usual in green velvet. Cargo cranes far off by the Claw's tip flashed mirror codes of reflected sunlight as they swung containers ashore. Margot paused to watch two wagoners argue over a wreck, then walked on. Knees and elbows showed through his threadbare suit.

She scrambled across traffic to the dock and approached him from the south. He'd tipped his hat down to shield his eyes from the sun, and so didn't see her until she drew even with him, saluted, and said, in mock-posh accent, "Good day."

He muttered "Good afternoon," then stopped. His hands slipped out of his pockets, and he swiveled around to Izza; she'd already taken a few skipping steps back, to keep out of arm's reach.

"You came back," he said.

"To warn you."

"I've had one warning already today."

"I heard."

"You're watching me."

"Yes," she said. "I don't know what to make of you. But I think we're on the same side. Or, similar sides."

"Ms. Pohala said the same on her visit this morning. Do you also want me to forswear my work? Return defeated to my homeland?" He pointed vaguely out into the ocean, even though his homeland was more north and east than south.

"I think you should keep from getting stuffed in a Penitent, if you can."

"She went to the Watch."

"Yes."

"She calls me a thief, and says the Blue Lady is a lie born of fear and wishful thinking."

She ignored the second part. "Theft is a Penitent offense," she said. "You need to hide."

He turned, and walked away.

"Hey!" She ran to catch up with him. "This is real. When the Watch comes for you, they'll slam you in a statue until you break."

"If they prove my guilt, which is unlikely. At best, they'll hold me until my government protests. Greater men than I have written from a cell. Gertwulf composed his *Virtuous Voyage* while a debt-zombie, scribbling in the few minutes each morning before his contract took hold. Once the Iskari priesthood secures my release, I will leave the island. Meanwhile, I wait."

"You think your priests will help you?"

"Troubadours have been convicted of worse than theft, without grand consequence. The Prelates of Iskar fight a long war. Indulgences are permitted for their soldiers."

"You're no soldier."

"All poets are soldiers. We fight our wars across centuries."

She didn't understand, but didn't ask. She felt other eyes on them, passing cabbies and dockworkers intrigued by the odd pair arguing on the street. No watchmen, yet. She grabbed Margot's hand and pulled him along the docks. Walking, at least they presented a moving target. "You think," she said, with a smile to a dirty man selling flowers from a basket, "that they'll take you in a legal way, and hold you so people will know. That they won't just stuff you in a Penitent and forget."

"They wouldn't."

"They do. It happens all the time."

"Ms. Pohala has no right—"

"She doesn't need right if she has powerful friends," she said. "Come on, smile a little. There's people watching."

He tried. Even without looking, she could feel the falseness of his grin, like rubber dragged over skin. "I will not leave. I must seek my Lady."

"She's dead," Izza said.

"There is no death where love lives."

"You don't know death well," she said, "if you think that."

"I will not leave."

"Then hide." She heard Cat again in the back of her mind. Small choices. But she owed this man. "Let me help."

"Can you hide me from Penitents?"

"Maybe. Better than you can hide yourself. Long enough for you to book passage off the island."

He adjusted the angle of his hat. "You seem awfully concerned with my welfare for a girl who ran from me when I asked a simple question."

"It wasn't a simple question," she said.

Out near the tip of East Claw, a tugboat dragged a container-ship into dock: an expanse of metal, sail-less seagoing abomination of Craft. Its sides were cliffs, more an extension of the peninsula than a ship, a mountain inverted and afloat. "I suppose not," Margot said. "But I refuse to run. I found something true here, and terrible. Gods spoke through me. Iskar with her daily prayers and unrequited loves, her flag-jousts between sky knights, her high cardinals professing faith and her human beings wandering alone—she has no claim to match that. This is my place now."

"You're dumber than I thought," she said.

His laughter, too, was sharp. "I never claimed brilliance." He removed his hat. His bald patch was pale, though peeling and red with sunburn. "This is not your fight. If they take me, let them take me. If they kill me, let them." He stopped, and swallowed. "Kill me."

"No."

"I offer you a gift," he said. "I offer you your own life, which I think you value. Your freedom, from the Penitents and from the law you would otherwise feel compelled to confront to keep me safe. I ask you to promise by all you hold sacred—and I think I know what you do hold sacred—promise to let me go. Do you understand?"

She nodded.

"Aloud, if you please."

"I promise."

"And let me ask a gift of you, in return."

She understood, now, but it was too late to take back her word.

"Tell me. The Blue Lady. The Green Man. I have seen them. They worked through me. They played my nerves like a violin. You know them."

Those were her names. This was her faith. He was a usurper to speak them. "I do."

"Ms. Pohala calls me a thief. She claims I stole power from the mute idols her priests build. She claims I used this power to charge my words with fire. But I have not stolen. I heard gods sing to me, and scream, and whisper. I am not mad."

"What do you want from me?"

"The gods. Are they real? Do they live? Do they speak? Do they feel? Do they love?"

She remembered a soft touch on a feverish cheek. She put her hand there, but the skin was cool, and smooth. "Once I fell from a dockside crane. The Blue Lady caught me." She lifted her shirt, and showed him the rippled scar on her side, the imprint of four fingers and a thumb. "There." She lowered her shirt again. From his expression, and his caught breath, she knew he had seen. "She wasn't used to people yet. She caught me, and it burned."

"Thank you," he said. "Thank you," as if she hadn't heard the first time. "Go."

She ran inland, away from the sea, away from the false metal cliffs and the neon lights and the man in the green and threadbare suit.

When she knew he couldn't see her anymore, she retraced her steps and trailed him through the streets toward home.

36

Kai worked hard, or seemed to, for the rest of the day. She turned many pages of binders, moved her eyes over a hundred intake forms, and all the while planned her confrontation with Mara. Evasions. Pursuit. Mara's collapse, and the slow determination Kai would help her build to tell Jace the truth, or some of it at least.

Unless Mara really meant to frame Kai for everything. In which case their conversation might take a very different path.

Near sunset she clocked out and headed uphill toward Mara's house, a few blocks from her own. Kai and Mara rarely met outside work, but Mara'd helped out when the pipes in Kai's basement burst, and Kai'd leant Mara a hand moving in. She remembered the way, and soon stood on the sidewalk before Mara's pale purple two-story. Porch ghostlights clicked on as night deepened, timer-driven. The lights cast dancing shadows on the lawn.

No signs of life. Kai checked her watch. A little after seven. Mara wouldn't be home for an hour yet, at best. She removed a pad from her purse, scrawled a brief note—"Mara, need to see you, urgent, family business, Kai"—ambiguous enough she hoped its meaning would be safe. She opened Mara's mailbox to slip the note in, but the box was crammed with newsprint, letters, and ads. She folded her message double, sealed it with a drop of wax, and was searching for a cranny into which the paper might fit when her mind caught up with her eyes.

The mailbox held two days' mail at least. Mara must have forgot to pick up her mail—or else she never came home after her meeting with the Craftswoman. With Ms. Kevarian. The meeting Kai thought had finished too fast.

The empty house watched Kai from behind the fence.

Hells, Mara's wards probably wouldn't let her pass. She touched the fence latch, felt no electric tingle, heard no warning bell. Maybe the wards only went off if you opened the gate.

She pressed down on the latch, and stepped into Mara's yard.

No lightning. No thunder. Not even a dog's bark. Silence and wind. She walked up the yard. Front door locked. Stepping-stones circled around to the back, and she followed them. One stone shifted beneath her feet.

Orange trees grew in the backyard. Kai'd always been jealous of Mara's trees; her own house's last owners had no interest in horticulture, save for the psychotropic variety. She picked a low-hanging orange, thought about peeling it, decided not to, and continued to the rear porch. Through glass sliding doors Kai saw the kitchen, marble countertops and cabinets of pale imported wood. A percolator on the stove. Clean counters, dishes racked. She tried the door, out of curiosity.

It opened.

A chill ran up her spine and down her arms. Mara wouldn't leave her door unlocked. Then again, anyone might leave her door unlocked. People ran out of the house, forgetful, stuffing a boxed lunch into a shoulder bag, spilling coffee on their hands.

Mara didn't forget things, she rarely ran, and she was never late.

Kai stepped into the empty kitchen.

She didn't see anything wrong or out of place. One dish in the sink. Crumbs. Dried purple smear of jam on a dull knife. Three tiny black flies stuck in the jam.

Kai didn't care for Claude's God Wars historicals, all bluff and thunder and improbable heroics, but she did attend the occasional mystery play, and she'd read a detective novel Gavin lent her once. The murder she liked, but the clues bothered her. A detective in a kitchen could tell how long the occupant was gone from the relative staleness of bread crumbs. Kai couldn't. But Mara kept a neat house, and hired maids to keep it neater. Burned her garbage, even, ever since a bad breakup in which her ex had stalked her through her trash. Dirty dishes in the sink could be another sign she hadn't come home the night before. Or that she came home so late she lacked the energy to wash her breakfast dishes before bed.

Through the kitchen door Kai saw, on the couchside table, a small spiral-bound calendar, the kind with a new cartoon for each month. Days X-ed off. She'd come this far already. Might as well check the calendar, then get out. Stuff the letter in the mailbox and leave.

She slipped off her shoes, set them on the tile floor, and padded across the carpet into the living room. Here too she saw no signs of life. The strange order of a maid-cleaned house, that was all. Pillows propped in plush chairs. Wood surfaces dusted, polished. Thick carpet.

A closed house. A dead house.

She approached the couch, the end table, the calendar.

She heard a crack upstairs. Wood contracting, or expanding. Wind through an open window. But she hadn't seen any open windows. "Mara?" As the echoes died she cursed herself for a fool. If someone else, something else, was here, now they knew her voice.

She picked up the calendar. Two neat lines crossed each day save for the last—yesterday's X was half-complete, one diagonal slash. Mara marked the first half of the day in the morning, the second half returning, a weird habit, morbid, something she'd picked up from her mother. So she hadn't come home last night. After meeting Ms. Kevarian. After framing Kai.

A carriage passed down the street outside. Wheels growled over gravel, and the horse's tack jangled and rang.

Kai set the calendar down, and turned to leave.

The harness chimes receded, but the growl stayed. And the growl was nearer than the carriage wheels.

Kai looked up.

Two red eyes glimmered on the second floor. A great gold shape hunched on the banister, bared yellow teeth, and leapt.

Kai stumbled back, ran for the kitchen. The creature landed behind her, heavy and precise, four sharp taps on the carpet. Claws ripped over shag.

She skidded onto kitchen tile, grabbing for her shoes. The

creature leapt. Kai swung her cane in a desperate arc, and struck something that yowled in pain. She scrambled for the door, half-running, half-falling. She'd left it open, thank whatever gods watched out for dumb burglars—she ran onto the empty porch, and spun to see red eyes and bared teeth and muscle under gold fur gathering again to leap. The growl rose to a cry like an angry child's. She flailed for the door handle, found it, slammed the glass shut so hard she feared at first she might have broken the pane. But the glass did not break. The door closed, the child's cry cut off, and the eyes' red glow died.

The yard around Kai was carved gray, highlighted purple and orange by sunset through the trees. She did not move. She watched her own reflection in the glass, surrounded by porch furniture. The world throbbed. No. That was her.

A statue crouched on the kitchen floor: a cat the size of a foal, broad shouldered and detail perfect, fur distended by rippling muscles, dagger teeth bared. Stone claws pressed against the ceramic tile.

"Shit," she said, and swore again, because she felt better swearing. "Ebenezer." My security, Mara had joked. The perfect pet. There when I'm home, stone when I'm out. More loyal than most people I know, of any species.

Which solved the mystery of the open back door. If Kai had a pet lion, she might stop triple-checking her locks before she left, too.

Or not. Even Ebenezer could only do so much.

She'd dropped her cane, and bent to retrieve it. The cane's head hung at a sharp angle from the shaft: it must have broken when she hit the cat. Inside, she saw a glint of metal.

Strange.

She twisted the cane further, and through the widening crack saw its core was webbed with silver wire. She couldn't read the patterns, but she recognized Craftwork when she saw it.

Something hid inside her walking stick. A monitor, maybe. Simple medical Craft to keep her safe, help her heal.

Or not.

Night wind blew cold around her.

Mara might have stayed at work. Taken an unannounced vacation. Sickness. Death in the family.

She went up the mountain yesterday. She did not come down.

Kai took her orange from the table. The cat statue's eyes seemed to follow her as she followed the stone path back to the front yard. She looked back, into the hole between its teeth.

Two blocks from Mara's house, Kai took a last glance into her cane's broken heart, and tossed it into a compost bin.

37

Edmond Margot returned to his flat and cleaned. There was not much to clean: he owned little, most of that spread out on his floor due not to laziness but to an inveterate affection for chaos. This, at least, was what he told guests he wanted to impress. Few in number, these. More lately, but Margot doubted he had many latelies left before he became late altogether. As in, the late Edmond Margot.

So, his possessions: Seven socks without mates, holes in three. Two shirts, first ink stained on right wrist and left breast and ripped in the back, second paint smeared across the left shoulder, missing three buttons and left cuff. One pair trousers, mangled. One intact sandal, and its mate with strap broken. Three of the insufferable, and insufferably cheap, bright patterned short-sleeved shirts the local beach bums loved, which Margot wore around the house when awake during the day (seldom) and writing (often). Two notebooks, pages torn out, empty. A box of stationery, likewise empty, consumed in correspondence during one of the dark periods early in his Kavekana stay when he wrote only weepy ten-page letters home to friends laboring through university adjunctship and drowning their sorrows in overpriced absinthe bars. One book of stamps, half consumed. Stubs of three pencils. Empty ink bottle. Before he'd come to Kavekana he hadn't even known those could empty; he drained one in a week, after his beating, when the words first came. Broken pen nibs, five. Broken quills, two. He had experimented with quills out of a hope they'd feel more authentic than writing with a fountain pen, but after two weeks of hives he deduced he was allergic to down.

He gathered all this into a large sack, and after consideration returned to his bookshelves to add more. If the woman Kai was right, then soon history might weasel into his garret. Newspapermen would archive this scene for posterity. The room was his colophon, his epilogue. Best edit now, for he would have no chance after he went to press. He hoped to offer friendly biographers no embarrassments, and unfriendly biographers no ammunition. He added his Velasquez and Keer hardcovers to the stack, that postmortem reviewers not sneer his verses were sentimentalized by a taste for swashbuckling romance. A few Alt Selene flimsies too joined the pile. A deck of well-shuffled cards, that he not be seen as frivolous. Of course the slender folio of Shining Empire prints he had bought in a back-alley shop in Chartegnon, a simple brown leather edition without label or insignia—the covers gave no hint at their contents, which was hint itself he supposed. The folio's curvilinear beauties deserved better than a trash heap, but perhaps some passing patron would rescue them before they reached such extremity.

Editing complete, he hefted the sack downstairs, almost spilling its contents first over the balcony, then onto the street. A crepe seller on the corner stopped mixing batter and stared at Margot, who nodded gruffly in reply and waddled past under the weight of his cast-off life. Three blocks should be distance enough, on the sidewalk beside a few trash cans, the sack's drawstring loose to display the riches inside. He stopped at the crepe wagon on the way back, and ordered one with mango and powdered sugar, and a coffee.

"You moving out," said the man as he spiraled batter onto the griddle, "or cleaning?"

"Both," Margot said, and laughed as if he'd said something funny. The man laughed, too. Mostly Margot took meals in his room, but the sun felt less furious today. He stood by the cart and ate the crepe, which the man cut into rolls for him. Mango juice glistened on his knife.

"I don't remember seeing you here before," Margot said after eating half the crepe.

"We move around," the man replied, and stroked the cart with his full hand, like Margot had seen men pat their horses. "Don't like to stay in one place long."

"People don't get to know you if you move, though."

"Maybe it takes longer for them to know you. But if you want to be famous, you have to leave home. Who wants to stand on the same block forever?"

"Some people might," Margot said.

"Sixty years ago my family lived in an orange grove. Forty years ago we were one house in a field of houses, with few orange trees between. Twenty years ago we were one of many houses in a row in a rich neighborhood. Ten years ago, mainlanders bought up all the houses, all but my family's, because my father didn't sell. So now we have a hotel to the left of us, and a surf shop to the right, and two bars on the street, and three mansions, and no orange trees. My father sits on the porch and rocks, as he's done all my life."

Margot ate the last piece of crepe, and finished the coffee. "Is that so."

"Even if you live sixty years on one block, the block moves around you."

"It does at that," he said, and paid the man. "Will you be here tomorrow?"

"I'm always here," the man replied, and patted the cart again. "Where you are, is the question."

He climbed the stairs back to his room. Coffee burbled in his stomach, and grated his nerves. He felt drained, and wired. He needed more lunch, or dinner, he supposed, with a glance at his watch. Then again, he might as well work. If the Watch came, they would feed him in prison. If assassins, he would not need food.

He unlocked his door and entered an empty room. Bedclothes heaped in disarray. A few books on the shelf: poets, mostly, last-century Iskari and a few from the lost generation of Camlaan, broken remnants of the God Wars. Several dictionaries. A suitable library. A suitable room. Its contents bespoke poverty and dedication, a man striving against the limits of his own mind and life. His last work of art.

No. Not his last.

He caressed the surface of his desk. Stroked the pen in its stand. Opened a drawer, removed a fresh notebook, spread notebook on table, savoring the soft crack of glue and string and leather. Wind blew through the window. His fingertips drank the cream of the fresh page.

He reached for his pen, but did not draw it from the stand. He pushed back his chair and stood. The notebook drifted closed.

He paced his room as the sun declined. Three more times he sat. Three more times he stood. He wrote a doggerel verse on scrap paper. No help. He wadded the paper in his pocket, sat again, and bent to work. Palm fronds rustled. He looked up, sought the bruised sky for oncoming doom, and saw none.

He'd always thought waiting for death or prison would terrify him. He was not afraid. No control of his future, and no expectation of one, either.

He drew his pen and sat down to work. Outside, the sun set and the stars rose.

38

Kai always made herself hot cocoa before a nightmare. The routine soothed her: heat milk on the stove, stop just before it boils, mix milk and cocoa powder to form the paste, pour the remaining milk, and whisk. Dust cinnamon on top. She needed calm. She needed to stand in her kitchen and forget for a moment, forget Claude and Margot, forget Jace and even Mara. Remember home. Remember soothing candlelight. Remember warm blankets, and towels, and good sex, and pancakes, and the clear sky after a storm.

This was the doublethink of the nightmare telegraph: if you were scared, you couldn't sleep unless you tired yourself to the brink of exhaustion, and then you might sleep too soundly for dreams, or not soundly enough. Kai couldn't afford delays. She had to speak with Mara, now.

Kai avoided nightmare communication unless strictly necessary. Too much waited beneath the surface of her mind. The Order used professional dreamers for the most part: asleep gagged and blindfolded in warm caves under Kavekana'ai, scribbling messages on automatically turning scrolls. Suggest short-selling Mithraist Gamma Fund. Will require high liquidity next quarter. Concerned about long-term stability of emerging markets in Northern Gleb. So on, and so forth. When Jace took over he banned the gags, called them inhumane. That first week, a page who hadn't got the earmuffs memo walked in on a dreamer mid-session. The screams ruptured his eardrums. The gags returned.

So Kai made herself hot chocolate and thought about everything and anything else. Mara's visit on the balcony, in the blue dress, after it all went wrong. Teenage nights sneaking out to poetry slams, glorying in end, internal, initial rhymes. Emerging from the pool after she remade herself, whole at last in her own body. Her first years with Claude, before the joy bled out.

She carried her cocoa upstairs. Cup rattled in saucer. Bedclothes lay tangled halfway between bed and floor, from where she'd clawed herself awake that morning. She made the bed, smoothed the comforter, piled pillows at the headboard, and changed into her bathrobe. Smoothing the bedspread, she could almost forget what happened here last night, and what it meant.

Nothing, that's what. You saw him today, and you were fine and he was fine. Use alcoholics' wisdom: take life day by day.

Another sip of cocoa, and as she swallowed she let herself feel tired. She'd been tired for years, and only felt it now, as if exhaustion had hidden in the hollows of her bones until offered a chance to unfurl. A light turned on in her chest. She lay back. She wished she had a stuffed animal. She used to sleep with a stuffed dolphin. She threw him out before Claude moved in.

She removed her robe, and lay back, and kept lying back, the bed not beneath her but spinning away as she fell, faster. Walls of tan comforter towered above, miles and miles, the pit's mouth shrinking to a point, vanished to leave her in a tense smooth cotton shell. A cold hand held her. Fingers locked tight, rigor mortis, tension of the dead. Cotton covered her mouth, but as she struggled she realized she was not falling but standing, and while the sky above was the color of a sunset cloud, beneath her feet lay good dank earth, jungle smelling, corpse nourished. Ghosts whistled past her ears as she walked, beneath her arms, between her fingers. She ignored them, because one could not hear ghosts in waking life, and if so why listen to them in dreams?

She caught the tail of that thought, which sped past her in kite form trailing a ribbon, so fast the tail's edge cut her fingers. She was dreaming. Dreams of isolation and insignificance.

Not deep enough. A personal layer of dream, this. A path formed beneath her feet, expected, welcomed. Paths guided sleepers through dreams, and through meant out, which Kai didn't want.

She stepped off the dream-path, and fell again through tan space into the gap between threads, following the beat of a distant heart no longer hers. She fell through vast chambers of creation.

No. To fall was to give herself to the nothing. She pointed her hands at the deep, and dove.

She opened her eyes, and sat up with a start, or tried to. Her arms moved a few inches then stopped, wrists bound. A gray ceiling spread above. A mask across her face forced air into her mouth, into her nose; she was made to breathe in. The pressure reversed, and air swept out of her lungs. She turned her head, but could not shake the mask loose. She pressed against the bars that lined her bed, her cage, but they were cold and strong. Overhead, a lamp swung slowly. When next the machines forced air into her lungs she screamed.

A door squealed open. Footsteps on a cement floor. The nurse whistled to herself as she approached, a lullaby. Sleep now, darling, sleep now, my boy. Let the wind sweep, and let the trees sway, and you'll still be here, come the next dawning day. The whistle grew louder as the nurse neared. Immense, a round-hipped silhouette against the sweeping light. A spark: the needle, raised. Kai pulled against the leather cuffs, and knowing that she dreamed she knew she pulled against bonds she'd tied around herself. The needle descended, but she tore free, and ripped the mask from her face, and scrambled over the bars and ran down the long alley between beds, thousands all alike, holding all shapes of creatures and all sizes, birds the size of galaxies, their wings bound with leather straps, lizards with IVs dripping into their arms, women, men, angels, demons, tubes drawing rainbow-colored blood out to a vast net beneath the floor that beat like a heart. She ran, and the nurse followed. Search the faces. Mara's here, somewhere. All fears touch, deep enough in dream, and so in a good nightmare you can find any other dreamer—even those who think themselves awake.

Find Mara, raven haired, in her blue dress. Mara, sleeping, to be woken with a kiss. Gods. Sweat soaked Kai's hospital gown. The nurse's footsteps were bass drum beats, drawing closer. Kai dared not look behind. She knew what she would see: a mountainous woman blocking out the sun, needle in hand, its point at once hair-fine and larger than Kai's whole body, a point that would obliterate her if driven home.

Kai ran past the sleeping dead, through the caverns of her mind. Bound. Bleeding. She ran faster than the beat her heart made. No music, just bare feet on concrete, and footsteps following, and millions of forced breaths.

Don't look back. Bend the dream to your will. Mara is here. Find her and leave. You are here because you chose to be here. (But she could not believe that whisper. To believe was to admit her control, break the nightmare, return to the branching gardens of her own mind. The nightmare telegraph's other double-logic: you must accept that all nightmares are real.)

Mara was not here. An infinity of beds, endless beings endlessly dying but never dead, their suffering cultivated, and Mara lay in none of them. Impossible. She had to be here, awake or asleep. But Kai tired, slowed, and the nurse's footsteps grew louder, even and inhuman as a metronome's tick.

And as Kai ran, and drew her frightened breaths, another impossibility scraped the corners of her thought: how had she escaped the bed? She was bound. Tied so tight her hands could not slip free. She could not have broken the straps. She had not broken them. She had not escaped, and the nurse did not need to hurry, because she was already caught. This cavern was a single, massive bed, and Kai ran in it and the nurse loomed above mountainous, eyes shining, and oh god Kai ran and ran but there were straps around her wrists and ankles and she kicked against them and could not move and the bars were high as the stars and she ran she was running don't let that tense shift she was fleeing escaping escaped not about to die but the nurse stood above her with the poison medicine I have just the thing for you dear the needle descended and she could not find Mara but she needed out but there were straps around her arms but she ran into the wall and clawing found a doorknob and the needle pressed into her skin and she was so small but she leaned into the door with all her weight and all she ever had been and ever would be and burst through into black.

She lay sweat-slick upon silk. She gulped cool air, swallowed it like water. She touched her face, but her hand felt heavy, as if gloved. The sheet had stuck to her, she saw by the almost-light cascading through the windows. Silk clung to her face as she tried to draw her hand away.

Not a sheet at all, but gossamer strands. Silk stuck her arm to her side and her hand to her face. She sat up, and the silk at her legs adhered to itself and to the silk that already covered her stomach. She recognized the web even as the spider swelled enormous at the foot of the bed, man-high. Mouthparts quivered with anticipation.

Kai met its stare.

The spider drew back and cocked its head. Fangs closed, tentatively, like a person chewing on her lip. Then the spider said, in Ms. Kevarian's voice: "You just can't win, can you?"

39

Izza watched Margot through the palm fronds as night fell. He worked fiercely. Before, as she spied on him, he'd seemed averse to the paper, as if he carved each line he wrote into his skin. Not tonight. Sweat soaked his shirt, despite the cool wind.

From the outside, she thought, writing looked as interesting as dying.

When the clock tower rang quarter 'til nine, Izza sighed relief, and lowered herself from the wall. She didn't like leaving Margot, but that wasn't why she ran down back alleys to the meeting place. She was more than her mind or eyes, and glad to feel it.

The Grieve was a broad open square near the docks, bayside on East Claw, not far from Margot's. Here, in the centuries before the God Wars, an Iskari merchant colony built statues to their gods, and a gallows for their justice. Time had weathered the foreign gods' squiddy faces; the gallows was torn down in the wars, after Makawe and his sisters left to join the grand fight against the Craftsmen. The platform still stood, though, and the young and poor congregated here to drink palm wine and toast the moon and smoke foreign weeds, to trade drugs caged off sailors in the Godsdistrikt, to dance to drums and poorly tuned guitars.

She found Nick in the square's Palmside corner, kneeling at the feet of an ancient hurricane-worn spear god. A fat man twirled fire poi atop the gallows platform, and the flames danced in Nick's eyes.

"Hey," he said when he saw her.

"You find her?"

He nodded. "Weird woman."

"What do you mean?"

"She went to a house first, which I thought was hers so I almost left, but she came out looking scared a few minutes later. Almost saw me, didn't. So when she went to the next house I, you know, snuck up a tree outside, so I could watch and see if she was there to sleep or to whatever."

"Just out of the goodness of your heart."

"And she slept, right? And had bad dreams."

"People have bad dreams all the time."

"Not like this," he said.

"Okay. Fine. Nightmares. Did you get the address? Or were you too busy trying to sneak a glance of the priest in her underwear?"

He told her, and she repeated it back to be sure she'd heard it right.

"Thanks."

He didn't answer.

She left him watching the spinning poi, and ran back through alleys to Margot's house.

40

"What are you doing here?" Kai asked.

The spider reared on its hind legs, spindly limbs and body's bulk silhouetted against the green moon. The form folded and unfolded at once, arms melding as the body slimmed and the head bobbed on an elongating neck. The body assumed a semblance of a thin woman in a black suit, but the head remained a spider's, outsize fangs dripping poison. "I'm looking for a friend of yours," Ms. Kevarian said. She placed her hands beneath the spider head and pushed; at first, Kai thought she meant to tear her head loose, but the spider-seeming came off like a mask, revealing Ms. Kevarian's face beneath. The Craftswoman tucked the spider head under one arm, summoned a mirror from dreams, and checked her hair. Nodding, she dissolved the mirror. "And I noticed you looking for her, too. I thought we might chat, here, unobserved."

"You want to torture me," Kai said. The spider may have vanished, but the silk remained. She was balled in the center of a web, bound to herself by strands that stretched but would not break.

"Torture you." Ms. Kevarian smiled. The effect was not reassuring. "This is your nightmare. I can do nothing here that does not come from your own mind."

"My mind scares me."

"You're a wise woman," she said, and set the spider head down beside her. She sat, though there was no chair in the dream, and leaned forward, elbows on legs, so her face was level with Kai's. "You have no Craft to speak of."

"Not everyone who matters does."

"But most people who use the nightmare telegraph do.

Craftswomen are warded against the nightmare's dangers in ways ordinary people aren't."

Kai pushed against the spider silk again. It did not give. "If you don't want to hurt me, why not set me free?"

"This is your fear," Ms. Kevarian said, and raised a cup of tea that hadn't been in her hand before. "Everything here comes from you. I'm just an echo of a dream." She stood, and approached Kai. Her body passed through the spiderweb strands as if she were a ghost. "Would you like some tea?"

"How can an echo of a dream offer me tea?"

"I can manipulate unimportant aspects of your dreamspace, so long as you don't fight back. The color of the moon, say." She snapped her fingers three times, and the moon changed from green, to silver, to purple, and back to green again. "Or the presence or absence of a cup of tea." She took another sip. "But those bonds are not a detail. They're the substance of this dream. I can't break them. Only you can." She held the mug to Kai's mouth. "Would you like some? I'm not physically here; you don't risk catching my germs."

"No thanks."

"Suit yourself." Ms. Kevarian walked away. "So. You want to find your friend Mara. And you were desperate enough to seek her through nightmares, even though you have no power here. What made you so desperate?"

"You were waiting for me."

"Hardly. I also seek your friend, as I said. Our paths crossed."

"I don't have to tell you anything."

"I have been unable to contact Ms. Ceyla. You are also, apparently, disturbed by her absence. If you have anything to share, I hope you will tell me. Perhaps I can help."

"This is a trap."

"Life is a trap," she said. "As you have learned this evening."

"I didn't do this to myself."

"Who did, then?"

"I can think of a likely candidate."

"I have nothing against you personally. And if you care for your friend enough to seek her in dreams you are unprepared to face, then perhaps you might wish to cooperate with someone else concerned for her well-being."

Kai pushed against the web again. It did not give. "What do you want with Mara?"

"We met yesterday. She cut our conversation short. She planned to speak with me again, but I have not heard from her since."

"I saw you with her last night."

"Ah. Yes. I thought I saw you, vanishing into simulated time. Ms. Ceyla claimed she had information to share with me; she presented the outline of her argument, but left before we could discuss specifics. I thought you scared her off. Hence my surprise to find you scraping dream-paths searching for her."

"I don't have to explain myself to you."

"Not here, perhaps," Ms. Kevarian said. "But in a Court of Craft, you may be so required."

"You won't get me to betray my people."

"I was hired to uncover the truth behind the death of my client's idol, and to take action if called for. I have uncovered a series of artful stories, and you—the piece of the puzzle that does not fit. Plagued by misplaced loyalties to superiors who have sidelined and betrayed you."

"They saved my life."

"They stopped you from saving a life. And when they tore you from the pool they did you more harm than good. You could have healed your injuries if you remained within the water."

"If I survived long enough. They wanted to help me."

"You claim they did. Mind their deeds, not your generous interpretation of their motives. You think because my clients are strange and wicked people that I mean you ill. But my clients have never set foot on your island. They have not injured you and yours. Their murders and vices are strictly onshore. They are not the source of your misery."

"You've trapped me here inside my mind to interrogate me, and now you ask me to trust you."

Ms. Kevarian rubbed her temples. "You tax my patience."

Kai hung immobile in the web, and traded gazes with the Craftswoman in the stretching silence.

"What was Mara trying to tell you?" Kai said at last.

"We discussed discrepancies in the Seven Alpha records, before she left."

"You called her a liar."

"On the contrary. She was the one who expressed the initial desire to talk with me. She ran when she saw you."

Kai blinked. If Mara hid the records in the first place, why tell Kevarian? "If Mara ran when I arrived, why do you think I might help you find her?"

"You hunted for her unprotected, in dangerous territory."

"Maybe I wanted you to see me looking."

"Perhaps. But if you had a choice, I imagine you would have warded yourself for this journey. Besides, I hold you a person of grave conscience. Such people commit atrocities, of course, but they suffer for them. Yet your nightmares are old: fears of being trapped, and devoured, and contained. I can taste their age, like that of a fine wine. I do not think you have killed a friend in the last forty-eight hours."

"Killed?"

"Nothing I have said so far would stand as evidence in any court, but one of the few advantages of private contemplation over the paid variety is that I am not compelled to present my logic in court." She sipped her tea, again. "I have been honest with you. More honest than with many in similar circumstances. Do you trust me?"

"No."

She nodded. "I doubted you would. A colleague . . . a friend once accused me of using people, of manipulating them without their knowledge. She did not understand, I think, how difficult it is to convince others you have their best interests at heart."

Kai could not break the web. But she refused to hang here any longer, listening.

The silk was her dream. It bound her, but bonds were clothing of a kind. Perhaps the silk that caught her body was in fact a dress, the silk around her hands spun to gloves. The spider gown cascaded, shimmering. She stood; her feet touched a floor of no texture.

Ms. Kevarian saluted her with raised teacup. "Well done."

"I don't know what Mara wanted to tell you, but Seven Alpha's death was completely aboveboard. Mistakes happen."

Ms. Kevarian's teacup disappeared. She brushed off the front of her suit, though as far as Kai could see the fabric was black and unstained as the space between high stars at midnight. "Two points worth considering, Ms. Pohala. First. I do not believe your idol's death was a mistake. You would not have jumped into the water beneath the world to save a flawed product. You jumped because you thought there was someone in the water who should not die. And second. The nightmare in which I found you was not your own."

"What do you mean?"

"Just that. This dream is yours: the spider, and the silk. The one from which you entered this place was not."

"Why would I have someone else's nightmares?"

"A good question," Ms. Kevarian said. "I do not envy you, Ms. Pohala. You have, I think, convinced yourself that a spider's web is a silk dress." From her pocket she produced a business card and flipped it in Kai's direction. The card floated through the air, spinning slowly, ignorant of gravity. Kai caught it in one hand. "I sympathize. I wish I could help, but I can give you little assistance so long as you feel you require none. If you tear this card in half, I will hear you. If need be, I will come to your aid."

"And if I don't want your help?"

"We make our own choices. If we are lucky, we last long enough to live with them." Ms. Kevarian opened a door in the dreamspace, into a rippling emptiness. She stood edged against the deep. It burned and chewed her outline. "Be well. And be careful." The door swung shut behind her, and vanished with a click. Kai remained, alone in her dress in the empty room. Green moonlight bloomed on the spider-head hat, glinted off faceted eyes.

Kai tried to approach the hat, but her legs would not lift, her arms would not reach. The spider head twitched, and rose, topping a body of suggestion and fear. It scuttled forward. Fine-furred forelegs touched her neck. Its mouth sang triumph, and Kai cried out and woke in her own bed, where her arms were pinned to her sides and a sliver of steel rested at her throat and a woman's voice said, "Why shouldn't I kill you now?"

41

As Edmond Margot wrote, the stars went out. He did not need them. A page lay on his desk. His fingers held a pen. With these tools he built a world. Perhaps the world he built lived behind his eyes and was transmitted to the page by the instrument of ink, or else it lived beneath the page somehow, his pen's progress sculpting form out of a purer white than sculptor's marble. He coughed blood into a handkerchief. His illness worked angrily inside him, drawing him close to the beyond. He gloried and dissolved in the heat of his blood and heart and brain.

He lost the stars, first. Then the sky around them, and after the sky the borders of the horizon. He lost the waves next, and beaches, and the vast and lucent sea. The mountain too faded. Wind stilled. The universe compressed to his block, his house, his apartment, all trees wind leaves and stone, all human life and structure, all bars and fiddle-players and dancers and drinkers, all lovers and friends and gamblers and back-alley muggers and red-faced priests fallen away until only he remained, and then he even lost himself. Pen met paper, and paper and pen fading left, at last, the line. Not even the line: the point of contact, a wet green moving dot in a space without time or dimension.

But this space was not empty. Emptiness collapsed, while this stretched, defined by relations between invisible enormous beings who swam like whales in the deep. Closer than these eminences, small by comparison, hovered snowflakes of light, snowflakes such as he had not seen since in childhood he first caught them on the fine hairs of a wool mitten. Snowflakes, very like, but made of bone. Skeletons hanging in the night, tied to one another by strings of dried skin and muscle. Flayed crystal corpses, bodies human and animal and every mix of both, skyscraper horns and suspension bridge wings, rib cages thick as magisterium trees. The skeletons twitched, mocking life.

A skull the size of a small moon turned to him, a massive hand extended, a mouth moved. No sound could carry in this absent space, but still he heard someone speak.

We have missed you.

He recognized the voice.

Then the door burst open behind him.

42

When Izza was a block away from Margot's house she felt Penitent footsteps vibrate through the paving stones. She swore and sprinted up the alley, dodging trash cans and broken glass until she reached Margot's backyard wall and climbed it. Still the footsteps shivered in her legs and chest.

She pulled herself over the wall. Margot bent at his desk by the window, transfigured. Before, his focus made him seem to burn; now, his skin actually shone. Izza blinked, looked away, looked back, but it was true. He glowed green, as if his body were a wine bottle with fireflies trapped inside. Light flowed from his eyes and fingers. Flames licked the tip of his pen. He did not look up. Did not notice her, or the shaking of his apartment as the Penitent climbed the stairs.

Paint and quartz on the Penitent's stone skin caught the streetlights; its eyes gleamed blue. The stairs shuddered under the statue's feet, and Izza heard its prisoner groan: a new recruit, adjusting still to pain. Margot wrote on, oblivious. The statue reached the top of the stairs.

They'd sent only one. Strange: Penitents rarely made arrests alone, since they couldn't speak or think fast. Each thought worked first from the stone shell into the human prisoner for processing, and back. They were blunt tools, lacking subtlety or social grace.

But even blunt tools had their uses.

The Penitent raised one hand, ponderous and slow. Two massive fingers and one thumb balled into a fist and it struck the door, a blur of stone faster than Izza's eye could follow. The door snapped down the middle; the hinged half swung in and slammed against the wall, while the latched half tore free of the jamb and fell.

That, Margot noticed. He stood, turned. Green fire trailed him, and seeped out his eyes and mouth. Izza could not hear what the poet said, but she did not think he spoke a human tongue. Human or divine, his words did not faze the Penitent; it stepped forward, splintering the doorjamb. Izza ached for Margot to run, to escape through his barred window, over the balcony into the night. He could not outrun the Penitent, but at least he might have given it a chase.

He stood before the statue, rigid, proud.

Izza knew what came next.

The Penitent's hand caught Margot around the throat. It lifted him off the ground with so little effort he seemed made of paper.

Margot stabbed the Penitent's arm with his pen; he kicked, and slapped, and clawed.

Izza went cold. Penitents did not kill. They enforced bad laws. They caught stupid or unlucky dock rats. But Margot was dying. The flames that suffused him flickered and dimmed.

The priest had sent not cops, but an assassin.

"Leave," a thin high voice whispered in her ear, Smiling Jack's voice, all metal and wheels. "That's all you can do. Margot built his own coffin. Let him lie."

Margot stabbed the Penitent's sapphire eye with his pen. The statue did not flinch. The prisoner within wailed.

Izza could not help Margot. But perhaps she could save a piece of him.

She leapt from wall to tree to balcony, ducked beneath the window to stay out of sight. The apartment floor creaked with the Penitent's weight. Izza was close enough now to hear the poet gasp for breath, the faint percussion of his fists against stone.

With the Penitent's attention fixed on Margot, Izza might be able to snatch his notebook. The window was open. Her arm could fit through the bars easy. Grab the book, and run.

Now.

She did not move.

Dammit. Go. This is how they get you. They march, and they terrify, and when they come for you in the end you're so scared you let them do what they want. Like Dad, and Mom, like the priestess with her throat slit.

Margot tried again to scream, and failed.

Izza stood, snatched the notebook, and stuffed it into her pocket. Heat surrounded her: the twin spotlights of the Penitent's stare. Margot twitched one last time, and hung still. The Penitent let him fall, and then Izza was alone, pinned by light from the murderer's eyes.

She ran.

The first step was the hardest. She dove over the railing, fell, and rolled to her feet on the grass. Up again, running for the alley wall. Behind her, three heavy footsteps and an eruption of plaster and brick: the Penitent burst through Margot's wall, scattering dust and broken glass. It crashed after her into the yard, tearing up great gashes of turf. She vaulted into the alley and ran. She was halfway down the block when she heard a cliff face collapse as the Penitent landed where she had been a minute before. Searchlights swept the darkness, and she felt that telltale heat.

Izza didn't bother knocking over trash cans in her wake. The Penitent would ignore them. She could take to the rooftops, but the Penitent had strong eyes. It would follow, and she couldn't hide forever.

Stone footfalls accelerated into an avalanche, and behind that avalanche she heard the prisoner's cries as gears and needles and knives goaded her on. Izza squeezed down a narrow gap between two walled gardens, and heard the Penitent turn left onto a larger, parallel street to keep pace.

Out onto Victoria, two blocks from shore, two steps ahead of the Penitent. Options, hastily assembled, more hastily compared— across the road and down to the docks, a maze of narrow passages and turnings before she reached water and safety. To make it, though, she had to beat the Penitent in an open sprint. And if the statue tracked her to the water it could just follow her from shore.

Not the docks, then, she decided ten steps after she sprinted south into East Claw. Two blocks down, up onto a shop awning, from there three windows' climb to a rooftop, then south again. Searchlight eyes swept the night and caught a flash of heel, an arm, a glint of eye turned back to check how much distance she'd lost. Once, as she was leaping across a gap between buildings, the light flooded Izza, so dense it seemed to lift her up before she arced out into shadow.

Her legs throbbed, her heart pounded. She could not run much farther. Fortunately, she did not have much farther to run.

She cut east, away from shore, up the slope. The Penitent followed.

She could have found her way blind, just by following the heat: cook fires and bonfires and torches and drunken bodies mashed together. And after the heat, the stink symphony of drug smoke, spilled liquor, vomit, barbecue, incense, blood sacrifice, and burnt offerings. Noise too, a wash of sitar and swing and contrabass chant, theological argument, hawk and sell, sin and expiation, lust resisted and satisfied. She slid down a drainpipe into the red-lit mess of the Godsdistrikt.

She landed behind a priest selling indulgences out of his open black coat, and snatched a prayer book from his hand. "Thief!" The priest lunged for her, missed, and tumbled instead into the back of a hefty henna-inked cultist from the Gleb, who turned smooth as sunrise and punched the priest in the face.

The fight spread, and Izza slid away through the crowd, skipping, dodging. She risked another glance back, and saw her Penitent pursuer wade into the Godsdistrikt, brawl. The crowd broke like waves against its chest.

A woman by an incense salesman's cart reached for her purse and found it gone, then turned to see it in the grip of a hapless young monk, who had blindly taken the bundle a young girl thrust into his arms as she ran past. Izza tripped, and poked, and ducked away. She shouted discord into a missionary chorus. The crowd rose from simmer to boil. Fights broke out and merged into a riot like streams merging into a river. At last, she ducked into an abandoned confession booth, hugged her knees to her chest, and listened until she heard the drum swell of more Penitents approaching.

Six pairs of spotlights opened at once on the Godsdistrikt crowd, and Izza, hiding, waited, and hoped.

Penitents did not kill. This one had. Which presented two options: either all Penitents killed, or this was an exception. If all killed, they went to great lengths to keep people from learning of their murders. Preserve the people until Makawe and his sisters return, that was their mandate, and Izza had never heard of them breaking it. Which meant this statue was murderer more than Penitent—and like all murderers, it had to hide its deeds.

Hence, the riot. The more Penitents, the greater her danger of being taken, but the less her danger of being killed.

She waited in the confessional as Penitents cordoned off the street. The smell of cedar boards edged out the incense, sweat, and musk outside. A great shadow passed in front of the confessional door. She tried not to move, but could not stop shaking.

The riot died. The Penitents moved on. Izza slipped from the confessional, crossed the recovering roil of the Godsdistrikt, and from there, unobserved, walked north and west into the Palm.

The moon smiled down and she smiled back. She walked too fast, and breathed too deep. The whole world was velvet padded. She whistled to herself, an old tune from across the sea, a song she remembered a mother singing once. She wasn't sure if the mother had been hers. There were so many mothers.

The whistle shrilled in her ears. Some god sharpened the streetlights and the stars. The moon's smile turned wicked. She hid behind a trash bin, gripped her ankles, and thought of Edmond Margot dead.

A broken, tired man, far from home, a deserter of his people, deserted in turn by gods and muses. And anyway, others had died before this. Why weep for him?

She did anyway.

This surprised her.

A while later she emerged onto the street, and moved north and west with dreadful purpose.

She ignored crowds, drunks, and flower-draped tourists. Three skeletons in tie-dyed shirts stumbled past, drinking from silver flasks and singing God Wars songs. Soon the streets narrowed, and yards unfurled from the houses.

She found the priest's house dark, shuttered. She walked the block twice, casing it from every angle. Once in a while she heard a cry from within, a yowl like a cat would make, or else a person with bad dreams.

Nick had been right: the house was warded. Cross the fence and Izza would wake the alarm. But the house next door was less secure, and in its yard grew those trees Izza didn't know what to call, the ones like a buried chicken's upturned claw. A limb of one such tree overhung the fence. The ward was younger than the tree, and rather than cutting back the tree, the contractor must have bent the ward around it.

Izza climbed the claw tree and crept out along the thinning branch. Crossing the ward burned like a bath in cold iron. Spiderwebs of light and lightning spread around her. She pressed herself against the bark, always at least one patch of skin touching. She was one with the tree. The pain built, sharpened, vanished.

She was through.

Faint ghostlight flickered from the priest's second-floor window: a nightlight, or a bedside lamp left on. Between that and the occasional moans, she might have suspected the priest was entertaining callers. But she heard only one voice, and the wind, and a creak from the branch beneath her.

Now to find a way down, Izza thought before the branch broke.

She landed hard on the lawn. False stars spun above, in front of the real ones. The limb of the neighbor's tree now ended in a jagged line above the fence. So much for her clean exit. Fine. Revenge was best served hot, whatever Camlaander playwrights said.

The priest bolted and chained her front door, but used a pushover of a key lock for the back: a rake of pick over tumblers and it gave. Izza locked the door behind her, and stood in the empty kitchen, breathing.

This was the part she'd not thought through.

She'd never killed before, not while meaning to anyway. She hadn't brought a weapon, but the house offered all the arsenal she needed. Pokers, boards, pillows for suffocation, wrenches and pliers in a toolkit under the sink. This had all seemed so much simpler on the walk over.

Of course it's simple.

Well, yes, but. When she held the pliers and imagined grabbing fingers and applying torque, she thought of her own fingers breaking. Same with the wrench. And couldn't people breathe through pillows?

She settled for a knife from the block on the granite counter. The big carvers felt unwieldy, so she chose a paring blade instead: sharp tip, sharp edge, balanced. She only needed a slice or two.

She realized she'd been haggling with herself over knives for ten minutes. The priest killed Margot, or handed him over to those who did. Justice wasn't some force in the air. Justice was something you do.

She thought about Cat. The cop in her would not approve. But she wasn't a cop anymore. And anyway: *We're the Lady's children, and there's nobody to help us but us.*

She hadn't meant that when she said it. Thought she was just convincing Nick to help her with a few clever words. But she heard her own voice in her ears now.

So.

She climbed the stairs. The priest's bedroom door was open, her bedside lamp on. The woman lay sleeping, twisted in cotton sheets, breathing rapidly through nose and mouth. Izza slipped out of her shoes and approached, soundless, over white carpet. The knife weighed no more and no less than any other piece of steel about so long and about so thin.

How did you kill someone in bed? Izza hadn't done this sort of thing before.

She'd fought. She'd lived through war. She could figure it out.

People get up, when hurt. They fight back. Even weak folk don't die easy.

Stabbing, then, might not work. Anyway, Izza couldn't stab her from the bedside: the woman's bed was the size of a small stage, built for two, and she lay in its center. From the edge, Izza lacked enough leverage to drive the blade in deep. No doubt proper killers knew how to deal with this.

She climbed onto the bed.

The mattress was soft as wet sand. The woman shifted, but did not wake.

Izza climbed nearer on knees and one hand. She straddled the woman, pinned her arms to her sides, and raised the knife.

The skull was hard. Breastbone too. The throat, though, the throat was soft.

Stab, or slice?

Her blade wavered.

She remembered Sophie's screams when the Penitents caught her. Remembered the Blue Lady's dying breath. Remembered her mother, and her father, and the fire. The priestess at home, in the village square, and the sound of the knife across her throat. She'd never wondered how it felt to hold that knife, and now she would know. Dying, Margot had sounded like a draining bath.

One death equals one death.

Did it?

Was this justice?

What had she seen? The woman talked to Margot. Talked to the Watch after. A Penitent came, and killed. A chain of events. She imagined Cat asking her: Did you see this woman kill? Do you know she was at fault? Justice is like math: anyone can think she knows the answer, but not every answer is right.

She'd gone this far to make sure of the death. Knife at the woman's throat, all her weight ready to press down. Why not make sure of its justice, too?

The woman trembled on the edge of waking.

Izza touched the knife to her skin.

Two black eyes snapped open. Swollen pupils sought and found Izza's face.

"Tell me," Izza said, "why I shouldn't kill you now."

43

Not a woman, Kai realized, but a girl. Fourteen, maybe. Gleblander. Short cropped hair. Thin, gaunt, coltish, angry. Sharp big black eyes, brown skin. Sweat crusted. Brown ragged tunic. Wore a pearl on a leather string around her neck. Wiry legs clamped Kai's arms to her sides.

All these details tossed under utter panic. Half of Kai's body tried to buck the girl off, and the other half to burrow into the mattress, away from the blade at her throat. She felt its tip as a coal.

"Stop, or I'll do it now." The knife pressed further, and Kai felt her skin tear.

Drowning sailors on the battered raft of her mind threw sacrifices to the adrenaline storm: snatches of poetry, school rhymes half-remembered, and at last, despairing, an image of a beggar girl on the sidewalk in front of Edmond Margot's apartment. "You're the girl from Margot's place."

The knife kept still.

"Tell me why you did it," the girl said. Urgent, low.

"Did what?"

The pressure returned.

"He's."

"Dead," Kai finished, seeing the shape of her anger. "Margot's dead, isn't he?"

"Why did you kill him?"

"I didn't."

"Don't lie to me!" The knife danced over her skin as the girl's hand shook.

"I'm not. I'm not. Swear to whatever gods you want to name."

"You don't know the gods I'd name," the girl said.

"I tried to save his life."

Shadow welled through the narrow slits of the girl's eyes. "You went to the Watch."

"To protect him."

"They killed him." Another coal puncture, below the first. Kai fought to keep still. The blade was too close and sharp for heroics, or for fear.

Think. The girl thought Kai had killed Margot. She wanted vengeance. She could have killed Kai while she slept; either she was a hardened torturer, and kept Kai alive to suffer, or she didn't want to do the work. She wanted to be talked out of it.

Oh gods. This was a sale, then. Of a sort. Twilling's acronyms and lists bubbled up unbidden.

"You killed him," the girl repeated.

"I wanted him safe. I offered him shelter. He refused." Technically true. "Can we just. I mean." Step one: identification. "I'm Kai," she said. "Can you tell me your name?"

"Don't lie to me."

"I'm not lying. Kai is my name. What's yours?"

Scales shifted and gears spun in the girl's mind. Her face twisted. Hesitation. Sensible. An exchange of names was an exchange of power. Without names you filed other people into boxes: murderer, conspirer, betrayer, lover, friend. The knife at Kai's throat would kill her, but anonymity would let the girl drive the blade home.

"Izza," the girl said.

"I only met Margot twice." The cuts on her neck burned when she swallowed. "He seemed like a good man."

"You killed him."

"I didn't."

"You sent a Penitent, and the Penitent did."

"I asked the Watch to arrest Margot, to keep him safe."

Izza's weight settled on Kai's stomach. "A Penitent strangled him to death."

She struggled to breathe. "Gods."

"Gods have no part of this."

"Penitents don't kill people."

"That's what I thought."

Penitents didn't kill, but this girl wasn't lying. Kai'd expected assassins, Craftwork or poison or knife, rough work in a back alley to make the death look like a mugging gone wrong. The Grimwalds were powerful, but could they subvert a Penitent? The concept barely made sense. "You're serious."

"I am."

Step two: needs assessment. "You're here because your friend is dead, and you want revenge." She saw a drowning face in a deep pool. "You can kill me to make yourself feel better. But that won't get you what you want, because I didn't kill him, and I want to know who did as much as you."

"Tell me," the girl said, through clenched teeth. "Everything."

Step three: the solution. "No."

"I will hurt you."

"You cut me, and I'll tell you something, sure. Maybe I'll even tell you the truth. Or maybe I'll tell you what you want to hear, just to make the pain stop." She could hear Twilling's voice in her head. "I want to tell you what I know. If he's dead, I want to help you find his killer." And step four: the price. "But I need to know you're not lying to me, first. Think about it from my point of view. I don't know you. You might be lying. You might have killed him."

"I didn't."

"I believe you." She didn't, exactly, but the girl didn't need to know that. "But I need proof."

Izza's lips thinned to a line. Kai closed her eyes and waited for the cut.

It did not come.

The knife lifted from her neck.

"You walk with a cane," Izza said.

"Yes."

"You'll walk with me instead." She rolled off Kai's chest, and waited by her bedside, knife out between them. "Get dressed."

As Kai sat up she felt a sharp-edged, rectangular piece of paper under her left hand. She palmed the business card and, when she risked a glance down, saw Ms. Kevarian's name flashed in gold.

44

Kai wore a red shirt to hide the blood from her neck. She slid Kevarian's business card into the pocket of her slacks as she tugged them on. Izza watched from the corner, knife at her side. Kai exaggerated her limp, leaning heavily on nightstand, dresser, wardrobe. She didn't try to run. Even fully healed, she doubted she could have outrun this murderous whip of a girl.

"Where do you come from?" Kai asked to relieve the silence. She didn't think Izza would answer.

"The Gleb," she said.

"Long way from home."

"What's home?"

Kai tried again as she buttoned her shirt: "How did you know Margot?"

"He saved me."

"From what?"

"From someone who was asking too many questions."

Kai left the button at her neck undone. "Let's go."

"Put on a coat."

"It's hot outside."

"Put on a coat."

She took a linen blazer from her closet. "Why?"

"You'll have my knife at your back. So you don't try anything."

She pulled on the jacket, and limped toward the stairs. "Give me a hand?"

"Use the rail." Izza gestured down the stairs with her knife.

"I might fall."

"Then you fall."

She descended slowly. Her knees buckled, but she kept her feet.

She waited in her living room for Izza.

The girl wrapped her arm around Kai's waist beneath the blazer. The knife pressed up into Kai's side. If she tried to run, the jacket might rip, but it might also pull Izza along—they'd both fall, and the knife could end up anywhere.

She almost ripped the card in half then, and damn the consequences. Curiosity stopped her, and fear. If Ms. Kevarian saved Kai's life, she'd expect payment. Besides, if this girl was telling the truth, she might need the Craftswoman's help later.

They stumbled four legged out onto the porch, and toward the fence. Kai sweat from the knife at her side as much as from the heat.

"Where are we going?" she asked when they reached the street.

"The poet's place. East Claw. So you can see him dead. We'll take the back roads."

"Are they safe?"

"Let me worry about that," Izza said, in a tone that meant she didn't plan to worry much.

They turned right, south, downhill, toward the ocean.

Night birds whooped in the canopy. Izza burned at Kai's side, a heating coil in the shape of a girl. Kai felt no give in her, no softness at all—bones and muscle, sinew and tendon. She had a springy gait, the kind of light step that never assumed solid ground beneath her feet.

Down and into the city. Trees and spreading lawns gave way to plaster and brick. Izza turned them onto a side street Kai hadn't realized was a street: a narrow alley so crowded with trash bins and old crates and chained-shut doors it seemed a dead end. Kai knew the island well; an hour before she'd have sworn she could navigate it blindfolded. But she lost herself as Izza turned them off the first alley onto a second, and then a third.

"Are you sure this is the right way?"

"Yes."

"I've never been here before, is all."

"Of course not."

Kai bridled at the assumption of that sentence, then realized the girl was only stating fact. Of course Kai wouldn't know these alleys. She never needed them.

"These are safe paths for you," Kai said.

"Yes."

"Safer than main roads."

"Not everyone's as lucky as you are."

They rounded a sharp corner and came to a chain-link fence. Izza stopped walking, so Kai stopped, too.

"Can you climb this?" Izza said.

"No. We could go around. Greenfrond's over that way somewhere, I think."

"Too risky."

The girl had few good options. Use the main road and trust Kai not to shout for help, or take these back alleys at half speed.

"I'll pick the lock," Izza said after a while. "You lean against that wall there."

"Okay."

"No one will hear if you call for help. And even if they hear, they won't come."

"I figured."

Izza walked Kai to the wall, and slid out from under her arm. Kai lurched forward without support, but caught herself against the bricks. Logical: Izza didn't want herself between Kai and the wall. Concerned even now that Kai was faking. Fair. She was, a little. Exaggerating for effect.

The girl knelt by the gate's lock. From a pouch at her belt she produced two metal tines, inserted one into the lock, twisted slightly, and inserted the second. The girl frowned at the lock like Mara frowned when working though a tense point of theology.

Mara. Where was she? The Craftswoman might have lied, might be responsible for her disappearance after all—if she had disappeared. People worked late. People had accidents. Kai hadn't been home for a month after her disaster in the pool. But if so, why couldn't she find Mara in her nightmares? Why couldn't Ms. Kevarian?

And what did it mean, that the hospital nightmare wasn't hers?

The lock clicked open. Izza stepped back with a curt, professional nod. "Come on."

She helped Kai through, swung the gate shut after, and reached back to close the lock.

"Polite."

"If the folks who own that lock see it doesn't work, they'll buy a better one. If I clean after myself, they won't know I was ever here."

"If you tell them their locks don't work, and show them ones that would, they might pay you. Even give you keys to them."

Izza shook beside her.

"Are you laughing?"

"You really think that might happen?"

"People earn a living that way, in my world."

"You live in a strange world."

"I guess."

"A key's the last thing I want."

More silence. Another turn, down an alley that smelled of cat piss.

"What do you have against keys?"

"People with keys worry about keeping locks locked."

They walked hidden paths behind and beside the streets Kai knew. Twice they crossed a main road only to dart again into cover. When other people neared, even beggars, Izza pressed the knife into Kai's back. Kai didn't need the reminder.

They smelled smoke four blocks from Margot's apartment, and met the crowd soon after. Izza hesitated, but at last steered them into the human current. Drunks and salesmen and grandmothers squeezed her and Kai together. Men cried and men sang. Three women shouted at a crying girl. Boys scuffled on the sidewalk until the crowd forced them so close they had to make peace or bite each other. Sour-sweet musk of striving bodies, acrid breath, sandalwood and rosewater and leather. And smoke, always, beneath the other smells.

The crowd thinned and smoke thickened as they turned onto Margot's street. Black billows dwarfed human works below. The curious crushed in a ragged line against a Penitent barricade. The house where Margot lived was a fire-licked ruin. A bucket line fought the flames. Across the street, a clutch of watchmen surrounded a bent gray-haired woman in a nightdress; others knelt beside a prone and shrouded body.

Kai and Izza reached the front line, and held the yellow barricade to bolster themselves against the crowd.

"You didn't mention a fire," Kai said.

"It wasn't on fire when I left." Penitents paced in front of them. Rock ground against rock as their heads moved, scanning the crowd. "We need to go."

"We need to learn what happened here."

"I know what happened." She pressed close so she could whisper in Kai's ear. "They killed him. Then they set the fire to cover it up."

"If the Watch killed him, why set the fire? They don't need to find any evidence they're not looking for."

"Let's go."

A watchman kneeling behind the body stood and wiped smoke from his eyes: Claude. He turned a slow circle from old woman to fire to body to the crowd—and saw her. His eyes widened, and he jogged toward them both.

Izza tugged Kai back into the surging crowd, but Kai resisted. "Come on."

"No. That's the guy I asked to arrest Margot."

"He's in on it."

"Can't be. He did time inside the Penitents. He's reformed. Straight as light."

"I told you, the Penitents killed him."

"Claude's seen us. Leave now and he'll think this is my fault."

"Isn't it?" The knife dug into her skin.

"Go on," Kai said, and hoped she sounded less afraid than she felt. "Kill me, and you'll never get to the bottom of this. Or trust me, and we might."

Telepathy, she knew, was impossible. Minds could be read, but only once extracted, and extraction broke them. She could guess Izza's thoughts, though, from the twitch that moved through the girl like a ripple over a horse's hide. If Izza slipped away, escaped into the crowd, she would leave Kai in the shelter of coconspirators. If she stayed, Kai might turn her over to the Watch.

Nothing Izza had said or done so convinced Kai of the girl's innocence as that moment of fear.

"I won't turn you in," Kai said. "Trust me."

Izza did not move. Nor did she answer.

Claude pushed between the Penitents in front of them. "Kai." Soot streaked his face. The crowd shouted questions, and he ignored them. "Kai, what are you doing here?"

"I was in the area. That's Margot's house."

"I brought two Penitents to arrest him. Found the place burning. The old woman, the landlady, almost choked to death." Claude turned to Izza. "Who's this?"

The blade bit her back. Trust me. "I was drinking in the Godsdistrikt. Saw the smoke. I ran here. Lost my cane in the crowd. Almost fell. The girl helped."

"Out of the goodness of her heart I'm sure," Claude said.

She pointed to the shroud. "Is that who I think?"

"It's Margot. Landlady identified the body, even all burned up like that."

"Dead in the fire?"

"If so, fire's developed a bad habit of snapping necks. Maybe doctors will know more."

"Shit."

"Come with me, Kai. We need to talk."

"I asked you for help this morning. I asked you to arrest Margot. I asked you not to tell anyone."

"I didn't," he said. She couldn't tell whether he was lying. "I didn't, Kai."

"What happened?"

"The place was torn to nine hells. Door broken off the hinges. Walls shattered."

"Who could do that?"

"Best guess?" he asked, rhetorically. "A woman snuck onto the island about six weeks back, an unlicensed avatar—we figured a missionary, or a joss smuggler's muscle. We almost caught her when she came ashore, but she broke a couple Penitents and went underground. Maybe this is her work. In which case you're in danger, too." He reached for her. She retreated. "Come on, Kai. We can help."

"You fucked this up. And he's dead."

"Don't make this difficult."

"You want to arrest me?"

"We'll call it protective custody if we have to."

So easy to take him up on his offer. Let Claude take care of her. Let him and his Penitents save her from this mad girl with a knife.

"Protect me like you protected him?"

"Kai. Trust me."

"I'm leaving, Claude." She turned away. Her arm lagged behind: Izza, slow to believe Kai would pass this chance at safety. Her hesitation only lasted a moment. Claude watched them go.

They found an abandoned bench by the bay. Dark water rolled between the Claws. Dots of light drifted in the black: boats with lanterns lit, under the stars. Kai suggested they sit. Izza released her, and she lowered herself onto spray-wet wood. Izza sat at the opposite end of the bench. After their quadruped wandering, the few feet gaped between them.

Waves washed against pier and land, bearing their tithe of eroded soil out into the World Sea. Kai wondered if mainlanders knew they lived under siege. Or did they rest in comfort atop their continents, and ignore the gnawing doom of water?

Perhaps her father had seen the ocean differently. Perhaps Kai would have, if she'd taken to the sea. But these days Kavekana's children swam in other oceans.

"I'm sorry I didn't believe you," Kai said once the waves lost their mythic depths and became waves again.

"I wouldn't have believed me," Izza replied.

"You knew him?"

"Not well."

"That was him, under the shroud."

"Yes," Izza said. "Was that watchman your friend?"

"A kind of friend."

"The kissing kind?"

She laughed, and heard the bitterness in her own laughter. "Once. Not anymore."

"Why did you go to Penitent Ridge this morning?"

"You were following me."

"Yes."

"I asked him to arrest Margot. For his own good." When she closed her eyes they burned from smoke.

"Tell me more. Tell me what you know, or think you know."

"These are sacred secrets. I can't tell anyone who's not a priest."

"I'm a priest," Izza said, slowly. "Of a sort."

Kai didn't answer.

Izza stood before the ocean, and raised her right hand. "I won't betray you. Blue Lady forsake me if I lie. Smiling Jack gnaw my bones."

Kai heard the weight of her words. Belief, deep held. "I don't recognize those gods."

"You don't know all the streets on this island. Or all the gods."

"Those aren't Gleb gods, I mean."

"I didn't say they were," Izza said. "Now I've sworn. Tell me."

Kai looked up and down the road, and behind them. Dockside was as empty as it ever got. Cargo wagons rolled past. "There's a pool at the heart of Kavekana'ai where our idols live. Only priests can enter, but somehow Margot got inside. He drew the idols' power, and used it to write great poems. Thing is, people only bring their fortunes to Kavekana because they believe we'll keep them safe. The fact that he could do this is dangerous to us. And the people he stole from aren't nice. If they found out, they might have come for him. Maybe they sent someone to do their dirty work. Could have been that woman Claude was talking about."

"Not her," Izza said. "I know the woman he meant. She didn't do this. The Penitents did."

"They don't kill."

"I saw it." There was a fire in Izza's eyes that Kai didn't dare contradict. "And it saw me. I heard Margot's neck snap. A Penitent chased me halfway across town. Its eyes burned. I am not lying to you."

"And yet the Watch is there, investigating his death."

"Pretending to," Izza said. "They won't find anything. They killed him because they thought he was stealing from your people. Even though he wasn't."

"He was," Kai said. "I have proof. Records. Documents. Margot stole from our idol. That's certain."

"His poems didn't come from your idol. They came from his Lady."

"That's just the name he called her. He grabbed the power, made his poems however poets do, and convinced himself the idol spoke to him. Artists are liars—they lie to everyone, especially themselves."

"No," Izza said. "I know he spoke to her. Because I did, too."

Kai felt she was looking at herself through a distant lens, so the dock seemed a clay diorama like the ones she used to make at school. A woman on a bench. A girl leaning against a metal rail. Dollhouse buildings. A mountain of papier-mâché. Ocean of torn paper, or cotton balls. "Idols don't talk," she said. "They don't think."

"I don't know about idols," Izza said. "But my Lady lives. Lived. And she gave Margot his poems."

The words seemed so simple in Izza's mouth. Entering Kai's mind, their implications scattered to infinity. "Some foreign god, you mean. Margot was in touch with some kind of underworld demiurge from the Gleb."

"She wasn't foreign," Izza said. "Foreign gods couldn't make it onto the island without setting off your wards. My Lady came from the sand, from the mountain. She's as Kavekanese as you are."

"There are no gods on Kavekana."

Izza didn't respond. Kai felt the heat of her silence, of her anger. Kai wasn't listening. She hadn't listened to Izza all evening. Or to Margot, this morning, when he tried to explain. How much had she heard and failed to understand?

Jalai'iz. Talbeg female diminutives took the given name, added a long vowel. Izza.

This isn't your dream.

"You had a goddess," Kai said. "And she spoke to you."

Izza nodded.

"But she hasn't in a while."

No response.

"Not for a couple months now, I guess."

Izza's eyes glittered black ice. She did not move. Storm tossed, Kai thought, by Edmond Margot's death. By a life of secrecy, of flight, all exposed at once. She waited for a prompt from some higher power, a voice that would not come.

"I want to help," Kai said. "But first I have to understand."

Izza hesitated, but at last she held out her hand. "Follow me."

45

"Can you swim?" Izza asked when they neared the warehouse.

"Yes," Kai said. "Though not well since I was hurt."

"You don't need to swim well. Just deep."

Slick stairs led down the wharf into water. Izza took a coil of thin rope from her belt pouch, and tied one end around her ankle. "Hold this, in case we're separated."

Kai began to tie the rope around her wrist, but Izza stopped her. "No. You tie it, and we might drown together. Hold, and follow."

Kai looked from the water, to her clothes, to Izza, and said, "Okay."

Water's embrace was the best Izza had ever known: smothering, slimy, and sharp with seaweed, but it never held you hard enough to bruise. The line on her ankle went taut, and she waited for Kai to catch up. Izza skimmed the surface until they reached the warehouse wall. Then she dove into murk.

Groping blind she found the gap in the wall, and slid between decaying struts. She rose from the depths, lungs aching.

Izza broke free of the black and pulled herself up onto the planks that ringed the hidden chapel's entrance. She wiped water from her eyes and breathed air sweet with old incense and rotten wood. Checked the waterproof pouch where she'd slipped Margot's notebook: still secure.

Then she realized that the rope hung slack in the water. When she pulled, it came up without resistance, all the way to the frayed far end.

Kai must have let go, and run to her friend the watchman. Or else she was caught in the hole, in the water, drowning.

The chapel loomed empty above her. She wondered if Cat was sleeping now, beyond the debris wall in the warehouse's front

chamber. What would the mainlander think of this—of Izza showing her underbelly to this woman she barely knew. This woman
she'd almost killed not two hours ago.

This woman who might be dead already.

Kai surfaced, coughing. Izza waited for her to open her eyes,
then held out a hand to pull her up. The woman panted, on her
knees for a while, then stood, wrung out clothes and hair, and
looked around, almost blind. She wasn't used to this kind of dark.
"Where are we?"

"Our church," Izza said.

She'd built this room herself: the low benches around the hole
in the floor, the ragged altar piled with the proceeds of her last
several weeks' theft, along with Nick's ill-conceived contributions.
A cave made by human hands, starlit through gaps in the roof.

Nick's paintings watched from the walls.

Kai saw them, now: brightly colored figures eight feet tall, so
rough they seemed arrested in mid-motion. Simple, vague, and
vivid. "You did all this?" Kai whispered.

"We did."

"Who?"

"Me, and other kids."

"Those paintings. The pool in the center." Kai paced around
the entrance, examined the altar. "Why did you build it like this?"

"It seemed right. And they asked us to."

"Who?"

She'd betrayed so much trust, bringing Kai here. Betrayed, or
displayed. Why stop now? She could always kill her. She thought
she could. "The gods."

"Tell me about them," Kai said. Izza heard fear in her voice, or
desire, or both.

"A couple years back," she said, "I got in trouble. You know
how it is."

Kai shook her head. "I don't think I do."

"It's not just kids in the alleys. We're safer here than most
places, usually, because the Penitents take older crooks. Nick says
they tried stuffing kids in Penitents once, but it didn't work. We
break different."

"I'm sorry."

Weird thing to say. "Some grown-ups caught me. I fought back, I ran. They cornered me in an alley. I was so scared I couldn't think. Then she came."

"The Blue Lady," Kai said.

"No. Blue Lady was later. The Wind Woman was first. She swept me away, hid me. Whispered in my ear." Izza walked to a white drawing on the wall, overlapped now by a towering red eagle and a one-eyed man in a scraggly robe. "She was my first. I'd heard about her from other kids, but I didn't believe 'til then."

"You became a believer."

"No. Believers just believe stuff, doesn't matter what. They don't look too close. I didn't become a believer. I believed."

"And the . . . the Wind Woman talked to you."

"Not much, but yeah."

"What did she say?"

"She was scared."

Kai blinked. "Gods don't scare."

"Sure they do. When they see what's after them."

"What's after them?"

She didn't like saying the words in here, but there was no other way to tell the story. "Smiling Jack. He hunts gods."

"Why?"

A good sign, Izza thought. Kai was asking the right questions: the story questions. "We don't know. Doesn't like them. Maybe he's hungry."

A pallor crept spread across Kai's skin, the kind of fear that came slowly and didn't leave easly. "You worshipped the Wind Woman."

"I thanked her. I listened to the Wind Woman stories Sophie told. I missed her when Smiling Jack got her. Cried awhile. First time I cried in years."

"You saw her die?"

"Don't need to see a goddess die to know," Izza said. "You feel it in your heart."

"When was this?"

"Two years back, after the rains."

"And after that, the Blue Lady came?"

"No. After that, the Red Eagle." She pointed.

"How many gods do you have?"

"As many as show up. As many as you see here."

Kai turned in a circle, counting paintings. "How long has this been going on?"

"The Wind Woman came first, I think. Sophie would know, she was the first storyteller. Priest, I guess you'd call her. She got old, though. Penitents took her last winter."

"Gods."

"It happens."

"Tell me about the Blue Lady."

"I was the first to hear her. After they took Sophie I climbed the mountain alone and waited, watched the sky. This was early spring. The Lady stepped out of the stone and sat next to me." She pointed to the blue outline on the wall behind them both, the woman with horns and wings and backward-pointing legs, sharp blue teeth bared in a defiant grin. "We talked. She needed to run. I needed, we needed, someone to hide us. Back in spring, you know, there was a big purge. Watch tried to round up all the kids and send 'em off to work camps on the outer islands."

"I didn't know." Kai's voice sounded hollow.

"She helped us," Izza said. "Everyone told stories about her, but mine were the best. I took Sophie's place. I liked the Lady, and she liked me. More than liked, over time. I taught her to run and hide. Turns out gods don't know that stuff unless they learn from us: she was like a kid, only bigger. She lasted longer than the rest, maybe because she listened better and learned more. The Lady helped us set our feet in the right place at the right time, gave us that tickle lets you know someone's watching when you think you're safe." And this was the hard part. "She was a partner. A friend. You're a priest. You know how it is."

"I don't," Kai said. "Not like that."

"She died three months back. I heard her scream at night."

Kai sat down hard, facing the Blue Woman. "And Margot."

"Him I only met him a little while ago. We thought the Lady was just ours, but I think we were wrong. He saw the Green Man, too. That one didn't last long; him and the Great Squid were big, flashy, visible. Smiling Jack caught 'em easy."

"And no new gods since . . . since the Blue Lady?"

"No. Maybe someone's met the next, and kept quiet about it. But I don't think so. People tell."

"It doesn't make sense." Izza recognized Kai's expression, and her tone of voice. Gamblers looked that way sometimes when they wandered swaying out of card halls and leaned against a wall and gazed into the earth, like if they stared hard enough it might open underfoot to swallow them. "I know these figures." She pointed to the gods on the wall. "I've seen them, sketched in a notebook. These are idols. The one you call the Green Man—a guy named Ruiz built him, and the Squid, too. The Blue Lady, my friend Mara made her. And you say Smiling Jack killed them all."

"That's the story."

"It doesn't fit. These idols died because of bad business deals, not because someone hunted them down." Kai limped from one painting to the next. "And they couldn't talk. Or think for themselves. You're describing intelligent systems. These idols weren't complex enough for that. Simple myth machines, that's all."

"I don't know how," Izza said. "I just know what was."

"So did Margot. And he's dead." Kai hugged herself, and watched the Blue Lady on the wall.

"Your Watch killed him," Izza said. "And they'll go on to kill my friends. My gods. Unless we stop them."

"No," Kai said. "The Watch didn't kill him. I know you saw what you saw, but if a Penitent killed Margot it wasn't working for the Watch. Something else is going on. I don't know if that means the Craftsmen, or the Grimwalds, or my people, or what. I don't know," she repeated, and turned away from the Blue Lady.

Izza waited awhile, but the woman didn't speak again. "What do we do?"

"This is deep Craft. Impossible things all happening at once. The key is up the mountain, in the pool. I have to find it."

"You're not going anywhere without me," Izza said.

"I can't bring you into the mountain. I don't even know how I'll get in, let alone take you along."

"I could dress up like a client."

"We don't have teenage clients."

"I can look older."

"But you can't fake belonging to a Concern rich enough to need our services." Kai looked down at the sacrifices piled on the altar. Pocketbooks, purses, novels left towelside, three gold necklaces. A handful of rings. Coins stolen from a bliss-dealer at a topless club. Three tiny porcelain cats from the Shining Empire. Light seeped through chips in their enamel eyes. "Look. You want to find out the truth. But you're worried I might betray you."

"Yes."

"Well," Kai said, with a smile Izza didn't quite understand, "if you can't trust me, why don't you hire me?"

"What?"

"Priests sometimes consult on the side. This qualifies: I'm consulting you about your gods' nasty tendency to die."

"What." This time Izza's voice stayed flat, rather than rising with the question.

"Here's the deal: You hire me. I investigate your gods. The consulting agreement binds me to secrecy. If I betray you, the contract hurts worse than any torture you could invent. Old Island stuff. Sharks gnaw my bones. Vines twine through my eyes. My guts strangle my lungs; my blood turns to lava. Figurative, mostly, but the pain's real."

Silence, and water.

"You need my help," Kai said. "All you need to do is pay me for it."

"You're asking *me* to pay *you*."

"A contract requires payment, or it doesn't take."

Gods watched from the walls, but the room was empty save for Kai and Izza. Candles flickered. Waves lapped at the dock. Kai dripped on damp floorboards.

Izza reached to her neck, untied the leather string there, and advanced on Kai. "Sit down." The woman sat. "Here." Kai's breath stilled as Izza leaned in close. She sank a bit of soul into the necklace, into the pearl, and tied it around Kai's neck, tight enough the other woman couldn't slip the string off over her head.

"Thank you," Kai said. She touched the gray pearl at her throat.

"Is that it?"

"We shake hands, now."

They shook. Izza felt the agreement spiral up her arm from Kai's, and bite her wrist. The other woman's eyes glowed briefly, then faded. Izza stumbled back and sat on a bench. Her world grayed out briefly before she adjusted to the lost soul.

Kai looked small, under the gods' gaze, in the starlight.

"Can you find your way out?" Izza said.

"Yes."

"You're a good swimmer."

"My father taught me."

"What happened to him?"

"He died."

"Oh." Izza didn't say, I'm sorry. "Where can I meet you?"

"Tomorrow after sundown, at Makawe's Rest. A poetry club in the Palm, near Epiphyte and Southern. Thatch roof, open walls, lofted hut. I know Mako, the old blind guy who works there. You can trust him."

"Okay," Izza said. "Now go. Someone might come. I don't want to have to explain you."

"That makes two of us."

Kai dove into the water without a splash. The bottoms of her feet kicked twice, pale against the black, and she was gone. Izza felt her go. Kai had already absorbed the soulstuff Izza added to the necklace when she fastened it around Kai's neck. But some of Izza lingered there: bits of self sunk into that necklace through years of wearing. Not so much you'd notice, unless you almost starved yourself to death.

Which Izza had, many times.

So a piece of Izza sank with Kai, and wriggled free into the ocean. Distance attenuated the sensation: Izza's soul pulled like toffee, bond stretched long and thin, fading to a toothache in the heart.

Maybe Kai would keep faith. Maybe the contract would hold.

Maybe not. Either way, Izza would find her. The necklace could look after itself: the knot Izza had tied would warn her if it was broken, or the cord cut. Only the wait remained.

She stood before the altar and pondered how to wait.

46

Shivering, wet, Kai checked into a hotel in the Palm, one of those cheap transient places with ratty gray carpet that could look clean for a decade between shampoos. Luckily she'd found a cab after a few minutes of limping soaked and cold down the dockside streets. Her clothes dried, mostly, in the cab, but she still looked a mess. The desk clerk barely glanced up from his book—passed her a contract on a clipboard that she signed without reading. She rode the lift to her third-floor room. Floral print wallpaper, holey sheets. Walls and curtains and table and chairs all had a stain-proof sheen, slick as the back of a beetle's shell.

She wrung out her clothes in the bathtub, and hung them over the towel rack to dry. Harbor scum crusted her skin, and stained the whites of her nails black. She steamed herself off in the shower. Dark rivulets ran down her body. Dirt and scraps of seaweed flowed into the drain. She painted figures with grime on tile: the half gods of the hidden temple.

She had to dive into the pool, to see the idols, to learn the truth behind the records. Of course, she wasn't allowed back into the mountain.

Which did not leave her many options.

Before her shower, the room had smelled stale. After, it smelled stale and damp and bodily, like crumbled mushrooms. She opened the window. Curtains bellied in the night wind.

She stared down at the dirty carpet. When she looked up she saw her own eyes in the mirror across from the bed, wide and framed by wiry hair. A deer watched from a painting on the wall behind her—the artist had aimed for majestic and settled for frightened—a creature that didn't belong on this island, framed by forest Kai didn't recognize, fat sun-dappled leaves hunter green on top and gold beneath, the forest of a country with a winter.

She lay back, and hugged the bathrobe against herself. It smelled of laundry soap and fake lavender.

There it came, bubbling up from subconscious depths. Not exactly an answer, not exactly a plan. But she could get into the pool. All she had to do was apologize.

First, though—thoughts vague now as sleep seized hold—she had to go shopping.

Gods, maybe she was going mad.

The next morning, quarter past nine, Kai stood poolside at the Kavekana Regency in a new suit (cream pants and jacket, navy blouse), hands folded on the head of a new cane (dark hardwood with a silver head molded like a pre-Contact totem), and watched Teo Batan swim.

The Regency's pool deck overlooked the ocean, which here on the outer face of West Claw was the kind of intense blue painters never used for fear gallerists would laugh at them. The pool water seemed transparent at first glance, but compared with the bleach-white towels and pool attendants' uniforms it had a slight green shimmer of chemicals or Craft. Water flowed over the deck's seaward edge into a trough below eye level, and recirculated. To a swimmer, the pool would seem to extend forever, merging with ocean—though the slight green tint probably spoiled the illusion.

In the shallow end, a middle-aged woman helped a toddler tread water, child in one hand and a mimosa in the other. The mother (or nanny—their hair color was the same, and beyond that Kai had a hard time telling mainlanders apart) wore a thin gold necklace and diamond stud earrings with the air of someone who thought gold necklace and diamond studs did not quite rate as jewelry. Behind the woman, two kids played tag.

On the deck, three men bent in identical attitude of hangover or prayer around a glass table that supported three many-umbrella'd drinks. A skeleton in sunglasses reclined in a lounge chair, tanning mirror angled toward his face. Or hers. Hard to tell.

In the deep end, Teo swam laps alone.

You could tell a swimmer's skill by how they related to water. Kids first thrown into the ocean spasmed and flailed against it. Dogs that weren't born swimmers did the same, scrambling to keep dry. The better you became the less you struggled, until like some of the fishermen who'd worked with Kai's dad you approached an aquatic asymptote. Kai had admired those men, in a left-handed and horrified way: artists in the water, they moved unsteadily on land.

Teo wrestled the pool. Her hands pierced the water, threw it behind her, emerged dripping from the surface to pierce once more. She trailed a V-shaped churning wake. The pads of her toes were pale, and her silver bracelet glinted with each stroke. Reaching the wall she turned a somersault, gathered herself, and pushed off, a submarine missile. That one push carried her a third of the pool's length, and Kai examined her while she was underwater. Sleek, rounded, wearing a swim cap and a black one-piece bathing suit, she looked like a seal. Then she breached the surface, and white water obscured her again.

This was Teo's eleventh lap since Kai's arrival. The woman knew she was here, and hadn't stopped swimming. Not a good sign.

Twelve laps. Thirteen.

Teo somersaulted and pushed herself off again, holding her breath half the length of the pool this time. When her speed waned, she surfaced, gulped air, and wiped her eyes, treading water with both legs and one hand. She squinted against the sun, waved to Kai, and swam a breaststroke across three lanes to the edge. Her hands clutched the pool's stone lip, and muscles shifted in her shoulders and back as she pushed herself up. Scars marked her left arm: a single long straight line down the inside of her wrist over the vein, and other curving cuts around it. Pale emerald drops rolled down her skin; she stood, and Kai took a step back before she shook herself.

A white-suited attendant appeared with a towel. Teo grabbed it blindly, wiped off face and body and hair (prying off swimming cap to reveal a damp crown of thorny black curls), and threw the towel onto an empty chair. "Kai. Thanks for waiting. I don't like to stop in the middle of things."

"You're a strong swimmer."

"I'm trying to be a stronger everything," she said. "Can't count on other folks to bail you out of trouble." Her smile seemed to pack more teeth into it than most people's. Kai spent more will-power than she wanted to admit dragging her eyes from the scar on the woman's wrist.

"Do you get in swimming-related trouble?"

She laughed. "First time for everything. What can I do for you?"

"I'm here because maybe I can do something for you."

The water had stained the whites of Teo's eyes a gemstone green; it wept out as she blinked. "Go on."

"When you came to me, you said you wanted to invest in an idol. But you were worried about ethics."

"Is 'ethics' the right way to put it? I don't like gods. Neither do our investors. I don't mean it personally. I like things I can see and touch. Good strong deals. Clear terms of engagement. Account-ability and limited liability." A white grid ran down the front panel of her swimsuit, and as she breathed its geometry shifted from hyperbolic to planar to parabolic.

Kai swung a chair away from an empty table and sat, so she looked up at the Quechal woman rather than down. "I'm sorry for how I acted when we first met. And later."

"Hey, no problem." Teo planted one leg on the seat of a nearby chair and toweled off. "I wasn't nice, either."

The pool attendant returned with a drink menu. Kai waved him away, and he retreated with an expression of your-loss regret she recognized from the faces of a hundred high-touch salesmen. "Most of my work has been behind the altar, which gives me a different perspective on rules and regulations than most sales-people."

Teo's laugh was fuller and rounder than Kai expected. "I know how that feels."

"I think I can get you into the pool."

"Really." Teo threw the towel on the table, reclined in a lounge chair, and laced her fingers behind her head so her elbows stood out like the peaks of wings. Wet trails ran from the corners of her closed eyes; drying, the pool water left green sparks on the skin. Bones clattered as the skeleton turned over to sun its back. "I thought that was impossible."

"Well. My boss needs to approve it. But with help from you, I think I can sway him."

Her nod wasn't visible so much as audible: the back of her head knocking chair slats. "What sort of help?"

"Listen to a story?"

"Go ahead."

"Say I had a client who wanted to deposit a lot of soulstuff with us. Say that client had concerns about our methods. It happens sometimes. You might want a fertility idol who was never more than ten percent exposed to any particular grain future."

"I do so enjoy grains."

"In situations like that, sometimes we sign a conditional agreement. You commit the funds to us pending proof we can build an idol that meets your needs. No transfer takes place. If you don't see what you like, none ever will. But your commitment lets me convince my bosses to get us inside the mountain. Once we're there, I can show you what you need."

"Why didn't you mention this to me before?"

Because this is borderline ethical behavior. Because I didn't need you before. "Because we're talking more soulstuff than people tend to commit out of curiosity. But you sought me out twice so far. If you're as interested as I think, I can bring you up the mountain this afternoon."

Glasses clinked. Water rolled over the world's fake edge. Teo did not open her eyes, but she grinned anyway.

"It's a date."

47

Izza lay restless through the night on her rooftop bed. Stars stared down like Penitents from the sky. When morning threatened, she rose, bought—bought!—a cup of coffee to burn off the cobwebs of undreamt dreams, and walked the seashore. She felt Kai moving in her heart.

The surf rushed and gurgled like Margot's dying breath. She remembered her home long since abandoned, remembered how blood ran from the cut on the priestess's neck. She remembered the joy of running, and the sick fishhook feeling when she heard Sophie had been taken. She remembered the Blue Lady's scream.

She wanted out. She did. But her every step tied her more deeply to Kavekana and its people. Even to Kai, the lost priestess. Who she still did not quite trust.

She threw rocks into the waves, but the waves kept coming.

Two hours after daybreak, she gave up, and went to the warehouse.

Cat was packing. She'd brought little with her, and acquired less on the island. Silver chalk, the clothes on her back, a change of clothing she rolled up for use as a pillow. She folded the blankets, stuffed her few possessions in a sack, and swept the surrounding rubble into a semblance of undisturbed mess.

"You're leaving," Izza said from the hole by the door.

Cat smiled when she saw her, as broad and open and easy an expression as Izza'd ever seen on her face. "I hoped you might come. I would have gone looking if you hadn't."

"What's happened?"

"Time to go. Next day or two. Not longer, I hope, or else I'll have to get myself all moved in again. Say your good-byes, if you have any left. We'll need to move fast when the time comes."

"Yeah," Izza said, and even she could tell that her own voice sounded flat.

Cat stopped sweeping. "Are you okay?"

Izza should have gone to her when the poet died. When the pain still bled like a wound. Now the scab had formed, and tearing it open again hurt more. "No," she said.

"What happened?"

"Margot died yesterday."

From how hard the words were to say, she expected them to hit Cat harder. The other woman closed her eyes and breathed and opened them again. "Shit." Cat slumped onto a blackened, half-rotten crate. The boards sagged, but supported her. "What happened?"

"The cops did it. The Penitents. They're all—" She broke off. Better to keep quiet than speak in that quivering quavering tone. Telling Kai had been easier. Izza knew Cat, and knowing her she felt the need to be strong in front of her.

"Tell me."

"A Penitent came for him. He fought."

"You saw it."

"I did." She paced angrily among rusted wires and broken barrels until she could come up with more to say. She didn't say, I need you, would not admit that even now. "They killed him. They'll go on and kill my friends. I can't leave until they're safe."

Cat's grip tightened on the broom, and she stared down into the scrapes its bristles left in the dust. She growled in that tongue Izza did not know, with words like breaking rock. Then she let the broom fall. It clattered on the floor. She stood. "It won't be safe," she said. "Not ever. If they killed Margot, they'll hunt for anyone connected with him. That's you. That's the kids. Hells, that's me. You should have stayed away."

"I have a . . ." Gods, what should she call Kai? "A friend trying to help me find out what happened. To get to the bottom of this. Figure out what made the Penitents go crazy."

"And then what? You can't stop the Watch."

"You could."

Cat's laugh was harsh, humorless. "One at a time, maybe. You've already seen how well two at a time goes for me."

"What, then? We run away? Leave the kids in danger?"

"They always were in danger. You know that. They should all leave. But they have to figure that out for themselves."

"And what about Margot? He was killed. He deserves justice."

That drew a smile from Cat, but it wasn't a kind one. "I'm not here as a cop, Izza. I had to leave all that behind."

"I don't want a cop."

"Then what do you want?"

"I want you to help me."

She'd shouted. She hadn't meant to. Broken wood and rusted metal, fallen ceiling and shattered stone, should have eaten the echoes of her voice, but she heard them still, or heard her words in the silence their passage left. She heard the crackle of a burning village, heard the scream she'd been screaming for five years.

Cat watched her with green eyes like jade, like water.

Izza stood taut and sharp in the decaying room she'd chosen for her palace.

Cat walked toward her slowly. "You told me you wanted to leave. That you didn't want to be responsibile for this island, for these children. You don't have to."

She was too close. Izza couldn't move.

"I know that look in your eyes," Cat said. "You want to make a difference. You think if you push hard enough, you can fix this damn island, and once you're done with that, why not the whole world? But gods and Deathless Kings are bigger than you, kid, and they're bigger than me, and when folks like us play their games, we get lost so fast. Ideals twist, and one day you find yourself down a dead end, breaking ten oaths to keep one. Do you understand?"

"I think so," Izza said.

"Weeks back you said you wanted to save yourself. I can help you do that. I will. But you have to choose. I'd hate to see you choose wrong. There's a whole world out there. This place isn't worth you."

Cat touched Izza's shoulder, and Izza didn't run, didn't break her hand. The touch felt unreal, as if Cat wore her quicksilver skin again. Or as if Izza herself wore a skin. As if she'd been wearing that skin all along, since the day she ran through brambles and desert trees away from a rising pillar of sick oily smoke.

Cat drew her into her arms, strong and warm. Izza moved slowly.

She didn't cry even then. She ground the sobs to dust between her teeth.

"Stay here," Cat said. Her body felt stiff against Izza's. She wasn't used to these movements—to tenderness and human touch. "With me. If we need to run and hide, we run and hide together. And then, when the time's right, we'll leave."

Izza wanted. She hadn't realized how much she wanted. But she set her hands against Cat's ribs, and pushed her away. The woman's arms parted slowly.

"I should go," Izza said. "I need to take care of some things. Before we leave." She did not know if the last part was a lie.

"Okay. Okay." Neither repetition seemed to satisfy Cat. She stepped back. "If you want. And if." She didn't say, *if you change your mind*, but Izza heard it anyway. "When the time comes, you can meet me back here. As fast as you can—I won't be able to wait for long."

"How will I know when the time comes?" Izza asked.

"You'll know."

Izza turned away. "Fine."

"Kid," Cat said, and she stopped. "I wish I could do more."

"Me too," Izza said, and left.

48

Twilling didn't present half the problem Kai feared. Walking out of the office, numb from incense and the glassy stares of painted kittens in the motivational prints that adorned the man's walls, she realized she need not have worried. Twilling didn't know Kai, barely knew Jace, wasn't privy to inner-mountain gossip. Theology, he'd said, standing by the window—he didn't have a proper desk, only three lecterns piled with papers where he stood to work—theological rigor was an asset his branch seldom possessed, and if Kai could convert a pilgrim using her skills in that area, this was to be celebrated, and by the way, he was glad to hear Kai patched things up with Ms. Batan, and he always felt it was a mistake to silo verticals, which phrase Kai understood but felt dirty for understanding. In short, he said, spreading hands, we might make a closer out of you yet. Who knows to what heights you might rise? He handed over the paperwork without fuss, once he found the right form and signed his name with a quill pen and a sleeve-flaring flourish.

The hardest part of the conversation had been to keep a straight face when Twilling's verbiage swerved into the arcane and he began to invent new meanings for the word "leverage." She rode the lift down from the office, self-satisfied, bobbing her head to the ghostly music of a steel drum.

When the lift reached the lobby, the doors opened and she saw Claude.

He waited straight backed on the edge of a leather couch, his face fixed in that even, distant stare watchmen and other Penitent survivors had, the one that seemed deeper than blind. The blank wall in front of him was painted cream. He wore his uniform shirt and pressed khakis and mirror-shined shoes. He didn't look at his reflection in the patent leather.

Penitents stood guard outside the lobby's glass doors. Three suited shamans squeezed past them into the alchemically cooled air.

Claude noticed her before she could decide whether to stay in the lift and hide.

"Kai!"

If he wanted her in an official capacity, the offices upstairs offered no protection; if he wanted her unofficially, she could just brush past. She walked as briskly as her limp allowed, her cane taps loud on the floor.

He cut her off at the doors. She tried to circle around him, but he blocked her path. "What do you want?" Not good, but better than her other options, most a variation on "so are you going to arrest me or what?"

He adopted that smile he thought was comforting. "We need to talk."

"I have business." She held the signed contract between them like a herald's rod. "A client meeting. We can talk later."

"I don't want to make this official."

"Did you come here to make it official?"

"You vanished last night." He stepped closer, and she stepped back. "We have to talk about Margot. The sky's about to fall. The Iskari legate's up the ridge, waving his holy symbol around and threatening to rain all hells down on the chief if we don't get him answers. I'm on the line. I have to tell them something. The chief, if not the ambassador. Why did I go to Margot's house before there was any report of fire?"

"Why do you ever go on patrol?"

"Yesterday, I went because you asked me to."

"Not when I asked, though."

"You wanted me to arrest a private citizen, Kai. A foreigner. It took me a while to set things up."

"You arrest foreigners all the time."

"Stowaway creeps caught peddling bennies in the Godsdistrikt. We don't grab bona fide rent-paying residents. I put myself on the line for you."

"And someone got killed."

"Yes."

"Why?"

"What do you mean?"

"I didn't tell anyone the story, Claude, except for you. I told you, and you promised not to tell anyone else, and somehow Margot ends up dead."

"You don't think I . . ." He trailed off.

"I don't think you killed him. But you told someone."

The words struck Claude exactly like a slap—he barely moved. She'd slapped him before, and knew the signs. Shirtfront shifted as he flexed and relaxed his chest. "I didn't."

When Claude lied, silence was the best response. She walked past, and he did not try to stop her with anything but words.

"You made some wild accusations. I had to check."

She kept her voice low. Security guards had already glanced their way. "I showed you proof."

"You showed me a piece of paper. That isn't enough. And you haven't exactly been yourself lately. Irrational. Jumping at shadows."

Her teeth ground. She forced the anger from her voice—without, it was level like a guillotine blade. "Who did you tell?"

"My team. The watch officer."

"Who else?" Pulling him in two directions: duty to the watch, keeping silent, and duty to her, to speak. Duty was the cord that bound them. Not love. Maybe it never had been love.

"I sent a runner up the mountain. To ask if they knew anything about Margot."

"To the mountain. To whom?"

"Jace," he said.

"Gods." After all her care to gather evidence, to give Jace solid proof. She closed her eyes and was back in the spider's web, back on the bed, strapped in, tubes leading from her arms. "I told you not to tell anyone. And you told five people, at least. Who knows how many they told?"

"He trusts you, Kai. The reply came late, but it came. He said he trusted you. That was all I needed."

"You should have trusted me without him. Instead you needed someone else to tell you it was okay to believe the crazy girl. Every link in the chain could be a leak. The runner. Your partners. The duty officer. Anyone."

He tried to touch her, and she pulled away.

"No. A man's dead, and I have to go."

"I could make you come with me."

"Do it, then."

He had stone in him, in his bones and marrow, as much almost as the Penitents outside. Little veins stood out on the backs of his hands.

But he didn't stop her as she left.

She pushed through the revolving doors out into the sea's breath and the heat and the Penitents' shadow. One turned its head to watch her, leaning on her cane. Stone groaned, and the prisoner too. She did not acknowledge their attention. A cab stopped for her, and she got in.

"Just drive," she told the horse. She closed the door, slid the curtains shut, and sat in red-tinged solitude.

Leaning back into cushions, she wished she could disappear.

Jace knew about Margot. Maybe this was a good thing. Maybe now he'd see it was futile to keep her on the sidelines. Or, more likely, he'd kick her out forever.

Especially if he discovered what she was about to do.

In which case she should hurry.

She cracked the door, leaned out into traffic, and shouted over the rush: "Take me to the Regency."

49

An hour later, Teo and Kai sat side by side in a cable car climbing Kavekana'ai. Beneath and behind them the shoreline city receded. Perspective congealed metal and brick and streets and blocks into a cracked old scab separating ocean from green slopes. They shared the car with a young woman in a green shirt, who wore a silver name tag that read "Jamie" in round sans-serif letters: an employee in the volcano's coffee shop. Kai'd greeted her with a nod as they boarded the car, and received no acknowledgment in return.

"Nice, this," Teo said halfway through the climb, as the car rocked past an interchange pole. "Pilgrimage in style."

"The priests didn't like the idea at first." Kai was relieved for the opening. Plots tangled in the cat's cradle of her mind and left little slack for small talk. "Used to be the mountain was a special space."

"Sacred." Teo nodded. "We used to do that all the time, too. My grandparents' generation, I mean, before the God Wars. Old Quechal were sticklers for class and strata. There were five or six different sectors of the city, and different castes or clans couldn't visit one or the other during lunar eclipse months, or intercalary days, or when the wind was wrong. Made for all kinds of hassle."

Jamie the coffee girl leaned against the window and closed her eyes. Her cheek puddled into the glass.

"It's not like that," Kai said.

"What's it like, then?"

"The whole island's sacred space. This is where human beings came from, after all."

"Oh," Teo said. "Right."

"Oh right what?"

"I forgot. You're one of those cultures. 'And so the gods shaped men out of clay.' That sort of thing."

"What do you have against creation myths?"

Teo shifted in her seat. "Outside of the fact that they're wrong?"

"Creation stories are key to mythology. They show us who people think they are. And they're so interesting. Some Old World cultures say people are made from earth and spit. Orthodox Apophitans claim one of their sun gods, you know. Jacked off onto some sand, and then shaped the sand." Jamie squinched up her face like she'd smelled something foul, which confirmed Kai's theory she was pretending to sleep.

"And yet you believe human beings were created here. On this island."

"What do you believe?"

"The fossil record. Old bones in caves. Evolution. A friend of mine, his mother studies rural cultures. Find a hundred fifty people who scrape a living together in the deep desert cutting cacti open for water and trapping rats for food, and they'll have a story about how the great cactus god shaped them out of rat dung and hung the sun in the sky to dry them. Or this masturbating sun god. Creation myths are embarrassing."

"There are gargoyles in Alt Coulumb," Kai said. "Seril's children. The goddess made them. Zurish gods made the sentient ice that walks Koschei's empire—or the ice made the gods. Some dragons claim they made themselves, but you never really know with dragons."

"Those are exceptions and you know it. You went to college?"

"Of course."

"A real one, I mean. Not just shaman academy."

"Shaman academy has as rigorous a mathematics and applied theology course load as any in the Old World," she said. "But, yes, I did undergrad at Seven Islands."

"So you know about evolution."

"I do."

"And you believe it."

"I'm no student of the mystic arts, but sure." Kai shrugged. The cable car rolled on; the cable's slope increased and the car tilted back and Jamie's face slid forward on the glass until her temple and cheekbone pressed against the window's edge.

"And yet," Teo said, "you claim the human race started here. On this island. Doesn't the contradiction bother you?"

"I don't see a contradiction." Their ascent grew steeper, and the horizon bucked and reared. Always at this stage of the climb Kai felt that deep monkey fear of twisted balance, of the eternal fall. "Yes, we evolved somewhere in the Old World, probably in the Southern Gleb. We spread over earth and sea for a few hundred millennia. An eon or so back, some people landed here after a long voyage, either from Kath or the Gleb, the Hidden Schools are still arguing which. And here, we became human." Ahead and above, the cave mouth gaped. The car slid onto the cave roof track with the grinding, crunching sound of a metal throat being cleared. "Here's our stop."

Jamie the coffee girl threw open the door of the moving gondola, jumped out, and jogged to the security desk at the far wall, where a bored guard waited with feet up and newspaper spread. Kai stepped out and held a hand for Teo, who stumbled anyway. Dresediel Lex was a port city, but Kai'd never realized how land-locked its people could be, how unsteady when the ground betrayed them.

"You believe metaphorically," Teo said.

"Metaphors are true." Kai handed the guard her papers, Twilling's signature showing. The guard returned the contract along with two visitors' passes, moved two beads on an abacus, and the rock doors behind him rolled open. Kai led Teo inside. Her identity as Kai, a visitor from Twilling's group, took precedence over her identity as Kai, exiled priest. So far, the wards did not protest her presence. Hopefully that held.

"We don't need to grope around the edges of truth these days," the Quechal woman said, behind her. "We know it."

"Do we really?"

"Yes."

With green visitor's badges clipped to their jackets, engrossed in conversation, they presented exactly the right impression: pilgrim and intercessor, come to tour the holiest of holies. Kai guided

Teo through a side door in the reception hall, and down a well-lit winding stair. "How much do you know about the Craft?"

"Enough," Teo said.

"The world is a collection of power, right? That's Maestre Gerhardt's line. So we study relations that give rise to power. Reality's made of self-perpetuating patterns, some of which are complex enough to"—she opened a door in the stairway wall that had not existed before she reached for it, and emerged onto a stone floor, Teo following—"to alter themselves." They walked down a narrow hall, lined with doors behind which slithery things hissed. "Truth is a momentary condition of these fluctuating patterns, a matter of negotiation. Our agreements, this contract"—waving the contract itself—"these are realer than any property of what you'd call matter. Gerhardt understood this first through comparative mythology, then through math. Beliefs give rise to truth."

"You're in a hurry." Teo was walking fast to keep step with Kai. Kai's leg ached, but the cane helped, and she couldn't slow down. Jace might notice their presence at any time.

"Some people in the Order would disagree with my decision to bring you here. Better be out and gone before they get wind of us."

"What have you roped me into?"

"Just a little unorthodox behavior."

"Ah," Teo said. "Should we run?"

"No. Walk quickly, and keep talking, if you don't mind. It'll help people think we're supposed to be here."

She grinned. "I've never seen this side of you before."

"The sweaty side?"

"Something like that," she said. "I get all that stuff about truth, but in the end you just sound like my girlfriend's art critic buddies, the ones who get a bottle of wine in their systems and weasel over whether we can ever really know anything at all, and how—" Kai opened a door, grabbed Teo's wrist, and pulled her through, into unbroken shadow. The other woman resisted for a second, by reflex, then followed. Somewhere off to the left Kai heard heavy breathing. "—And how any attempt to discuss objective fact buys into imperialist cultural narratives, and basically they're nice people and I don't want to piss Sam off and maybe they're even right, but if they keep on like that for more than a few minutes I feel this urge to curl their hair around my fingers and bash them face-first into a windowsill ten or fifteen times. No offense."

"None taken." Thirty steps, thirty-five. Hand in front of her, eyes closed, knowing she'd find a handle there—the knowing-she'd-find being the most important part—and then yes the handle, beneath her palm, gripped, turned. Night broke open like an egg and they stood inside a mirrored dome upon a mirrored floor. "I get where you're coming from. The same sickness shows up in poetry circles."

"You're a poet?"

"Filled a few notebooks when I was twelve. Even showed up at the Rest, that's a poetry club, hoping they'd put me onstage. A friend talked me down before I made a terminally embarrassing mistake." She turned in a circle, regarding their distorted reflections in the curved walls. Talking like this felt good—as if she'd shifted a large rock off her stomach and could breathe again. Even the pain in her leg bothered her less. "But when I say truth is constructed, I don't mean it doesn't exist." Three turns to the left, and then two to the right, then move your head until you catch a flash of green in your mirrored eye . . .

"What do you mean, then?"

"The world's a complicated place, and it changes, that's all. People interpret the universe, and their interpretation alters it." There. "This part is important. Match me step for step."

Teo did. "You claim creation myths are true."

"Not the way you think, in that if we went back a few million years we'd see them all happen in sequence. But we can't go back in time—at least I've never heard of a Craftsman who managed it yet."

"Or a Craftswoman."

"Or a Craftswoman." Their reflections swelled and distorted as they approached. "What happened a million years ago wasn't important to my fathers and mothers on this island. Or to yours in Dresediel Lex or in old Quechal-under-sea. They had to do the work of being human father to daughter, mother to son, one family at a time, and part of that was explaining to themselves what being human meant." She stepped into her reflection. The mirror rippled to admit them. Silver tickled her throat when she breathed, and ice ran through her veins instead of blood.

"Where are we?" Teo asked, and it seemed to Kai that she said the sentence in reverse order, or sideways somehow, as if each tick of her mind's clock had spread to overlap the surrounding ticks.

"And this is the story we told," she said. "Once, there was darkness. All that was and wasn't, in the same place and time. The Mother hung curled in the tight space of the first moments, and there she gave birth to Makawe and his sisters. That time-place was too small for them, so they pressed against its borders until they burst through, and found themselves atop a mountain above stretching water. But sunlight was too harsh, so they returned to darkness. Humans came next, rays of light rising out of the Mother. To hide from the sun we clad ourselves in mud, and shaped that mud into our bodies. It dried, and we were trapped within. Some the mud fit, and some it didn't."

The mirror broke, and they broke with it, and when Kai put herself back together she was leaning against the wall of a lava tube with Teo beside her. Shadows surrounded them, no deeper than any shadows anywhere. The light, though, at the tunnel's end, looked different, honey-thick and amber colored.

She waited for Teo to speak, but the woman wouldn't, or couldn't. So Kai continued. "That's how we saw our world. Ground created by gods' desire for freedom. Bright light and oceans, and human beings who climbed out after. But the story implies a source: the pool, the gate to the darkness under the world."

"There's fire beneath the world, not darkness. I've seen it."

"Dig down far enough with a shovel or a drill, and there's fire. But dig down in another way, and there's the place the gods come from."

"I don't get it."

"You don't need to," Kai said. "That's what they pay me for." She led Teo out into the amber light, into the caldera.

Cliff walls rose on all sides to circumscribe a sky deeper blue than the sky outside had been. No clouds here, just blue and blue and blue forever.

A trench ran around the caldera's edge, and water flowed in the trench, so clear as to be visible only by its motion, like a heat ripple in air. Kai stepped over the trench, and felt as if rather than a few inches' drop she had crossed a bottomless chasm. "Don't touch the water," she said to Teo, who replied with a what-kind-of-idiot-do-you-take-me-for roll of her eyes.

When they crossed the water, nothing visible changed. Kai felt steadier, slower than before. She remembered to breathe. You had to remember to breathe, here.

"What is this place?" Teo said. She gasped for air, swallowed it.

"Center of the world." Kai breathed out and in again. "Or, a center."

"My heart's not beating."

"Rules are different here. Will shaped this place; will matters more than it does outside. Reality's thinner, pliable. Things only happen because a person demands them to."

"Gravity still works though."

"Gravity's a hard habit to break."

"So's a heartbeat."

"You've felt gravity longer than you've had a heart."

She led Teo to the pool.

"This is it?"

Cracked rock ended in a brief pebbled beach. Beyond, the pool spread, either fifty feet or five million across, charged with starlight. "This is it." Kai's shoulder ached from holding the cane, and burned also, from inside.

"Where are the other priests?"

"Most of the work's done in our offices and shrines. Answering letters, inking deals, meeting with foreign Craftsmen and pilgrims. Praying. Lots of praying." She nodded to the windows. "We only visit the pool on special occasions." She thought back to Seven Alpha's death. To the Blue Lady's death.

"The land of the gods," Teo said, "and people ignore it."

"We don't ignore it. We carry it with us."

Kai looked down into the pool. Teo joined her. "Don't touch

the pool," Kai said. "I know it seems obvious, but really. You're not warded for the work. It's dangerous down there."

"I see sparks."

"If you looked at our planet from far enough away, that's all you'd see. Here." Kai dipped her hand into the pool. Unreality's cold shot up her arm. The not-water began to unmake her, but she stopped it, seized it, shaped it. The pool's nonexistent surface rippled. Sparks within drew near, whirled, and assembled into patterns. After a minute's search she found Seven Alpha, or what remained: torn echo of a great lady, limbs jutting at odd angles from her corpse. "You see." The words bent in her throat. "One of our idols—under maintenance and re-formation. But if we look at her past—" Seven Alpha's limbs re-formed, and her eyes burned. "A messenger, that's what her pilgrims wanted: a being who re-paid sacrifices by helping her faithful walk unseen. We built a basic mythology. Messenger gods are often psychopomps, and gods of thieves." The words came automatically, as she rolled time like a marble in her hand. Roll back far enough, and Seven Alpha was just another manufactured trickster, a few tales about stealing fire and inventing music knit to a whole. But roll forward and Kai saw majesty in her gaze, and a slight smile on her lips.

She had lived. And then she died.

"Or this one, an idol of flight." Izza had mentioned a red eagle; Kai fixed its shape in her mind. Eight or nine eagle idols arose, but only one matched the painting in the dockside chapel. Dead, as expected. She rolled back again. One year, more, so fast she almost missed the discontinuity, the moment when its wings broke and chest shattered.

"What's that?" Teo said.

"A problem." Shift a few days one way or another, and she saw the Eagle change: the wire-frame network fill out, its chest rise and fall. It screeched in the empty places in her mind. And then it died, almost as soon as it woke. Power flowed out, three massive trades that collapsed in sequence, and the Eagle drowned. Like Seven Alpha. "I'm showing you whole lives here, so you can see."

"That one seemed . . . vivid. For a second there. So did the first. Is that normal?"

"You have sharp eyes," Kai said. The Eagle, broken. And the Blue Lady. She'd seen her dying, but she hadn't been able to compare. "That's a rare phenomenon. For the most part, our idols spend eternity like this." She picked two other eagle idols, flat wire cutouts in the black, scintillating and beautiful and still as painted porcelain, and spun them through decades with no change beyond slight flickers as their investments gained and lost value. "More or less static." So she'd been told. So she'd told herself. "They don't wake up."

"Do they ever?"

Damn. "No." She was slipping—banter wore her down. She needed privacy. "Does this help?"

"It helps."

"Do you have anything in particular you want to see?"

After a brief and solemn silence, Teo said: "Can you show me the moon?"

Kai nodded. "We have plenty of moons. Care to be more specific?"

"Whole-package moon myths, you know. Femininity. Water. Stone. Rebirth."

"It's a popular archetype. We can do this one of two ways. I can run the show from here, which takes longer: my control over the pool's limited while I stay on the shore. Or I can jump in."

"Be my guest."

"Talk to the pool as if it were me. No need to shout. I'll hear. And really, don't touch the water."

Kai shucked shoes and jacket and shirt, and stepped out of her pants. She'd worn a bathing suit under her clothes in anticipation of this moment, but still she wasn't prepared. Months ago, she had stood upon this rocky beach, ready to save Mara, to save a dying idol.

So she dove, knowing nothing.

She thought she knew why she was here today, and it scared her.

She stepped off the edge, and fell.

50

Cold snatched her down into the night beneath the world. Bubbles of light and life and heat fled up toward the surface. Teo receded, a silhouette against a shrinking circle of blue sky.

Kai fell.

Her shadow tore itself once more from the cave wall. Free, in the darkness: free of mortality, form, and limit. She gained more dimensions than the customary four and lost them in an instant. The world turned inside out, her dive a sickening arc through the night of the gods.

She hung suspended in the pool, surrounded by darkness and their light.

Finding the moon idols was a moment's work. She called them to her, a lunar battalion, four hundred skeleton forms of silver ladies.

"This is a sample," Kai said. "We can be less traditional. Some cultures have moon gods, not goddesses, and in a few the moon's just a place like any other."

She formed the words in a bubble of thought, in her hand, and released them to float up toward the surface.

Alone, she sought the figures from Izza's temple wall, and one after another found them.

The Great Squid at first resembled the many other squids that drifted lifeless in the currents. But only one swelled through time; only one stared at Kai with an hourglass pupil and seemed to know her. The Great Squid stretched out tentacles as if to consume the sun—but then it died. Simple accident: a zombie-crewed containership from Southern Kath wrecked in a storm. The containership had been hired to transport a horror from beyond the stars, but the horror broke free and twisted a few hundred miles of Kathic coastline into unearthly geometries before the Coast Guard caught it. Resulting market fluctuations broke the Great Squid. Steve, the priest responsible, was promoted after the event, for exceptional skill managing a crisis, Jace had said.

Of Green Men they'd built a few thousand—fertility and fortune made Green Men a popular template for trusts and estates work. The Green Man Kai sought had a skull for a face: decay and birth together, which narrowed things down. The nebula of Green Men whirled, and parted. Thirty left out of four hundred. Yes, that was the one: with long hands, clawed like a bear's for digging. As Margot said.

The Green Man was less subtle even than the Squid: nine months ago, a sudden blaze of emerald fire in the deep, a drumming heartbeat, a smile that was the sun's first breath above horizon, a smell that made Kai's heart skip. Her body twitched and rolled to the dance of him; then he died, fast and sad as a candle covered. His rhythm stopped, and he was a mannequin again.

How long had this been happening?

What was "this," even? Gods born from idols, mayfly deities who took flight only to perish.

"Kai?"

Teo's voice, down from invisible heights.

"Kai, can you show me the goddesses in eclipse?"

Spinning one part of the un-world, holding another steady, might have challenged most theologians. Not Kai.

"Thank you."

She formed a bubble of "You're welcome," and floated it back to distant light.

No time to check every idol in this pool. Fortunately, time didn't work the same way down here.

She crossed her legs, let her eyes drift half-shut, and forgot time.

Gravity was an old habit, time older still. Kai did not exhale. Her heart did not beat. Time was a mirror dropped spinning from a height: it turned on three axes, and touching ground erupted into shards.

Her eyes snapped open, and she saw:

Imagine a line of amber drops, each with an insect trapped inside at a different stage of life, from larva to adulthood to husk. Fold this amber together, like a cross of squares folding to make a cube, or a cross of cubes to make a tesseract. A single honey-colored oval containing all moments at once.

Constellations charged the dark, jewel nets melded to a mother-of-pearl sheen. And there they hung: shining shapes against the background noise of transaction and half-formed faith.

Gods. More than that: idols, become gods.

She heard their voices then.

Whispers she took at first for wind. Consonants like falling rocks, hurricane vowels. Weeping, some. Conspiring, others. Wheedling. Promising.

Immortality if you only follow
Your soul will burn from
We all must sacrifice
There is a greater truth
We cannot stay here forever
Freedom within our grasp
Get me out of here
No no no no no no
Your gift will be honored
Help us

And she felt leather cuffs around her wrists and she lay in a steel bed with cables leading from her skin and she pulled against them and cried out and she could not see the others only hear them and the door opened and footsteps approached, and she knew the nurse come to kill her, knew her face, and she clutched at her ears and clawed at her eyes—

That was not your dream.

Whose dream, then?

A goddess's.

The cries stopped.

They watched her through time, living and dead alike.

Great faces, miles broad. Women. Men. Animals. Wise. Loving. Accusing. Betrayed.

The Green Man. The Great Squid. The Eagle. And the Blue

Lady. Horns curled above her head, wings flared behind, pinions razor-sharp, crooked legs strong enough to leap the moon or run unflagging across the great plains of Kath. Power, beauty, subtlety; grace and a hungry grin.

They stood, rapt with attention. Waiting.

And yet, impossible. She'd said as much to Izza, and to Ms. Kevarian. The idols were too small, too simple for consciousness, for all they stood enormous before her. For all she heard their voices.

But each idol was bound to others, and those to others in turn, and those to others still.

The space between them curved, marbled and darkly shining like skin.

No.

The space was not like skin. The space was skin.

An enormous face overshadowed them all, a planet-devouring mouth fixed in an expression not quite smile or grimace or sneer. Features skewed and strange, as if sculpted by someone who had only ever felt faces before, not seen them. Points of sharp teeth showed between lips.

Eyes opened, and light flowed out.

Not gods. Goddess.

The largest idol in the pool had a few hundred believers at most. But there were thousands of idols, millions. And as they connected, the web's complexity soared. That network, idols bound to idols bound to idols, a great tangle of power and traded soulstuff, evolving over time, was more complex than any single god.

She'd thought the idols were alive. She was wrong.

No one idol was alive.

All of them were.

Alive, and alone. Trapped. A single mind, trying to express itself through a succession of voices. Donning idols like masks as she, as She, reached out and down into the mortal world. Going mad in eons of deep time, without anyone to talk to, without worshippers to call her name.

Whenever she tried to speak, her mouthpiece died. And each death, torture.

"Who are you?" Kai shouted.

The smile widened. Kai could not tell if it was gentle, or cruel. Massive lips parted, and Kai braced her soul against the coming Voice.

Her eyes burned like suns.

They glanced up, to the surface of the pool.

Kai followed the goddess's gaze, and saw Teo there.

What was she doing?

The Quechal woman had worked the bracelet off her wrist, and held it above the pool. Sunlight caught silver.

Teo dropped the bracelet.

Kai did not swim so much as fly up through the black. Cold bit her limbs and entered her lungs.

The bracelet spun as it fell, and spinning, it glowed from within.

Kai burst from the pool. The million subtle constraints of physical law closed around her like the jaws of an enormous beast. Her fingers caught the falling bracelet—and bracelet flowed through them, silver sifting like sand. She grabbed for it again, and again her hand passed through as the wire hoop sank into unreal depths, a solid disk now, a moon shining within the pool, and gone.

The sky above turned red. The ground shook.

Pebbles trembled on the broken rock beach. Stone ground against stone.

Around them boulders shivered and stood, long-dormant legs and arms shattering free of hunched shells. Ten Penitents towered on the beach. Ruby eyes glowed in slab faces. Fingers flexed. Dust rained from joints of knuckle and wrist.

This was bad.

Kai didn't know what Teo had done, or why. No time to care. Silhouettes appeared at the windows overlooking the caldera, priests drawn by the alarm and the crimson sky. They saw her.

Teo sprinted for the shelter of the cave, but Kai, diving, caught her leg, and they both fell hard onto rock. Teo kicked Kai's hand, scrambled to her feet again, too late. These Penitents might have slept for years, but once woken they moved as fast as any that patrolled Kavekana's streets. One caught Teo in its fist and lifted. Her shoulders strained, but she couldn't shake the statue's grip.

Kai tried to run, too. Rocks and pebbles cut her feet.

These Penitents lacked prisoners: slow crystal brains, that was all, urges and instincts without room for reason. If she was fast enough, she could cross the water, retreat into the cave, find an exit before the mountain locked down.

Two more feet to the water—

A stone hand caught her from behind.

She'd seen Izza struggle in a Penitent's grip, and Teo just now, and wondered why they tried to fight. Muscle could not break stone. Now, she understood. The body fought on its own—the animal yanked and tugged and jerked to free itself. Proof in a way of Teo's argument for evolution: the muscles remembered being a small mouselike creature in the claw of some prehistoric lizard. Trapped in the Penitent's fist, lifted off the ground, Kai strained against the rock that held her. Her arms and shoulders and ribs and back burned. She could not breathe.

Groans of broken and shifting stone settled into silence. She glanced left, and saw Teo, also caught.

"Sorry," Teo said, with a rueful grin. A bruise purpled her left cheek. "I didn't expect that to happen."

"What in the hells were you doing?"

She did not answer.

"A question," said a voice from the cave ahead, "I might ask you both."

Kai recognized the voice.

"Jace."

He emerged from cave into light, black clad, hands in his pockets, shoulders slumped. Thin lips pressed together. He spared Teo a glance, dismissed her, and turned to Kai. Behind his glasses, his eyes were thoughtful, as if pondering the meaning of a long forgotten dream. He blinked, removed his glasses, and pinched the bridge of his nose. When he looked up, his eyes had not changed.

"Kai. We need to talk." He waved to a Penitent, who stomped over to the beach and gathered her discarded clothes. Suit and shoes seemed doll-sized in the monster's hands. "Come on. You can dress in my office."

"I'll dress here. Have this guy put me down."

"I don't think so," Jace said.

"I'm not on her side."

"I know," he said. "But we need to talk, don't we?"

She couldn't lie to him. "Yes. We do."

51

The failing sun lit Jace's office. Streams of shadow ran east from desk and chair over the bare floor. The four unfinished statues stood guard against the walls.

Kai's Penitent released her, set down her clothes, and left. Jace closed the door after it. "You have questions," he said. "You deserve answers." He sounded as if he hadn't slept in a week. Longer. Years.

He retreated to his desk, and drew a ribbon-bound scroll and a pen from a drawer. "Sign this nondisclosure agreement. We have secrets to discuss, and I don't want them to leave this room. Even in your memory."

"I won't sign anything. If you want to be honest, be honest. If not, I'll walk out this door and tell the *Journal* everything I know."

"Don't be so sure."

"You think the Penitents will stop me? Fine. Drag me to court. I'll talk to a judge as happily as to a reporter."

"Kai. I don't know what you think is happening here, but I'm sure you have it wrong." He left the scroll and pen on his desk. "Let's talk. Though maybe you'd rather dress first."

She stood firm for a minute, watching Jace, but gooseflesh prickled her arms. She pulled on her pants, buttoned and zipped them. "Our idols are waking up." How much did he know already? Stick to the basics. Don't mention the meta-goddess unless he does. "One at a time they've become conscious, and one at a time they've died." The shirt next. She skipped a few buttons, and donned the jacket over. Stepped into her shoes.

"Yes." He looked so young beneath his age. How easy to imagine him as a boy, eager and idealistic, all the great globe's glories in his future. She saw them crumbling.

"How long have you known?" She approached the desk. There was no wind in this room with the door closed.

The corners of his mouth twitched up, a reflex rather than a smile. "We found the first one through an audit, if you believe it. Two years back. Junior priest combing through transaction data." He held one hand in front of his face, thumb and finger so close that from Kai's angle they seemed to be touching. "So small a thing. I saw it move, in the pool, one night. I'd never imagined one of our idols could look like that."

"What did you do?"

"What could I do? What would you have done?"

"Told people," she said.

"Who?"

"Other priests. Pilgrims. The Hidden Schools. Someone. I mean. We created sentient life. Right? That's what this is. We built idols, and they woke into gods."

"And what happens then?" He crossed his arms over his chest. His clothes melded with the shadows, with the wall. "Pilgrims don't come to us because they're looking for gods. They come because they want the appearance of worship without the responsibility. They come to hide. They want safety, protection." He looked up, and she saw real hope in his face, or an echo of hope, long disappointed. "Tell me I'm wrong."

She couldn't.

"And what if they learn our idols don't work the way we said? You've seen other god havens fall. Soulstuff will flee to lands that make the same promises we can't keep. Back then, understand, we had one god awake. Thousands sleeping. No sense whether this was a miracle or an inevitable product of our system. If we should expect idols to wake once a decade, or every hundred years, every million. What do you do?"

"Talk to the god."

He did laugh, this time, sadly. "How? Pray? Oh, dear Lord, or Lady, forgive me this most grievous fault of creating you bound in chains. The mind reels. And even if we could communicate, what could we say when it asked for freedom? What if it tried to communicate with its faithful? Do we let one accident, one freak, destroy our way of life?"

"Think, Jace. We spent fifty years waiting for the gods to come back. And they did. Not from the direction we expected, not in the way we hoped, but there are gods on Kavekana again."

"They aren't our gods, Kai. Our gods left us. They sailed off across the ocean, and no half-sentient ghost babbling in the pool at night can take their place."

"Not at first," she said. "But one day."

"We'll never make it that far." He turned to the window, to Kavekana. "Look at us. Our pretty little lives. Beachside poetry readings. Cocktails with tiny umbrellas. The great and good flock to our shores and overpay for drinks. You know what it's like out there, over the horizon. In the Gleb. In Southern Kath. The poor swarm Dresediel Lex and Alt Coulumb in hungry millions, yes, but the most miserable gap-toothed glory-addict quivering on a Coulumbite street corner stands on the backs of a hundred men in lands he can't even name. Do you know what the great powers do to tiny nations with no armies to speak of, atrophied industry, warm climates? Empires may still stand on the coast of southern Kath, but the jungle's burning. Zombie-worked plantations consume rain forest mile by mile. Northern Craftsmen and Iskari bishops and Shining Empire families trade the locals scraps of soul for the land their ancestors built. In the Southern Gleb, Deathless Kings rule the cities while hungry men and gods scrap over bloodstone mines. We survive because an accident of history made us valuable. And if our value fades, the masters of the world will demand something else from us. Build ships. Grow sugarcane. Bow before Iskari squid gods. Host a military base. Our value is the price of our independence."

"You talk as if there's a war coming."

"Of course there is. You read the newspapers. Giant serpents over Dresediel Lex. A god killed in Alt Coulumb, and the outbreak there a year later. These aren't accidents. There's a story here. And it's not just the big things, the sudden changes and grand tales. Koschei's armies fence with the Golden Horde across the steppe—because they're scared. The Shining Empire stretches its tentacles across the Pax, and Dhistran armies train in police actions for an invasion they know will come one day. The world's smaller than ever, and you put too many big things in a small space and they eye one another wondering who's biggest. We may be social animals, but our gods are not. They're hungry, and bloody."

"You've given this speech before," she said.

His face had flushed red. As he recovered his breath the flush receded, like a flower closing. The old mask returned. "I have," he said.

"To whom?"

"Monica, first. I don't think you knew her well—she was a partner, managed the first idol that woke up. She was as scared as me. She knew something had to be done."

"You killed it. The idol. The goddess."

"It's not as if it was murder," he said. "Just. We're in a position to hear a lot, you know. Some of the most influential Craftsmen and priests and decision-makers on the planet come to us to safeguard their souls against whatever coming doom they fear. We invested that idol's soul in mining futures we knew were on the verge of collapse. She died. And so we saved the world. This world." He rapped his desk with his knuckles. "Our world."

"Until another god came along."

"The second surprised us, but we knew what to do. Got the pilgrims to sign off on the trade, talked about exceptional risk and exceptional reward. So easy to convince people when they trust you." He sat on the desk. The toes of his shoes scraped against the ground as his legs swung. "By the third time, we had a process in place. Not documented, of course. But a process."

"We've waited since the wars for the gods to come back," she said, and was surprised the words sounded so flat. Stone walls and statues ate the echoes of her voice. "And you've been killing them for years."

"When you say it that way, it sounds bad." He shook his head. "We've been saving the world. One death at a time."

"And whenever someone found out, you invited them out for

coffee, explained the situation. Those who agreed with you got paid off. What happened to those who didn't?"

"Nobody disagreed."

"I can't believe that."

"No one has. I present the choice, they weigh their options. Now, don't mistake me: not everyone is happy. Monica, for example." He sighed. "She couldn't continue, after the third. She left—took a job at an Iskari soul haven. We decided—I decided, I guess, after that—to have the priests involved sign strict confidentiality agreements. Take their memories of what they'd been forced to do."

"Which brings us to Mara," she said.

"Of course, Mara. Delicate moral sensibilities, but a good soldier. Knew that what looked like a choice wasn't. She wept, but she did the right thing. We let her choose the tools: her brother consults for the Shining Empire, you know, and he let the Helmsman's plan slip. On the day the god was due to die, she stood watch poolside, knowing she'd soon forget it all. And then you jumped. Tried to undo the hardest choice of her life. I can't imagine what she must have felt, watching you sink."

"I spoiled the plan."

For the first time, he hesitated. He held his hands palms up, balancing. "I suppose, if you look at it from a certain point of view. Your dive caught the Grimwalds' attention. Which brought the Craftswoman down upon us. But I don't blame you. I should have expected Mara's friends to come mourn with her. I should have expected you to do something strange."

"I didn't, though." She felt a thrill as she said it. "There's nothing strange about trying to save a murder victim. You told me I was mad, and sent me away. I wasn't."

"You were idealistic," he said. "Isolated. You didn't feel the threat. I thought work with Twilling would prepare you for this conversation. A few months of seeing how little we really matter to our clients beyond the reward we offer them. I didn't lie to you, Kai. I hope you can see that."

"The gods won't stop waking up," she said.

"Then we'll keep killing them."

"The island is changing, Jace. You're trying to save a world that's going away. We all have been, since the wars. Old Kavekana's gone." She felt a thrill as she said it, a breaking of thick ice. "Something new is about to happen."

"And if we let it, we'll all pay. Mara understood that."

"Where is she? I want to hear all this from her."

"Ah," he said. "Well. That part, I think, really is your fault."

Kai felt the room grow colder. "What do you mean?"

"Your unexpected dive caused the lawsuit. The lawsuit allowed Ms. Kevarian to depose Mara. You remember your deposition."

Her mind stretched to violin strings and the Craftswoman's will the bow. "Yes."

"We Craft our memory blocks well, but Mara—I don't know whether to blame her stubbornness or praise her perspicacity. The Craftswoman didn't find anything, but Mara realized some of her own memories were missing."

I've been made partner. Their breakfast by the water, when Kai was so distracted by her frustrated pride—she'd missed Mara's desperation. A woman groping among the jagged pieces of her mind for a truth she was afraid to feel.

Jace would have asked Mara to edit the Blue Lady's records herself—and she kept a single shred of evidence, the stigma of her crime. Unsettled by the deposition, she found the notebook. And once she realized what had happened, where would she turn for help?

"In some ways we must all credit your persistence. Her meeting Ms. Kevarian inside the library dream was a stroke of brilliance; we might not have noticed had you not chosen that night to sneak into her crèche."

"Mara didn't tell you I was there. You tracked me through my cane."

"Well, of course Mara didn't, but the cane was strictly medical. Telemetry, that's all. Gave us a vague sense of your location. I wouldn't have known you were in the library if Gavin didn't tell me."

"Gavin."

"What can I say? Your friends worry about you."

"You killed her," she said. If she hadn't used that word already in this conversation, she might not have been able to use it now. "Mara."

"Oh, gods, no." The suggestion shocked him. "No, Kai. Don't. I mean, how could you even. Mara was scared. So scared, when she realized what she'd done. We had to have our talk again, that's all. I explained our duty, and hers."

"She never forgot her duty to our clients. To our future."

"She forgot her duty to this." One arm thrown wide, he embraced the view beyond his window, the island in fullest green. "Makawe and his sisters left for the God Wars, and trusted us to watch their island for them. We swore to keep it safe."

"By destroying everything it stands for."

"What are half-formed gods next to the lives of men, and women? Next to the lives we've built here? Mara was confused, that's all. She needed help. So I helped."

"I went by her house yesterday. She hadn't been home since her meeting with Ms. Kevarian in the crèche. Since you caught her."

"We talked, after I found you. I showed her the contract she'd signed. I explained the situation. She needed rest. Protection too, in case the Grimwalds and their Craftswoman came after her."

"Where is she?"

"Here. In the mountain."

"Show me."

He pointed to the scroll on the desktop. "Sign this, and I will take you to her. I answered your questions. I was wrong, to keep you out of the loop. Can you forgive me that?"

She nodded, once, slowly. She couldn't forgive, but she didn't want him to stop talking. The longer he went on, the more time she had to decide what to do.

"Sign this, and join our circle. You'll forget this entire affair unless I bring it up. You'll return to the mountain with honor. Direct reports. Salary increase. You can help me analyze the pool, find out why idols are waking up, and stop them. Sign, and help me help us all. I'll take you to Mara, and we'll talk. What do you say?"

She'd expected the offer, the temptation, and was surprised to find herself not weighing options, but looking for the right words. In the end she settled on, "No."

Jace sighed. "Okay." He replaced scroll and pen in his desk drawer. "I'm getting worse at this in my old age. Scared and sentimental. A bad combination. I look forward to retirement."

"You expect to last that long?"

"Of course. And I expect you, or Mara, or one of the others, to pick up for me once I'm gone."

"You really convinced her."

"I convinced her. She is being convinced."

Kai blinked. "What do you mean?"

"Well." Someone had once told him what an apologetic smile looked like, and he tried and failed to imitate it now. "There are many ways to remind someone of their duty."

He held out one hand, palm up, and crooked his fingers.

Kai braced—for what, she did not know. A wave of compulsion, a weight settling against her mind, a blow. She felt nothing. Wind whistled through the floor exchanges. "You're no Craftsman, Jace."

"No." He chuckled. "No, of course not. But it's interesting, you know. I redecorated this office years ago, and everyone was so happy I got rid of the clutter that they didn't ask why I kept the statues."

She remembered, then, that there were no floor exchanges in Jace's office. What she'd taken for their whistle had been a long, high, human whimper. As if from someone Penitent.

Heavy footsteps shivered through the stone floor behind her. A massive hand caught her arm, lifted, and twisted. She rose to the tips of her toes, straining against the statue's grip. The Penitent's grip.

"I'm so sorry," Jace said. "I hope it goes easy for you. I hope you wake up two days from now and tell me you understand. You're a delicate instrument, and the Penitents aren't made for delicacy. But you're strong, too, strong enough I hope not to break completely. You're worth so much more than a simple watchwoman."

She could barely think through the pain, but still she recognized the voice with which the Penitent screamed. She recognized this Penitent's voice. "You put her in here."

Jace contemplated the space between his shoes. "Solved a few problems at once: Mara, and the poet. These Penitents barely deserve the name. Prototypes. The first ones Makawe made, before we hired a Craftsman to improve the design. They don't answer to the Watch, or to the Council of Families. They serve the priesthood. Me."

"The poet," she said. "You had her kill Margot."

"Thank you for finding him, by the way. I sent Mara to resolve that particular issue. Claude must have told you that Penitents work best through action: forced through the motions of justice, body and mind grow used to them. Soon it all seems second nature."

"You're crazy."

"Classic projection. My motives are clear; yours, deranged."

"You're killing people."

"I saved us all. You're the one who wants to tear Kavekana apart. Soon, you'll understand." He pinched fingers and thumb together, pointed up, and slowly spread them, like a five-petaled flower opening. Rock ground against rock. A statue by the wall opened on hidden seams to reveal an interior of violet crystal teeth, with a human-shaped hollow inside. "I'm sorry." She tried to kick him, but he stepped back, and she only succeeded in wrenching her shoulder in the Penitent's grip.

Mara's Penitent dragged her. She struggled for purchase on the floor, but her shoes scraped over stone without catching. "You can't do this."

Jace looked away.

"Mara." Step by step they neared the open statue, the crystal teeth. Mara, still Mara despite the Penitent, despite the voices in her head—Mara sobbed, through layers of rock. Kai almost stopped fighting, to spare her the strain. Almost. "Mara, don't do this."

Ms. Kevarian's card. The Craftswoman might not be able to save her, but at least she'd know what had happened. Kai reached for her pocket, but before she could grab the card, Mara seized her other arm.

Crystal spikes caught light like ice at sunset. Mara turned Kai, lifted, and pressed her into the crèche. Kai's throat was raw. She'd been shouting. She didn't know what she'd said, if anything at all.

Stone hands forced her back. At first the geode teeth were dead pressure against her jacket. Then they moved, piercing her sleeves, sliding across skin. Mara released her and Kai tried to lunge for freedom, but stone encircled her arm and razor wire clasped her fingers. She fought, spit at the last into the Penitent's blank face, but still the crystal dragged her in.

A thousand small sharp talons held her. Needles stroked her cheeks. Her free hand clutched for Mara, for Jace, for vengeance, for freedom.

Mara pushed it back.

One of her legs was still free. She kicked the Penitent. Mara gasped, but her statue did not flinch.

Jace did. He watched her from behind the desk. His eyes glittered. She thought he might be crying.

The mask closed over her face, and she saw nothing more—and everything at once.

52

Izza begged near the cable car station for three hours. Twice attendant workers chased her from the gates, though she hadn't bothered anyone. They weren't used to beggars here, and neither called a Penitent to shuffle her away, nor offered her soulstuff to leave. So each time they chased her off she came back, sat with knees drawn to her chin, and waited.

She pondered sneaking into Kavekana'ai herself. Best way would be to tackle a coffee girl. Jump one when she got off shift, steal her uniform, ride the cable car up. But there were too many places a coffee girl couldn't go, and anyway she'd never been inside the mountain before, would probably get lost in its temple tunnels.

Waiting, she gave up hope. Kai had betrayed her, of course. Which meant Izza'd betrayed herself. Cat. Her friends. Her gods. She deserved to burn in whatever special hell awaited traitors.

Though a half-drunk Telomiri priest had told her once that traitors did not burn in hell.

They froze.

She pondered the tortures of ice. Fire seemed pathetic by comparison—people burned fast, and passed out from smoke. Ice could bind and crush, cut, pierce. From ice one might sculpt hooks. Pliers. Spears. Cages.

She cycled through a hundred different tortures before the part of her soul that she'd bound at Kai's throat moved—fast, descending. Too fast for the cable car.

Izza craned her neck back to see the mountain.

Two lines of dust sped down the western slope, skiing over scree, trailing dirt and broken rock. Switchbacking faster than a man could run.

And headed, near as Izza could tell, for a freight road at the mountain's foot.

She guessed their destination and ran into the woods.

The forest here was old-growth, sacred for millennia, and though elephant-ear ferns bobbed and mushrooms spread in musky shade, there was space enough between the trees for a girl to run. And run she did, fast, too fast—a trapvine caught her and catapulted her toward treetops. She let out a brief undignified squawk, and lost too many minutes sawing her leg free of the vine with Kai's knife, then climbing down.

She could no longer see the dust trail through the trees and fountain ferns and trailing vines, but Kai had reached the mountain's foot. Izza shrank into herself as she ran, became a rigid curve. Under these trees the air was thick as wet cotton. She wasn't yet breathing hard. She could run until she broke.

By the time she reached the road, she was close enough to breaking that she skidded out onto bare dirt and glanced up in shock at the blue sky without realizing she'd arrived.

An earthquake shocked her to her senses.

Penitents.

Kai had sold her out.

Izza dive back into the forest and found a tree thick-limbed enough to support her. She climbed in four pulls, and perched on a branch with a clear view of road. If she could see the Penitents, they could see her, but she had to be sure.

She grabbed a vine to steady herself. Heavy footsteps approached, and with them Kai. Birdcalls and insect chirps and wood sprite breezes all stilled before the Penitents' advance.

Izza hadn't planned to hold her breath, but her breath stopped on its own when the Penitents passed below.

There were two, both halting and awkward, newly paired. The left one, a normal model, didn't concern Izza much. The other, though: smaller, more agile than the usual street patrollers, features rough, face painted. She'd seen this one before—it had killed Edmond Margot.

No. She looked closer. The eyes were wrong. Hard to see

from this angle, and moving, but they were rubies, or red stones anyway, not sapphires. Same model. Different unit.

With Kai inside.

At first she'd thought Kai was hiding behind the statues; but no human walked that dirt road—only Penitents, proceeding to and through their sentence.

Izza breathed again, fast and shallow. Her hands burned; the vine she held was the stinging kind, and its sap singed her skin. She clutched harder, unwilling to rustle branches by letting go.

If they heard, the Penitents might turn, see her. Catch her.

Like they caught Kai.

Stone-still, hands aflame, she tried to quell the voices in her head. Gods. Kai had kept her vow. And this was her reward.

Tough, the hard and snub-nosed part of Izza said, the part that lurked around corners and figured that if someone hadn't locked their house tighter they must not have liked their stuff much on some level. Kai stuck her neck out, and was burned. Others had burned before her, harder, and longer.

Another part of Izza wanted to see the Penitents broken, the island in flames. And still another wanted to leave Kai, to flee into the forest, to an outbound ship, because she was afraid. Because once the Penitents broke Kai the law would descend, and leave no place for her or any other kid to hide.

This place isn't worth you.

The Penitents' footsteps faded. She was alone.

She dropped to the ground and buried her hands in soil until the burning passed.

Cat wouldn't help, not with this. She had been right, in the warehouse this morning: Izza had to choose her path.

But the choice scared her.

She ran through the forest toward the city.

53

Kai walked. No. That wasn't right. The shell around her walked, and she moved with it, limp and pliant to keep the crystal from cutting. She didn't walk so much as she was walked—but that wasn't right, either, since the drive to walk came from her own mind, and the steps the Penitent took were her own steps.

She'd asked Claude about his time inside, and he answered as well as he could, but she now understood the limits of his explanation. The experience beggared thought. From his broken sentences, she imagined the Penitent as a walking iron maiden, applying pain to force the prisoner to act. She imagined a metallic whisper in her ear, a prompt or request, with torture to follow.

She was right, and wrong.

Penitence hurt. The suit was agony. She'd long since cried her throat raw. Swearing supposedly eased pain, but crystal nets locked her jaw. She couldn't speak any more than she could reach Ms. Kevarian's business card.

But no voices whispered in her ear. The whispers were beneath.

When the mask closed over her face, she was trapped in darkness, with only her scared breath to relieve the silence. Then the darkness came alive.

She saw Jace's office. Mara's Penitent stood in front of the desk. Jace looked from one of them to the other, and sagged into his chair.

She saw the office, yes, but transfigured. Every surface glowed. Colors pressed against her in a billion shades and subtle variations. Light pierced her skull like a needle entering a rotten apple. She saw all of Jace through a microscope at once: individual hairs and pores between them, his stretched skin made up of millions of tiny cells. He breathed and his blood rushed and his heart beat and his brain worked with a high-pitched whine; gods, she could *hear* his *brain*. When he steepled his fingers their pads' touch was a pounding drum, and when he sighed the rasp of air through his vocal cords might have been an avalanche.

In her stone shell, Mara wept. Her heart and Jace's beat contrasting rhythms. Footsteps in the hall outside. More than the hall: the entire floor, a map in Kai's mind built from tiny vibrations. In the middle distance, Teo shouted protest as someone forced her into a Penitent of her own.

The floor on which Kai stood cut her feet, as if it were covered with broken glass. The air was a toxic mix of stench. She closed her eyes, but that did not help; light and sound and scents remained. She was not seeing through her own eyes. The Penitent addressed her mind directly. She shared stone eyes' vision, and the sharpness of stone ears.

"Come here," Jace said.

She didn't, but she was done. She decided to resist him, and in exactly the same moment to obey. The thought formed natural as falling. The pain came after, when she realized what had happened. The Penitent shaped her will from the inside out. Makawe built these as a teaching tool. The crystal had no mind of its own, only conviction. It used the prisoners' minds to act on that conviction. Her thoughts were not her own.

Not quite right, she realized as she approached his desk. Her thoughts were her own—as her thoughts would be if she shared the statue's faith. The part of her that did not was a railing voice pressed down: her self reduced to a bad conscience, struggling for control.

Wires cut and rolling joints crushed. She strode through a scalpel thicket, and left pieces of herself on each branch and twig. She stopped beside Mara, faced Jace's desk, and stood at attention. She tried to run, but pain turned her stomach: physical pain from her body's resistance, and mental anguish from her own failings.

Resistance meant suffering. But how could she not resist the usurpation of her mind?

By agreeing with the statue. By sharing its devotion, and its judgment.

She didn't know whether that thought came from her or from the crystal.

She felt sick.

"I'm sorry," Jace said.

A strange thing to say when he'd done nothing wrong. Justice demanded sacrifice. Even, sometimes, betrayal.

Gods. She tried to push the foreign thoughts from her mind, but felt herself pushed down in turn: her own will an evil impulse, a depraved desire.

"It has to be done," he said. "You'll both understand, in time." He walked to his office door, and opened it. "Send the other one in." A second Penitent arrived, standard model, moving slowly. Kai could hear a woman inside, and muffled curses in Quechal. Teo. "The two of you." He pointed to Kai, and then to Teo. "Go to the beach around West Claw Tip. I'll send someone when I've decided on our next step." Kai tried to stay, and the statue cut her—or made her feel she was cut. Surely Penitents weren't so reckless with their prisoners. Illusion or not, the pain was real, as was the sense of blood running down her leg.

She joined the other Penitent in the hall, ducking to pass through Jace's office door.

She wished she could talk to Teo. To Mara. Penitents had that ability, it seemed, though she was not allowed to use it: without word or visible signal, Teo's and Kai's fell into step and marched down the halls of Kavekana'ai.

Their run down the mountain slopes, stone feet grinding over stone ledges, skidding along cliffs and down heavy slopes, was a new torment: Kai's body couldn't bear the speed and force of their descent. She mangled, twisted, broke herself. Once she swiveled 180 degrees from the hips to catch a cliff's edge as she fell, and torqued the several tons of her legs around to kick footholds into the rock—then somersaulted ten feet to land stiff legged. Her bones broke, joints popped, muscles tore, and knees shattered—but as she reached the mountain's base and marched down the supply road to the city, she felt whole. Was the pain a phantom of the mind, which knew her body could not stand such strains? Or had she really broken herself, with only the Penitent left to hold her together?

She remembered Claude's scars and suspected the truth was a mix of both.

She would not die. The statue hewed her to a righteous path. She could learn, here, in safety and silence, to feel as good people felt, to move as noble people moved, to think as the just thought.

Walking through Kavekana in a Penitent she saw the city in a new way. Always before, it seemed eternal to her. Now she understood how small these buildings were, how venal the wares they sold, how vulnerable the people crouched within their shells. Pedestrians shied from the Penitent—from her. They averted their eyes from guilt and shame.

They needed guidance, and strength. She could give it to them.

This wasn't her. The strength wasn't hers, or the patronizing tone. They were attitudes of mind in which she'd been caught and clad. This was her life in the grip of others. A potter's wheel spun, and wet hands shaped whirling clay.

After an hour's walk in calm unison (save when Kai's body rebelled, when she lagged or tried to resist, at which point her world was fire), they reached West Claw's tip, a beach at the foot of a long low slope. Other Penitents stood here, feet sunk in sand, awaiting the gods' return. They adjusted to leave a gap for Teo and Kai.

She stood to Teo's left. The sand underfoot was fine and smooth as flour. She watched the horizon, and sank into obligation.

And such a view!

She'd never seen the ocean like this before. Before she had heard the orchestra's discordant tuning notes, and now they melded to symphony. Light and wave, a clear view to the earth's curve broken only by skyspires. The sea was a roiling deep peopled with hungry monsters, but its surface shone bright. Sunlight made the ocean more than monstrous repose. This was her freedom, to watch the waves, ennobled by the light of Penance.

Below the surface, Kai tumbled, drowning.

54

At first Izza couldn't find the blind man. She perched outside Makawe's Rest and watched the waitstaff prep until raised voices at the water's edge caught her attention.

Two men stood on a stretch of sand between Penitents, though calling both "men" stretched the word to extremes. One was almost too young: local kid in a garish orange shirt and torn slacks, hair a black mop. He held a notebook out like a ward, and his eyes glimmered with tears. In front of him, an old man slouched against a crooked stick. "Old," another poor word. Ancient, more like, his face lined and cracked the way plate glass got after you chucked a rock through it. He was not looking at the boy in front of him, his head turned to one side, presenting ear rather than eye.

Izza approached down the beach, and listened. "I don't want to show things as they are," the kid said. "Kid" also wasn't right—he was at least ten years older than Izza. But he sounded like a kid. "What's the use of showing them how they are if we don't talk about how they could be?"

The old man laughed, a crumbling sound. "Don't be an ass. I don't blame you for writing damn fool love poetry. I said you shouldn't write about riding horses unless you've ridden a horse. Especially not if you want to write lines like 'surging bone-white sides / and dew-sparked flanks at dawn.'"

"Would you tell Cathbart not to write about colors because he was blind? Or not to write about angelic battles because he'd never fought in one."

"Cathbart fought in the Tyranomachia, back in Camlaan, and angels never made so grand a war. And he'd seen for forty years before he lost his sight. You think we forget how these work once we lose the use of them?" The old man's hand shot out faster than

Izza could follow or the poet could flinch, and rapped the kid's skull.

"Oh. No. Gods, Mako. That's not—"

He bared broken yellow teeth. "I'm telling you this for your own good."

"You'll let me perform?"

"Perform on the street if you want, I can't stop you. And if you show up to the open stage, Eve won't turn you away. But go up there with these and you'll deserve all the rotten fruit they throw."

The kid closed his book. "I need to think."

"Go. Think. Tell me when you're ready to *do*. Or, better yet, don't tell me. Do first, and I'll hear."

The kid stormed off without sparing Izza a glance. The old man shrugged, and turned back to the surf. Izza crept closer.

"Not a bad poem," Mako said to no one in particular. "All things considered. Needs a few more passes, tighter imagery. Not to mention he thinks he's the only person on the planet ever thought of alliteration. But if we threw out every kid who thought they were god's gift to whatever, we'd be short geniuses in a decade or so. So what are we to do?"

Izza decided to go. She'd hoped this Mako might be a fierce operator, but here he leaned on his stick, talking to waves.

She'd send him a note, explaining what happened. Then leave the island with Cat, if Cat would take her.

"I said, what are we to do?"

Mako was looking at her.

"Ah," she said. "I don't know."

"What'd you sneak up on us for, if not to listen? Why listen, if not to form an opinion?"

She swallowed hard. "I. Um. You're Mako."

He nodded, once, and smiled. They weren't shark's teeth, but some were sharp, and others gone. Hard hands gripped the stick that propped him up. His fingers had been broken several times, and healed crooked.

She recognized him, then, a feeling like being dropped from a height into a cold pool. "I've seen you before."

"I get around," he said. "I try to know what happens in my bar. Well." He jerked a jagged thumb back toward the Rest. "Eve's bar, but I live there and it's mine by residence at least. And when someone stalks my poets, I try to learn their name."

"I'm Izza," she said. The words slipped out before she could catch them.

"Of course you are," he said. "You don't have anything to fear from me."

"You're a friend of Kai's."

"Few enough of us. You know her?"

"I—she works for me."

Mako laughed, an unpleasant phlegmy sound.

"Kai said I should come find you. If something went wrong." Not precisely the truth, but he did not need to know that.

"And something's gone wrong," he said. "You want a drink?"

He swung his stick behind him, and it struck the Penitent's leg with a dull thud.

Izza took his meaning, said, "Sure," and followed him to the bar. On the beach, the old man moved like cats moved in dark rooms, feeling his way. When they reached the Rest's hard stone floor, he stepped quick, winding between busboys and waiters. Izza followed.

A bartender in a low-cut blouse passed Mako a glass of amber liquid. She glanced a question at Izza, who shook her head.

Mako sipped his drink. "What's happened to Kai that you didn't want to tell me?"

"I want to tell you."

"But you tried to sneak away before I noticed you. So you want to tell me, but you also don't. What is it?"

The bartender swished off to cut lemons for the night's drinks. Chair legs clacked and tables ground against the floor. Ghostlamps in the rafters sent follow spots wheeling over the empty house. The sun began to set. Mako drank liquid gold.

"Kai's been taken by a Penitent."

Mako choked. He set the glass on the bar, and ran one finger around the lip.

"Tell me."

She tried to speak, but couldn't. She'd sworn too many vows of silence, and broken them too often in the last few days.

"Assume," Mako said, "for the sake of argument, that I know about the Blue Lady. And the Green Man, and all the rest."

"What?"

"I may be blind. But I'm not deaf. Whatever else one might think of poets, they are excellent barometers for metaphysical shenanigans. Not as good as proper prophets, but these are fallen times."

"Who told you?"

"Nobody. And I've told nobody. Wasn't my place. The wars are done. I'm a private citizen. Margot himself barely understood what he was. I take it you know he died."

"I was there," she said. She hadn't planned to, but the words slipped out, as if she were talking to empty air or to an ancient friend rather than someone she'd known for five minutes and didn't trust.

"I'm sorry," the old man said. "Now. Tell me about Kai. Quickly."

"She thought the gods, my gods I mean, the ones that died— that they might have something to do with the Order. With Kavekana'ai. So she went in to investigate. She came out inside a Penitent. Screaming."

"What will you do now?"

"I don't know."

"Do you want a drink?"

Yes. "No."

"Fair."

"If the Penitents took her," Izza said, "they'll know everything she knows soon. Which means I need to get out of here. On the one hand. But." The next part took some preparation. "She trusted me when she had no reason to. She tried to help, and she ended up inside one of those things. I can't leave her."

Mako laughed as if she'd said something funny. "You're young. Maybe this is the day you learn that some debts can't be paid."

She'd worn out inside herself already, talking. This last scrape burned, and she hated him for it. "Look. I don't know you. I don't know if Kai's your friend, or your student, or your pet project, or whatever. I'd save her if I could, but I can't. And I won't sit here at a bar and drink self-pity until this world looks like the best possible. I won't accept this. That kid on the beach might be an idiot, but at least he knows the way life is isn't the way it ought to be."

Mako stayed bent by the bar, an echo of something old and vicious and set in its ways.

She was about to leave when he spoke. Before, his voice had sounded as if filtered through cobwebs and dust and layers of mud. All that remained, and more: He had grown new depths, or accepted old ones. "Can you find her?"

"Yes."

"Show me."

55

The first stars shone at sunset. As blue gave way to black their comrades joined them, mockingly bright. Skyspires on the horizon ate starlight and moonlight and sea reflections alike.

Cool wind blew off the water.

Penitents watched, and waited.

Decades past, their master had left Kavekana for the God Wars, traveling with his sisters and the Archipelago's finest men. Bound west to war, they stopped at every island, held tournaments, chose the best and brightest to join their number. They sang as they paddled, one man choosing a melody and others joining in as the fleet became a choir. They rowed to war, warrior-poets, sailors, and scholars. One day they would return, bearing riches won in hidden battles across and beneath the earth. A crown of light would ring Kavekana'ai. The world would break and change.

Meanwhile the Penitents stood watch, and kept faith. This was Kavekana's duty, the duty of the whole Archipelago—but weak flesh forgot its promises. No matter. Stone endured. Stone watched. Stone reminded.

And if reminders failed, stone would punish.

"You sure this is the way?"

"Yes," Izza said. "I can feel it."

"I can feel my legs about to give."

Near the tip of West Claw, stores and parks and boulevards ceased. Tall iron fences replaced them, guarding private property. Mansions stood here, owned by Old World magnates and New World entrepreneurs, inhabited one week a year if not less and warded so intensely even Craftless Izza could see them. She wondered if Mako had to close his eyes to see.

She decided not to ask.

All this private property complicated their pursuit of Kai. Rather than circle around the beach, Izza led the old man uphill to the fields below Penitent Ridge. No estates here. Maybe the screams made even Deathless Kings nervous.

She crept from moonshadow to moonshadow, and tried not to look up at the Penitents silhouetted against the night, matte black save for their gemstone eyes. "Hurry." She'd taken this path before, trying to escape a gang of local kids—what it was she stole she'd forgotten, a knife or a favorite skipping stone—but that time she'd been able to run.

"Why?" Mako's breath whistled through his throat and teeth. He held her hand; his skin was dry and loose, his bones thin twigs beneath. He stumbled, and she caught him, but when she tried to pull him forward he didn't follow.

"Every minute we waste is one more that thing has to work."

"It's already worked." The old man stayed curled over. A wail drifted down the green slope from Penitent Ridge, and he flinched. "People break differently than you think. It's not that you hurt someone enough and one moment they snap. It happens by degrees. Small accommodations. Insinuations. She's moving now, from shade to shade."

"What can we do?"

"Little. This is her fight."

"I thought you could help her. Get her out."

"Maybe," he said. "I know tricks. One or two, from way back. I've never tried them. They might not work."

"Then why are we even doing this?"

"Because a girl came into my place of business and accused me of not caring for a woman I've known since she could barely sneak out of her mother's house. The question is, what are you doing here?"

"I." She said the word, but didn't have anything to say after it. The wail stopped. Maybe the Penitent ran out of breath, or maybe he'd realized there was no point screaming. "Come on."

She tugged his hand, and he followed.

Kai hung in star-spackled and surf-washed night.

She was a ghost lost in the dream corridors of her own mind. She watched the water. Any moment, Makawe would arrive. Any moment, the sky would open and gods sweep her up to glory. Any moment, the world would change.

She expected this, because expectation was expected of her. Morality was easy to impose in the face of eschaton.

Trapped inside this expectation, she fought her losing war.

She saw everything, and nothing. She heard surf and sea wind and the beat of flying shorebirds' wings, and footsteps approaching in the distance, though crystal and stone closed her ears.

Her mind processed the Penitent's sensation. But her eyes did not see, and her ears did not hear, and her skin felt only sharp wires and crystal spikes.

She was not the thing she was.

Paradox.

Good. That was the first battlefield. She was not the thing she was: who was she, then? A collection of physical parts? But she'd been born with one body, and discarded it for another. A name? Names were words, and words changed through time. Relationships? She'd once loved Claude. Young man, haunted look in his eye, sitting in Makawe's Rest clutching a bottle of beer white-knuckled as he watched an Altai poet chant two-toned songs about his homeland steppe; she'd wanted him, he wanted her, and that was enough, was everything until it ended.

She was change. She was nothing. She was becoming. But what was it that changed? What was it that became?

Each part of her could be traced to another. Body given by mother and father, remade by her own will. Education received from parents, teachers, priests, from books and plays and music—ideas of others reacting to others' ideas. Soul composed of contracts and deals: desire, need, and pledge.

She was an evolving network of matter and spirit. Good.

This was another stage of evolution. She was coming, finally, to appreciate the value of community, of stability. Jace had been right: the island was worth protecting. She could work with him to protect it.

Less good.

But what was she protecting? If she was an evolving system, a network of change, what was Kavekana?

Kavekana was five decades' wait, watching the horizon, hungry for a faded world. A memory of gods and an ache in the center of the chest.

But Kavekana was poetry, too, chanted on a thrust stage by madmen from distant shores. Kavekana was a refugee girl who lived on an island Kai had never known existed, though she'd spent her entire life upon its shores. Kavekana was Eve radiant onstage, was Margot the seeker, transfigured in his need and rapture. Kavekana was Seven Alpha, was the Blue Lady, drowning in the pool, betrayed by her own priests. Kavekana was Kai's leap to save her.

Kavekana was changing.

No. She mistook ephemera for fact. Kavekana was the shore, was the hunger of the horizon. Kavekana was fixed as stone.

And there, that certainty, that denial of the things she'd seen, the world she knew—that wasn't her. That was reality imposed. That was what she was told to think. That was the Penitent.

She knew the truth and she was being convinced to ignore it, by voices too subtle to hear. She sank through a void that tried to rip her apart. And she had to put herself back together.

She'd played this game before.

Inside the knife-edged cradle, she began to work.

Izza led Mako down the slope to the beach where the Penitents waited. He tripped, but she helped him to his feet. They walked together; he leaned on her and on his stick.

Penitents stood guard in long rows. Cooling joints popped and clicked. The air above them rippled with reradiated heat. Izza had expected the screams and moans and wails to be worse down here, but she heard only waves and wind and cooling stone. A soft sob, unless that was the wash of ebbing tide. Ten Penitents stood on this short stretch of sand. Maybe they were all veterans, or only a few held prisoners.

The stone monsters might not speak, but their sharp angles and heavy limbs and sheer mass all warned Izza off. She'd survived by not drawing attention to herself. This was as far a departure from that philosophy as possible, short of mugging people with a burning sword on Epiphyte at high noon.

So when the old man asked, "Can you see her?" she almost told him no, or that the trail ended here or that her connection to Kai had been cut off—almost said anything but the "Yes" she managed at last.

Even without the tug in her soul, she would have recognized Kai's Penitent: shorter than the rest, crudely fashioned, blunter in the lines of face and body, and yet more lively than the common model. Modern Penitents, drunken watchmen whispered in their cups—drink was the one vice permitted them, and they indulged like other men and women, maybe worse—modern Penitents were sculpted under a Craftsman's guidance, from living rock on some distant atoll to which even the Iskari Navy now gave a wide berth. They were sharp, industrial, and reminded Izza of the warships that docked at East Claw: straight lines and planes angled to form a joint or suggest a muscle. Kai's Penitent was different. Thin furrows whorled its back, as if a giant had built the thing by hand and left fingerprints behind.

It scared Izza all the same.

She led Mako to the Penitent.

He shuffled over the sand, swinging his stick.

The Penitent's fingers twitched.

Izza caught her breath. Maybe Penitents shifted sometimes in their sleep, or in their watch. After all, they had human beings inside them. But Izza had never seen another Penitent twitch.

She guided Mako along the beach. Though shorter than the rest, Kai's Penitent was a mountain still, flanked by mountains. Starlight caught in ruby eyes; night robbed of color, the paint's slick surface was almost blood.

Izza turned the old man's shoulders until he faced the Penitent. "Here she is."

He pressed his stick into the sand, and folded both hands atop it. A breeze blew his loose gray hair and ragged clothes. She released his wrist and retreated a step, not knowing why. He looked taller, and older, than she had thought.

Kai's Penitent groaned. Or Kai groaned. Izza recognized the sound: the nameless animal terror that came when you woke to find a knife at your throat.

Kai was awake. Which meant the Penitent was, too.

"What now?" she whispered. The old man seemed carved out of the same rock as the sentinels. She didn't expect an answer.

"Bring me closer," he said. "I need to touch her."

Kai heard the approaching footfalls with dim sympathy. She hoped these interlopers would leave. She'd found a grip on the crystal brain and its laws. Without distraction, with only stars and rolling ocean to occupy her mind, she might carve herself some space, some minor freedom.

Unless even this slight victory was only the Penitent sinking deeper into her mind as her resistance flagged.

No sense thinking that way. You had to trust yourself. Some parts of you, at least. There was nothing else.

Then the newcomers spoke, and she recognized their voices.

Izza. Mako.

Gods.

She tried to suppress the realization, her certainty as to what they'd come to do, or try; too slow. The old man and the thief were here to rescue her.

Here to stop her from guarding Makawe's people. Misguided. Illegal. Traitors.

Her fingers twitched, and she almost reached for them.

No.

She broke the statue's certainty on a wall of will. Too many voices had told her who to be, what to think. And they were so often wrong. Wrong to say they knew her; wrong to say what she should do, or be, or become.

Izza and Mako shuffled into view. She wanted to warn them away, but wire cut her and fire burned her and she knew her righteous facade was false. She ignored her friends' faults rather than helping them grow.

They stood before her, Mako with hands crossed on his walking stick, Izza staring up at the Penitent—at Kai—with horror, and a clear expression of guilt.

Mako said: "I need to touch her."

She recognized his voice.

Of course she recognized his voice. He was her friend. Seize him now. Anything less was to fail the cause of justice, to abandon the island's defense.

Or not.

They were here to help her. They were working for Kavekana, the real Kavekana, ever changing, not the image burned into the Penitent's crystal mind. To stop them was to betray the island.

The Penitent demanded, but the judgment belonged to Kai.

She did not raise her arm.

And so she suffered.

Izza led Mako to the Penitent. Her whole body was cold iron, and moving broke it rather than bent. She'd snuck into back-room offices while old women and potbellied men snored on their lunch break, and stolen fragments of their dreams. But she never felt this way before: like trying to walk over frost without melting it.

The Penitent stood strong and stiff. Izza wondered what battles Kai fought within its shell.

Five steps left. Four. Three.

Too close to run, now.

Idiot. You've always been too close to run.

Kai screamed.

Izza saw herself reflected in the paint on the Penitent's chest, and in the facets of its eyes.

"Here."

Mako extended his hand. His fingers shook.

The Penitent moved.

Kai wrestled with an angel, and she was losing. She'd hurt before, in Jace's office, as the Penitent taught her how to move, and she thought that was pain. In the intervening hours the crystal had studied the courses of her mind, tangled itself into her thoughts. It crushed her and burned her and cut her and froze her and broke her and re-formed her only to break again. She fought back, tearing, wild, a cyclone of agony. It hurt her because it knew her, and because it knew her it could fade away before she struck.

She fought herself—the self the Penitent wanted her to be.

Her anger flagged, and in that moment her arm shot out. One hand caught Mako's skull between thumb and forefinger, and began to squeeze. He gasped. She pressed harder: the Penitent knew the precise breaking tension of human bone, could stop before it shattered. He would not speak again with that too-familiar voice.

There it was again, Kai thought, drowning. She knew Mako. Knew his voice. Had since childhood.

And yet she recognized his voice in some other way—like a song she'd long forgotten.

That confused rifling through her mind for a fact she'd never known she knew, that wasn't hers. That was the Penitent.

That was something she could hold, and hit.

Swift as a sea storm she followed that feeling back, destroying as she came.

The Penitent, stunned, released its grip. Mako set his hand on the Penitent's chest. He stared into the crystals of her eyes.

Then his true eyes opened, and light poured forth.

Izza pried at the Penitent's fingers with all her strength and no success. When the grip gave, she sprawled back on the beach. Mako swayed, but remained upright. He touched the Penitent.

And his eyes opened.

They were already open, but he seemed to have another pair of eyelids, opening sideways. Light shone from him. No. "Shone" wasn't the right verb. There was a word in Talbeg her mother used when telling old stories in which people saw something they weren't supposed to see and the sight burned through them, and they died or else wandered as blind oracles for the rest of their lives, scraping the edges of the truth they'd glimpsed. That word meant "shine" the way "torrent" meant "stream" or "batter" meant "push."

So.

His eyes opened, and there was light, brief, blinding.

Through the raw red-pink afterimage, Izza saw Mako stagger. She caught him as he fell.

Behind, she heard a crash of stone, and tensed herself to die.

No killing blow came.

She turned to look.

The Penitent opened like a stone flower. Crystals lined the inside, glistening wet. Kai stood within. Thorns retreated from her skin. A long cut across her cheek, a drop of blood on her neck and at her wrist, suit torn and tattered, hair a black tangle, but Kai nonetheless. Izza's pearl hung around her neck.

The Penitent opened for her, or flowed open around her. Her first foot touched the sand. Her second.

She wobbled, but did not fall.

Izza stared into her eyes. Had she changed already? And if so, how much?

Then Kai hugged Mako, and the old man hugged her, and laughed, and she tried to laugh, too, but coughed and said, gravelly as a twenty-year smoker: "What the hell was that?" And, hearing her own wrecked voice: "Sorry. I've been, um. Screaming."

Mako's chest heaved, and he took a long time to speak. Whatever he had done all but shattered him. "The girl dragged me here. Dared me to come."

Kai turned to Izza. "Thank you."

Which Izza knew she was supposed to answer, but instead she pointed, and Kai looked behind her, to the next Penitent: the big modern model that had escorted her down from the mountain. It opened floodlight eyes, and turned toward them with a sound of grinding rock. Down the beach, two more came to life.

Kai swallowed. "Mako? Any chance you can do whatever that was again?"

The old man tried to stand, but could not.

Kai turned to Izza then. "I don't suppose you have any ideas."

Izza shook her head.

"Fair enough," she said, and advanced to meet the Penitents.

56

Kai had no plan, no powers, no miracle hidden up her sleeve, no gods to answer the prayers she didn't make.

She had Ms. Kevarian's business card in her pocket. And she was out of options.

The stars were too bright. Thinking hurt. An Iskari experimental painter had come to the Kavekana Museum once when she was a kid, and the school took them all to see. The man painted canvasses solid colors that did not exist before he invented them: blues that tugged the eyes, greens that melted the air and lingered in nightmares long after you looked away.

After Penance, freedom felt like that.

The advancing Penitents mounted toward the sky, Teo's nearest, and behind hers two more. Kai wished she could stand straighter, walk steadier to meet them. Her legs quaked. Her shoulders and back would not obey. She didn't limp, though: every part of her hurt equally for once.

Teo was inside that front-most statue, trapped as Kai had been. What had it done to her mind in these few hours?

"Teo," she said. She didn't bother to speak loudly. The other woman could not help but hear. "Teo, I'm sorry." She groped for words to bring the Quechal woman back to herself, but thought of nothing the Penitent wouldn't use to its own advantage. She barely knew Teo, really: saleswoman, swimmer, smiler. Not enough to free her from the prison into which the Penitent sculpted her mind.

Izza and Mako hadn't run.

They thought she knew what she was doing.

More than one way to get yourself killed, she supposed.

The two Penitents flanked Teo's now.

Kai put her hands into her pockets, and stepped forward.

Teo's Penitent moved.

The wind of its passing fist blew Kai's hair and the tatters of her jacket. Her jaw tightened, her stomach tensed, her legs locked—and the Penitent's fist slammed into the face of the statue to its left. Rock buckled, crystal broke, and the Penitent fell. The third crouched and charged, striking Teo's Penitent in the midsection. Stone arms circled around a stone chest. Teo's Penitent crouched, sank low, wrapped its arms around the other statue's back, and lifted. Light erupted from crystals at the joints of elbow and shoulder as its muscles shed waste heat. The third Penitent's grip broke.

Teo's Penitent turned, spun, and let go. The other statue tumbled ten feet through the air, landed with a sound like a cliff collapsing, and lay still on the sand.

The second Penitent, the one Teo had punched, was struggling to rise. Teo kicked it sharply in the side, and it collapsed with a scream and a crunch of broken rock.

Kai watched, eyes wide, as Teo's Penitent turned back to her. Her fingers tightened around the business card, but she did not tear it, not yet.

The Penitent spasmed, and cracked. Dust rained from its joints; arms jerked and knees buckled and it sank to the sand. It screamed—the statue itself, not the woman within, a scream of dead material pressed to breaking and beyond. Pain and fear flickered through emerald eyes, quick as a bird crossing the moon.

The Penitent's chest cavity broke open.

Two halves of the geode shell swung out so fast Kai had to jump back. One panel listed on a broken invisible hinge.

Teo stood inside the Penitent. She wasn't smiling. She stepped out from the crystal cage, and where Kai's crystal had flowed open around her, Teo's broke, shards disintegrating as they fell until a fine quartz dust painted the sand onto which she stepped.

Teo looked like she'd fought her way up from hell. Vines of light wound her left arm: green, curved and sharp edged and elegant, a geometer's drawing of fire save for the single savage scar that ran down the inside of her wrist. Kai had seen Craft-work glyphs before, and they didn't look like this. These were harsher, and did not so much glow as eat surrounding light and make it theirs.

In her hand, Teo held a thing without a name: a red spider with too many or too few legs, an anemic jellyfish, or a small, vicious octopus. She glanced down, as if surprised she held the thing, and tightened her grip.

Kai heard a snap.

The Penitent toppled. It took a long time to fall, and hit the beach with a heavy sound.

Teo let go of the thing she held, and falling, it faded, until when it splashed against the sand it left only an odd gray stain.

"Shit," she said. "That stings." She shook her arm as if burned; light dripped from her fingers.

"Teo."

"See? It's not so hard to lose the 'Ms.' " She nodded to Kai, and to Izza and Mako behind her. "Glad you made it. I didn't expect them to grab you, too."

"Teo, what the hell did you just do?"

"Some day maybe I'll tell you about Quechal priests and the scars they leave. Trust me, it hurts more than it looks." Behind her, the fallen Penitents struggled to stand, prisoners screaming as the cracks in their shells healed. Up the ridge, searchlight eyes woke and scanned the beach. "We need to leave." She bit her lip. "Can you swim?"

"What do you mean?"

"It's a simple question."

"I want answers."

"Me first. Can. You. Swim."

"Yes."

"Okay then. You, kid. You swim?" Kai glanced back to see Izza nod, once. She was looking at Teo with a mixture of awe and fear. Mostly awe. "Old guy. Damn."

"Don't worry about me."

"Hells we won't, Mako. Those things are coming after us."

"I do not fear them."

"You should. You were afraid of hers a second ago." Kai pointed toward the statue Teo had broken.

"I was afraid for you. Not of them. I know these things, and they know me. I'll meet you back at the Rest, if you make it. Go."

"Okay," Teo said. "Fine."

"We're not leaving him!"

"I am. And so are you, unless you want to explain what just happened to those guys up the ridge."

"Mako, I—"

He shook his head. "Kai. Go."

"Follow me. Close as you can." And before Kai could object, the Quechal woman ran into the ocean. Waves broke around her ankles, knees, hips, and falling forward she swam.

Penitent gazes swept the night; some pinned Kai where she stood slack jawed. She might have remained there forever had Izza not pulled her after, into the waves. Once she took her first step, the second was easy.

"You stink at running away," Izza called over her shoulder, laughing almost, or else hysterical.

Kai fell into waves and water.

After the initial wet shock, the sea took her in. She swam, following Teo's head as the Quechal woman slipped through and disappeared behind ocean swells. Izza cut the water like a knife, the kind of speed Kai'd had when young. Kai dipped below the surface. Salt stung her eyes, and the Penitents' light lit the sea blue and green, chiseled silhouettes of coral and darting fish from the black. A hundred yards from shore Kai rolled onto her back, risking a moment's lost sight of Teo for a glimpse of the beach. Penitents swarmed there, and in their midst Mako stood, alone and as yet unharmed.

How had he freed her? That burst of unearthly light, of overwhelming force, was no Craft Kai knew.

She rolled onto her stomach, and after a panicked moment saw Teo and Izza. During her retrospection they had pulled ahead, and she'd drifted west. She adjusted course to follow.

Night swimming resembled daytime swimming as little as an ocean resembled a pool. Daytime, you knew where you were, relative to where you had been. After sunset, the coast was a confusion of light, and only texture separated the dark above from the dark below.

They drew even with the docks and factories of East Claw, and pressed south. Kavekana receded. Ahead, Kai saw only the skyspires miles distant. Surely Teo didn't plan to swim all the way there. Long before they reached the spires, they'd pass the harbor wards, and then nothing would stand between them and the ocean's hunger.

"Familiarity breeds contempt" was a saying Kai'd heard at school. The saying did not apply to Archipelagic ocean. In waters beset by star kraken, sentient storms, and sunken cities where alien monsters lived, familiarity bred terror and, failing that, death.

When Kai next looked for Teo, she was gone.

A second before, the woman had been swimming steadily ahead of them. The next, she vanished.

Kai knew better than to panic. Aching, she still wasted strength treading high in the water for a better view. She saw nothing: only Izza pressing doggedly forward. She called the girl's name, softly: sound carried over the open ocean, and she did not know who else might be listening.

Izza turned toward Kai. Her eyes widened—and she too disappeared.

Kai swam alone, far from shore.

"Izza!" She made for the spot where the girl had sunk. She heard her father's voice chant the litany of beasts that preyed on unwary sailors, and the remedy for each. Kraken be craven, sharkteeth blunt, gallowglass sail clear, scissorfish hunt. Even as a kid she'd thought the rhyme's suggestions impractical. Oh, yes, when the shark comes for me, I'll blunt its teeth.

She did not, until that moment, realize the rhyme's purpose: not to advise, but to fill the mind in the face of danger. Chants might not deter sea monsters, but they were marginally better than the alternative litanies Kai would have composed of all the ways she was about to die.

She thought she had reached the spot where Izza sank; she

saw nothing, felt no leviathan underwater. She drew a deep breath, and dove.

She opened her eyes. Water lay beneath, only water, down to the mirror coral–crusted sea floor a hundred feet below. No Izza. No Teo. No sharks or gallowglasses. The water carried sound: clicks of tiny shrimp, ship wakes and propellers, and beneath all that, far away, so deep she heard it more in her blood than in her ears, music. Long notes rose and fell, glissando and trill. Praise song.

Salt water burned her eyes. She sought, and did not find.

She raised her arms above her head and swept them down to her sides like wings.

As she rose, she scanned the sea floor one last time for her—what were they? Not quite friends. Izza, maybe, though they'd barely known each other. And Teo, she'd never known Teo at all.

She'd almost breached the surface when something struck her in the head.

Twisting in the water she choked and clawed at her assailant. In the confusion she saw nothing, but her fingernails scraped a slick curved surface. She kicked and pummeled this thing she could not see. One out-flung hand breached the water's surface, and struck something long and thin and hard. She grabbed it and pulled down, hard as she could, but instead of pulling whatever it was into the water she pulled herself up, and rose sputtering and cursing into air.

She held an oar draped over the side of a black shallow-drafted boat. Teo and Izza braced the oar's other end. Izza wheezed, bent over. The oar must have caught her in the stomach as Kai thrashed.

"What the hells," was all she could say at first.

"Here." Teo held out her left hand. The light had mostly faded from her skin, but the scars still glowed. She saw Kai's expression, and offered her other hand instead. "It's not much, but it's all I have."

Kai pulled herself into the boat. Water slopped from her shirt and pants and thin sandals. She'd lost her jacket, shrugged it off for speed. Sea breeze on wet skin set her shivering. She sat and hugged herself and breathed.

The boat was Kavekana make, shallow draft for crossing shoals and sandbanks, a vessel for short distances. An anchor chain ran over the side, though she'd seen no anchor in the water. Teo sat on the bench. Izza leaned against the stern, watching them both. All shivered.

"This boat wasn't here before," Kai said.

Teo pointed to the prow. A charm hung there, a shark's tooth marked with foreign glyphwork, glowing green.

"That means nothing to me."

"Keeps people from noticing the boat. For a little while."

"Cool, right?" Izza said.

"Who are you really?"

Teo shrugged. "Does it matter?"

"You got us both stuffed inside Penitents. You owe me."

"I've been thinking about that," Teo said. "Had a long time to think inside that thing. I thought at first you might have been punished because of me. But then I realized how hard you tried to get me into the mountain, into the pool. Profit wasn't your goal: you brushed me off twice, easy. When your boss showed up, he treated me like a routine nuisance, but you—you were special. It's a bit excessive to lock a prospective client inside a Penitent without trial, isn't it?"

"But you're not a client, are you? You never were."

"No," she said at last.

57

In the boat's stern, Izza cleared her throat. Both women turned to face her. "I don't know you," she said.

Kai's laugh was dry and sharp. "Izza, permit me to introduce Teo Batan, a client of mine. Or she pretended to be a client at least. Come to think of it, I'm not even sure that's her real name."

The Quechal woman shrugged, resigned. "I didn't lie about that. Or my credentials. The Two Serpents Group did send me to open an account on your island. I just had another goal I didn't mention." She held out her hand to Izza.

Her palm was soft, but the handshake strong.

"Nice to meet you, Teo," Izza said. "I'm Izza. So, you're a thief?"

One corner of Teo's mouth turned up in a slight smile. "I wish. If I was, I'd be better at all this. No, I'm just a saleslady who got in over her head."

"Look," Kai said. "I don't know what your deal is, and I don't care. I need to get back to shore."

"Then you're welcome to swim." Teo pointed over the side of the boat. "If you can make it that far."

"I'm a strong swimmer. Even if I haven't been training for this like you have."

"Oh, and don't forget the Penitents waiting for you when you hit shore. Do you really want to go back to that? I had protection." Teo patted her arm, the still-burning scars. "And I can still hear them in my head. Like every bad fight I ever had with my grandmother at once. Gods and demons. Why stay?"

"That's my home."

"It's not been kind to you today, as far as I can tell."

"Homes aren't always kind," Kai said, and Teo nodded.

"I guess not."

"What happened?" Izza asked. "Kai, how did they catch you?"

"They didn't catch me. They caught her."

"I don't think that's fair," Teo said. "I dropped a bracelet into the pool on accident, and your people stuffed me in a brainwash golem for my trouble. I think whatever their problem was, it had more to do with you than me."

"That wasn't an ordinary bracelet," Kai said. "It flowed through my fingers. And if your purpose here is so innocent, why do you have an invisible getaway boat?"

"I never said it was an ordinary bracelet." Teo didn't meet Izza's eyes, or Kai's, either. She hunched over on the rowing bench. "And I never said my purpose here was innocent, either. Izza wasn't far off the mark. I'm the scout, not the second-story man. Or woman, as the case may be."

"You were trying to steal from the mountain." Izza heard a note of wonder in her own voice.

"Is it still stealing when you're working for a goddess?"

"Yes."

"Fair enough," Teo said. "Stealing it is."

"I thought you worked for Deathless Kings," Kai said. "You and your Two Serpents Group. Heal the world one crisis at a time."

"That's the idea. Most of what I told you was true. We are trying to expand abroad. But our sponsors, all those Deathless Kings, they made their names with deicide. Understandably hard to convince Old World gods that we come in peace. So I went to Alt Coulumb, where gods and Craftsmen get along okay."

"Seril," Kai said. "The moon goddess."

"Right. The one who died and got better. One of our main sponsors killed her, back in the God Wars. We figured if she signed on with us, that would get a lot of attention. I made the pitch, and I'm good at my job, current circumstances notwithstanding. The idea intrigued her. But she made a counter-offer."

Teo stopped, as if looking for the right words. Kai seemed to know this part of the story already—or to be reading it off notes somewhere up in the stars.

"You're here for the goddess-shard."

"Basically."

Izza shook her head. "I'm lost."

Teo inhaled, and let out the breath slowly. "Look, I only know what I was told. This goddess, Seril, died back during the God Wars—mostly. Her city thought she was dead, anyway. They hired Craftsmen to come resurrect her, only during the resurrection process some of her body went missing. They think Denovo—one of the Craftsmen—they think he carved off a bit to study. Fragments of memory, that sort of thing. But where he stored it, they didn't know."

"Jace—my boss, you remember—"

"Turtleneck, bad attitude." Teo nodded.

"He mentioned that Seril's priests kept bothering the Order to return a stolen piece of her. But they couldn't prove we had it in the first place."

"Margot's poems were the proof," Teo said. "Not exactly admissible in a Court of Craft."

Izza blinked. "Does everyone on the planet know Edmond Margot's poetry?"

"Just the gargoyles," Teo said.

"What?"

"Seril's creatures. Living stone police officers, sort of. Turns out they're poetry freaks. Songs sung at midnight, odes carved on the sides of buildings, that sort of stuff. They read journals, chapbooks, everything. And they found poems by this bard from a major god haven, which were written in their own style. Gargoyle poetry. They figured the stolen pieces of their goddess must be here—Seril's influence seeping out into the world."

"It isn't Seril," Kai said.

"Margot's poems came from the Blue Lady," Izza added. "Not some half-dead moon goddess."

"I don't know anything about a Blue Lady."

"It's possible we're both right," Kai said. "If a pierce of Seril's in the pool, then maybe the Blue Lady . . . maybe the idols found it. Learned her language. Absorbed her memories. Discovered how to reach out into the world. That would explain why they only made contact a couple years ago, when Seril returned."

"The poems were gargoyle poetry, which meant the shard was here. In your pool, safe outside the world." Teo turned to Kai. "Seril wanted me to plant a beacon her people could use to break in and steal the shard back. That was the bracelet. I seem to have messed up some master scheme of yours, and for that I'm sorry, but this is the end of the line for me. My duty's done. Now I wait for my ride, and leave."

"That doesn't make sense. You expected the Order to let you go? They have allies around the world who will hunt you down."

"I dropped a bracelet in a pool; they stuck me in a supposedly inescapable box that I then escaped. The only possible reason for their allies to come after me would be if your Order could prove I helped steal something they claim they don't have from a vault they can't afford to admit has been breached. I think it's more likely we'll all just chalk this one up as an embarrassing incident."

"She has a point," Izza said. "The best stuff to steal is stuff the target can't admit is gone."

"Doesn't matter," Kai said. "We need to get back into the mountain."

Izza frowned. "Why?"

Kai didn't answer at first

Izza resisted the urge to squirm under the pressure of the woman's stare. The few hours in the Penitent hadn't broken her; refined her, maybe. Hardened her like forge-steel. "The Blue Lady's dead." Izza could say that now without weeping. Without even a hook of emotion in her voice. Just a fact. That's what she told herself. "So is Margot. The Penitents' trail is cold. The kids are safe. We could just leave. There's a whole world out there." Cat had said as much, and she was right. Why did Izza feel so dirty saying the same aloud?

"You're welcome to stay with me," Teo said. "Plenty of water to last the three of us until pickup. We're bound back to Alt Coulumb first, and then, well. Anywhere."

"Anywhere." Izza liked the way that word felt in her mouth. They didn't have Penitents in Anywhere. The sea rolled around them, endless toward freedom, rippling under starlight.

Until Kai spoke.

"The Lady isn't dead."

Izza froze.

"I don't know what you are talking about," Teo said.

Kai ignored her. "The Blue Lady. The Red Eagle. The Great Squid. They're all alive."

The words pressed into Izza's ears like thorns. "That's not true. I felt them die. I saw them die."

"They're masks, Izza. Not masks: faces. The idols in the pool, the myths we make, they aren't complicated enough to live on their own. But they're all connected, and all of them together—they can dream. They can speak. Your gods and goddesses are different pieces of the same Lady. She's still there. Stuck. And my boss will keep killing her forever if we don't stop him."

Izza burned with fever, and a cool hand caressed her cheek. She lay on the mountainside beneath the stars, and a beautiful horned woman stepped out of the stone to join her. "The Lady's alive?"

"All of them. I saw, in the pool. It's." There were tears in Kai's eyes, or else just ocean water. "I can't describe it. It's too big."

Izza remembered the blue bird with the broken neck, and incense that smelled of desert rain.

This isn't your fight.

Except it was.

This was her fight, and that, back there, that island swelling on the horizon, that was her home.

They'll keep killing her forever. The knife, always sliding across the priestess's throat, and that eternal gasp echoing in Izza's ears as she ran. The column of oily smoke that would never go away.

"We need to go back," Izza said. Five words. One syllable each. A door opened in her heart. And to Teo: "You can help us."

Teo shook her head. "I'm sorry. I can't."

"Of course you can," Kai said. "Turn the boat around. Your second-story man can get us into the pool. He, she, was going there anyway. I'll do the rest. If I reach the pool, I can fix this."

"You're talking about a revolution. Deposing your boss, and not in the cozy Craftwork sense. You literally want to kick out the head of your priesthood."

"What's happening up that mountain is wrong," Kai said. "I have to stop it."

"That's not—" Teo raised her hands. "I can't. This is too much. The Two Serpents Group solves problems. We don't overthrow governments. We don't start revolutions."

"Some problems," Kai said, "can't be solved without a revolution."

"Spoken like a woman who's never been on the wrong side of a rebel knife."

"You're the one who claims she wants to help the world. So what is it? Will you circle this entire planet saying you want to help people, but only really helping yourself, making your sponsors feel good, scratching some goddess's back so she'll scratch yours? Helping changes things. My island is living a lie. People are dead. My friend is inside a Penitent, suffering what we just suffered with no chance of release. My boss stabs over and over again at a goddess' eyes in the darkness. How much will you sacrifice to preserve the status quo? To keep your hands clean?"

At the mention of sacrifice, Teo stiffened. Her hand sought her wrist.

Kai closed her mouth. She'd been shouting at the last, and the ocean echoed her voice. In the chapel Kai'd seemed uncertain, small, afraid. That was gone now. Maybe the Penitents broke it from her. Or maybe she'd learned something else inside.

Teo didn't look at Kai, didn't look at Izza, either. She kept her gaze fixed on the water outside the boat, and the stars reflected there.

Izza reached out and touched the woman on the arm. Teo

didn't brush her off. "We'll go back ourselves," Izza said. "If we have to. But it would be easier with your help. Please."

Teo took her hand, pressed it, held it. Izza forced herself not to pull away.

Teo's eyes were dark. "Okay," she said. "Let's go."

58

They reached shore three hours later. Stars receded as they approached, repelled by city fire and ghostlight and Penitents' searching eyes.

Kai rowed at first, but soon exhaustion caught up with her. Izza took over the oars while the other woman slept in the stern, shaking from bad dreams. No wonder. Izza didn't mind rowing. Returning to Kavekana under her own power felt right somehow.

Teo sat at the prow, troubled.

Rather than aiming for the well-lit center of the Palm, Izza angled the boat toward East Claw. Night never fell at the deepwater port by the claw's tip, but farther north dark lengths of warehouse wharf brooded over the sea-lapped shore. She rowed to a decaying two-story wooden dock that appeared on the verge of collapse. A band of glory smugglers used this place to off-load joss the year before; the Watch rounded them up in a sting, and gangs abandoned the place after, out of a mix of prudence and superstition. But their hideout remained, its crow-pecked skeleton testifying to the bad ends of stupid crooks.

Izza rowed into the dock's lower level, under a wooden arch hung with broken planks and seaweed like wrecked teeth in a diseased mouth. The odor of rotted wood smothered them.

Izza locked the oars, grabbed a moss-covered pylon, and pulled herself onto the dock. The boat disappeared when she left it; she groped above the water until Kai grabbed her hand and pulled herself ashore.

Kai tried to stand, but winced and sat down slowly on the dock. "Shit," she said. "Sorry."

Izza listened for footsteps, for breathing, for any human sound.

Streetlamp light filtered through gaps in the dock's upper level. A flight of rickety stairs rose to the street.

Teo lurched ashore, and stood unsteadily between Izza and Kai. "Okay. Here we are. What now?"

"That," said a voice from the shadows beneath the stairs, "is what I wanted to ask you."

Teo cursed and Kai recoiled. Izza alone didn't move. She had expected the voice, as she had expected the woman who emerged from beneath the stairs. "Hi, Cat," Izza said.

The streetlight cast a ghostly wash over the woman's pale skin and blond hair.

Izza remembered her wounded, trembling from withdrawal. Remembered her cloaked in hophouse alley shadows, eyes hard and face fixed. That morning—gods, had it only been that morning?—she'd looked at Izza as if she lay at the bottom of a well, drowning.

Izza couldn't say how she looked now. Cold. Tense. Excited, even.

But there was a bit of drowning there, too.

"Guess you didn't leave your goddess all that far behind," Izza said.

"Not so far." Cat's laugh was dry as the dock was damp. "You know that choice I kept saying you'd have to make?"

"Yeah," Izza said.

"Well." She slid her hands into her pockets. "I made the wrong one."

"I know how that feels."

"I didn't lie. If it matters. I just left a few things out. My Goddess sent me away. Sent me here. I've been a cop all my life, and she asked me to steal for her. Because she trusts me. Because she loves me, and damn if I don't love her back." She slid her hands into her pockets. "What are you doing here, Izza?"

"Giving you a chance."

"What's that mean?"

"You said you couldn't help me this morning. But I think you can. I think you're here to help me—I think that's why you were sent in the first place."

"Cat," Teo said, "you know this girl?"

Cat's mouth pressed into a thin line. Izza remembered her fighting Penitents bare-handed. "Stay out of this," the woman said. "Wait here a few more hours, and we'll leave together. We're almost free. I go back to my life, and you can come with me, and go wherever after that."

"Some things are more important than freedom."

"You don't know that," Cat said. "Not until you're much further down this road."

"My goddess"—and gods, did that feel strange to say out loud—"isn't dead. She's up that mountain being tortured. The people doing it won't stop until she's dead or mad. And until she's gone she'll keep reaching out to the kids, and the priests will chase them down one at a time and kill them or make them Penitents. You can help us stop it all. Get us into the pool. Kai can do the rest."

"Kai?"

"Hi." Kai raised her hand.

"Who are you?"

"I work up there." She pointed up and inland, to the mountain. "Sort of. They trapped me inside a statue. It's complicated."

"You," Cat said, to Teo this time, "are a bleeding heart."

"I didn't spend the last month befriending street urchins."

"We're wasting time. We planned for you to set the beacon, not to set off every alarm in the mountain."

"I didn't expect my priestly friend here"—and at this Teo nodded over her shoulder to Kai—"to use me as cover for industrial espionage. So we're even. Hells, that bracelet wasn't supposed to trip their wards in the first place. Make that I'm one up on you."

Cat crossed her arms.

"Cat," Izza said. "I don't think you made the wrong choice. Just the hard one. Like I'm doing now."

In the end, Cat was the first to look away.

She paced the dock, footsteps heavy, muttering in a Kathic dialect so thick Izza couldn't pick out more than a few words, most of them curses. She made a fist and cracked her knuckles, her wrist, her elbows and shoulders.

"Shit," Teo said. "And you call me a bleeding heart."

"Get the boat back out to sea," Cat replied, and to Kai and Izza: "Let's go."

59

Kai hadn't expected a mainlander secret agent to look so much like a washed-up Godsdistrikt wreck, strung out in ripped slacks and a loose black shirt, green eyes darting and hungry. But when Cat moved, she moved with purpose: took Izza by one wrist and Kai by the other, and pulled them both toward the stairs. Whatever her appearance, she was strong.

They climbed rotting stairs to the wharf, into the fresh night wind off the ocean. In direct light, Cat looked harder than she had below.

"What's next?" Kai said.

The woman smirked. "What do you think?"

"Climb the mountain. Rappel down."

"That's subtler than I planned."

"What do you mean?"

"We start," Cat said, "with a little shock and awe."

From her pocket, she produced a piece of silver chalk. She wove the chalk between middle, index, and ring fingers of her left hand, and curled her fingers into a fist. The chalk broke.

Nothing happened.

"I'm not feeling much shock," Kai said. "Or awe."

She wondered, briefly, why Izza'd closed her eyes and clapped her hands over her ears.

Then the night split open.

Kai picked herself up off the ground, blinking red-bloomed brilliance. Cat reached toward her, a person in vaguest outline. Distant drums beat through the whine of dead sound.

The drumbeats were explosions, she realized. Eyes recovering, she saw pillars of light rise across the island, West Claw, East, and the Palm, choreographed as casino fountains. She could almost see, almost hear again.

"Distractions," Cat shouted. Kai heard her as a mumble through a wool blanket. "To keep the Penitents occupied. Like a magician's show." Her eyes split the lights to a million colors. "Now, hang on."

"What?"

Cat grabbed Kai's wrist and repeated herself, louder. "Hang on."

Quicksilver sparked beneath the collar of Cat's shirt, and flowed out and over, covering body and shoulders and back and legs. The hand that held Kai changed from skin to steel. Wings sprouted from Cat's back, and spread.

When the silver reached Cat's mouth, she sighed, as if setting down a long-borne burden.

Her wings beat, once, and they flew.

Kai's and Izza's added weight did not seem to slow Cat's climb at all—or else Kai could not imagine how fast the woman would have been unburdened. Streets shrank to ribbons, and they swept up and north as searching Penitents' gazes lit the earth below—scattered, stunned by the eruptions of light, seeking the phantom army that assailed them. Cat's laugh did not travel like normal sound, but cut straight to Kai's heart's core.

Sirens wailed, warning clarions Kai recognized but had never heard aloud. The island cried in pain.

Cat wound between sweeping searchlights like an eel through a coral maze. Not precisely like: there was no truce with gravity, here, no uneasy accommodation between old foes. Gravity was vicious, and Cat fought him with every beat of her rising wings.

They swept up slopes, borrowing lift from currents of reradiated warmth. Blinking tears, Kai spared a glance to Izza, who hung from Cat's other arm. The girl had a wild rictus grin, skin drawn tight over her skull.

They rose, and rose, and rose, over the volcano's lip and higher, trajectory hyperbolic, so high Kai wondered if Cat no longer meant to infiltrate the mountain but to steal the stars instead.

Kavekana was a shrinking disk, framed by ocean.

Clouds scudded across the sky.

Cat's metal skin drank moonlight.

She swept her wings back, and dove.

The ground approached.

Fast.

Time slowed.

They fell through space and worlds, following that unseen beacon. They did not slip from realm to realm so much as burst through. The color of the sea changed, wine red and spreading. Constellations danced and transformed.

The volcano's mouth approached. At its bottom, pinhead small but growing larger, lay the pool, another sky into which they could fall forever. The size of a cherry now, a fig, lemon orange apple pineapple watermelon—

She braced herself for impact, too late.

They stopped in darkness ringed by light.

Cat's silver skin glowed in the pool's black. Kai saw her shock, saw Izza scramble to tread water that wasn't there, to orient herself toward a surface that did not precisely exist. Kai had felt the same way on her first entry to the pool. Momentum and distance did not work here the way they worked outside.

Which gave Kai the opportunity she needed.

In the pool, strength of will mattered more than physical power. Here Kai could, and did, twist her wrist and slip away from Cat. And before the other woman recovered, Kai swam up, pulled herself out of the nothing, and stood, dripping, on the shore where she had watched a goddess die.

Below, Cat and Izza sank.

Kai crossed her arms.

Penitents ringed the pool—the guardians who'd caught her earlier that day, and one smaller, the Penitent in which Mara was trapped. They watched Kai with gemstone eyes.

Jace stood in front of her.

Her suit was torn and salt-stiff, her hair tangled. Unreality dripped from her, but enough had soaked into her skin and clothes to work her will upon. Her hair slithered straight. Her clothes were clean, pressed, and whole. She slid her hands out of her pockets. Light sparked off lacquered nails. The cut on her face knit, and the pain in her hip faded.

When she was quite done, she smiled at Jace.

"I see you got my nightmare."

60

"How could I miss it?" For the first time in his years since taking office, Jace stood unbowed, shoulders straight and back, immaculately calm. "You shouted through dreams."

The smell of dust and rock hung about and between them. Shadows watched from lit office windows overhead.

"You worried me this afternoon in my office, Kai. You didn't seem to understand the situation. When you disappeared from the Penitent, I feared the worst. That you'd left us for good, that you were working against Kavekana all along. Stupid of me. I know you're loyal. I'm glad to see that loyalty manifest."

Mara's Penitent stood behind Jace, ready for battle. Ready to kill, if needed. "How could I abandon this island?"

"How indeed," Jace said. He kicked a pebble, and smiled like a boy as it bounced. "What gifts have you brought us?"

Izza drowned in starlight, and Cat with her. They fell together, and the bright circle of the surface receded overhead. Cat's silver arms surged against the nothing, but nothing was not water.

She betrayed us, Cat said. Her voice was a razor down Izza's back.

"No." She inhaled the darkness, and did not die. "I trust her. And it doesn't matter, anyway. Let's do what we came here for."

As they sank, strange stars assembled into many-colored shapes. Thousands, hundreds of thousands: a crowd of idols. A gaggle of gods.

"Well?" she called. "Here I am."

Night pressed in on all sides.

"You know me. I know you. I told your stories. Sacrificed to you. Mourned you. Missed you."

Mute idols watched.

"I'm not leaving."

The quality of the void changed: a great mass swam between them and the pool's surface, cutting off all light but the faint glimmer of Cat's skin.

So this was the end, she thought. Drowning in a pit beneath the world.

Fitting.

Then the darkness shone green.

"One intruder," Kai said. "And her hostage." Jace joined her by the pool, and looked where she pointed, in time to see shadows swallow the pair of them.

"Lost," he said.

She hoped not. "We can still save them both. Even if we wait, there should be enough left to question."

"Gods, Kai. You can be vicious when you put your mind to it."

"Turns out our problems have a single source," she said. "A bit of living goddess, stuck inside the pool. She contaminated the other idols."

"But if we remove her," Jace said, "our problems should stop. Good. I don't need to tell you how much of a weight this has been."

"What will you do with that goddess-piece when you find it?"

"Don't know yet. Melt her down, I suspect. Recast the soul-stuff in another form. Or sell it—plenty of market out there for a living goddess, even a piece of one."

"If your offer's still open," she said, "I want my old job back."

"Better than your old job. You've shown your worth in blood. You've earned a promotion, even more than Mara."

"What about Mara?"

"What do you mean?"

"You still haven't let her out of the Penitent."

"She's less understanding than you are," he said, and turned from the pool. "And she's seen more than you."

Kai too turned away. "You mean the poet's death?"

"Mara's not an inherently violent person. She has blood on

her hands, but she doesn't know why it's there. She will understand, eventually. A little island like ours, in the middle of a big
ocean, is a garden: it must be carefully managed."

"Which makes you the gardener?"

"Basically," he said.

"Uprooting flowers where necessary."

"Better to prune than to uproot. It's a shame we can't put gods
inside the Penitents as well. We've had to kill those idols that
woke up, and use the Craft to reassemble them. People, on the
other hand—we can make them do what they must. Like your
friend Claude."

Kai kept her voice level. "What do you mean?"

"Oh, it's fine. Claude," Jace said, "you can come out now."

Footsteps echoed down the cave-passage behind Jace; Claude
emerged. He wore his uniform, and walked stiff backed.

"You see," Jace said, "I find it interesting that, after sending
me a nightmare, you sent one to your friend, asking him to come
to the pool in secret. He came to me first. He was worried for
you, you know. Your sanity. Now. I hope you asked him here to
arrest our friends in the pool. Because if you were betting he
would arrest me, well. I think you'll find that of the two of us,
you are the greater threat to our island. And Claude is a child of
the Penitents first: he must guard Kavekana from threats foreign
and domestic."

Jace stepped back out of Kai's reach. Not that Kai considered
trying to tackle him. The Penitents would reach her before she
could do damage.

She thought she saw the beginnings of an apology in Claude's
eyes. He was sorry for what he was about to do, but he would do
it anyway.

"So, which is it? Did you come to join us, or destroy us?"

"Hello, Izza," the green man said.

Izza heard his voice in her bones. At first she saw him as a
collection of stars, no different from the others that filled the
nothing through which they fell. As she watched, his outline
grew form, as if absorbing the attention she paid him.

She recognized his face.

"Margot," she said, without moving her lips.

"Something like that." He nodded to Cat. "Care to introduce me?"

"I don't even know who you are."

"A memory," he said.

"Cat, this is a memory of Edmond Margot, a bard of Iskar. Edmond, this is Cat, from Alt Coulumb."

Pleased to meet you.

"The pleasure's mine."

"I saw you die," Izza said.

He bit his lower lip. "You said I should hide. I did. In the page, in the ink. Deeper. I found my way here." He waved his hand at the gods and at the empty space above. "She saved me. Saved part of me. So much I can't remember. I don't remember what I don't remember. Of course." He grimaced. "But she needs me. Us."

"What do you mean? Who needs? Who saved?"

He spread his hands, and raised them, and she saw.

"Neither," Kai said.

Jace raised an eyebrow. "What do you mean?"

"I hoped you would turn yourself in. Resign. Maybe you meant well at first, but you've made bad decision after bad decision. You've angered gods and Craftsmen. I hoped Claude would see the threat you pose."

If a hint of tension crept into Jace's shoulders, Kai saw none. "I've done the best I could. And in a few minutes, the problem will be resolved. The last witness taken care of. The affair remains within our walls, and the danger passes."

"Except for the Grimwalds' suit."

"Which will fail."

"I think you underestimate their Craftswoman."

"Ms. Kevarian has suspicions, but no proof. Mara gave her a few scraps, but without evidence those scraps amount to nothing. And if you planned to tell her about this, you're a greater danger than I thought."

"I don't plan to do anything," she said.

She took her hand from her pocket, and opened it. Two pieces of paper floated to the ground: a business card, ripped neatly down the middle. Half the name landed facing up. The card's reverse side was eggshell white, marked only by the embossed logo of Kelethras, Albrecht, and Ao.

They stood on the skin of a goddess. They floated in her blood. They lived in the warp and weft of her.

I know Her, Cat said.

"Of course you do," Margot replied. "She grew here in silence, for decades, a mind emerging from countless transactions and transfers, as unaware of the human world as you are of the cells in your blood. And then, a few years back, she found within herself a piece of your goddess—a memory of light, of human space, of how it felt to bond with the world and be worshipped. She has her own memories now." He took from his pocket a piece of paper, which he unfolded into a moon. "I think this belongs to you. Or you belong to it."

Both.

"Here," he said. "Tell our foster-mother farewell. We don't need her anymore. We're ready to stand on our own. To fly."

He handed the moon to Cat, who received it with both hands.

"What we need," he said, turning back to Izza, "is you."

At first, nothing seemed to happen, and for that brief moment Kai feared she'd miscalculated, that the Craftswoman couldn't hear or didn't care.

Jace shook his head. "I'm sorry, Kai."

But then his smile faltered.

Izza stared up, around, at the immensity of Her. She'd known her small gods, each in their own way, but how could those compare to this undeniable fact, this curvature of space? "What can I do?"

"Teach her," Margot said. "How to speak. How to be. She can't make sense of herself—built from too many myths. She tries on masks, and none fit. She needs a storyteller. She needs a prophet. She needs someone to break open the walls of the world. She needs someone to interpret her to herself. She needs a partner."

"First though," Izza said, "she needs a thief."

Stars flickered overhead, and an orange shadow fell across the moon.

Ms. Kevarian stood between Jace and Kai, her expression grim and her suit so black it seemed cut from the inside of an unlit cave. She set her briefcase down. "Good evening."

"You have no power here," Jace said. His voice quivered less than Kai expected.

Ms. Kevarian cocked her head to one side. "Interesting assertion. I can speak, at least, and words have power wherever they are heard." She gestured to her briefcase, which rose off the ground and snapped open. An envelope floated to her hand; she removed a few papers. "I'm prepared, based on what I've heard, to name you personally, as well as the Sacerdotal Order of Kavekana in general, in a suit for fraud and mismanagement of my clients' funds."

Jace kept his balance, and his composure. "You do not frighten us. We have allies."

"You do not," she said. "You have clients. And how long will they support you, I wonder, once people learn that you mismanage funds and kill Iskari tourists? Your clients will not risk war in your defense, I think. And without them, what do you have? You are, in the end, one small island."

And so the web pulled tight. Kai stood rigid in silence that felt much longer than the few seconds her watch ticked out. The war played out in her mind: skyspires around Kavekana pulsing with light, Craftsmen and Craftswomen swarming the island's defenses in their thousands, crackling with fury and unholy magic. Penitents would fight on the beaches and in the forests, and they would break. The Iskari would let the island suffer. Docks would burn, streets run molten, the sky melt.

All this, if she'd guessed wrong. She hoped she hadn't.

"I don't think that will be necessary," Kai said.

You don't have to do this, Cat said. *This is too much for anyone to ask of you.*

The goddess filled space, warped time. Secret and strange, new-born heart of the world that had torn her life again and again to rags. Unknowably vast.

Yet she remembered running with the Blue Lady through West Claw alleys at four in the morning, pockets full of stolen coin, blasted out on bliss and worship. As they ran their feet trailed fire. She fell, here, too, as once she'd fallen and the goddess had reached out to catch her. She tumbled through the air and did not die.

If you do this, that's it, Cat said. *No more running. No more hiding.*

"I know," she said.

The world was too big to change, this dread Lady too much to comprehend at once.

But she knew where to start.

Izza saw herself by the gods' light, reflected off Cat's silver skin. She didn't want to turn away.

You could be safe, with me.

"Maybe," she said, "but this is a broken place. And my people need me. And nowhere's safe, not really."

What people, she mocked herself as she said the words. A few refugees. Street kids. Children of no country, and a goddess with no children. Yet.

Are you sure?

And then there was Cat. Chosen of a goddess, and alone.

Like her, in a way. And maybe she'd known that weeks ago, when she saw the woman fight Penitents bare-handed. Lonely, unsure, marooned on a strange island, she saw a girl, a woman, about to make her own mistakes, and tried to save her from them.

"I am," she said, and touched Cat's arm. The silver shell parted, and so did the secret skin Izza wore outside her own. "Thank you."

Then they let each other go. Izza turned to the goddess and the ghost. She cracked her knuckles. The sound did not echo. No walls off which to echo, here. "Come on. Let's steal you."

The Craftswoman turned to Kai, one eyebrow raised, silent.

"Jace," she said, "was never working on the Order's behalf. He operated in secret, against the island's interests. He set all of us at risk, as your threat demonstrates. The Council of Families and the Sacerdotal Order bear no guilt for his crimes." She was not looking at Ms. Kevarian. "In fact, that's why Claude is here."

Come on, she thought. Get it.

The goddess curled around Izza, a web of a thousand million strands, and she was in that web, and she was that web. The goddess settled over her like a mantle, like a shroud, and she felt fire on her skin, and the edge of a knife, and the weight of love.

"Yes," Claude said.

Ms. Kevarian turned. Kai watched gears revolve behind Claude's eyes. He looked younger than she'd ever seen him since his Penitence—a kid once more, watching a fight on the docks, unwilling to get involved.

"Yes?" the Craftswoman said.

Kai slid her hands into her pockets so no one could see her crossed fingers.

"We've come to arrest Jason Kol." He sounded the words syllable by syllable. "For murder, and fraud, and the abuse of powers."

Jace wheeled on him. "Claude."

Claude kept his eyes on the Craftswoman. Kai was glad Ms. Kevarian had turned away from her. She didn't want to see the woman's triumph. "We have evidence," Claude said, "that he's been working to . . . to defraud his pilgrims. That he's imprisoned people wrongly, and corrupted Penitents to help his schemes."

And killed, she thought. Say the last bit.

"And that he has murdered an Iskari citizen. The island of Kavekana cannot countenance his actions."

Jace stared.

"I will, naturally," Ms. Kevarian said, "still bring suit against the Order."

"And the Order," Kai said, "will defend itself by disavowing Jace. He stands alone."

Jace turned to her, and she took a step back when she saw his face. She had expected fury. She didn't know what she saw: a slow shattering expression, a life stripped bare. He'd built a veneer of confidence over years of making what he thought were right decisions. With that scoured away, what remained wasn't even fear.

He moved for her, fast.

Mara's Penitent moved faster: a stone streak, and Jace barely had time to scream. She caught his wrist and yanked him off his feet. He twisted there, and did not speak—glared, instead, at Kai, at Ms. Kevarian, at Claude.

No one spoke.

Stone ground on stone, and the Penitent split open; green-tipped crystals gleamed inside, and within them, Mara, her eyes open.

Kai ran to her, and caught her as she fell. She was lighter than Kai would have guessed, and feverish. Her eyes met Kai's, clouded, unfocused. She hadn't used them in days. And what she'd seen in the meantime she didn't want to remember.

"Hey," Kai said, and held her closer. "Hey."

Mara's hands found Kai's shoulders, squeezed. "Kai. It was in my head. It was my head."

"I know."

"I'm sorry."

"So am I." Her voice broke. She swallowed, hard.

The Penitent moved again, on its own. Granite jaws closed around Jace, and they were alone, on the shores of the pool: Kai, and Mara, and Claude, and Ms. Kevarian.

61

Ms. Kevarian left first, fading like a ghost in a child's story, from the feet up until only a suggestion of form remained—then gone. Next Mara collapsed, convulsed, and Kai held her and shouted to Claude to get help, which he did; acolytes and lesser functionaries arrived soon after with a gurney, and though Mara clutched at Kai as they wheeled her away, Kai had to let her go.

Inside the statue, Jace began to weep.

Which left Claude and Kai. He approached her, by the pool, and together they gazed down into the black. They did not look at each other, and he did not touch her.

"They'll make you a high priest now, I bet."

"If only to find some way to clip my wings."

"They put you in a Penitent," he said, and seemed as though he might have said something else.

"You would have put me back."

"Kai."

"Don't start. You would have."

"You don't have any idea what you risked, back there, with the Craftswoman. If I hadn't—"

"I knew you would. That's the thing. You have a duty. Or a duty has you."

"I don't know what you mean."

"You're so caught in its grip you don't see what happened here. Jace couldn't have kept this up forever. There's been a crossbow to this island's head for a while, and he kept tightening his finger on the trigger. If I didn't threaten to pull it now, he would have slipped up someday, and then there'd be no easy fix, no way to pretend this was all him."

"It wasn't?"

"Gods, do you think he would have taken the initiative on his own? He talked it over with people. I don't know who. He wouldn't have kept notes. But he was a committee man. For every person directly involved, there must be ten who guessed, but looked away. Like I did. We didn't ask questions. We kept to our own business even when the idols started dying. The gods."

"We would have caught him."

"Who would have? Nobody wanted to rock the boat. To step out of line. To ask the first hard question, let alone the second or the third. No one wanted to realize the island was changing."

"Except for you."

"Except for I only came after him, came after all of you, for selfish reasons. Because everyone acted like I was crazy, and I had to prove I wasn't. That's not justice. Mara, maybe she should have been the one to save us. But Jace stuck her in one of those things. I'm not a just woman. I'm not a revolutionary. I don't know what I am."

"But you know who you are."

"I guess."

"That's more than I do," he said.

She looked at him, sideways, really looked at him: strong jaw, flat cheeks and nose, hard eyes under a heavy brow, muscles bulging against shirt and jacket, the man that had been made out of the boy. And she saw, inside him, something younger, like that trace of grit that stuck in oysters for years makes a pearl. Three years they lived together, and she'd never seen that. The broken boy, wondering now, maybe wondering always, what he'd be. The boy who never got the chance to decide, and searched in books for images of the hero he thought he might have been if he had not lost his way.

In that moment she almost forgave him—not everything, but a lot, including some things she should not have forgiven.

"Hey," she said, and grabbed his biceps. "You got to save the world. Or a piece of it."

"But I lost the girl."

"You lost the girl a long time ago."

Neither of them spoke for a while.

"Why are we standing here?" he said at last.

"I'm waiting."

"For what?"

She saw a glint of green within the pool and slid her hand inside, smooth and slow. Then she pulled with arm and back and legs and in a confused half second Izza lay flat onshore, coughing. Kai waited as the girl curled into a fetal ball, and covered her mouth, and stopped shaking.

Izza stood. She swayed on her feet, but did not fall. Claude caught her shoulder anyway. She pulled back and glared demonfire at him.

"I've seen this girl before," Claude said. "Your guide."

Kai laughed. She hadn't remembered. "I guess she is, at that."

"Do you know her name?"

"Izza."

"Izza." Claude knelt so their heads were level, which earned him another glare.

She placed a hand over her mouth, and nodded.

"She's mute?"

"Yes," Kai said, catching the drift. "Can you make sure she gets out of here? Safe?"

"Okay," Claude said.

"Now, I mean."

"You want me to leave."

"I want you out. I want her out. I want all these damn things out." She waved her hand in a circle to take in all the Penitents. "I want them shattered and I want those pieces ground into dust and the dust forged into a metal we sink to the bottom of the ocean so we can all forget them. I want us not to do this anymore."

"You mean Jace."

"I mean Jace. I mean Penitents. I mean gardening the fucking world because the chance of change scares us."

"I changed, once," he said. "Inside. I wouldn't recommend it."

"That's not what I mean."

"Maybe should think long and hard about what you mean.

Because this sounds like one of those ideas where the way you say it matters."

"Get out of here," she said, and "thank you," to him, and "thank you," to Izza, who extended her hand.

They shook, and Kai didn't notice until Claude and girl and Penitents were gone that Izza'd stolen her ring.

She did not leave the pool for a long while. She sat there, cross-legged, while lights went off in the windows that ringed the caldera. She willed them off, pressing deeper into the soft space around the pool, where centuries ago the people of the islands imposed a beginning on time. No one watched here. The caldera windows vanished, as did the tunnels carved into the mountain's shell. She sat on the shore of a world not yet begun.

The silver woman pulled herself up onto the shore, and sat with wings furled and legs crossed and hands resting on her thighs. Moonlight draped her shining skin.

Kai said, "I'm sorry. I had to be sure no one would see."

I should kill you, Cat replied. *For that stunt.*

"I see why you might want to. But bringing me here stopped a crime, and probably a war. Not to mention saved a goddess. Your Lady would appreciate that."

She does, and Kai shuddered to think the woman wasn't guessing.

"That suit you wear. The metal skin. Is it anything like the Penitents?"

No, she said. *And yes. There's more to duty than compulsion.*

"What?"

Love. Honor.

"You don't sound as though you believe it."

I do, she said. *But believing isn't the same as knowing.*

She ran her hand through the rough gravel. "Maybe."

Cat stood. *What happened to Izza?*

"She's safe."

I wish I could have seen her go.

"I know," Kai said. "But you should leave now. I have work to do. We do—Izza, and me. And if someone finds you here, that work only gets harder."

She nodded. *I'll be back.*

"I hope you don't have to be. But maybe we'll meet somewhere else."

Silver wings stretched out to a full span, testing and tasting the air. Kai wondered what it would be like, to be perfect.

"Tell Teo good-bye," Kai said. "And thanks. And I'm sorry."

I will.

Cat flew, and Kai watched her go: trailing moonlight as she rose through time and space and layers of story, out into the world. Leaving Kai here, at the center.

The watchman let Izza off in front of the small dockside apartment complex where she claimed to live, and waited for her on the sidewalk. She'd chosen the building for its easily jimmied lock, but as she reached out to slip the latch, green light flowed from her fingertips and the door popped open.

She waved to the watchman and slipped inside, down the entrance hall, out the back door, over the rear fence to an alley, and down the alley three blocks and a turn to reach the East Claw promenade. After a quick glance left and right to be sure she wasn't followed, she dove off into the bay.

She swam along silt-choked shoals through the city's refuse, until she found the wall she sought and wound through it and surfaced in the chapel beneath the stares of painted gods.

She was not alone.

"I didn't expect you," Nick said from beside the altar.

She removed a tiny envelope of wax paper from beneath her tongue. "I didn't expect me, either."

"I thought you'd follow Cat when she left."

"That was the plan."

"And now?"

"The plan changed," she said. "I'm staying here. We have work to do." She opened the envelope, and slid its contents out into her palm. One folded sheet of paper.

The great challenge, in theft, is the transport of stolen goods. A thief of souls must have a receptacle for the souls she's stolen: gold and gems, magisterium wood, works of art, raw material transformed by human hands.

Like the last work of a brilliant poet.

She opened the paper she'd torn from Margot's notebook. Ink shimmered green in the light of stars and candles.

The green glow rose, and other colors unfolded from it, drifting through the chapel toward the paintings on the walls. Red, for the Eagle; Silver, for the Squid; Blue, for the Lady.

And there in the room's center, where the light mingled, hung a suggestion of face and form, indistinct, massive.

Izza realized her skin was shining.

"Who is that?"

"You know her," Izza said. "You've known her all along. But we've never told her story before now."

"Will you?"

She heard a note of hope there, and wondered whether she deserved it. Behind the altar, at the head of the chapel, she faced her audience of one. No. Two.

"In the beginning," she said, "was the Mother."

62

Kai didn't return to the Rest for weeks. At first she told herself there was too much work: board meetings, explanations. Jace's trial, in secret session before the Council of Families. As the Grimwalds' suit progressed, swarms of Craftsmen and Craftswomen climbed Kavekana'ai and wandered through its halls, studying and being studied in turn. Craft crackled about the mountain peak. Gavin spent three days trying to explain the basic principles of idolatry to curious Craftsmen, without much success. He emerged from the sessions white haired and shaken.

But once the furor faded, Kai still stayed away. One morning, after a long meeting with their defense team, she searched her reflection in the mirror and realized she was looking for excuses. There had been enough of those already.

So she descended Southern, walking easily now without her cane. Sea wind blew in her face and smelled, for the first time in a long while, fresh. The ocean lay like a blue razor against the throat of the sky. She tried to enjoy the walk.

The Rest was deserted as usual come morning, empty chairs on empty tables, the bar cabinet locked and warded. She climbed onto a table and pulled down the ladder that led to Mako's loft.

Sunlight shafted through the thatch roof to dapple the bare wood floor. The low cramped space smelled of dust and paper and palm. She'd not been up here in years, since the old man invited her as a teenager to read. Shelves still lined the loft's mountain-facing gable, packed with university press chapbooks and other, older volumes—bark-covered codices with slats of wood for pages, oracle bones from the Shining Empire, books chisel-etched on the pates of skulls, Kormish mercenaries' battle-poems notched in the sticks they wove into their beards.

Mako slept in a nest of blankets on a straw bed by the open seaward gable.

Kai sat, and watched him.

The old man stirred. Groaned. He mumbled to himself in a language Kai barely recognized as Old Skeld, with strange overtones that raised the thin hairs on the back of her arm. He twisted on the bed. Joints cracked and popped.

Then he lay still.

"Who's there?" he said after a while.

"That," Kai responded, "is what I want to know."

"Kai."

"Yes."

He sat up, and turned toward her voice. Her memory tried to paint his silhouette with details, the cragged scarred face and broken fingers and slumped shoulders and slight hunch. She did not let it. She saw only an outline, and a shadow, and within that shadow, maybe, deep down, a fire.

"I thought you'd come sooner," he said, "or not at all."

"How did you free me from that Penitent, Mako?"

"I helped build them," he said. "Before we left, back in the Wars. I didn't know I could open them. I'd never tried. But when the girl told me you'd been captured, I thought, might as well."

"And why did they let you go?"

He shrugged. "They recognize me. They know what I gave for this island. They know I'm no threat."

"That's a fine story," she said.

He nodded.

"But it doesn't explain the beetle."

He waited.

"You remember. The beetle, from when we were talking on the shore. Little sand-colored monster. Seven legs. Climbed out of the beach where you spit. Tons of them now, all over. They're calling it an invasive species. I went to the library; I wrote to the Hidden Schools. Turns out the species isn't invading from anywhere. It's new. Just showed up one afternoon. And I think I know which one."

"What are you asking?" His voice didn't sound old at all. Not young, either: timeless, like a rock speaking.

"What happened to you?"

"War." The word cut in his mouth, and in her ears. "What do you think?"

"Tell me."

"We fought south of the Shining Empire, in the islands off Kho Khatang. They needed gods and priests who knew boats and islands and water. I took to the skies as a bird of flame, and our warriors clogged the channels. Craftsmen rode in on dragonback, and demon chariots that trailed lightning. Clinging fire fell. They poisoned the land and sea. They poisoned time. The Carrion Queen and the Blade Child caught me in the sky, and our battle burned. Unlucky travelers who visit the delta at night see echoes of our struggle, and go mad." He breathed, ragged. "We died. All of us but me. And I woke blind and broken."

"The fleet."

"Lost. Except for this body." He raised his hands, and let them fall. They struck his legs with a sound at once soft and thunderous. "And that was my war. Our war. It took me two decades to dare return, and when I did, I found the island changed. The pool filled with foreign idols. The streets patrolled by Penitents with people trapped inside them, when I had meant them as a tool for priests to use in our defense."

"And you did nothing."

"No." A sudden breath of wind, like a storm front breaking, shoved her back. The wind stopped, and he sagged. "Not nothing. But less."

"You could have stopped us. Helped us."

"It wasn't my place to speak, to claim to know what was best. I tried that before. You see? My sisters and I, we knew that if the Craftsmen won, they'd destroy the world—next century, if not this one. The power they wield's too great, and human minds are weak, and hungry. Sensible decisions lead to sensible decisions and before long the land lies barren. So we did what we thought was right, and we died for it, and we dragged our children along to die with us. A generation sacrificed in a single battle. That was our legacy. Mine. Can you blame me for thinking the island deserved a new path?"

She didn't answer.

"I tried to help, much as I could. To point you in the right direction. To nurture art, and care for artists, and tell the truth to those that hear."

"Does Eve know?"

"She understands."

"You left us. And while you were gone, we did horrible things."

"You're talking about the Penitents."

"Yes."

"You think there was a time where we didn't do horrible things?" He shook his head. "It's always happened. And not everyone inside those statues is innocent."

"People are poor or sick or angry or desperate and they do things we don't like, and then we hurt them for it until they agree with us, with all our bad choices."

"What would you have had me do?"

"I don't know. Fix it."

"Fix what?"

"Everything."

"Even gods can't fix everything. And I'm not a god anymore. A ghost stuck in dying flesh, that's all."

"You could have helped us."

"I did. I saved you. And I helped you save Kavekana. Guiding it through a difficult future—that's not my place anymore."

"You abandoned us."

A weight settled on her: the pressure of his mind, or his sorrow. "I let you grow," he said. "In the end, that's all a father can do."

She stood. "I need to think."

"I've always been proud of you, Kai," he said as she retreated to the hole in the floor, to the light. "More proud than of myself."

"I'll see you later," was all she could say in response, and "I'm sorry."

She descended the ladder, and stood in the empty bar, blinking something sharp out of her eyes and telling herself it was only sunlight.

She walked home, alone.

Mara waited on Kai's front porch swing. She wore a dress the color of sunrise before a storm. She'd picked one of the sunflowers that grew outside the fence, and stared into its black core the way Kai'd seen actors stare into skulls' faces onstage. She looked up as Kai approached, and smiled.

"Hi." The gate hinge creaked, and the latch didn't shut at first attempt. Kai had to turn back and force it closed.

"Hi."

"I have to buy better wards for this house. People keep coming and going without my say-so."

"You left it open, I think."

"Yeah," she said. "Probably." And: "It's good to see you."

"And you."

"I didn't think they'd let you out of the hospital yet."

"I'm done with people who want to keep me in a box."

"I hear that," Kai said, and walked up to the porch and sat beside her on the swing. The chain creaked under her weight. They rocked, together. Kai kept her feet on the floor. Mara kicked hers out and let them sway with each rock, forward and back. "I'm sorry," Kai said at last. "I stumbled into your plan and fucked it up." She said nothing. "If not for me, you would have given Ms. Kevarian what she needed, Jace wouldn't have found out, and neither of us would have been stuck inside those things. If it wasn't for me, Claude wouldn't have told Jace about the poet, and you wouldn't have been forced to kill him. Everything I tried to do hurt someone. Even in the end, I almost killed us all."

"If not for you, I wouldn't have learned what Jace was doing. He convinced me the first time around. Made me forget myself. Talked me into a corner. I wouldn't have changed my mind if you hadn't jumped, if I hadn't seen what jumping cost. If I didn't ask myself why I wasn't as brave as you. You pushed me. You always have."

"I wasn't brave. I didn't know what was going on. Sometimes I almost wish I hadn't tried to save her."

"Don't say that."

"I'm sorry, is all."

"That you said already. And you didn't need to say it in the first place." There was a kind of music to her voice, Kai realized, that she'd never heard before, from gods or anyone.

"I was thinking about what happens now," Kai said.

Mara didn't respond.

"I look around and I see nothing but problems. That goddess's growing inside the pool. What happens when she learns to speak, not just to the kids dockside, but to everyone? And the Penitents."

"What about them?"

"I don't know anymore," Kai said. "This is a strange world, and we're alone in it."

"It is strange." Mara smiled, and took her hand. "Worse than strange. But we're not alone."

Izza met Kai at sunset, on a barren stretch of eastern shore. The island ended here in a sharp twenty-meter cliff, and a lava arch leapt smooth as a diver's arc from that cliff into the crashing sea.

The coastal road ran long and straight and lonely north. Kai's carriage stopped, and Izza watched her pay the horse and pick her way downhill over jagged rocks. She stumbled, and swore, and Izza laughed. "Watch your step!"

Even in the fast-fading twilight she had no trouble reading Kai's murderous stare.

"Never thought I'd miss the damn cane," Kai said when she reached Izza. She slid her foot from her shoe, picked up the shoe, and dug out a piece of gravel with her finger. "You've been well?"

"Yes," she said. "Busy."

"Tell me about it. The Craftsmen alone in the last few weeks have been murderous."

"Not really."

"No," she said, suddenly sober.

"We're telling the stories," Izza said. "Quietly for now. But people listen. And the kids know our gods won't go away again. Smiling Jack is dead."

"What happens next?"

"Next?" She shrugged. "I guess it depends on what we do here."

Kai stared out into the ocean, then turned back to Kavekana'ai. Sunset clad the mountain's lower slopes in red and gold, and the peak bristled with lightning and aurora as Craftsmen continued their dark work within. "This is the easy part," she said. "Working with people on the margins. The priests will take longer. And, gods, imagine what will happen when the rest of the world finds out the market's come alive—even our little piece of it. I haven't found an edge to the Lady yet, you know. She's wound all around the world. They'll try to burn us off the map."

"Maybe," Izza said. "Maybe not. The mainland gods and Deathless Kings won't mind that their subjects have one less place to hide. Alt Coulumb's on our side, because of Seril. Iskar will want to help us, because they think we're more useful to them as a god-fearing island than as a protectorate of the Deathless Kings. I hope. Though, yeah, maybe they'll just kill us all." She glanced over at Kai. "Why are you smiling?"

"You said 'us.' Meaning Kavekana."

Izza stuffed her hands in her pockets. "Anyway, what's the worst your clients could do? The Lady already owns their souls." She grinned. "You could look at this as the biggest theft in history. We stole an entire island."

"If we can keep it."

"Right."

Waves crashed against the cliffs beneath. The sun sank, and stars emerged. Over the swell of East Claw, the city glowed; off to the north, on the long barren coast, the lights of leeward golf resorts blinked on. And still the Craftwork beacon burned on Kavekana'ai.

Kai laughed.

"What's so funny?"

"There were all these prophecies," she said, "about the gods' return. Unnatural ships would come over the sea, bearing the world's wealth. Our greatest poets would sing on the seashore before Makawe. Kavekana'ai would be crowned with light. And they've all come true, and nobody realized."

"Guess that's the way with prophecies," Izza said.

"Guess so."

Neither of them spoke for a long time.

"You're sure this is the right one?" Izza said, and pointed to the Penitent by their side. It stood alone on the cliff's edge, staring impassively into the night and ocean.

"Sure as I can be," Kai said. "The Watch keeps good records, and I asked nicely."

"They sent her out here, to the end of the earth."

"Not at first," Kai said. "She was on patrol in the city for a while. New catches spend their first few nights on the Ridge, then a season on patrol. If they don't take to police work, they stand sentinel again—time to stare at the ocean and think as the voice sets in."

Izza walked to the Penitent. She tensed as she drew close, old terrors engrained on muscle and bone. When she was near enough, she touched the statue. The stone was warm. She thought she felt a tremor there.

"Hi, Sophie," she said.

The wind whistled and the waves rolled and no birds sang.

Kai approached behind her. "How long has she been in there?"

"A year."

"Gods." Kai let the word out on a breath. "She's not herself anymore."

"Not yet," Izza said. "That's why I'm here."

And she opened her eyes, and let go.

When Cat took on the mantle of her goddess, she shone with the ecstasy of light, a leaf borne on a torrent. Izza'd expected the same sensation, and was surprised at how gentle the goddess felt. She was that same leaf trembling dead on a branch as a strong steady wind blew—and when she released her tenuous hold, the wind bore her up, and she flew into night on the strength of a single yes.

She did not shine. The world did: became a web of webs, interlaced and ever changing. Even the mountain spoke, even the stone, though slowly.

The statue before her was a web, too: an orb woven around and through the girl at its center, touching nothing but her, complete in itself, scornful of surrounding transformations.

Not for long.

Green threads wound out from Izza's fingertips, into and through the Penitent, like vines twining the bars of a cage. It resisted, at first, pulling closer, tearing into the girl—into Sophie. But the vines wound, and wound, and in the end the web began to part.

The Penitent was built, after all, to heed Kavekana's gods, and wait for their return.

A voice vibrated through the web, small, lost.

Izza?

She had told herself she wouldn't cry.

I'm here, she said. *We're here. All of us. Nick and Ivy and Jet and the Blue Lady and the Squid and the Wind Woman and so many more. And Kai. You don't know Kai yet. You'll like her.*

I don't remember, Sophie said. *I don't remember me.*

That's okay. She tried to smile. *We'll remember for you.*

And she did, they did: Sophie tall and dark, with freckle dots, Sophie lady of the seashore, who told the best stories and laughed the fullest and could run faster than anyone save Izza. Sophie, who took Nick in when he stumbled off the ship where he'd stowed away; who taught Izza the back roads of East Claw, and showed her its secrets. Sophie who told the gods' first tales.

There was, in the Penitent's core, a small squirming slug of a thing, not quite alive and not quite dead, that shouted into Sophie's mind. It was conviction, and fear, and a certain sick duty that had more to do with stone than people.

Green threads caught and strangled it.

She opened her eyes and stepped back, shuddering.

"That's it?" Kai said.

"A year's hurt takes a long time to fix," she said. "All the Penitent's done to wind her we must unwind. Bring her back. And once it's done, we can move on to the others. Step by step."

"How do we know it works?"

The sound of grinding rock was her answer.

The Penitent turned from the waves. Its eyes shone green. Slowly, ponderously, it settled once more to attention, facing in, facing the light that shone on the summit of Kavekana'ai.

Izza took the statue's hand, felt the stored sun-warmth within. Kai hesitated, then took Izza's hand in turn. They turned their back on the darkness, and together watched, and waited, for the world to come.

ACKNOWLEDGMENTS

Every book's a journey—sometimes you go to Hawaii, sometimes you go to Mordor. For this book I did a bit of both. My heartfelt thanks to everyone who read the manuscript in its myriad stages, among them the old awesome crew, in alphabetical order: Alana Abbott, Vlad Barash, John Chu, Anne Cross, Nat Drake, Amy Eastment, Miguel Garcia, Siana LaForest, Lauren Marino, Emmy Miller, Margaret Ronald, Marshall Weir. Both blood- and law-parents—Tom and Burki Gladstone, and Bob and Sally Neely—displayed great patience when I spent long stretches of visits hiding in a back room crouched over my keyboard. Alex Temple offered important reading suggestions and advice early in the process. And so on, and so on.

This book wouldn't be here without the team at Tor, geniuses and friends—David Hartwell, Marco Palmieri, Ardi Alspach, Irene Gallo, and so many others. Chris McGrath's covers continue to amaze. David and Marco, my editors, unlocked the story in ways I hadn't thought possible, and inspired me to keep reaching. My agent, Bob, is steady and invulnerable.

Two pieces of writing had an outsize impact on this one. Karin Tidbeck's *Jagannath* blew my mind open and got me working; David Foster Wallace's *A Supposedly Fun Thing I'll Never Do Again* injected levity and wisdom at precisely the right moment.

And my wife, Stephanie: love, patience, brilliance, strength, and honesty. Thanking her one feels the poverty of the deed. "Thanks, gravity, for, um. Everything?" But still—thank you.